UNCOVERED
in
MERRIWEATHER

UNCOVERED *in* MERRIWEATHER

A Jane Austen in Wisconsin series
Book Two

Michelle Cox

Woolton Press

Copyright © 2025 Michelle Cox
All rights reserved.
No part of this publication may be reproduced, distributed, or transmitted in any form or by any means, including photocopying, recording, or other electronic or mechanical methods, without the prior written permission of the publisher, except as permitted by U.S. copyright law. For permission requests, contact Woolton Press at WooltonPress@gmail.com.

The story, all names, characters, and incidents portrayed in this production are fictitious. No identification with actual persons (living or deceased), places, buildings, and products is intended or should be inferred.

Published: 2025
Printed in the United States of America

Print ISBN: 979-8-9987571-1-2
E-ISBN: 979-8-9987571-0-5
Library of Congress Control Number: 2025909277

For more information, address:
Woolton Press
285 N. Cambridge Ct.
Grayslake, IL 60030

DEDICATION (POSTHUMOUS)

Peter Nicholas Bonnet (1839–1926)
and Mary Catharine Luis (1853–1919)
. . . the first of us.

OTHER BOOKS BY MICHELLE COX

<u>The Henrietta and Inspector Howard Series</u>

A Girl Like You

A Ring of Truth

A Promise Given

A Veil Removed

A Child Lost

A Spying Eye

A Haunting at Linley

A Christmas at Highbury

<u>Stand-Alone Novels</u>

The Fallen Woman's Daughter

<u>The Merriweather Series</u>

Matched in Merriweather

Uncovered in Merriweather

PROLOGUE

There it was again. A cry. Edmund perked his ears. Yes, it was definitely a cry, but of what? It was almost like the meow of a kitten, which delighted him. Though he was only seven, he was particularly good at finding batches of kittens tucked away in the hay barn, usually in the upper loft, hidden by many a mama cat.

He dropped the cottonwood leaves he had been collecting and pressed into the weeds nearer the creek. They had decided to have a leaf race there, and Edmund knew that cottonwood leaves made the very best sort of racers. Beating Louisa would be easy, but May might be harder.

Normally, they played war or Cowboys and Indians, but it wouldn't be the same without all the Kerwyns, especially Ray. He and Ray were always the captains of the two teams, but Ray had been made to stay behind today to help his dad fix fences. None of the other Kerwyns—besides Louisa and May, that is—had been able to come out, either, so they had decided to race leaves instead.

There it was again. The cry. Though now it was more of a whimper. And it wasn't a cat, Edmund decided. It was more like . . . well, like a baby, maybe. He quickened his step and, avoiding the giant thistles, plowed into the Queen Anne's Lace instead.

"Hello?" he shouted.

The crying stopped. "Mama? Mama!" Then the crying started up again, more frantic now.

Definitely a baby! "Here, baby!" Edmund called excitedly.

Pushing through the weeds, Edmund hurried in the direction of the cry, only to almost trip over a little creature. Edmund stared at it. It was indeed a baby! Well, not a *baby* baby, but more like a toddler. Maybe two years old, Edmund guessed. It had long black hair and very chubby red cheeks streaked with tears and dirt. Must be a girl, Edmund decided, going by the hair and the dirty shift it–*she*–was wearing.

Startled by Edmund's sudden appearance, the baby locked her big black eyes on Edmund and promptly began to scream.

"Shh, baby! Shh! It's okay," Edmund cooed, using the voice he usually reserved for calming calves and dogs and, well, almost any creature. "Shh, baby, look." He crouched in front of her and held out his hands, palms up. "I won't hurt you." He wished he had something to give her.

The baby kept crying, fresh tears streaming down her cheeks.

Edmund stood up and scratched his head. He looked around for the others. "May?" he called.

No one answered.

The baby continued to cry unabated. Edmund remembered, then, that he had half a peppermint stick in his pocket and pulled it out. Unfortunately, it was covered with lint and likewise a few hairs. He quickly popped it into his mouth to clean it. After sucking for a few moments, he pulled it out. Looked okay. He spit out the lint and held the candy in front of the baby.

The baby stared at it.

Edmund waited for the baby to take it, but she did not. She must not know what it was. Bending closer, he touched it gently to the baby's lips. The baby's eyes lit up in surprise.

"Here, you take it," Edmund encouraged, but the baby did nothing, just blinked at him. But at least she had stopped crying. "Here." He wedged the stick in the baby's chubby hand and stood back, waiting to see what the baby would do. Ater a few moments she put it to her mouth, and then her tiny tongue came out and gave it a little lick.

Edmund pealed with laughter. "You look just like a baby possum!"

The baby continued licking and then tried to gnaw it.

"May!" Edmund called again. "Come see what I found!"

This time he heard a rustling. "Where are you?"

"Over here!" he shouted.

More rustling, and then a girl of eight finally pushed through the weeds. She was covered with sweat, as was he at this point in the afternoon.

"What is it?" May asked.

"Look what I found!" Edmund pointed at the baby.

May's eyes grew wide as her gaze shifted from the baby to Edmund. "A baby! Who is it?"

Edmund shrugged, still grinning. "How should I know?"

"And what is she eating?" May placed her hands on her knees and peered more closely.

"She was crying, so I gave her some candy."

Horrified, May snatched the candy from the baby. "You can't give a baby a peppermint stick! Don't you know that?"

The baby began to wail.

Edmund frowned. "See?"

May hesitated, then gave the sticky candy back to the crying baby. "What if she chokes?"

"She won't choke."

"What are you guys doin'?" came another voice from the weeds. "How come you always leave me behind? When are we gonna do the race?"

Louisa appeared. "Hey!" She stared at the little girl. "Where'd you guys find a baby? In a cabbage patch? How come you didn't tell me?" She looked from her big sister to Edmund and stuck out her lower lip. "And, hey! Why does *she* have candy? Do I get some?"

"Be quiet, Lou," Edmund said. "I'm trying to think."

"About what?"

"About what to do with this baby."

Louisa flopped down and rested her head on one hand. "Are we doin' the race or not?"

"Wonder where her family is," Edmund mused. "Think she belongs to the Warehams?" He nodded in the direction of the Wareham farm, whose pasture abutted the Kerwyns'.

"They don't have any kids. You know that, Ed."

"Well, maybe they got company."

"Maybe."

"I guess we can't leave her here." May picked up the baby. Startled, the girl resumed her wailing and squirming again, despite May's efforts to pat her hard on the back. "Shh!" May said. "It's okay. You're a feisty one, ain't you?"

Edmund slowly held out his hands. “Come here, Possum,” he said softly. “Come on; you’re okay.” Gently, Edmund took the crying baby from May’s arms, staggering for a moment under weight of her. He was not very big himself. “She’s heavy!” he said as he shifted her onto his hip. “There you are,” he said soothingly. “You’re okay now, aren’t you? Shh. It’s okay now.”

Miraculously, the baby stopped crying and instead stared at him, only a few hiccups escaping and the candy stick still grasped tightly in her little fist. Her tiny dark eyes were filled with fright, and Edmund felt a crush of pity for her. She reminded him of a small animal inadvertently caught in a trap meant for bigger prey, and he desperately wanted to soothe her.

“That’s it, Possum,” he said softly.

“Possum?” May’s nose wrinkled.

“Don’t she look like a baby possum?”

May peered at the baby more closely. “No.”

Edmund began to walk.

“Where are you going?” May called.

“Taking her to your ma.”

“Why not take her to yours?”

“’Cause yours is closer. Anyway, your ma will know what to do, most likely.”

“Aw!” Louisa whined, reluctantly getting to her feet. “What about the race?”

“Be quiet, Lou!” May scolded.

“Come on, Possum. Let’s get you home,” Edmund said and gently rubbed the baby’s back as he tramped through the weeds.

CHAPTER ONE

"But you must remember *something*," Kate called from where she was propped up on the sofa in the front room of the Kerwyn farmhouse.

"Honestly, Kate, I don't," replied a frazzled Mrs. Kerwyn, who was busy churning wet shirts through the kitchen laundry press. "Louisa, go out and bring in some more wood. If we don't get that stove hotter, these'll never dry." She pulled her gaze from the tub of dirty suds and inspected the clothes hanging from temporary crisscrossing lines.

Louisa dropped the socks she was folding and let out a disgruntled harrumph. "Why can't Kate? It's not as if it's taxing to walk outside and grab a couple of logs."

"In this weather? She'd catch her death again. Go on."

Despite the fact that Louisa was all of twenty, she stuck her tongue out at Kate before moving toward the back door and pulling on a pair of black rubber farm boots. She didn't bother to buckle them.

"Mom, I can help," Kate insisted and set aside the afghan that Mrs. Kerwyn herself had tucked tightly around her legs. Kate had no real desire to ease the burden of her lazy older sister, but she was sick to death of lying around.

When she stood, however, she did feel a little weak. Leaning one hand on the arm of the sofa to steady herself, she glanced quickly at her mother, hoping she hadn't noticed.

"Oh no you don't!" Mrs. Kerwyn exclaimed over her shoulder. "You lie back down. You know what Doc Hodges said."

"I know, Mom, but I've been lying in bed for nearly two months. If I don't walk around a little, I'm going to forget how." She concentrated on not wobbling as she made her way to the kitchen.

"Pneumonia is tricky, Kate." Mrs. Kerwyn kept her weak gray eyes on the rollers, careful not to get her fingers caught. "Takes a long time." Mrs. Kerwyn might have been considered pretty at one time, but her frizzled strawberry blonde hair had thinned, as had her frail body, and her eyes now had permanent dark circles under them.

Kate pulled out a kitchen chair and eased herself down. "Well, I'll just sit here, then. How about that?" She picked up the socks Louisa had dropped, folded them, then rummaged through the rest of the clothes on the table to find more. She knew she couldn't push her mother too hard, as Caroline Kerwyn was overly protective when it came to sickness, having had two children die from the flu during the epidemic eight years ago.

It had been hard on all of them to lose Eula and Fern, but it had been hardest, of course, on poor Mrs. Kerwyn, who, in Kate's opinion anyway, had never been quite the same. May had also left to marry her sweetheart, Will Dresden, that year, which had further added to the family's sense of loss.

"Well, do you?" Kate asked, pulling a few small towels out of the pile.

Mrs. Kerwyn eased a wet shirt out of the rollers and shook it. "Do I what?"

"Don't you remember anything else from when you found me? What was I wearing?" Kate asked, hoping the answer might provide a clue as to her origins.

"Lord, Kate. How should I know?" Mrs. Kerwyn reached into the bag of clothespins and began pinning the wet shirt to the line. "That was fifteen years ago."

"You're not talking about all this again, are you?" Louisa banged through the back door and dropped an armload of logs onto the empty wrought-iron rack. She then pounded the snow from her boots on the braided rug, a few strands of her long blond hair coming loose from the bun she normally wore.

Kate gritted her teeth. "Yes, we *are*, Louisa. No one asked you to be a part of it, so you can mind your own business."

"Why does it matter so much to you?" Louisa shrugged out of her coat and hung it on the peg by the back door.

It was a good question. Why *did* it matter? Kate supposed she just wanted to know, definitively, to whom she had once belonged. She had grown up thinking that she was a Sauk Indian, but, according to nearly every book on the subject in the Merriweather Library, the Native Americans were very family-oriented, loyal, and honorable, despite their reputation for being vicious, bloodthirsty savages. It seemed impossible that they had simply abandoned her. Had they *meant* to leave her behind like some sort of cursed creature? Or had she wandered away and gotten lost? But if that were the case, why had they not searched for her? And how had she come to be wandering by the Wareham farm?

As a child, she had been happy enough as a Kerwyn, but as she grew older, it became more obvious that she did not belong, not just in her looks but in her temperament.

"You were wearing a brown shift, I think," Mrs. Kerwyn mumbled, a clothespin between her lips.

"And there was nothing on the ground near me? A blanket maybe? A basket?" Kate looked from her mother to Louisa.

"Don't look at me!" Louisa exclaimed. "I was five, so no, I didn't notice. What are you hoping for? A tidy little basket with a letter outlining your name and family history, complete with a desperate appeal to 'take care of our darling child'?"

Kate threw her a wicked look. "Why are you such a shrew, Louisa? It's no wonder you aren't married yet."

"Me? You're one to talk! At least I have Vernon. You'll never find a man with all that vinegar in your veins!"

Kate opened her mouth to deliver a blistering retort when there was a quick rap on the back door, and Edmund ducked in.

"Oh, Ed!" Mrs. Kerwyn set down her bag of clothespins. "You and Gus done already?" She wiped her hands on her apron and glanced nervously at the clock on the wall. "Good gracious! I haven't even started supper yet."

"No, Mrs. K, Mr. K sent me in for a thermos of coffee. Said to tell you it's gonna take a little longer to rebuild that stall than he thought."

"Well, here, sit down by the stove and warm yourself. Louisa, make some coffee."

Louisa let out a deep sigh and rolled her eyes before doing as she was bid.

Edmund's brown eyes grew large at the sight of Kate, half hidden behind the pile of laundry. "You're up! How are you feeling?" He moved anxiously toward the table but then stopped when he noticed he was tracking snow across the floor. "Oh! Sorry, Mrs. K."

"Here, you sit there, Ed." Mrs. Kerwyn nodded at one of the kitchen chairs and went to grab the braided rug by the door. "Put this under your feet," she said, bending in front of him. Ed obediently lifted his feet, and Mrs. Kerwyn shoved it under. "There we are. That'll do. You want something to eat?"

"No, I'm okay. Thanks, Mrs. K."

"Well, at least have a biscuit." Mrs. Kerwyn went to fetch one from the stone canister on the counter.

Edmund looked approvingly across the table. "You look better, Possum. Stronger. Are you?"

Kate smiled, her anger at Louisa dissipating. Edmund always had that effect on her–making her feel calm. He was the brother she wished she had instead of the brutish Ray. Edmund, an only child from the farm next to theirs, had grown up with the Kerwyns, and they had whiled away many a summer day romping through the woods and fields outside of Merriweather proper.

It was Edmund, of course, who had come to her aid when she ran off to live in a badger hole on Christmas Tree Hill when she could no longer stand Ray's relentless harassment. Edmund had helped to make the dwelling not only habitable, but rather cozy, though he had betrayed her slightly by finally informing the Kerwyns as to where she had disappeared.

When she heard where her daughter was, Mrs. Kerwyn herself had several times made her way to the badger hole to plead with Kate to come home, but to no avail. Kate stubbornly refused to leave, having found that independence suited her quite well, thank you very much. She liked living on her own and probably would have remained thus had she not become desperately ill. After finding her unconscious, Edmund had, for the second time, rescued her and carried her home.

"I do feel better, yes." Kate threw a sock at him.

His face immediately broke into a crooked smile, and he threw it back. "Good. I've been missing your caraway bread. When you gonna make some? You're weeks behind, you know," he teased.

"That all I'm good for? Making bread for you?"

He shrugged and shot her a tiny wink, though his eyes looked fatigued, Kate noticed. He practically lived at the Kerwyns these days, helping her father to get the harvest in after Ray, fed up with what he called his father's "relentless slavery," had secured a job in town at the feed mill and taken up residence at Ruby's Boarding House. After stubbornly waiting days for Ray to change his mind and come back, Mr. Kerwyn had been obliged to telephone Edmund and ask if he would come over and help, which he did, despite the fact that he had a widowed mother and his own small farm that needed caring.

"Do you remember anything, Edmund?" Mrs. Kerwyn asked, setting a small plate with two biscuits and a steaming cup of coffee in front of him. "About the day the three of you found Kate?"

"Thanks, Mrs. K," he said, eagerly picking up one of the biscuits. He took a bite and leaned back. "Not much." After pausing to think, he looked at Kate. "I remember you had long black hair, all tangled. Cutest little button nose. No shoes. You were crying. Kept asking for 'Mama.'" He reached for the coffee. "Me and May took turns carrying you." He blew on the steaming mug. "I was probably only about seven, though, so May did most of the carryin'. Why?"

"Because she's obsessed," Louisa said disdainfully from the other end of the kitchen. "She's always been an attention-seeker, Ed, you know that. I wouldn't put it past her to have gotten sick at Christmas on purpose."

"Attention-seeker?" Kate exclaimed, her hot temper flaring. "You'd know all about that, wouldn't you, Louisa?"

"Girls! That's enough," Mrs. Kerwyn said tiredly. "Kate, we've already told you all we know. After the kids brought you home, we got you cleaned up and fed and then called the sheriff. He came out, asked us a bunch of questions," she recited, obviously not for the first time. "By the look of you, he thought you might be one of the Sauk tribe up near Prairie du Chien. Asked around, but no luck. Put out a national wire, but–"

"No one claimed me," Kate finished, able to repeat the old story word for word. But if something had happened to her parents, wouldn't *some* relative have claimed her? It seemed odd . . .

"Yes, that's all we know. Sheriff Norris suggested taking you to Madison or Milwaukee to one of the orphanages there, but, well, by then, we couldn't bear to part with you. Wanted to keep you."

Like a pet, Kate sometimes thought on restless nights. She knew this was unfair, but now that she was on the cusp of womanhood, she simply couldn't rid herself of this burning desire to know more.

"I guess I just want to know what happened to my real family," Kate muttered.

"I thought *we* were your real family, Kate," Mrs. Kerwyn said sadly, wiping her hands on her apron again, a nervous habit.

"I know, Mom. You are. But I . . . I want to know who I really am. Wouldn't you?"

"Can't say that I would, Kate." Her mother retreated to the icebox and began rummaging.

"You're upsetting Mom!" Louisa snipped. "Stop asking her about it! If you really want to find something out, why don't you go talk to the sheriff? Seems he'd have more information than us."

Kate considered. *Why hadn't she ever thought of this before?*

"The thing I've never understood about that story is that there *isn't* a Sauk tribe up near Prairie du Chien." Edmund bit into another biscuit. "Not anymore, anyway."

Kate looked at him sharply. "What do you mean? There is! I've read about them!"

"Well, there might have been once upon a time, but there isn't now. There haven't been any Indians in southwest Wisconsin for about a hundred years. I was telling the story to Uncle Bill the other day for some reason, and he said that story's all hogwash. Upper Wisconsin, maybe, but not lower. So, I don't know what Sheriff Norris was talking about. Maybe he didn't really inquire up there." He took a sip of coffee. "Who knows? You might not be an Indian at all."

Not an Indian? Kate just stared at him. She had spent her entire life thinking she was an Indian, so much so that she had insisted on wearing her thick black hair in braids until she was nearly fifteen to match what the kids had taken to calling her at school, thanks to Ray. *Indian Kate*. And yet, this was the second person to suggest otherwise. The first had been Frank Churchill, who guessed she was perhaps Slavic–an idea she had quickly dismissed at the time.

"You and your mother going to the potluck this year, Ed?" Mrs. Kerwyn asked as she set butter and milk on the counter.

"*I* am, I reckon," he said, glancing over at Kate, who was frowning absently at the wall opposite, her thoughts whirling. "Don't know about Mom. She don't like to go out much anymore. 'Specially in the cold."

"Well, I don't blame her." Mrs. Kerwyn reached for her mixing bowl. "I've a mind not to go myself. Won't be the same without Lou Merriweather, will it? Still can't believe he's gone." She opened the flour canister and scooped some into the bowl. "Poor Leola, what a blow. To lose your husband so young."

"But we're still going to go, aren't we?" Louisa begged. "I told Vernon we'd be there!"

"Yes, I suppose." Mrs. Kerwyn let out a weary sigh.

"Can I go, too?" Kate asked suddenly.

Mrs. Kerwyn looked up from her mixing, her brow furrowed. "Oh, Kate, I don't know. You're not strong enough, I don't think. Normally, you're the one begging to stay home."

"But I missed the funeral," Kate urged. "I don't want to miss this, too." While it was true that she did not like crowds, nor did she enjoy making small talk, this might, she quickly realized, be her one and only chance to question the sheriff. From what she remembered, he was usually there with his wife, as was Chief Meyers, the mayor, and all the city council members. Besides the Harvest Fest and the Independence Day celebrations, the annual potluck was the biggest event in town, and a most welcome one during the long, dark days of winter. And while Kate was not overly sentimental, there *was* a part of her that wanted to express her condolences to Melody upon the loss of her father. It was she, after all, who had given her the chance to sell her baskets and make some extra money when she was trying to survive in the badger hole.

"Might be a chance to talk to Sheriff Norris," Edmund suggested with a tiny wink. Kate looked at him quickly, a smile creeping across her face. Typical Edmund. He had ever been able to tell what she was thinking and feeling–sometimes before she was even aware of it herself.

"Oh, Kate, don't go bothering people." Mrs. Kerwyn began beating flour and milk together with a whisk. "Just let well enough alone."

A surge of irritation erupted in Kate's chest. How often had she heard this as a child? Even when she had finally worked up the courage to tell her mother what Ray had done to her in a closet when she was ten, not long after Eula and Fern died. Ray had teased and harassed Kate from the moment she came to live with the Kerwyns, but that day he had taken his torment a step farther. He had trapped her, unawares, like a wild animal and had, well . . . he had had his way with her. Months afterward, when she had finally told her mother what had happened, Mrs. Kerwyn had been disbelieving and dismissive, telling her to "let well enough alone," which Kate found to be almost more devastating than the crime itself.

Thankfully, "the incident," as Kate began to call it in her mind, only happened the once, though not for the lack of trying on Ray's part. Still, it had changed Kate as profoundly as the death of the girls had changed Mrs. Kerwyn. Kate became ever more alert and wary, unable to be completely at ease unless she was alone. Or with Edmund. Large crowds were therefore a nightmare, which is why she retreated so often to her attic garret and why the badger hole had been so inviting.

"Are you sure you're feeling up to it?" Mrs. Kerwyn's voice was tentative.

"Of course I am," Kate said firmly, though in truth she suddenly felt a bit lightheaded. But it was not due to her weakened state. It was the realization that she might not be who she thought she was. The thought filled her with unnamed dread. Many a time, Mr. Kerwyn had opined that Kate's dark looks and stubborn demeanor were her Indian blood coming out. He did not say it meanly, but proudly, as if pleased to have an exotic bird among his surviving flock of blond, blue-eyed children.

But if she wasn't a Sauk Indian, who was she?

CHAPTER TWO

"I'd have to agree, Mrs. Ehlers," Mrs. Kerwyn conceded. "This *is* the best strudel I think I've ever tasted." She took another bite of the pastry. "Who did you say made it? Mrs. Manning? Now, Kate here makes a very good strudel herself, don't you, Kate?"

Kate nodded absently, not really paying attention to the conversation. She had succeeded in getting herself to the annual potluck dinner, which was no small feat, as Mrs. Kerwyn had faltered not twice, but three times in the space of a week as to whether or not Kate should attend. The latest vacillation had occurred just last night, and it had been Edmund who had finally convinced Mrs. Kerwyn, promising that he would look after Kate (*as if she needed looking after!*) and that he would drive her back home if she grew tired or felt ill in any way. Kate was grateful for Edmund's intervention, but she was becoming increasingly exasperated with her mother. She was perfectly fine! Well, almost.

Kate scoured the crowd again, hoping to spot Sheriff Norris. She wanted to waste no time in finding him in case he left early. Edmund, who had at first stood dutifully at her side, had gotten sidetracked by several other young farmers and was now drifting toward the long tables of food.

Kate took a few steps from her mother, still engaged in a deep conversation with Mrs. Ehlers, and peered into the corners. Half the town seemed to be here, and she had to quiet her desire to escape into the cold air outside. Imogene and Esmerelda Kaufmann were clustered in a corner, and nearby were what looked to be all of the Merriweathers: Mrs. Merriweather and Melody's little sister–*what was her name again?*–were sitting glumly at a table, while Melody, of course, was chatting away with a little crowd gathered around her. Her brother, Fred, stood awkwardly on the periphery, looking a bit lost and forlorn. Near to him was Mrs. Haufbrau, speaking animatedly to several town ladies, and next to *them* stood Frank Churchill and Julius Fairfax, who were also in the thick of a little group, Frank eagerly engaging everyone around him while Julius stood silently at his side, unobtrusively munching on what looked like a cucumber sandwich.

Only Harriet was missing. Kate would welcome a chat with her friend right about now. Throughout the whole of Kate's illness, Harriet had loyally come nearly every day to visit, but she had since dropped off as Kate grew stronger, no doubt busy with her work at the Merc and now the preparations for her upcoming wedding to John Schneider.

Perhaps she was simply late, Kate guessed, and perused the crowd again, remembering that she was supposed to be looking for Sheriff Norris. Finally, she spotted the tall frame of Mrs. Norris. The sheriff stood near her, discussing something with Mayor Hopkins. Kate watched them, her courage suddenly failing. *What had she been thinking?* Was she just going to march up to Sheriff Norris and ask him to recount an incident that had happened fifteen years ago–especially one he probably considered trivial?

Sheriff Norris was an exceptionally fat man, almost completely bald, with small, dark eyes that were nearly squeezed shut from the layers of bags beneath them. Though it was a social event, he was in uniform, his brown shirt straining to hold in his large stomach. Kate's eyes fixated on the shiny gold star on his chest. The mayor moved away, and for a moment the sheriff was alone.

This was her chance . . .

Kate glanced sideways at her mother and then, taking a slow, steadying breath, made herself walk toward the sheriff. He unfortunately spotted her before she reached him, however, his beady eyes tracking her and making her feel awkward and self-conscious. It seemed to take forever to get to him, her legs heavy, as if she had forgotten how to walk. When she finally stood in front of him, he looked her up and down, taking a deep puff of his cigar as he did so.

"What can I do for you, little lady?" he asked.

"I . . . I'm Kate Kerwyn." Kate swallowed hard. "You probably don't remember me."

The sheriff's eyes narrowed as he studied her for a few moments. "You're that kid I picked up, aren't you?" he said through clamped teeth, his cigar firmly planted between them.

Kate blinked in surprise. "Yes, I . . . I am."

The sheriff offered no help, just waited for her to continue. When she did not, he asked in a mocking voice, "Can I help you with something?"

Kate shook her head, breaking her momentary paralysis. "I . . . I was hoping I could ask you about . . . about the time I was found."

"Like what?" He frowned.

Kate let out a quick exhale. "I was told you went to Prairie du Chien and inquired with the Sauk tribe if I belonged to them."

"Yeah?"

"Well, I've . . . I've recently found out there *wasn't* a Sauk tribe, or *any* tribe, up there."

"Yeah?"

"Well . . ." Kate looked around uneasily. "Well, why did you say that?" She forced her eyes to return to the sheriff's. "Why did you tell that to the Kerwyns? All these years, I've believed I'm was a Sauk Indian, and now I find out I'm not?"

The sheriff let out a disgruntled sigh. "Look." He took another puff of his cigar. "I *did* ask a few Indians when I was up there. Wasn't no tribe, per se, but there was a few stragglers. Carryovers. Rejects or runaways from the tribe, you might call them. There's always a few of 'em roaming around. Or lyin' on street corners, more like." He took another puff and looked at her through squinted eyes. "You never know. You *could* still be an Indian. More likely, though, by the look of you, you're from a gypsy family. Coulda been passing through and maybe didn't have enough to feed you and left you behind."

"That can't be true." Kate's stomach tightened.

The sheriff shrugged. "Happened quite a bit after the Crash, 'specially in the cities, but it happened around here some, too. Parents killing themselves or abandoning the kids. Plenty a people went plum crazy back then."

Hot tears sprang to Kate's eyes. "Then I could be anyone."

"Well, far as I'm concerned, you're a Kerwyn. You got lucky. I was all set to take you to St. Joe's in Milwaukee, but when I came to fetch you, Mrs. Kerwyn says, 'No, we'll keep her.' 'You sure?' I says. 'Yes, we're sure,' she says. So, I don't know what you're complaining about."

"I . . . I'm not complaining." Kate's throat ached. "I just wanted to know."

"Well, now you know," he said gruffly.

"Who's this, Ted?" Mrs. Norris snipped, joining the conversation and giving Kate a quick once-over.

Mrs. Norris was as different to her husband in physique as a couple could possibly be–while he was short and fat, she was exceptionally tall and thin. It reminded Kate of the rhyme about Jack Sprat and his wife, though in this case it was reversed. Mrs. Norris had very pale skin, a hooked nose and a cleft chin; she looked exactly like what Kate imagined a witch would. All that was lacking was a disfiguring wart. But while the couple in front of her were opposites in bodily shape, they seemed to be of one mind in their disdain for the general public.

"That kid I picked up aways back. 'Member? Kerwyns took her in."

Mrs. Norris gave her another look up and down. "Oh, yeah?"

"Spent her whole life thinkin' she was an Indian," Sheriff Norris said amusedly, as if this were all a big joke.

"Indian?" Mrs. Norris scoffed. "She ain't no Indian. I told you that at the time, Ted. More than likely you were from one of those immigrant camps that used to be down at the bottom of Magnolia in New Grimsby," she directed at Kate. "Don't know what they were. Romanians or Hungarians or something like that, maybe. Some kind of foreigners. They're all gone now, thankfully." She raised an eyebrow. "What does it matter, anyway? Got a good home with Gus and Caroline. Not all girls is so lucky. Ted can tell you that, can't you, Ted? Number of runaway girls he's come across in his time. Most of 'em turn up dead. Or worse. Would make you sick, some of the things he's seen."

Kate did feel sick. She wanted desperately to get away from the Norrises. She looked around for Edmund, but she didn't see him. "Well, thank you," she mumbled. "I need to find my mother." She needn't have bothered with any niceties, as the sheriff had already turned his attention to Chief Meyers.

Kate wandered in the direction of Mrs. Kerwyn, who was still in conversation with Mrs. Ehlers. Before she could reach her, however, Kate was intercepted by an excited Harriet Mueller. Both her affianced and her mother were in tow. All three of them had plates piled high with food.

"There you are!" Harriet exclaimed. "Your mom said you were here somewhere. I'm so glad you're feeling better."

Kate smiled weakly, grateful that her friend had finally arrived.

"Yes, how are you, dear Kate?" Rosemary Mueller inquired kindly. "We've been ever so worried about you, haven't we, Harriet?"

"I'm well, thanks, Mrs. Mueller. Hello, John." Kate said to the young man at Harriet's side.

John Schneider took a moment to shift the food in his mouth to one side and mumbled, "Hello."

Kate did not actually know John all that well, as he had been several years ahead of her in school, but he had always seemed nice enough. And her father always said the Schneiders ran a good farm. One thing was for sure, Kate decided as she observed John staring puppy-eyed at Harriet: he was head over heels in love with her friend, which made Kate glad. She was grateful Harriet had seen sense in the end and avoided Melody Merriweather's misguided attempts to marry her off to Wesley Elton.

"Didn't you get any food?" Harriet asked. "You'd better hurry if you want any of the hashbrown casserole. It's almost gone." She popped a pickle into her mouth.

The last thing Kate wanted right now was food.

"I'm not all that hungry."

"You okay?" Harriet asked. "You look white as a ghost. Is Ray here?" she asked in a low voice. Only Harriet knew the full story of what Ray had done.

Kate blanched further before remembering that Ray would never come to something like the potluck, even if it meant free food, as for one thing, he would have to face his father.

"No, I . . ." Kate faltered. "I guess I'm just tired."

"Oh. Well, I guess that makes sense. I saw you talking to the sheriff. Everything okay?"

Kate hesitated. Normally, she wasn't one to share her feelings, but she longed to tell Harriet everything the sheriff confirmed. Still, she was loath to do so in front of Rosemary and John. However, they did seem somewhat preoccupied with their food . . .

"Yes, I was . . . I was asking the sheriff for more information about where I might be from, who I might be. Turns out I've been wrong."

"Wrong?" Harriet took a big bite of a meatball. "About what?

"About me being a Sauk Indian from Prairie du Chien."

Harriet's brow creased as she chewed.

"Mrs. Norris thinks it's more likely that I was from one of the immigrant camps that used to be down near you in New Grimsby. Which makes more sense, I suppose," Kate mused. "If I had really been from Prairie du Chien, how would I have been found all the way out by the Wareham farm?"

"What's this now?" Rosemary asked, setting down a large piece of strudel.

With a tired little sigh, Kate quickly related the story to Mrs. Mueller.

"Hmm," Mrs. Mueller said when Kate finished. She wiped her mouth with her hankie. "I do seem to remember a story about a little lost girl now." She studied Kate anew. "Funny how I never connected the story with you." Her wrinkled eyes were unusually bright. "Yes," she murmured. "You'd be about the right age."

"What is it, Mom? Do you remember something?" Harriet looked hopefully at Kate.

"Well, I do recall that there *was* a family, name of Espo or something like that, who lived in that camp. The father was killed in the same mine accident as my Earl, and the mother died of diphtheria not long after. The kids were all picked up by a relative from Shullsburg, if I'm not mistaken. Maybe you were one of them?"

Kate's heart skipped a beat, and she tried desperately to remember. *Espo? Espo?* It didn't ring a bell. "Well," she finally said, "if that were the case, why didn't the relatives take *me*, too?"

Rosemary shook her head sympathetically. "I don't rightly know, Kate. Maybe you wandered away and got lost?"

Kate thought about this. "But once they discovered I was missing, why wouldn't they have come back for me?"

"Maybe they did, but couldn't find you?" Rosemary shifted her plate into one hand and used the other to pat Kate on the arm. "Or maybe they aren't connected with you at all. It's just that when you mentioned the families who used to live down our way, it came to me that maybe they *could* have been your people, just as Mrs. Norris suggested." She moved the plate back into both hands. "I guess I didn't think of it before.

You've always been a Kerwyn to me. And at the time that it all happened, I was overwhelmed with my own grief, as, like I said, Earl died in that accident, too."

"Yes, I'm . . . I'm sorry, Mrs. Mueller," Kate mumbled.

"Ah, well. 'Time heals all wounds.' Isn't that so?" She smiled at Harriet. "Me and Harriet got along alright, didn't we?"

"We did, Mom." Harriet gave her mother a quick return smile and then turned her attention to sampling a deviled egg.

"Did you ever think to ask out at the Warehams?" Rosemary suggested.

Kate folded her lips in quick irritation. Of course they had asked at the Warehams. Many times. The Warehams, however, had not noticed anything unusual on their property, nor had they heard anything. And now they were both practically senile, so it was no use asking them yet again. How they were still living on their own on that big farm was a mystery to all.

Kate pulled her eyes from the Muellers, hoping to spot Edmund in the crowd. It was getting more difficult to see through the haze of cigarette smoke. Finally, she saw him. He was standing very near Frank and Julius, which was odd, but what was even more odd was the fact that he was talking–and laughing!–with a pretty young woman.

"Who's that?" Kate asked Harriet.

Harriet popped a baked chestnut into her mouth. "Who?" she garbled.

"The woman talking to Edmund. I don't think I know her."

"Oh!" Harriet swallowed. "Her name's Mary Crawford. She's a friend of Frank's. She and her brother–he's the one talking to your sisters–are from Chicago. Frank's asked them to help him with the cottages. Henry, that's the brother, is some big architect, and Mary's an interior designer, whatever that is." She looked at John, who gave a little shrug. "I think it means she arranges the stuff inside," Harriet mused. "You know, like the furniture."

Kate studied the young woman. She was tall and slender, but not overly so, just enough to give her a commanding, elegant presence. She had very fair skin, beautiful bobbed, black curls, and a pleasant smile. She was wearing a long, slim burgundy skirt with a matching jacket, cropped at the hip, and a white blouse with a bow at the neck. And gloves! Who wore such an outfit to a church basement potluck?

Now, the woman leaned close to Edmund and whispered something, which made him laugh yet again. Kate felt a little stirring in chest. She wasn't sure she liked this new young woman.

She shifted her gaze to the brother, Henry, who was also dressed as if he were . . . well, going somewhere other than here! He was wearing a dark gray suit with polished Oxfords and a burgundy silk tie that curiously matched his sister's dress perfectly. He was apparently also quite entertaining, if Louisa and Nettie's loud laughter was any indication. However, the two of them, Kate knew, would laugh at just about anything, especially if spoken by a man, so this was no real proof of Henry Crawford's wit.

Unfortunately for Kate, Frank caught sight of her and let out a little cry of joy. "Ah, Kate Kerwyn!" he exclaimed, dramatically throwing up an arm in welcome before moving towards her.

Oh, God, no! Kate's head suddenly began to throb.

"We were just talking about you!"

At this, most of the entourage stopped chatting and looked in Kate's direction. Kate wished a hole would open up in the ground and swallow her. Her eyes darted to Edmund, but he was unfortunately at the back of the little group, Mary Crawford's arm looped tightly through his as he tilted his head toward her to hear what she was saying yet again.

"Allow me to introduce one of our local artists, Miss Kate Kerwyn." Frank's voice held real pride as he approached, the little group following. "Kate makes the most exquisite woven baskets, and she also has a very fine hand at illustration," he added. "Kate, these are my friends Mary and Henry Crawford."

Kate tried to turn to Harriet for support, but the Muellers and John were already back in line for more food! *How much could Harriet possibly eat?*

"Charmed, I'm sure," Henry Crawford said, pulling Kate's attention back. He held out his hand, and after hesitating a moment, she took it. He was not very tall, just her height, actually, but he was extremely handsome—possibly the most handsome man she had ever seen. Her guard went up immediately, however, when he raised her hand to his lips and kissed it. Her insides squirmed. *Was he mocking her?*

"You really must show us your baskets," Mary added, disengaging from Edmund. "Edmund here has been telling us all about you."

Kate shot Edmund a dagger, and his crooked smile instantly withered. With his close-cropped brown hair and worn tweed jacket, he appeared as opposite of Henry Crawford as a man possibly could. He shuffled slightly under Kate's gaze.

"He's been telling us all about how you live in a hole! Is it not charming, Henry?" Mary drawled. "Dear Frank, you have the most delicious acquaintances. Why have you not told us about them before?"

"Well, you are here now, are you not?" Frank smiled his big jovial smile. "And right at the beginning of our grand project. Tomorrow, I will take you and Henry to see the cottages so you can observe what is to be done."

"Splendid! And will you come, too, Edmund?" Mary gushed and batted her eyes at him. *Batted her eyes?* Worse was the fact that Edmund actually blushed and looked at the floor.

"That's mighty kind of you, Miss Crawford, but I've work to do," he bleated like a lost lamb. *Why was he acting this way?* He was normally so confident and strong, but he seemed now like a bowl of mush.

"A pity," Mary said sweetly. "But what about you, Miss Kerwyn? Or may I call you Kate? I do hope you'll call me Mary!"

"Yes, Miss Kerwyn, will you accompany us?" Henry was not quite as overeager in his request, but his deep green eyes held hers, almost as if he could see right through her. It made her feel exposed and weak, shabby. Quickly, she shifted her gaze away and focused instead on the dark curls near the nape of his neck, which was thick and strong. She imagined this was how a Roman emperor might have looked. She found it hard not to stare. He was utterly fascinating, but at the same time, he filled her with a sort of nervous dread.

"No, I . . . I think not." She cleared her throat.

"Oh, but you must!" Henry insisted. "And then perhaps you could show us some of your work."

Again, she could not tell if he was mocking her.

"No!" she said sharply and then regretted it. Feeling everyone's eyes on her again, she began to struggle a bit to breathe. She needed to get away from here, away from these people, away from all the eyes. *It was horrible!* She looked behind her toward the door.

In the next moment, she felt Edmund's strong, familiar arm around her, and she gratefully leaned into him.

"You okay, Possum?" he asked quietly.

She nodded. "I need some air. Help me, Edmund," she mumbled so that only he could hear. She felt herself sag then, but Edmund held her up and began to lead her toward the other end of the hall.

"She's been ill," he explained over his shoulder to the little group. "She just needs some air."

"Shall I come, too?" Mary called eagerly. "She might need a woman's touch."

"No," Edmund called over his shoulder again. "She'll be okay. I've got her."

* * *

Edmund succeeded in getting Kate outside and shuffled down the sidewalk with her until there was a break in the bare shrubbery. He leaned her against the church's brick exterior. She tilted her head back, gasping for air.

"Just breathe slow. Deep. That's it."

Kate tried to follow his instructions, but her mind was racing uncontrollably. Too much information, too many people. Henry's piercing green eyes on her, Mary looping her arm through Edmund's, Sheriff Norris's easy dismissal of her, Rosemary's revelation. She struggled to force her mind to be a blank and fought the urge to gasp for breath. Instead, she tried to breathe slowly, in and out. Over and over she did this until her breathing regained a semblance of normality. She leaned her hands on her knees. The frigidity of the air seemed to help.

"I'm okay, Edmund," she finally said, peering up at him. "You can go back in."

"What happened?" His expression was one of extreme concern.

"I don't know," she tried to say calmly, thought her heart was still beating hard. "It just got to be too much. Too hot and too many people. I just needed some air." She had no desire to tell him everything, particularly because she hadn't figured it all out herself. *She needed time to think.*

"Are you feeling ill? Should I go find your mom? Or should I drive you home?"

"No, I'm fine." She stood up straight. "Really. I just . . . I'm fine. I just need a minute alone. You go on in."

"I'm not leaving you out here!"

"Honestly, Edmund. I just need a moment."

"You sure?" Edmund's brow wrinkled.

Kate nodded.

"Okay," he said uneasily. "But here, take my jacket." He slipped out of his tweed jacket and draped it gently around Kate's shoulders. It smelled so much of him–like fresh hay mixed with clover and sweat–that her eyes momentarily closed in comfort.

"If you're not back in five minutes, I'm coming back out." He wagged a finger and turned back toward the church hall.

Kate watched him go and let out another deep breath. Why *had* she panicked? Her eyes swept the lawn. The moon was bright and illuminated the tombstones of the graveyard across the way. Was it Henry Crawford–the way he had stared at her, as if he knew all of her deep, inner thoughts, as if she were naked in front of him? Suddenly hot, she shrugged off Edmund's coat. She didn't trust this Henry Crawford, nor his sister, either, the way she was flirting–yes, flirting, Kate was sure!–with Edmund, who was too gullible to notice. Who were these strangers, really, and why had Frank brought them here? And why did Frank insist on calling her an artist? She *wasn't* an artist! She was no more an artist than the next person. She had made her baskets to survive in her badger hole. That was all. They had nothing to do with art.

Making her way to the edge of the churchyard, she gripped the metal of the iron fence that surrounded it. Her eyes flitted over the graves, and she let out a deep sigh. It wasn't really Frank or the Crawfords that had upset her so, she knew. It was the new information given to her by Rosemary Mueller. She had a name now. Or maybe a name. Espo.

Espo. Espo. Espo.

Try as she might to force it, the name meant nothing to her. Had these Espos really been her family, and might they really be living in Shullsburg, Wisconsin, just thirty miles away? What would happen if she went to Shullsburg to look for them? She let go of the fence and began to walk along it. Would they recognize her if she knocked on their door? Would they want to? After all, they had rejected her once, might they again?

She glanced back at the church hall. She should return before her mother noticed she was missing. She dreaded going in and being the center of attention, but she couldn't just remain out here.

No, she would have to go back, and, she realized with a groan, she had not yet spoken to Melody.

CHAPTER THREE

Melody looked around the church hall filled with what seemed to be half the town and let out a deep breath. She was already exhausted, and the potluck had begun not but an hour ago. She hadn't expected so many people to come up and share their memories of her father. Hadn't they already done this enough at the funeral? However, if she were honest, she hadn't taken in much of what was said to her at the funeral, being in such a state of shock as she had been.

Louis Merriweather had quietly passed away on New Year's Day, effectively sealing that day, at least for the Merriweathers, to forever be one of sadness rather than the one of hopeful resolve normally afforded that holiday. The whole town had grieved the loss of one of their most stalwart residents, and despite the frigid temperatures that first week of January, hundreds had turned out for the wake and funeral. So many had turned up at the luncheon afterward, in fact, that the Ladies Aid at St. Mary's had run out of broasted chicken and had had to resort to turkey-and-dressing sandwiches.

"Never in my life did I see a more well-attended funeral, Melody," Mrs. Dixon was saying now. Melody hadn't even noticed her approach. "I told that to your mom at the time, I did. The only one that even comes close would've been little Jimmy Dalsing's. That was an awful tragedy, wasn't it? How's she doing, poor thing?" Mrs. Dixon's eyes traveled to where Leola Merriweather was sitting forlornly at a table with Bunny.

"She's holding up," Melody fibbed. In truth, her mother was not "holding up" very well at all. She was lower than Melody had ever seen her. She ate hardly anything these days, and Melody had frequently found her sitting alone in the front room for hours at a time, seemingly not aware that the room had grown dark around her. Even Helenka's frequent attempts to engage her in conversation failed. And when Mums *did* speak, she tended to be irritable and short. Melody was trying to be patient, but it was hard, as Mums seemed not to realize that Melody–and Bunny and Fred, too–were grieving as well.

"And what's to happen with the Mercantile?" Mrs. Dixon asked, her tone shifting ever so slightly now from sympathy to what one might call gossipy interest. "Not gonna close, is it?"

"Not if I can help it!" Melody said cheerily but then instantly regretted it, as in truth, the Merriweathers were divided on the subject.

After the funeral, Mums had closed the Merc for a whole week out of respect. In the weeks that followed, however, she had been reluctant to reopen and spoke of shuttering it permanently. Alarmed, Melody had pleaded for it to remain open, saying that it was what Pops would have wanted. Surprisingly, Fred had backed her up, saying that not only was it a Merriweather institution, but it had the potential to be even more profitable if managed properly. And, since Pops had left behind a small life insurance policy, they were not *quite* as overstretched as they had been just before his death.

Mums had finally acquiesced, "for the time being," but she remained uncertain, routinely blaming the Merc for Pops's poor health, saying that it had sucked the life out of him, just as it had his father before him. Melody was of the opinion that it had probably been the cigars and whiskey he consumed every day of his life that had sucked the life out of him, but she had refrained from saying this aloud.

"Well, I'm glad of that!" Mrs. Dixon exclaimed. "Heitman's doesn't hold a candle to the Merc!"

"Thanks, Mrs. Dixon." Melody absently brushed her hair back.

"I'll just go over and say hello to your poor mom," the older woman said, patting Melody on the shoulder. "You let us know if you need anything, won't you?"

Melody gave a little nod and decided she would go get some desperately needed lemonade no matter who came up next, but when she saw Mr. Van Dyke approach, she stopped herself.

"How are you holding up, Melody?" he asked in his gentle way, taking her hands in his.

Melody looked into the older man's sad blue eyes and felt a wave of sadness herself. She had been doing her best to put on a brave face, both at the Merc and here tonight–which was seeming more like a second memorial to her father than a typical potluck–but at the sight of Mr. Van Dyke, she crumbled a little.

This past Christmas, Mr. Van Dyke had taken up a collection amongst the other business owners and given it to Melody as a gift to help save the Merc. She was deeply indebted to him, though he claimed that it was a repayment–a grossly inadequate one, he added–for a favor

Louis had done him many years prior. Melody still wondered what it possibly could have been, but since Mr. Van Dyke did not elaborate, she did not feel like she should pry.

Her father, she was discovering, had done countless favors for people over the years, none of which he had ever felt the need to expound on. A larger-than-life character, he had always been the heart and soul of any party, but Melody hadn't known the depth of his charity and compassion. Everyone, it seemed, had a story to tell, and while these tales were a comfort, in a way, they were also painful. It made Melody realize that there was a part of her father she would never fully know. And it made her feel ashamed of her own selfishness in the past. But, likewise, they inspired her to be a better person and pick up just where her father had left off.

"I'm fine, Mr. Van Dyke." She gave him a sad smile. "Thanks for asking."

"Anything I can do?"

"Not that I can think of."

"You'll let me know, though, right?" He patted her hand. "I'm just down the street."

"I know. Thank you. I–"

"Ah! Young Melody Merriweather!" Mayor Hopkins boomed, coming up now. "How are things? Doing okay?" He patted his large middle.

Mr. Van Dyke dropped Melody's hands and stepped aside, giving her a small wink.

"Still can't believe ole Lou's gone!" The mayor wagged his head back and forth. "Sure isn't the same here tonight without him, is it?" Without waiting for her answer, he went on. "Did I ever tell you about the time he and I snuck down an old mine shaft? The boarded-up one on the other side of Christmas Tree Hill? Think we were only about ten or eleven–"

Melody *had*, in fact, heard this one, and after a few minutes of polite attention, she surreptitiously let her eyes roam while the mayor yammered on. Mums was still talking to Mrs. Dixon, or rather, Mrs. Dixon was talking to *her*. Mums looked embarrassingly uninterested. Bunny, of course, had disappeared. Melody glanced in the other direction and spotted Fred politely conversing with Mrs. Haufbrau.

Remembering she was supposed to be listening to the mayor, she turned her attention back and nodded accordingly at various parts of his story, smiling when necessary.

After a few minutes–the mayor still droning on–she looked out over the crowd again. This time, she was surprised to see Cal Fraiser hovering near. Her heart skipped a little beat, but she looked away, determined not to give him the satisfaction. He had said he wasn't coming tonight, and yet, here he was. It was just like him to be so . . . so frustrating.

Ever since her father's funeral, Cal had been acting differently. At first, she put his aloofness down to respect for her grief, or possibly his own grief, but as it continued week after week, she wondered if it was perhaps something else . . .

Though they had started as almost enemies, Cal critiquing her every move when she first took over the Merc, there had been a softening of sorts over time, especially after the fire and after she admitted that she had been wrong about Harriet and John. So much so that she was *sure* he had been about to say something at their Christmas Eve party . . . something perhaps intimate or flirtatious, maybe even committal. It had all the makings of a romantic moment, if the fluttering of her own heart had been any indication, but said moment was lost when Douglas Novak had arrived on the doorstep and ruined everything. Cal had promptly retreated to a corner, glaring at her intermittently until he had finally slipped out without even saying goodbye.

And then her father had died, further killing the precarious, coveted moment. And now there seemed to be no chance of it resurrecting, despite the fact that she had purposefully put herself in Cal's way so many times since that it was almost embarrassing–rearranging the cheese display to be alphabetical; counting the sheets of white butcher paper, supposedly for inventory purposes; sweeping the back entrance more times than she ever had before, which previously had been none; and various other meaningless tasks. Was it because Fred was hanging around now that Cal had become so reticent? If so, it was yet another reason to be irritated with her annoying older brother.

Fred had taken a leave of absence from Harvard following Pops's death, and in the beginning, when their grief was still raw, it had been nice to have an extra pair of hands at the Merc, especially with Imogene gone to live in Frank and Julius's restored mining cottage to serve as a sort of docent, or, more accurately, as a living prop. But as time had ticked along, Melody and Fred were beginning to butt heads on the running of the family store. It bothered her that Fred had just waltzed in and assumed that because he was older–and male–he was in charge. Why couldn't he just go back to school?

She glanced back at Cal again. He was still staring at her in that moody way of his as he pushed back a dark lock of hair. She wasn't sure if it was annoyance she saw in his eyes or if it was maybe . . . if it was maybe . . . She pulled her gaze away, her heart beating a little faster now. It was the same look he had given her at the Christmas party. But why, then, did he practically ignore her at the Merc? And why not come over here right now instead of sulking in a corner? She was tempted to go over to *him*, but–

"Wouldn't you say, Melody?" the mayor asked with a booming laugh.

Startled, Melody turned her attention back to the man in front of her. "What? Oh, yes!" She forced a smile.

"And then Lou pulled that bucket up out of the well, what do you think was in it?" Mr. Penrose asked merrily. Melody hadn't even noticed that a little group had gathered around them, nor did she have any idea how the story had gone from the mine shaft tale to one about a well. "An old shoe!" He laughed, and the others joined in. "Shoulda seen the look on your dad's face!"

Melody gave a false little chuckle and looked back to where Cal had been standing–but he had disappeared!

Her eyes darted quickly around the crowd until she eventually spotted him talking now with Harriet and John. With them, she noticed irritably, he was all smiles. For a brief moment, Melody was tempted to squeeze out from the group surrounding her and join her employees, but before she could, she saw Cal give Harriet a kiss on the cheek, shake John's hand, and head toward the door.

And then, before she knew it, he was gone.

With a sigh of frustration, she turned her attention back to Mayor Hopkins, who had unfortunately started yet another story. Melody tried her best to listen attentively this time, but she couldn't help but feel like the bride who doesn't get to enjoy her own wedding for fear of offending the guests. Except, she thought wryly, she was without a groom. And a maid of honor, for that matter, who might fetch her a drink.

"Here you are," Frank Churchill said and miraculously handed her a cup of lemonade. "Thought you might be thirsty." He smiled. "Big crowd tonight, isn't there?"

"What a godsend you are!" Melody took a long drink and tried to force Cal from her mind. "How did you know I was thirsty?"

"Well, you haven't moved from this spot for over an hour. And, as I've told you before, I'm your fairy godfather." He waved his fingers. "Enjoying yourself?"

"Well, you know." She gave him a faint smile. "We came thinking it would be good for Mums to get out." She tilted her head toward where her mother was still sitting forlornly, a full plate of food in front of her. "But I think it might have been a mistake."

"We spoke to her for a bit, didn't we, Julius?" he said.

Julius, always a man of few words, nodded.

"She seems quite low, poor dear. Perhaps we shouldn't have moved out so suddenly?" Frank suggested. They had been the Merriweathers' lodgers while Pops was in the hospital.

"I don't think it was that. It's just Pops."

"Perhaps I should bring my friends, the Crawfords, round to meet you all. I was hoping to introduce you this evening, but they left early."

"Yes, I saw them. Who are they?"

"Acquaintances from Chicago. We've asked them to come aid us on the redesign of the cottages. They'll be perfect, you know. Henry had a terrific idea to perhaps have a little gift shop in one of them. We could stock the cider, which would be another outlet for you. Or maybe a small café. What do you think?"

Melody considered. This might be a very good idea, indeed. "Why not? I think–"

"Melody, we should go now," interrupted Fred. He gave Frank and Julius barely a glance and instead glared at his sister.

"Now? I haven't even eaten anything yet!"

"Well, I can't help that. Mums says she has a splitting headache. She sent Bunny over to tell me. So, come on. We need to go."

"May I be of any assistance?" Frank asked with genuine concern.

"I think I can get my own mother and sisters home!" Fred snapped.

"Fred!" Melody exclaimed, shocked by her brother's rudeness. For reasons she had yet to unravel, Fred seemed to have an aversion to Frank and Julius. Though Julius had given him his room back and Frank had been nothing but respectful graciousness–*and* despite Pops himself approving–Fred continued to hold a grudge against the half-brothers. Even after they had moved out of the Willows and into the restored apartment above the Merc, Fred still did not seem to like them.

"Not to worry," Frank said, giving Melody a quick wink. He leaned closer. "I'll see you at the shop, and we can discuss things later."

Melody gave him a grateful smile before following Fred to where Bunny was helping her mother on with her coat. Except for the townspeople's additional kind outpourings of sympathy, it had been a thoroughly disappointing evening. She hadn't gotten a scrap of food, but worse, she had not had a chance to talk to Harriet or John or Rosemary. Nor Kate, whom she had seen standing next to them for a time. She had specifically wanted to tell her that not only were they low on her baskets, but that she had money waiting in the register from the sale of her others. And then there was Cal of course, who had slid out before she could speak to him. But he was a different problem altogether and one she didn't have time to think about right now.

One thing was for sure, however, she determined as she glanced over at Freddy again, his jaw set hard. She was going to get to the bottom of why he was so cranky. She knew he was grieving, but his grumpiness and his impatience seemed to be getting worse.

The sooner he went back to school, the better.

CHAPTER FOUR

Fortunately—or unfortunately, as it turned out—Melody did not have to wait long to discuss Fred's departure, as he himself brought the subject up at dinner the very next day.

Dinners had become rather muted in the months since Pops's death and the eventual departure of all of their lodgers. It was one of Pops's last acts of charity to insist the Kaufmanns stay at the Willows until new arrangements could be made, despite Mums's opinion to the contrary. Mums disliked poor Imogene and often said so out loud, but at least, Melody mused, she had had a strong opinion. These days, Mums was apathetic about almost everything.

"I've come to a decision," Fred declared grandly. He had just recently taken to sitting in Pops's chair at the head of the table, which annoyed Melody. It was not only disrespectful, but presumptuous as well.

"About what?" She was sure it had something to do with the Merc, probably a critique of something or other. Just this morning, he had barricaded himself in the office to work out a new system of tracking inventory. Personally, Melody wasn't sure what was wrong with their current method, which consisted simply of looking at the shelves, noting what needed to be ordered and then ordering it, but of course her opinion didn't matter. She braced herself for an argument.

Fred took his time responding, pausing to spear another bite of tender roast pork–one of Helenka's specialties–and swiping it through a pool of gravy. Despite his criticisms over the years of Bunny being overly dramatic, Fred had a flair for it at times as well. He leaned back now and dabbed his mouth with his napkin.

"I hope it's about when you're going back to school," Bunny said irritably. "I'd like to get back to my evening practice."

Since Fred had come home, he had asked–no, insisted–that Bunny refrain from practicing after dinner, as it gave him a headache when he was trying to relax and read the paper. *Relax and read the paper? Since when?* It frustrated Melody beyond belief that he was so obviously trying to turn himself into a carbon copy of their father.

Fred frowned. "As a matter of fact, that is exactly what I wanted to announce." He scowled at Bunny, clearly annoyed that she had stolen his thunder. "I'm not going back."

"What?" Melody exclaimed. "Why?"

Bunny likewise groaned.

Mums stopped pushing food around her plate and actually looked up. "What did you say, Fred?"

"I said I'm not going back to school, Mums," Fred repeated, a little louder.

"But why?" Melody was stunned.

"I think that's obvious, Mel. The Merc needs help, and I'm here now."

"No, it doesn't! I was doing pretty well on my own, thank you very much."

Fred sopped up some mashed potatoes with his roll. "You've done a good job in the interim, Mel, I'll say that, but there are a lot of improvements that could be made."

"Yes, I know that, Fred, but it's not like I had any money to make changes. I've tried as best I could." *How dare he!* She had more than done a "good job"; she had literally saved the Merc from going under. And she now had a vision for the future, courtesy of Frank Churchill, who had convinced her to focus on local products and craftwork for the new age of tourism he and Julius were hoping to usher into Merriweather with the renovation of some of the cottages on Magnolia into working historical sites.

Fred gave a little chuckle. "Yes, but selling crude baskets made by a hermit girl, and soaps made by the village idiot, and . . . and cider brewed by crazy old Rosemary Mueller isn't going to do it. What we need to do is apply sound Harvard business practices." He pounded the table softly with his fist. "Let's face it, Pops wasn't the best bookkeeper in the world. And," he hissed in a whisper meant only for Melody, "the fact that he borrowed money from loan sharks is saying a lot."

"Well, Uncle Joe didn't help matters," Melody hissed back.

"But it's Pops's fault for trusting him with all of his money!"

"What are you two whispering about?" Bunny interrupted. "Didn't anyone ever tell you that's rude?"

"Yes, what are you saying, Freddy?" Mums pushed her plate away.

"I was just saying that I'll be damned if I let the Merc and the Merriweather name fall into the dustheap of history. I plan on staying to bring us back to our former glory!" He raised his glass, but no one else joined in the salute.

"I wasn't aware we were in *need* of resurrection," Melody snipped.

"Me, either." Bunny set down her fork.

"Well, I don't know. Perhaps it *might* be a good idea for Freddy to stay," Mums said with pathetic eagerness. "I couldn't bear for him to leave just now. What would we do without him?"

"Mums, it would be foolish for Freddy to quit with just one semester left. It was Pops's greatest wish that he finish law school. And, as a lawyer, he'll be a much better financial resource to the family."

Mums pursed her lips. "Well, that *is* true, Fred. And Melody was doing well enough at the Merc. There *was* the fire, but that wasn't necessarily her fault. Perhaps she should continue on while you go back to school."

"I will at some point, Mums. But right now, a man's gotta do what a man's gotta do."

Melody rolled her eyes. "A *man* would do his duty and finish school!"

"Temper, temper," Freddy admonished and waved his fork at her.

Melody threw herself back in her chair and crossed her arms. "Well, what am I supposed to do now that you think you're in charge? Be a shopgirl at your beck and call?" Of course he was swooping in now, *after* she had been forced to give up her lovely life at Mundelein. Had it really taken Pops's death for him to feel some sort of family responsibility?

Almost as if he had read her mind, Fred tossed his napkin onto his empty plate. "You might as well go back to Mundelein, Mel."

"Go back to Mundelein? But why?" Mums seemed genuinely confused.

"Don't be ridiculous, Freddy." Melody tossed her napkin, too. "We don't have the money for that. You just want me out of the way. And, anyway, it's the middle of the term!"

"Well, what does *that* matter? You're not really there to get a degree, are you? Look, you can have *my* college money. Or maybe you can get some kind of scholarship. Family hardship and all that. Who knows, maybe you'll meet some rich guy and marry him. Isn't that the whole point of that school? Whatever happened to that kid you were seeing? What was his name?"

Melody drummed her fingers on the embroidered tablecloth. Figures Fred would bring all this up again. And in front of Mums, who did not blame Douglas for essentially ruining Christmas (at least for Melody) and instead blamed Melody for rejecting him! It was maddening!

It hadn't been *her* fault that Douglas had turned up on their doorstep on Christmas Eve. She had written him a perfectly respectful letter in which she had refused his many offers of matrimony once and for all, thinking that this would be the end of it. But, no! He had not accepted her answer and had recklessly driven all the way to Merriweather from Chicago to confront her. His parents must have been furious! And of course, having no clear plan and nowhere to stay, Douglas had accepted Pops's invitation to sleep on the couch. Likewise, he had further ruined Christmas by accompanying them to church the next morning and then accepting Mums's cheery invitation for him to dine with them as well.

Melody had tried her best not to be alone with Douglas, but he had finally found his chance when he spotted her trying to creep up the stairs for a quick nap after their big Christmas dinner.

"There you are, Melody! I've been looking for you everywhere!" he hissed, rushing up the stairs after her.

Melody reluctantly turned. "Oh, hello, Douglas." She forced a smile. "I was just going to lie down for a bit. A little too much for dinner." She patted her stomach.

"Melody! Stop avoiding me! We have to talk!"

Melody bit the inside of her cheek. It *was* silly to keep running from him. She would just have to be firm, though she *thought* she had already done that in her letter.

"Oh, alright." She leaned against the wall. "Go on."

"Here? On the staircase? Can't we go somewhere . . . well, private?"

"In case you haven't noticed, the house is rather full." Melody came down a few steps. "Maybe the pantry? But I think Helenka is in the kitchen preparing something for this evening," she murmured. "And the back porch is too cold . . ."

"Can't we go to your room?" he pleaded.

Melody sighed. It *was* perhaps the only private place left in the house, but she was loath to lead Douglas to her bedroom–not because of the impropriety, though if Mums were to find out, she would be furious (however, if the light snore coming from her room was any indication, Mums was having her own little lie-down). And it wasn't because Melody feared that Douglas would do anything ungentlemanly–he was, in her mind, akin to a cuddly little kitten–but because she would have nowhere to retreat if the conversation grew uncomfortable. She could hardly waltz out of her own bedroom, leaving him in there alone, if the topic at hand became too heated. Which, she predicted, it might.

"Fine. But we have to be quick. And quiet," she emphasized. "Mums is right next door."

Douglas followed her on tiptoe into her room and paused just inside the door, his eyes darting everywhere at once.

Melody leaned against her desk, facing him. "Well?"

Douglas stopped observing the sacred inner sanctuary of his love and gazed at her. Melody quailed under the pain she saw there.

"Why, Melody? Why won't you marry me?" he begged. "Is it something I did? Something I said? Didn't say? Didn't do?"

Melody's stomach churned, and she closed her eyes briefly, trying to gather strength. "Douglas, it isn't you. You're perfectly sweet. Perfectly charming. It's me. I . . . I'm needed here. And I *want* to be here, especially with my dad being sick."

"I can wait! I really can. I'm sorry if I pressured you. I won't anymore! I promise."

Melody pinched the bridge of her nose. "Douglas, it's not that. I . . . I just don't love you in that way," she said softly. "I'm sorry."

Douglas's face crumpled. "But why? We were so happy back at school. What's changed?"

Melody didn't answer.

"There's someone else, isn't there?" he asked abruptly.

An image of Cal rudely appeared in her mind, but she banished it. "No, Douglas. There's not."

"Promise?"

Melody considered. She would not be lying if she answered that there was nothing between her and Cal, because there wasn't. "No, there's not, Douglas."

Douglas put a hand briefly over his eyes. "Can I have my ring back, then?" he asked, lowering his hand. His face was hard now. "It was my grandma's engagement ring."

Melody felt suddenly nauseated. This was the other reason she had been dreading this conversation. "Oh, Douglas. I don't know how to tell you this, but I . . . I had to pawn it. I'm so terribly sorry!"

"Pawn it! Why?" He stared at her incredulously.

Melody pulled her eyes from his and studied the black-and-white celebrity photos she had clipped from *Vogue* in her younger years and taped to her dormered ceiling. She stared at Clark Gable and then Barbara Stanwyck. *Had they ever had these problems? Oh, what had she done?*

She returned her gaze to Douglas, her stomach still churning with guilt. "My dad borrowed money from loan sharks to keep the Merc afloat," she said in a rush, "and I needed cash to pay them off. I tried raising the money by brewing and selling cider, but it wasn't enough, so I . . . I pawned the ring. I'm so sorry, Douglas."

Douglas ran his hands through his hair and began to pace in the little space. "Well, where is it? I'll just have to buy it back. My mother will kill me if I've lost it!"

"Melody! Is that you?" Mums called from her room. "Who are you talking to?"

"No one, Mums!" Melody called back.

"Well, be quiet!"

Melody rolled her eyes and turned her attention back to Douglas. "Oh, Douglas!" she said in a lowered voice. "It . . . I don't know how to tell you this, but someone has already bought it." The fact that it had been Wesley Elton who had purchased it just to thwart her made it all the worse.

"Bought it!" Douglas ran his hands through his hair again. "Who was it? I've got to get that ring back."

"His name is Wesley Elton. He works at the bank. He's a bit of a crumb, though, so I'm not sure if he'll sell it back."

Douglas looked at her with what seemed utter defeat. "Oh, Melody. How could you do this to me?"

For a brief moment, Melody wavered. Almost instantly, however, her resolve returned. She couldn't possibly marry someone she didn't truly love. She loved Douglas as a pal, but not as a woman should love her husband. "I'm sorry, Douglas. I . . . I was desperate. I'll pay you back for the ring. I promise."

Douglas groaned. "It's not just the ring, Mel. It's you. I want *you*."

Tears were pooling in her eyes now. "I'm sorry, Douglas," she repeated. "Truly, I am. We had some fun times. Ones I'll never forget. But I'm not the girl I was back then. I've changed." She brushed a tear away. "I guess it just wasn't meant to be."

"It *was* meant to be! I'll show you. I'll wait for you."

"No, Douglas." She took his hands. "It's no use."

Douglas stared at her for a few more moments and then dashed out of her room and pounded down the stairs. Melody did not immediately follow but stood there trying to collect her thoughts. When she heard the front door bang and his car rumble to a start, however, she ran down the stairs. He couldn't leave on Christmas Day! But by the time she got to the front porch, his car was already halfway down the street.

Melody knew it had been the right decision, but it still hurt. She had gone over it so many times in her head, tortuously thinking of all she could have, *should have* said to poor Douglas. Several times she had attempted to write him a letter, but it always ended with her tossing it, unfinished, into the waste basket. Neither had he written to her, apart from a plain white card expressing his sympathy after her father's death.

Melody let out a deep breath. "His name was Douglas, Fred. You know that. But I don't see what he has to do with any of this. I'm not going back. You are!"

"Why isn't there ever any discussion about *my* future?" Bunny declared. "If there's college money no one seems to want, why can't I have it for Julliard? Miss Elliot claims I have a very good chance of getting in, that I have a talent that shouldn't be wasted."

"Who the hell is Miss Elliot, and why should you take her word for it?" Fred scoffed.

"Miss Elliot is my *piano teacher*, which you'd know if you weren't so self-absorbed, Freddy."

Fred drained his wineglass. "She probably says that to all her students."

Bunny stood up. "You know, for once I agree with Melody. You're a pretentious brat!" she declared and exited in a huff.

"I don't see why you all have to argue!" Mums moaned as Helenka came in and began clearing the table.

"Pretentious brat, am I?" Freddy hissed to Melody.

Melody gritted her teeth. "I never said that, Freddy."

Helenka exited with a load of dirty dishes.

"But you think it, don't you?"

"What does it matter what I think? You've made *that* perfectly clear."

"It is banana pudding for dessert," Helenka announced to no one in particular as she returned to the dining room, now carrying a silver tray with three bowls of heaping pudding topped with whipped cream and garnished with a cherry. She looked worriedly at Mums, who was already getting to her feet.

"None for me, Helenka. I couldn't possibly eat another bite."

"*Pani*," Helenka urged, setting a bowl at Mums's place anyway. "Just one bite, no?"

"I'll have some!" Fred said eagerly, but Helenka was not listening. Having failed at enticing her mistress into dessert, she was now helping Mums out of the room, one arm around her middle.

Fred rose and reached across the table for one of the bowls still sitting on the tray. "I guess I'll have to help myself. You want some?" He glanced at Melody as he dipped a spoon into the pudding.

"No," she said, pushing back her chair. "I'm not hungry. I'm going up."

"I don't see why you're so sore, Mel," he called. "I'm doing this for you, you know. Sacrificing myself for all of you. It's what Pops would have done."

Melody paused, her hand on the stair rail. She turned to look at him. "Sacrificing yourself? No one asked you to, Fred. This doesn't make sense, and you know it. You're just being pigheaded. And this is *not* what Pops would have done. He sent for *me* when he got sick, not you. And there was a reason for that, if you'd only think about it for half a minute."

With that, she marched up the stairs and shut herself in her room for the rest of the night.

CHAPTER FIVE

Melody awoke with a jolt the next morning and glanced at the little round alarm clock near her bed. *8:20! She had overslept!* She groaned and threw off her covers.

She struggled to get her feet into her slippers but then kicked them off again when she realized she hadn't time to go down for breakfast. Instead, she went to her closet and pulled on a blouse and her work skirt. Despite having gone to bed early, she hadn't gotten to sleep until the wee hours, and even then, had slept fitfully. All night, she had tossed and turned, thinking about Freddy's announcement.

Dressed now, she threw herself onto her vanity stool and began to frantically brush her hair. Her thoughts had run the gamut during the course of the night, going from insisting that she remain in charge of the Merc and demanding that Fred go back to school to capitulating completely and returning to Chicago, if only to watch him fail. But she couldn't do that, she thought, as she carefully applied some lipstick. As much as she would love to see Fred humbled, she couldn't bear to let the Merc fail.

But then she had conjured up memories of the balls, the spring tea, dancing at the Aragon, and their rides up Lake Shore Drive in Charlie's Buick Century or Douglas's V8 Sport and imagined how wonderfully delicious it would be to step back into her old life—to have her only care be studying for a silly test or advising one of her court on the best way to attract a certain Loyola boy's attention. What a contrast it would be compared to her daily worries at the Merc about money, not to mention having to order supplies, bargaining with the farmers over the sums she paid them, setting mousetraps, scraping the mold off the cheeses in the case, and dealing with annoying housewives who complained about prices and anything else that occurred to them, such as if the apples or turnips they bought rotted too soon. As if that was *her* fault! No, she would be all too glad to hand this all off to Fred while she waltzed the night away and watched the sun come up over the lake with her friends.

Downstairs, the dining room was deserted. Helenka had already cleared away breakfast. Melody was tempted to simply dash out the door, but then a thought struck her. Why was she hurrying? Fred was there. He would no doubt have choice words for her when she finally turned up, but would it matter if she took the time to have a cup of coffee? After all, he fancied himself in charge now, so let him handle the morning's business. His custom these past weeks was to simply lock himself in the office for most of the day, letting Melody handle the daily operations as well as the staff. Well, let him do it. It would be good for him to see what he was really getting into.

She pushed through the swinging door into the kitchen, expecting to find Helenka there, but she was not. She must be upstairs already, either making beds or tending to Mums. Helenka had gotten into the bad habit of carrying breakfast up to Mums instead of Mums joining them as she always had. It made Melody sad all over again. Her mother used to be the first one up every day, bright and cheerful, with a long list of to-dos for the day. Now it was a struggle just to get her to come down for dinner. *Oh, Pops! Why?*

Morosely, Melody poured herself a cup of coffee. Maybe she really *should* go back to Chicago, she considered. She could return to her gay life at Mundelein and pretend that Mums and Pops were still back here, still alive, still happy. She might even be able to resurrect the old foursome–her and Cynthia and Douglas and Charlie. Maybe she could get Douglas to accept a friendship instead of a love affair, and everything could go back to the way it was–football games and dances and holding court in the grand parlor of Philomena with Mundelein's most elite and fashionable girls clustered around her. Maybe she could even get a job at a sweetshop or a soda fountain on Saturday afternoons as a way to pay Douglas back for his ring.

Right now, everything went to paying the bills and buying supplies. With the Merc on such a tightrope, she hadn't dared to pocket any money for herself. But if she had a little side job in Chicago, she could surely keep that money until she had enough to pay Douglas.

She set her empty coffee cup in the sink and went to get her hat and coat. Maybe she *should* let Fred take over. After all, maybe he wouldn't fail. Maybe his "sound Harvard business practices" would turn the Merc around more than *her* farcical ideas would. She wished she could discuss it with Frank, but she could already guess what he would advise: stay the course and be part of Merriweather's revival.

Melody slipped out of the house and began walking down Ridge. Though there was still a trace of frost on the ground, the trees were beginning to bud, and she could see flowers beginning to poke through the dead autumn leaves against the white picket fences. They cheered her.

As she turned onto High Street, she tried to view Merriweather as an outsider might. It had definite charm, she decided, and felt herself wavering yet again. It wasn't at all a bad place to live. She had grown used to running the Merc and to, well, to stepping into her father's shoes. Admittedly, they were big shoes to fill, but she had grown immeasurably in confidence since last fall. She was proud of what she had accomplished so far, and she repeated the retort she had thrown at Freddy last night–that it was *her* whom Pops had asked to come back and help, not him. She could always come back after she graduated. It wouldn't be forever, after all. Unless, of course, she met someone in Chicago and fell head over heels.

But that, she mused, was unlikely to happen. No, this was where she belonged, she resolved, and Fred wasn't going to push her out, as if she had no say in the matter.

When she finally arrived at the Merc, she stood for a moment enjoying the display in the big front window. Her latest window design filled her with not a little pride. Instead of the rakes and shovels and seed packs they normally showcased as part of their "Get Ready for Spring" display, she and Harriet had arranged one that featured a pastel bunting draped across the window with Kate's baskets assembled on the ground and atop boxes draped with pastel cloth. Artfully arranged throughout were the luxury hats and gloves she had ordered last fall, and at the center of it all was a bicycle!

It was Melody's latest idea for a product they might stock. There used to be a bicycle shop in town–Brietbach's–but they had gone out of business shortly after the Crash. Now, if one wanted a bicycle, you had to go all the way to Madison. It had been a stroke of genius on her part, Melody thought proudly.

She pushed open the door, the shop bell tinkling. "Sorry, I'm late!" she cried.

"Oh, hello, Melody!" Harriet was behind the counter, a feather duster in hand. There was no sign, of course, of Fred. "We were getting worried, weren't we, Mrs. Haufbrau?"

Mrs. Haufbrau merely grunted and returned to looking over the receipt book at the back counter, her favorite task.

"We were just talking about the wedding," Harriet explained as she returned to jabbing her feather duster between the jars of candy sticks.

"Have you decided on a date?" Melody shed her hat and coat and reached for her apron.

"Oh, yes!" Harriet gushed. "We finally decided late last night. June 11! I'm to be a June bride! Mom thinks it's a bit too fast, but I don't. Do you, Melody?"

"Yes, it's too fast," Mrs. Haufbrau called without looking up.

"Well, I don't know." Melody tied on the apron. "Have you talked to Fr. Eggert? What does he say?"

Harriet glanced nervously at Mrs. Haufbrau. "Well, he says it's okay as long as . . . as long as, you know." She blushed.

"People will talk," Mrs. Haufbrau chirped matter-of-factly, still absorbed in the receipt book.

"Well, anyway." Harriet's voice was lower now. "We've already gotten so much done. Mom is sewing my dress, and John's to buy a new suit. His brother, Walter, is to be the best man, and I'm having two of his sisters for bridesmaids." She looked guiltily at Melody. "I'm sorry I didn't ask you, Melody! I wanted to, you know. Well, actually, I wasn't sure I should, seeing as you're my boss. Though I know we're friends, too! But it was on account of John having so many sisters. Already there's been hurt feelings. We chose Frances, 'cause she's the oldest, and then Irene, 'cause she's the next oldest–after Walter. So, you see. You don't mind, do you, Melody?"

In truth, Melody *was* a little hurt. She had assumed that she would naturally be a part of the wedding she had helped bring about . . . although, she supposed that wasn't really true. She had been the one trying to actively break the young couple apart, at least in the beginning. And besides, she wouldn't be a very jolly addition to a wedding party right now, nor did she probably have the time, she convinced herself.

"That's alright, Harriet." She forced her best smile and began straightening the copies of the *Saturday Evening Post* in their rack.

"Oh, I'm so glad you understand!" Harriet gushed again. "I've been dreading telling you." Her face had resumed its earlier brightness. "And now we have to come up with another groomsman. John only has the one brother, and I have none, of course. We're thinking maybe a cousin? Mom says it doesn't have to be even, but what do you think, Melody?"

"In my day," piped up Mrs. Haufbrau, "we only had two witnesses. That's all that's necessary. Anything more is just a show. A pageant. And that ain't what a marriage is. And if you don't know that by now, you're in for a sad awakening." Mrs. Haufbrau closed the receipt book. "But I guess you wouldn't know, would you? Having no father all these years."

Harriet glanced at Melody, slightly raising her eyebrows. Mrs. Haufbrau had been even more insufferable than usual these past weeks and months. She seemed to have taken Louis Merriweather's death particularly hard and was still fully arrayed in black, even though the rest of them had progressed to wearing a simple black armband. Likewise, the fledgling comradery that had blossomed between them after the fire seemed to have well and truly fizzled. Melody tried to have compassion for her in the wake of her father's death, but Mrs. Haufbrau's grief was starting to affect business, as she was quite short and temperamental with customers lately. Melody knew she should take her aside and have words, but she had no idea how to approach the situation. She couldn't very well scold a woman twice her age! Fred, of course, was of no help.

"Well, anyway," Harriet went on, "Mom says it's okay, so I think we might just leave it as is. That or ask his cousin Virgil."

Harriet proceeded to ramble on about what each Schneider, old and young, was proposing to wear to the wedding, and Melody felt her mind drift. Harriet had asked for her opinion on two topics, yet did not seem to notice or care that Melody had not had a chance to reply to either. Harriet, she was quickly realizing, had plenty of people to advise her on her upcoming nuptials and was not in need of her help.

Mrs. Owens entered the shop then, and Harriet quickly shoved her feather duster under the counter. "Oh, hello, Mrs. Owens! Can I help you?" Harriet was in a perpetual good mood these days.

"Just came in for some flour, Harriet. And some milk. How's your mom doing?"

"Oh, she's good," Harriet replied, moving to help the woman. Melody took her place behind the counter and noticed two blocks of cheese sitting at one end.

"What are these?" Melody called.

"Oh, goodness! John delivered those this morning with the eggs! I forgot to take them back to the cooler. Here, I'll take them."

"No, you tend to Mrs. Owens. I've got this."

She was, in truth, glad of an excuse to go back and ask Cal why he had left the potluck so early. In her fretful musings last night about whether to stay or go, Cal had several times factored into the equation, though he had annoyingly factored into both sides. In her current mood, she was leaning toward him being a reason to go. Why should she stay and moon over him? He wasn't all that great, anyway, she decided, and tried to call to mind all the handsome Loyola boys who would be hers for the taking.

She paused just outside of the office (she refused to call it *Fred's* office, though *he* did) and considered going in and trying to get him to see sense. If he wanted to waste his life working at the Merc, she would not stand in his way, but it made sense to finish his degree first. Plus, she was certain that once he was back at Harvard, all his old pleasures would be more than enough to convince him otherwise. But what if he refused to see reason? Could they successfully comanage the Merc? She didn't see how that would work, and yet she refused to be reduced to being his subservient employee. Likewise, she wasn't about to let herself be packed off to Chicago like an inconvenient child if she didn't want to be.

But now, she decided, was not the time to discuss it and lowered the fist she had poised to rap on the office door. For one thing, the cheese she was carrying had grown warm and spongy, and, more importantly, this might be her only chance to speak to Cal alone.

She rounded the last aisle of canned goods and entered the butcher shop area. Cal was bent over the back worktable, carefully slicing a lamb loin–if she wasn't mistaken. Recognizing different cuts of meat was not her specialty. She set the cheese blocks on top of the display case. Cal did not look up.

"Harriet forgot to bring these back to the cooler this morning with the eggs."

Cal continued slicing.

"Want me to put these in the there for you?"

"No, I'll do it in a minute."

Melody pressed her lips together. She moved toward the end of the counter so that she could see him fully and leaned against it. "I saw you at the potluck."

He didn't respond.

"I thought you weren't going," she prodded.

"Yeah, well, I changed my mind." He began arranging the chops on a white enamel tray.

"How come you left so early then?"

Cal's shoulders shrugged. "I don't know."

"I was . . . I was hoping to talk to you."

He glared at her. "Well, you seemed pretty busy. And I had to get back. Had other things to do."

Other things? What other things? "Is someone ill?" she asked, trying to draw him out.

He looked up at her finally, a dark lock hanging over one eye. "No, no one's ill, Melody. Not that you'd care."

Melody felt as if she'd been slapped. *What was that supposed to mean?*

Cal went back to slicing. "Heard you're going away."

"Who told you that?"

"Fred mentioned it to me at the potluck."

How dare Fred! She crossed her arms tightly. "Well, that's not true! I . . . we're still discussing it."

"I meant to ask you about it that night, but like I said, you were occupied. Too busy I guess to talk to one of the employees. 'Specially when you're rubbing elbows with the mayor."

"I don't think of you as an employee!" Melody blurted, though she *did* suddenly remember referring to Harriet that way that night. "And I wasn't 'rubbing elbows' with the mayor!" she exclaimed. "He wanted to tell me some story about him and my dad. I've heard it a hundred times before, but I couldn't just walk away from him."

Cal stared at her for a few moments and then tossed his head, flipping back his errant lock of hair. "You know what? You *should* go back, Melody."

Melody stared at him, stunned. *Not him, too!* Did *no one* want her to stay?

"It'd be the best thing for you. To get away from here. Study whatever it was that you were studying before."

Melody tried to remember what she *had* been studying. English? What good was that? She cleared her throat, feeling like she was suddenly sliding down a slippery slope. "I don't know. I kind of like it here now."

Cal let out a little snort. "Thought you couldn't wait to get back to all your friends in the city. And your beau. What's his name? Doug?"

"It's Douglas. And he's not my beau. He's just a . . . a friend. I've tried to explain that!"

Cal examined his thumb. "You sure?"

"Of course I'm sure! I would have introduced you that night if you hadn't just bolted out."

"Look, it's none of my business, but he didn't have the look of a 'friend' to me."

Stunned again, she exclaimed, "You're right. It isn't any of your business!"

"Sometimes you just can't see what's in front of your face, can you, Melody?" He scowled–actually *scowled*–at her!

"*Me?*" She bristled. "That describes you perfectly, Cal Fraiser!" *Was he really this dense?*

"Oh, I think I can see what's in front of me just fine."

"Well, if I left, you'd . . . you'd have Fred for a boss!"

Cal shrugged again. "Makes no difference to me."

Melody tried desperately to think of something to say, some way to hang on to whatever this was. "Well, what about the cider?" She knew this was a grasp at straws, but it *was* actually a concern. "I can't just . . . just abandon it!"

"Fred's here now," Cal said cooly. "I reckon he can handle it. So, you see, there's really no reason for you to stay, is there?"

He was looking directly into her eyes, as if searching them for . . . for what?

Her heart was beating unnaturally fast. *Was this a test?*

She pulled her gaze away. She refused to beg him for his affection.

"No, there's not." Turning on her heel, she headed back toward the front counter, brushing a few stray tears as she went. No one seemed to want–or need–her to stay, and no one seemed appreciative of all that she had done, all that she had sacrificed. She glanced at her father's office door through blurry eyes.

Well then, fine.

She would leave and let them all stew in their own juices. She was more than happy to leave this backwater town and return to the delights of Chicago. She would write Cynthia with the happy news as soon as she got home. No, she decided–she would go home now and do it. After all, Fred was here. Let him handle everything.

CHAPTER SIX

"Why do I need to help?" whined Minnie.

"Because I said so." Kate let out a tired sigh.

Mr. and Mrs. Kerwyn had left for a whole week for Des Moines to attend the wedding of Mrs. Kerwyn's cousin Estelle. Kate could count on one hand the number of times her parents had left the farm overnight; only the fact that Estelle was "like a sister" to Mrs. Kerwyn had induced them to attend. Up until the minute they finally drove away, Mrs. Kerwyn had still been of two minds as to the prudence of such a trip. After all, it was still winter, she fretted, and more than once declared that she had never heard of someone getting married in February.

Mr. Kerwyn, however, who would have gladly given their regrets when the invitation had first arrived–refused to abandon the journey, having already made all the arrangements. Eventually, he had managed to get his wife into the car, but only after she had tearfully embraced each of the children and given the hundredth repetition of everything that had to be done while they were away.

The running of the farm was left to Edmund, while the inside duties, which included caring for Minnie, were distributed between Louisa and

Nettie and Kate. Of course Louisa did little besides lie on the sofa and read magazines, and Nettie, by virtue of having a job in town, promptly declared herself exempt despite the fact that working at Ben's Bakery took only a few hours a day.

"Finish drying those and then you can go," Kate said sternly.

"You're not my mom!" Minnie whined.

"No, but I'm in charge of you."

"No, you're not! Louisa is!" Minnie stuck her tongue out at Kate and ran from the room.

Kate felt her pulse rising. Minnie could really be a pill sometimes. Mrs. Kerwyn had had her late in life—maybe a little *too* late, as the last of Mrs. Kerwyn's energy seemed to have gone into the growing of the baby, so much so that when Minnie was finally born, there was little left over to actually mother her. Indeed, Minnie was being raised in a haphazard sort of way and, consequently, was spoiled rotten. She was much too much under the influence of Louisa and Nettie, who thought it amusing to goad Minnie into precociousness.

Kate picked up the flour sackcloth Minnie had tossed and began drying the dishes, gritting her teeth at the memory of what she herself had been expected to do at eleven—weeding the garden, plucking chickens, canning corn, ironing clothes, and any number of chores Minnie had never been made to do.

Kate carefully lifted a stack of plates back into the cupboard, her mind again straying to the Espos. Her *real* family. Or her supposed family, anyway. There was no proof she was connected to this Espo family, but it did make her wonder. Had her father really been *a miner*? Well, what was wrong with that? She picked up a mug and began wiping it. But if they were in Shullsburg, why would they not have come back to look for her? And why had the Kerwyns not tried harder to find *them*? After all, they had plenty of children of their own. Had they just kept her to be their servant? Kate knew that was unfair, though Louisa and Nettie *were* horribly lazy.

The front door banged, which was odd, as they all used the back door, even Edmund. Surely he wasn't tromping through the front room with muddy boots? She turned to scold him but then abruptly stopped–

It was not Edmund in the kitchen doorway, it was Ray, his muscular body filling the space. Kate's first instinct was to flee out the back door, but she stood her ground, as she had painstakingly schooled herself over the years not to cower in front of him.

"What are *you* doing here?" Kate wiped her hands on her apron.

"Is that any way to greet your big brother?" His face held his usual sly grin. She hated his sly grin. She imagined he reserved it only for her to remind her of her shame.

"Hey, Ray!" It was a male voice. "Where should I put this stuff?"

Ray turned. "Just throw it there. We can take it upstairs later."

Kate heard the thump of something being dropped and then a young man with greasy blond hair entered the kitchen.

"Who we got here?" he asked with a smirk as he looked Kate up and down. Several of his teeth were missing.

"This is my sister, Kate."

The young man gave a look of surprise. "Your sister?" His eyes darted between them. "Don't look anything like each other."

"She's adopted."

"Ah!" He turned his gaze back at her appreciatively. "Not blood then?"

"Nope."

"Who are you?" Kate forced her hands to her hips.

"Name is Lee."

"Lee's going to be stayin' with us for a while. Least until Mom and Dad get back."

Kate was about to protest when she heard feet pound down the stairs.

"Ray? Is that you?" Louisa called and burst into the room. She embraced him tightly. "What are you doing home?"

Ray gave a little shrug. "I quit."

Lee guffawed. "No, he didn't. He got fired!"

Ray elbowed him. "Shut up, Lee." He looked back at Louisa. "Doesn't matter whether I quit or got fired. The point is, I'm back! Got anything to eat around here?" He peered around the kitchen. "We're starving."

Louisa looked at Kate expectantly. "You heard him, Kate! Get them something to eat."

"Why don't you?" Kate retorted.

"I have a terrible headache! You know that. Or were you not listening to me before?" She pulled out a chair and sat down. "Sit down, Ray. And Lee, is it? Tell us all the news from town!"

Kate, bristling with fury, retreated to the icebox. It would be better, she guessed, to appease them than to fight them. She removed the meatloaf she had made last night and cut some slices. Not very carefully, she placed them between slices of white bread, topped each with ketchup, and carried them to the table.

"Thanks!" Lee said eagerly and took a huge bite. Ray, however, didn't even look at her, as if she were a nameless servant. He was constantly doing that, turning his attention on and off so that she never knew what to expect, which succeeded in keeping her always on edge.

"Not much goin' on in town that I know of." Ray took a bite. "Not much goes on down at Ruby's. Not with all the dregs that shack up there."

"Hey!" Lee said, his mouth full, "I live there! I'm not a dreg."

"Well, everyone 'cept you and me, then." He winked at Louisa and took another bite. "You know what I was thinking? I was thinking we should have a little party."

"A party!" Louisa exclaimed. "Oh, what a good idea!"

Kate's stomach lurched. A party was the last thing her parents would want, nor did she think she could endure another crowd of people so soon after the potluck.

"Who should we invite?" Louisa asked eagerly.

"Couple of boys from the mill." He shrugged. "It don't have to be big."

"How about the Crawfords?" Louisa suggested. "They're new in town, so maybe this would be a good way for them to meet people."

"The Crawfords? You mean the ones that have been staying with those two pansies above the Merc? I don't know. They seem full of themselves. They wouldn't want to come to a farmhouse party. All we got is hooch, basically."

"You're wrong!" Louisa insisted. "They're not like that at all! I talked to them for an age at the potluck. You'd like Henry. He's a good laugh."

"Well, alright." Ray shrugged again. "I'll take your word for it."

"Are you two crazy?" Kate finally spoke up. "Mom and Dad would *not* want us to have a party. Louisa, think. You know this."

"Don't be such a stick-in-the-mud, Kate! It's not like we're doing any harm. Are you worried about the extra work? All you ever think about is yourself."

Kate ignored the jab, but her stomach continued to roil. It wasn't just that her parents would be mad if they had a party, Mr. Kerwyn would be furious that Ray was here at all. And even though Ray claimed the party would be small, she had a feeling it would quickly get out of hand. And to invite the likes of Henry and Mary Crawford, with their elegant clothes and fine manners? It was bad enough that they had been invited to the Potluck in the church basement, but to have them *here*? Kate glanced around the kitchen, trying to see it through their eyes. It would be too awful!

Kate undid her apron and tossed it on the counter. "Well, you do what you want, but I'm not going to be a part of it."

"Don't then!" Louisa called as she banged up the stairs. "No one wants you, anyway!"

* * *

By the very next day, everyone except Kate was excitedly preparing. For once, Louisa and Nettie were in the kitchen preparing food.

Kate cringed at what her mother would say when she found out they were taking things from the last of their winter stock in the cellar. Kate was trying her best to remain in her room, only venturing out to make lunch for herself and Minnie, who was determined to disobey her as well. Despite having been told to stay in her bedroom, the girl was laughing and running around downstairs.

Trapped as she was, albeit by her own hand, Kate decided to attempt work on her baskets. She had done little with them since she had returned from the badger hole. First it had been her illness that had prevented her, and, then, when she had recovered sufficiently enough to turn her mind to them again, there was no good place to lay out her supplies without them getting in the way. That, and the fact that Minnie was always messing with them. *Honestly, sometimes that girl was little better than a toddler!*

Kate sat on her bed now, trying to weave together two different colors of jute she had purchased at Rhomberg's. The sun had already begun its descent, however, and it was getting harder to see in the dim room. She wanted to get up and switch on the light, but she was reluctant to let go of the braided strands. She peered at her work, concentrating intensely when she heard a car door bang. She jumped, and the strands slipped through her fingers, ruining her latest pattern.

Kate got up, her insides clenching, and went to her tiny window. A group of people were tumbling out of a car, laughing and shouting their hellos. Ray appeared on the lawn to greet them. They were obviously friends of his. She let the curtain drop and slumped back onto her bed.

As more and more people began to arrive, the noise from below started to intensify. She wondered if she should go down and fetch Minnie, but she had no desire to be a part of any of this. She heard a loud bang and prayed that nothing would get broken. Picking up her strands of jute, she tried to figure out where she had left off. Before she had gotten very far, however, there was a light rap on her door.

"Kate?" called a voice.

It was Edmund.

Kate again dropped her work and scrambled up. "Edmund?" She opened the door a crack. "What are you doing here?"

Edmund smiled, his dimples showing. "Well, I've come for the party. Ray invited me this morning when I stopped over to do the milking."

"Oh."

"Louisa told me you were up here. 'Sulking' is the word she used." Another smile tugged at his lips. "Can I come in?"

"Oh, yes. Come in." She opened the door wide and returned to her bed, plopping down on it. "You know you don't need to ask."

Edmund stepped inside. He seemed taller somehow, but it was probably the fact that not only was his head bent to avoid the dormered ceiling, she was looking up at him from a seated position. As children, they had spent many hours in this room playing or reading or hiding during endless games of hide-and-seek, but it felt strange to be up here with him now, as adults.

He closed the door behind him. "Why aren't you downstairs, Possum? Are you not feeling well?"

"No, it's not that. I just don't feel like socializing, I guess you could say." She picked up a few strands and tried again to weave them.

Edmund watched for a few moments. "Working on something new?" He gently eased himself onto the end of the bed, careful not to disrupt anything.

"Well, I'm trying." She kept her eyes on the project.

"I don't know how you do it."

"Do what?"

"Create something from nothing."

She glanced at him briefly and was about to return her attention to her basket when she paused. If she wasn't mistaken, there was something new in his eyes. Something more tender than before, and she felt a corresponding something deep within her. She studied the tiny, familiar scar near his right eye, his dimpled chin, his smattering of freckles. She had seen his features a hundred thousand times, but tonight they seemed different in some way. Her pulse picked up a little, which unnerved her, and she pulled her eyes back to her work.

"You do the same," she said, giving a little shrug. "You put specks in the ground, and you get corn and wheat and vegetables. Something from nothing."

Edmund gave a little laugh. "I s'pose you're right."

She had not meant it to be funny, but she couldn't help but smile, too. "Anyway, it was you that encouraged me to try. Remember? That day you found me in the badger hole?"

"I do!" He laughed, fingering a strand of jute. "You know, Kate," he said more seriously, "I was thinking that . . ." He suddenly looked uncomfortable. "That maybe–"

He was interrupted by a quick, loud knock.

"Kate?" called an unfamiliar woman's voice. "Are you up here?"

The door opened, and Mary Crawford's head popped round it. Her eyes grew large at the sight of the two of them on the bed. "Oh! I do beg your pardon!" she said and quickly closed the door.

Edmund jumped up and hurried over, throwing it open. "Mary!" he called, clearly expecting her to be halfway down the stairs, but, no, she was still right outside the door. He nearly knocked her over in his haste to call her back.

He took a step back, staring at her. "I . . . I didn't know *you'd* be here." He quickly smoothed his hair. "You look different," he added admiringly. "I mean, in a good way. Doesn't she, Kate?" He glanced over his shoulder and then looked back at Mary as if she were some sort of goddess.

Kate, too, could not stop staring at Mary's exquisite silk evening gown in the deepest emerald green she had ever seen. It was accentuated with silver jewelry, a glistening silver belt that hugged her thighs, a silver hair clip in her black bobbed curls, and even silver T-strap heels. Her lips were a bright red, and her rouge a perfect pink. She was a vision of loveliness, like she had just stepped out of the pages of *Vogue*. Is this what she imagined one wore to a farmhouse party? Kate wondered, looking down at her plain blue housedress.

Mary laughed prettily. "Well, thank you, kind sir. Louisa stopped in just this morning and asked us to come," Mary replied. "So sweet of her, and luckily, we had no other plans. So here we are!"

"Your brother is here, too?" Edmund asked, rubbing the back of his neck.

"Well, of course he is! I couldn't come unchaperoned, now, could I? Not like the two of you here in this cozy den. Have I interrupted anything scandalous?" She flashed a devilish grin. "Oh, *please* say that I have!"

Edmund blushed deeply and gave an uncomfortable little grunt. "Ha! No, nothing like that! We were just talking, weren't we, Kate?" He glanced at her quickly and then back at Mary. "Do you want to come in? Is that aright, Kate?" He threw her an anxious look.

Kate did *not* want Mary Crawford to enter her inner sanctum, but she saw no way to say so without being rude, especially as she was practically in the room already. "I suppose so, but it's pretty small."

Mary stepped into the tiny dormered attic space. "How utterly charming!" she declared, looking around. "A perfect little space. And what is this?" She studied the various materials strewn across the bed. "Are you working on a basket? How splendid! The artist at work. Oh, I *do* wish Henry could see this. Would you mind if I asked him up?" she asked, moving toward the door.

"No!" Kate snapped, louder than she had intended. "I mean, no," she repeated in a lower tone. "Please. I'm feeling a little tired." She set her materials down.

"Oh, surely not!" Mary declared, turning back. "Are you not to join us below? You're the one I came up here to find!"

"Thank you, no."

"But why not? It's most entertaining. I've met your brother, Ray, and he says he's going to start a bonfire soon!"

"You're hardly dressed for a bonfire!" Kate couldn't help but scoff.

"Kate!" Edmund exclaimed. His tone was slightly scolding, which infuriated her. *Who was he to chastise her?*

Mary let out an amused little chuckle. "Well, all the better to feel the benefit of a fire, don't you think? Though, I did bring a coat. Really more a wrap, but I'm sure I'll be fine." She laid a hand on Edmund's arm as if it were the most natural thing in the world. "You're staying for the party, aren't you?"

Edmund did not respond immediately, and Kate saw his Adam's apple bob a couple of times. He was staring at her like a man possessed.

"I have a mind to . . . yes," he faltered. "I came up to get Kate, you see." He gestured weakly.

"Ah! So, you have two envoys, Kate! How popular you are!" she twittered. "Come, we'll make up our own little party, shall we?" She held out a slender manicured hand to Kate.

Kate frowned. "I'm not coming down. You two go on ahead."

"But why? Don't you like parties?" Mary entreated, her bright red lips pursed.

"Not particularly."

"None? You must like birthday parties, at least?"

"I wouldn't know. I've never had one."

"Never had one!" She looked at Edmund with wide eyes.

"Well, since I don't know when my birthday really is, we've never celebrated it."

"Ah, yes! Frank was telling us that you were an orphan." Mary paused, thinking, and tapped her lips with her elegant fingers. "But surely you have *some* date by which you mark your age."

"Mom picked March 15th."

"Ooo! The Ides of March. How perfect for such a gothic heroine stuck up here in the attic."

Kate had no idea what the Ides of March were or what it meant to be gothic, so she did not respond. Instead, she flashed Mary a grimace and picked up some twine.

"See what I mean?" Mary gave a pretty little laugh. "Well, I have obviously failed in my quest to abscond you. Edmund, it's up to you to convince her."

Edmund cleared his throat, looking uneasy. "Can't you come down for just a little bit?" he implored.

Kate's brow creased severely. She was still a bit annoyed with him for scolding her.

Mary retreated to the door. "Well, I'll let you two discuss the matter further in private. I sense some unrequited tension between the two of you. It's utterly delicious, but I'll only ruin it if I remain."

Unrequited tension?

Kate looked to Edmund, who seemed equally confused by this comment.

Mary stepped out into the hall but then turned, one hand still on the knob. "But Edmund, do try your best," she said sweetly, as if he were hers to command! It infuriated Kate all over again. Worse, Edmund seemed all too willing to obey.

Mary flashed another smile and then retreated down the steps.

Before Edmund could even speak, Kate cut him off. "Just go," she said bitterly.

Edmund did not leave, however, but slumped back down on the bed. "What's wrong, Kate?" he asked heavily, as if she were the problem.

"You know very well what's wrong, Edmund! You know I don't like crowds, especially a crowd of Ray's friends. And he's not exactly in Dad's good graces right now. Dad would be livid if he knew Ray was back home and having a party. Especially with Minnie roaming around."

"Well, that *is* true." Edmund scratched his head. "But there's not much we can do about it now. It's already happening. And wouldn't it be better if we were both down there keeping an eye on things?"

Kate considered. Perhaps he was right . . . maybe she *should* be keeping an eye on things, though she doubted anyone would listen to her if things got out of hand, especially Ray.

Edmund stood up. "Come on; we'll be a team," he encouraged and held out his hand. It was rough and calloused, so different than the slender white hand Mary had held out. As much as she wanted to take it, she hesitated.

"Come on; we should at least try to find Minnie," he insisted.

Kate swallowed her fear. "Oh, alright." She took his hand, and he wrapped it around her small one, as he had done a hundred times before, but this time, as he led her down the stairs, it felt different somehow, like there was a current between them. Kate wondered if she was the only one who felt it, but when he gently caressed the side of her palm with his thumb, she was sure he felt it too. Was this what Mary had meant by "unrequited tension"? But wasn't the phrase usually "unrequited passion"?

Before she could decide, however, Edmund pulled his hand from hers. They had reached the bottom of the stairs.

Kate stood frozen, horrified by what she saw. There were people everywhere, none of whom she recognized, all talking and laughing loudly. In one corner, a group was playing cards on an end table they had moved from its proper place beside the couch. Plates of food were stacked on any available spot, and several had fallen on the floor, their contents littering the rug. Bottles of beer and cider were scattered everywhere.

Kate felt the familiar knot of panic in her chest. Ray was sitting on the sofa, several people squished in beside him. He was holding up a bottle of something, and when he brandished it to fill the glasses of those around him, Kate was horrified to see that it was their father's special cognac! He had carried this prized possession home from the war, and it only came out for a wedding or a funeral, the last one being poor Eula's and Fern's.

Ray spilled some as he haphazardly poured it into several glasses held up to him.

Kate was about to say something when Ray boomed, "Drink up, everyone! Come on, grab a glass." Several more people obeyed. "This is the old man's crap whiskey. He thinks it's so great because its French. Well, fuck him! And fuck the goddamn French!" He knocked his back without a flinch, as if he were drinking water. "Come on! Drink, everyone! Here's another." He started sloshing more into glasses.

"Ray! What are you doing!" Kate cried, unable to keep silent any longer. "That's Dad's!"

Ray's eyes immediately darted to her and then to Edmund, still beside her. "Where've you two been? Not upstairs alone, were you?" He grinned his sly grin. "Finally decided to stop sulking?" he said to

Kate. "Come on, Ed. Have a drink!" Ray poured some whiskey into a spare glass and held it out.

Ed shifted uncomfortably. "Uh, that's okay, Ray. I'll just grab a beer."

"Come on!" Ray slurred. "Can't even have a drink with me? For old times' sake? 'Member when we used to steal bottles of beer after haying and drink them under the wagon?"

"Well, uh . . ." Edmund glanced uneasily at Kate, whose face was rigid. "Nah, that's okay."

"Fuck you, then," Ray slurred. "I'll drink it myself."

"Come on, Ray." Edmund took a step toward him. "Don't be like that. Okay. Maybe just one. I wouldn't want to use up all your dad's special stuff, though."

"Now, you're talkin'!" Ray was suddenly jovial. He quickly poured another glassful and handed it to Edmund. "Here's to the old man." He briefly held up his own glass. "Bastard," he said bitterly.

Edmund looked over his shoulder at Kate, who was still standing at the foot of the stairs. She glared at him. Edmund gave her a sheepish look and then downed the cognac.

"Whoo-hoo!" Ray shouted. "Another!" His eyes flashed defiantly at Kate. "What're you looking at? Why do you always look at me that way?" he snarled. "You want one?" He held up the bottle and laughed. He looked around at the people beside him, and they obliged him with laughs of their own.

Utterly disgusted, Kate slowly shook her head. "I've got to go find Minnie," she muttered.

"Kate, wait! I'll go, too," Edmund called. "After this round."

Kate ignored him and made her way to the kitchen, stepping over several beer bottles littering the floor. One spot of the rug was wet and stained with something dark. Rage and fear were bubbling up inside her, not only because of Ray, but because Edmund had so easily abandoned her. *And* because it would probably fall to her to clean all of this up before her parents returned.

She pushed through the swinging kitchen door, and though she had braced herself for what she was sure to be a horrible mess, she was still stunned by what she saw.

Louisa and Henry Crawford were kissing passionately! In fact, it was a little more than kissing. Louisa sat on the counter, her dress up and her legs wrapped around Henry as he leaned against her, his face buried in her neck.

Good Lord! Kate quickly retreated, hoping they hadn't seen her, and, flustered, hurried toward the front door, grabbing her coat off the rack.

The frigid night air hit her like a brick wall, but it was a welcome balm to her hot face. She was sure she was beet red.

She slipped into her coat and peered across the lawn. Down by the barn, a bonfire was roaring, around which stood another whole group of people! Mechanically, she moved toward the fire, trying to see if there was anyone she might recognize. Where was Mary Crawford? Or Nettie? Or Minnie, for that matter? Kate looked around uneasily. As she drew closer, she scrutinized the faces all aglow. Finally, she did recognize at least one person–poor Vernon Tierney. He was laughing and joking with a few other young men.

Kate had never been overly fond of Vernon, thinking him a bit dull and not a little stupid, but she did feel sorry for him now, knowing that

Louisa was currently inside with another man. She stood silently for a few moments, gazing at the flames, before deciding to return to the house. She would find Minnie, drag her off to bed, and then hide herself away in her room.

She trudged back across the frosty lawn and slipped quietly back into the house–not that there was any need for stealth given the noise of the party–and made her way to the dining room, which was full of people, too. Who were they all? Kate arched her neck to try to see beyond a group of chatting young women and finally spotted Minnie at the far end of the table, dejectedly playing a game of solitaire.

"Minnie! There you are." Kate wriggled past the women. "I've been looking for you everywhere!"

"No one will play with me!" Minnie complained.

"That's because this is a grownup party. No one wants to play with a little kid."

"I'm not a little kid! I'm eleven and a half!"

"That's still little. Come on, it's time for bed."

"Aw! No! I want to stay up! You can't make me!"

"Remember what Mom said? If you don't obey, you'll miss dessert for a whole week. Is that what you want?" Kate frowned at her, her hands on her hips. "Come on, this isn't any fun anyway. I'm going to bed, too."

Minnie cocked her head. "Honest?"

"Yes, honestly! Come on. Pick up those cards, and let's go."

Minnie begrudgingly swept up the cards and wrapped the loose rubber band around them. Kate took her by the hand, not wanting to take any chances of losing her again, and led her back toward the front room. She breathed a sigh of relief that Ray was no longer there. He must have gone outside or possibly down to the cellar, though God only knew why.

She paused in her escape, however, when her eyes alighted on the group that had remained on the sofa. One of them was Edmund, with Mary sitting tightly beside him. Granted, their proximity was likely caused by the people squeezed on either side, but by the look the two of them gave each other, one would never suspect they were in any way discomforted.

Kate watched unobserved. Was it possible that Edmund was forming an . . . an attachment to Mary Crawford? It seemed ridiculous in the extreme, and yet how else could one explain the overt excitement in his eyes? She knew she should look away and retreat up the stairs with Minnie, but she could not. Her world was fracturing for the second time in a week, and she could not make her feet move.

Her misery was abruptly broken by the sound of the front door slamming.

"What the hell is going on here?"

Kate dropped Minnie's hand. Her father!

Her momentary paralysis broken now, she hurried into the foyer and saw her father standing just inside the door, his hat pushed back to the crown of his head–a sure sign that he was angry–and his hands on his lower back. Mrs. Kerwyn stepped from behind him, her expression transforming into one of disbelief as she observed the mess. One of her gloved hands covered her mouth in dismay.

"I said, what the hell is going on here!"

Most of the crowd remained frozen, but others began to scurry. Louisa, looking somewhat disheveled, hurried in from the kitchen. Henry Crawford slunk in behind her, wearing an annoying little smirk as he adjusted his emerald bow tie. He had managed, Kate observed wryly, to likewise pull on his suit coat, as when she had previously seen him in the kitchen making love to Louisa, he had been merely in shirt sleeves.

"Oh, you're back!" Louisa tried to say gaily, though her shrewd blue eyes were worried.

"Louisa, what's the meaning of this?"

"Well, it was Ray's idea, Dad! Just a little party."

"Ray? What the hell is he doing here?"

"Well, he . . ." Louisa's voice dropped. "He's moved back home, I think."

"Oh no he hasn't. Ray!" Mr. Kerwyn bellowed.

Several more people scurried away. Kate could hear various cars starting outside.

Ray came swaggering in through the kitchen door with Lee but stopped short when he saw his parents. He was still holding the bottle of French cognac, and rather than try to hide it, he defiantly took a swig.

"Mom, Dad," he slurred, swaying slightly. "Thought you were in Des Moines. Would have invited you had I known you were in town." Looking at Lee, he burst into laughter. Lee, however, his face creased with fear, began to back away.

Mr. Kerwyn grabbed the bottle from Ray and, noting that it was almost gone, grabbed Ray by the shirtfront and began to shake him. Ray's eyes flew open in surprise as he tried to wriggle free.

"Gus!" Mrs. Kerwyn cried. "Gus, don't!"

Mr. Kerwyn continued to shake Ray. "You good-for-nothing bastard! How dare you!"

Ray pushed his father, and the older man's grip released. They faced each other, panting.

"You get the hell out of here!" Mr. Kerwyn snarled. "Everyone, get out!" he shouted, and the few stragglers squeezed past him and slipped out the door. "Go on, get out!" Mr. Kerwyn shouted directly at Ray.

"Gus! It's freezing! Let him at least stay the night," Mrs. Kerwyn pleaded.

"No. He doesn't deserve to be called my son," Mr. Kerwyn said bitterly.

Ray's face finally contorted into what looked like anger at his father's disownment. "Okay, then. Fine. Fuck you, Dad." He stormed past his father. "Come on, Lee."

Lee hurried from the corner and followed Ray out the front door. Louisa put her hands over her eyes and began to cry.

"Stop your bawling!" Mr. Kerwyn cried. "I'll deal with you in the morning."

With a final wail, Louisa roughly pushed past Minnie and Kate and stomped up the stairs.

"Where's Nettie?" Mr. Kerwyn demanded of Kate.

"I . . . I don't know, Dad."

Mr. Kerwyn wiped his brow with a bandana and picked up the bottle of French whiskey Ray had dropped while Mrs. Kerwyn, still in her coat, made her way to the kitchen. Kate winced when she heard the resultant little cry of dismay.

"You go on up, Minnie," Kate said worriedly. "I'll go help Mom."

CHAPTER SEVEN

"There you are!" Cynthia Forsythe exclaimed, popping her head into Melody's dorm room. "I've been looking for you everywhere!"

The lovely dormered room Melody had previously shared with Elsie Von Harmon, now Stockel, in Philomena Hall was already occupied by two new girls, so Melody had been given a smaller private room at the end of the hall. It had granted to her as a kindness, but Melody wasn't quite sure she liked being alone.

She twisted in her desk chair as Cynthia waltzed in and shut the door behind her. "Hi, Cyn," Melody responded and then turned back to the open books on the desk, propping her chin on her fists.

"What are you doing up here?" Cynthia peered over her friend's shoulder. "You aren't actually *studying*, are you?"

In truth, Melody *was* studying. Or trying to study. She was, however, finding it very difficult. She should have never listened to Freddy and returned mid-term. She was horribly behind, even though Sr. Bernard had mercifully placed her in somewhat easy classes, namely Shorthand, World

Geography, and two gymnasium courses–Swimming and Equestrian Studies. Still, none of these appealed very much.

Swimming in the beautiful art deco pool hidden beneath the Mundelein skyscraper was pleasant enough, but horseback riding through Lincoln Park in February was not ideal. Likewise, she was discovering, she had neither the aptitude nor the interest in either geography *or* shorthand, and, worse, it was impossible to see how any of these subjects might be of use in the real world. She certainly didn't see herself as a teacher or a secretary. Then again, she had never seen herself as the manager of a shop, either.

But she wasn't the manager anymore, she reminded herself; Fred was.

Perhaps it *had* been better to begin now, she considered, as otherwise she would have had to endure that many more months of Fred lording it over her, not to mention Bunny complaining and Mrs. Haufbrau snipping and the Merc losing money and her mother crying and . . . and . . . Cal critiquing her every move.

She turned a page of her geography book, and the map of the Orient gave way to one of Africa.

Why was he always making it out that she was the one acting the superior, when it was really *him*? It infuriated her! He hadn't even said goodbye. Not really. Just a smug (*was* it smug? Or was it perturbed? Who could tell? And who cared?) wave from behind the counter when she had walked through the Merc for the last time just over three weeks ago now. Like Cal, Mrs. Haufbrau did not seem upset in the least that she was leaving, merely wished her well and had then gone back to her receipt book. Harriet, on the other hand, had actually shed a tear and promised to write.

Her family had likewise been oddly unemotional. Bunny had given her a perfunctory hug, though her dark expression seemed to indicate annoyance, or maybe resentment. Helenka, too, had seemed out of sorts when she wished Melody good luck–perhaps because she knew that the brunt of caring for her mother would now fall entirely on her? Melody had tried the night before her departure to encourage Bunny to help more with Mums while she was gone, but Bunny had only rolled her eyes and walked out of the room. Only Mums seemed sad that Melody was leaving and had cried accordingly, though she quickly recovered herself, saying that it was only for a few weeks and that time would pass quickly. Melody had been about to correct her but then thought better of it, deciding to let her believe the delusion.

As for Fred, he had been unusually quiet on the drive to the train station. Melody had been tempted to go over yet again the list she had left in the office regarding the Merc's daily and weekly requirements, but she had not the heart. He wouldn't listen anyway. When they finally reached the station and Melody's luggage and trunks had been carted to the platform by porters, Fred's mood finally improved. When the train finally chugged into the station, he slipped a ten-dollar bill into her hands and wished her luck, reminding her to look for a rich husband. She was pretty sure he was teasing, but his words stung.

Well, fine. If that was the way they all wanted it, she was happy to go. Happy to get away. If the Merc failed, it wasn't her fault.

She had remained morose and melancholy for the better part of an hour, but as the train picked up speed, hurtling her closer and closer to Chicago, her attitude began to shift. A lightness came over her as she left the cornfields and woods behind, as if she were shrugging off a heavy burden. Mile by mile, she became more and more excited to get back to her old life.

And it had been wonderful–at first, anyway–to be back. Melody had missed Mundelein more than she thought. It was a tiny campus, consisting only of the magnificent skyscraper with a whopping thirty floors and two mansions-turned-dormitories–Piper and Philomena Halls. These staid old homes, with their dark wood, Tiffany stained glass, converted gas light fixtures and inlaid Dutch tiles around the fireplaces provided a perfect contrast to the sleek art deco design of the modern skyscraper, successfully marrying the old and the new.

The Skyscraper, as it was called, was divided into several floors of classrooms, a dining hall, a hidden greenhouse on the sixth floor, a library, a chapel, and even a subterranean swimming pool. The upper floors served as a convent for the Sisters of the Blessed Virgin Mary, the order of nuns assigned to the administration of the school by Cardinal Mundelein. It was an institution where the daughters of the city's wealthy elite were schooled in proper etiquette and decorum–as well as academics for the few who actually desired some sort of profession.

Though the campus was small, it seemed larger due to its close proximity to Loyola's sprawling campus. The all-women's and the all-men's schools fit perfectly together, like brother and sister, with the students often attending each other's social and philanthropic events.

Sr. Bernard, Mundelein's president, had warmly welcomed Melody back despite Melody's hijinks the previous year, the most egregious being her masquerade as a nun to help her friend Elsie elope, which, in retrospect, felt like a hundred years ago now. Sr. Bernard had mercifully not mentioned this or any of her other pranks during her interview and was instead overwhelmingly kind and sympathetic regarding her recent loss. When she shared that she and the sisters had been praying for the repose of her father's soul, Melody had nearly broken down.

Without Melody even having to ask, Sr. Bernard had offered a reduced tuition because of family financial hardship, the only expectation being that Melody would work in the library a few hours a week whenever she felt up to it. Melody had of course agreed, but wondered how she was going to have time, especially since she still intended to procure a weekend job at a candy store or a soda shop to pay Douglas back . . .

She had not immediately seen Douglas upon her return, for which she was grateful, but when she had, he had acted startled and confused. His face had gone all red, and he had–

"Melody!"

Melody jumped.

"Have you been listening to me?" Cynthia complained. "You're a million miles away!"

Melody turned from her books to attend her friend, who was now perched on her bed, her long legs crossed, the dangling foot rocking impatiently. "I asked you what you're wearing tonight!"

Melody's brow creased. *What was tonight?*

"Don't tell me you've forgotten!" Cynthia uncrossed her legs. "Loyola's Winter Ball?"

Ah, yes. The ball. She *had* nearly forgotten, which was more than a little upsetting. It was *the* social event of the year and the thing that Melody had most despaired missing when originally called back to Merriweather. And now, by a strange twist of fate, she was back in time to attend, but, sadly, it no longer held the significance it once had.

She was finding this to be the case with any number of things, actually. A sort of apathy concerning things that had once been of the utmost importance. After running the Merc for almost half a year, starting a cider-making business to fend off her father's debtors, managing her ragtag band of employees, mitigating a fire, and ultimately losing her father, she was used to bigger problems than, say, a particularly onerous math assignment, a dull essay topic, or some boy failing to turn up for a study date as arranged.

She tried to care about all of the gossipy goings-on, but she found it hard. More often than not, her mind instead wandered to whether or not Fred had ordered enough cider bottles for the upcoming season, as she had instructed, or if he had remembered to pay the Schneiders for their last two months of eggs. Knowing Tom Schneider, John's father, he wouldn't speak up and ask for it. He would simply wait patiently for–

"Melody!"

She jumped again. "Yes!" she blurted. "I mean, what was the question?"

"What are you wearing tonight?" Cynthia's tone was one of exasperation.

"Oh." Melody tried to think. "Probably my green Chanel. How about you?"

"I haven't decided." Cynthia flopped back on Melody's pillows, evidently convinced now that Melody was finally firmly in the conversation. She put her hands behind her head and stared up at the ceiling. "Probably the red. But maybe the white Vionnet. Oh, what do you think?"

Melody sighed internally. "The white, I think." In truth, she didn't think it mattered.

"Me too!" Cynthia sat up suddenly and threw her legs over the side of the bed. "Oh, Melody, I just have a feeling about tonight. Something big is going to happen; I'm sure of it."

Melody did not say so, but she had the opposite feeling. That nothing at all would come of the evening. She was, in fact, dreading it. It was the first time, probably in her whole life, that she was attending a dance without an escort. Her fantasy about resurrecting the old foursome–as friends only–had immediately been dashed when Cynthia had reported, on her very first day back, that Douglas was now dating Vivian Anderson in earnest.

"The nerve!" Cynthia had exclaimed, referring, of course, to Vivian, not Douglas. "She's only doing it to rattle you. As soon as she heard you were coming back, she dug her claws into poor Dougie and won't let go for heaven or earth. It's too, too terrible! Are you sure you don't want Charlie to speak to him? I think he'd take you back in a second, Mel. He hasn't been the same at all this semester. Just mopes. Oh, do let Charlie talk to him!"

"No, Cyn," Melody had said with a frustrated sigh. "It's all over between us. I've told you all this. Douglas is a chum. And nothing else," she added pointedly as she tilted her head at Cynthia in warning. And besides, she realized now, it wouldn't have been fair to ask him to reform the foursome, even as friends, when she knew how he felt about her. It would be too cruel.

Cynthia had eventually accepted, begrudgingly, Melody's changed feelings, but it did not stop her trying to find Melody a date for the ball. She had Charlie ask all of his fraternity brothers, but, unfortunately, at this late date, everyone already had a partner. Melody–somewhat grateful that Charlie had come up empty-handed–had insisted she was happy enough to stay behind. Cynthia, however, would not hear of it and insisted that she come with her and Charlie. "It'll be just like old times," she had gushed. "Well. Sort of. Come on, Mel! That's why you're here!

To have fun. You're turning into Elsie these days–studying half the day and night."

In the end, Melody had agreed to be the third wheel to Cynthia and Charlie's twosome, realizing that it would probably take less effort to simply attend for an hour than to continue to come up with excuses that Cynthia would inevitably continue to knock back.

Melody stood up and stretched. "Well, I suppose we should get dressed. If we're going, that is."

"Goodness, yes!" Cynthia exclaimed, hopping up from Melody's bed. "It's nearly seven o'clock!"

* * *

Loyola's annual Winter Ball was held each year in the campus auditorium inside Cudahy Hall. Maroon and gold banners hung from the ornate plastered ceiling, and paper streamers in the same colors crisscrossed the room. On the curved proscenium stage with its triple illuminated arches, the college's orchestra was playing a mix of traditional waltzes and a variety of the increasingly popular swing tunes.

Taking in the ornate hall, Melody felt glad she had decided to come. It was, after all, as Cynthia had reminded her earlier, one of the reasons she had looked forward to returning to school. She hadn't realized, however, how similar the auditorium was to their own little Merriweather Opera House, though no "operas" were performed there anymore. In fact, it was more of a movie house these days, though she *had* seen a production last summer of *You Can't Take It With You* put on by the Merriweather Players. It had really been quite good. It was the last thing she had seen with her father before–

"There they are!" Cynthia hissed in her ear. "See them?"

Melody blinked. She was not sure who Cynthia meant by "them," but she obediently followed her friend's gaze to where Vivian Anderson stood with a gaggle of girls and guys, some of whom had been part of Melody's former circle, or "court" as she had been fond of calling them. She had never liked Vivian Anderson, and it frustrated her that not only had she essentially taken over Melody's former role as social queen, but she was doing it so very badly! Vivian, she knew, had a mean streak and delighted in excluding anyone who didn't meet her elite standards, while *she,* Melody liked to think, had tried to use her influence to include the lost and the lonely–Elsie Von Harmon the best case in point. And look how *that* had turned out! Elsie was now happily married and living in a big house in Palmer Square!

Though maybe, Melody reflected now, she was giving herself too much credit. She looked at Vivian again, laughing coquettishly with those nearest her, all of whom were hanging on her every word. Maybe she had been just as superficial and vain as Vivian. She let out a sigh. Where was Cal when she needed him to put her in her place? She smiled a little at the thought as she looked out over the dance floor and wondered what everyone at home in Merriweather was doing.

She chanced another glance at the little group and now saw that Douglas Novak had joined them. He was dressed smartly in his black tuxedo, but he kept shifting awkwardly from foot to foot, as if his shoes were too tight. Noticing him, Vivian put her arm through his and briefly rested her head on his shoulder before shooting a dart directly at Melody, as if she had been aware all along that Melody was staring. Vivian made a point, then, to turn her head in favor of the person standing nearest her and laughed at whatever was being said.

"What a crumb," Cynthia muttered. "Just ignore her. She's just doing it to make you jealous!"

The odd thing, however, was that Melody *didn't* feel jealous. Just a little sad perhaps. A little bit for herself, but more so for Douglas. It was clear he wasn't at all interested in Vivian Anderson, nor was she with him, but he was somehow now entwined with her. Yet another scrape he had gotten himself into. Perhaps, Melody considered, if she put her mind to it, she could help him get away from Vivian and match him with a nice girl who would be perfect for him . . . someone perhaps like . . . She thought for a moment. Maybe Susan Hastings? But, no! What was she thinking? The idea of matching her old beau with someone new was absurd!

As if on cue, Douglas suddenly caught her eye. She smiled at him, but he did not return it and instead gave her a hasty frown before looking away again, as if his current predicament were her fault, on top of everything else. Clearly, he was still angry, either because of her rejection of him or because of the lost ring. Maybe both. She wished she could talk to him alone to at least tell him her plan to pay him back . . .

"I believe this dance is mine," Charlie said cheerfully, holding out his arm. Melody hadn't even noticed him approach.

"Oh, Charlie, do you mind if I sit this one out?" Melody begged, suddenly not in the mood to dance. "You and Cyn go." She tilted her head toward her friend.

"Cyn?" He let out a pretend scoff. "I can have her any old time! How often do I get the chance to dance with the prettiest girl in school?"

"Hey!" Cynthia exclaimed.

"Just pulling your leg, old girl." He kissed Cyn on the nose. "How 'bout it, Mel?"

Melody gave a little smile. "No, honestly. Go on. Maybe the next one."

"You sure?"

"Sure, I'm sure."

"Well, come on, then, Cyn. Guess I'm stuck with you."

Cynthia laughed and took his arm. "You mean *I'm* stuck with *you*!"

Melody watched the two of them begin to jitterbug and then let her eyes roam the room. Everyone seemed so young. Some of the girls looked younger than Bunny! She tried not to look in Vivian and Douglas's direction, but she couldn't but notice that they were now on the floor, too, Douglas looking miserable.

"May I have the next dance?"

Melody turned, surprised. Beside her stood a dashing young man she had never seen at any Loyola gatherings or parties. He was tall and thin, with perfectly combed blond hair and a trim mustache. There was something authoritarian and mature about him. He couldn't possibly be a student . . . Was he a professor? But fraternization between professors and students was strictly forbidden, she knew. And even if he *were* attempting a clandestine encounter, he would not be so clumsy as to suggest it at a school event.

He held out his hand in a way that did not expect rejection. Intrigued by his confidence, she laid her hand in his. Gently, he led her to the dance floor just as the jitterbug ended and a waltz began. He put his hand gently on her back and, after pausing for a moment to join the rhythm, began elegantly twirling her around the room. His command of the waltz was impressive; she was quickly becoming interested in tall, mysterious stranger.

"Might I know your name?" he asked without looking at her.

"Melody Merriweather."

"Allow me to introduce myself," he said, finally meeting her eyes. "Eustace Sinclair. Enchanted to meet you, Miss Merriweather."

His eyes were a dark gray. She had never seen this color before, but they were mesmerizing.

"Yes," she faltered. "The same." *The same? What kind of comment was that?*

"You are obviously a Mundelein student?"

"Yes, I am. Are you? A student, I mean? Here? At Loyola?" She was babbling like an imbecile! She felt tongue-tied and nervous, which was an utterly new feeling for her around the opposite sex. Usually, she was in command with any boy she spoke to (besides Cal, of course, who didn't count), but then again, this was not a boy she was dancing with; this was a *man*.

Eustace let out a little laugh as he peered down at her with those arresting gray eyes. "A student?" He sniffed. "No, my uncle is on the board. We dined this evening, and he suggested I attend the ball in his stead. Daft, really, but I didn't want to disappoint. Not quite my thing, though." He glanced around at the paper streamers, which now seemed cheap and childish. "I promised I would dance one dance, and so I am." He returned his gaze to her. "And I must say, I'm very glad now of my promise."

Maddeningly, Melody felt herself beginning to perspire. "Well, if you're not a student," she said slowly, trying to not sound ignorant, "what is it that you do? Are you a professor?"

Eustace laughed in full this time. "Do I *look* like a professor? No, I am an art critic."

An art critic? Melody was certainly intrigued. How did one make money as an art critic? "How very interesting," was all she could think to say.

"It can be. Are you fond of art?"

"I . . . well, yes. But I confess I don't know very much about it."

The dance ended then and the two of them politely clapped. Eustace bowed elegantly. "It was an honor, Miss Merriweather, but, having fulfilled my obligation–"

Obligation?

"–I really must go. I've made arrangements with friends downtown. Meeting you, however, was an unexpected surprise. I had not anticipated you."

Melody felt herself blush.

He bowed again and lightly kissed her gloved hand. "Adieu."

Melody watched him walk away, wishing that he wasn't, when he suddenly turned back. Melody's pulse quickened, and she suddenly wished had a paper fan in her possession. *Why was it so warm in here?*

"You must forgive the impertinence, Miss Merriweather," Eustace said, approaching her again, "but might I inquire if you are otherwise engaged tomorrow evening? I have tickets at the Blackstone, if you would be so kind as to do me the honor."

Melody's mind went blank. Tomorrow? Tomorrow? Was she engaged tomorrow? Did it matter? She would cancel whatever it was. "No, I'm fine. I mean, yes, I'm free. I think."

Eustace smiled. "Splendid. *Romeo and Juliet* is playing. The reviews have been exceptionally positive. Where might I call for you?"

"I'm at Philomena Hall. Just across the way on Sheridan?"

"Yes, I know it. I'll pick you up at seven. We'll dine at the Empire Room first, yes? And then on to the theater."

The Empire Room! Melody had always wanted to go to the Drake Hotel and had had many fantasies about having a wedding reception there. Indeed, back when she had crafted elaborate fantasies for her gang, a reception at the Drake had frequently figured in.

"Yes, alright," she tried to say coolly, elegantly, but she couldn't stop from smiling. *Like a little girl!* she admonished herself. "Seven o'clock."

He took her hand in his again and kissed it. "Until tomorrow then, Miss Merriweather." He gave her a final tilted bow of his head and elegantly disappeared into the crowd.

"Who was that?" Cynthia exclaimed breathlessly, coming up behind her.

"I'm not exactly sure," Melody murmured. But she *was* sure about one thing–for the first time since returning to Chicago, she felt hopeful, almost happy.

Later that night, when she eventually returned to her solitary room, it was lovely to drift off to sleep thinking of something other than the dusty old Merc and a certain cantankerous someone–and by that she did *not* mean Mrs. Haufbrau.

CHAPTER EIGHT

Kate pushed open the rusty black gate of the Magnolia Hill cemetery with a screech. She had managed to get away from the farm by offering to walk into town to do errands for her mother. Predictably, Mrs. Kerwyn had fussed at the proposition, but she had finally acquiesced when Kate pointed out that the sugar canister was nearly empty and that she wasn't actually ill any longer.

Kate had considered asking Edmund for a ride, but she didn't want to take him away from helping Dad. Now that it was March, with the ground beginning to thaw, it would soon be time to plant, and her father was keenly feeling Ray's absence, though he would never admit it. The prodigal was back at Ruby's, and Edmund was again dividing his time between the two farms. Several days a week, he arrived at the Kerwyns before dawn and stayed well past dark.

Kate let her eyes travel over the tranquil space. If it hadn't been a cemetery, she would have thought it quite beautiful. A couple of big weeping willows and various pines stood tall at the far end, while a giant pin oak in the very center shaded a lonely bench. An army of daffodils had popped up along the fence line and were likewise invading inward, a few growing between the headstones themselves. It seemed a sad irony to Kate that something so fresh and new and lovely as a daffodil could grow amidst the crumbling graves, beneath which lay decaying bodies.

She let out a deep breath. The cemetery somehow seemed bigger on the inside. She had come with the intention of looking for any deceased members of the Espo family. The idea had come upon hcr a few days ago while she was sweeping, and she had not been able to get it out of her mind since. If Rosemary's story was true, wouldn't her parents' graves be here? She would at least have names to go on then. But where to start?

She set her grocery basket on the bench beneath the oak. The most logical choice was to do it in as organized a way as possible, so she returned to the gate and began walking along the row bordering the fence. This method worked with the first and second rows, but when she attempted the third and fourth, it became harder, as the stones began to lose their orderly neatness.

When she eventually reached the "old" section, which contained graves from the 1800s, it became nearly impossible to proceed in an organized fashion, so Kate did the best she could to wander around the obelisks and other markers, whose engravings were hard to make out. There were a few giant marble mausoleums–one of them for the Merriweathers, of course. Kate did not see the point of spending that much money to mark the spot where your bones would lie and rot, but, then again, she didn't understand most of the things people with money did.

After searching for over an hour, Kate had covered most, if not all, of the graves, yet she had not come upon a single Espo. Perhaps Rosemary had been mistaken about the name? That or they were not buried here. She returned to the bench and sat down wearily. There was St. Peter's

Cemetery, but that had been filled decades ago, and also a small cemetery on the outside of town that serviced the non-Christians. Had they been buried all the way out there?

Her mother, she knew, would worry if she wasn't back soon. But having escaped from her chores, she felt a sort of desperation to at least discover *something*. Perhaps there was someone in the cottages on Magnolia who could tell her more or at least confirm the existence of an immigrant camp. She checked her wristwatch. Nearly three. She would have to hurry.

Kate cut across Liberty Park and proceeded down Chestnut until she came to Magnolia. Harriet and Rosemary's cottage was midway along the street, so Kate turned left toward the lower end. She approached the cottage closest to the Muellers, but when she got to the door, she hesitated. What was she going to say? "Hello? Do you remember an immigrant family whose father died in the mine accident and whose mother died of diphtheria, leaving a bunch of orphaned children?"

She backed down the steps and stood in the street. Perhaps she should go home and rehearse what to say. But, she countered, who knew how long it would be before her mother let her come back to town? No, it had to be now.

She forced herself back up the two steps and rapped quickly on the door. After a few moments, it was opened by an elderly man with a hunched back. "Yes?"

Kate shifted. "Hello. My name is Kate Kerwyn, and I–"

"Who?" The man held a hand to his ear.

"Kate Kerwyn!" she shouted.

The man pondered this for a moment and then squinted at her. "What is it?"

"I'm wondering if you could tell me about any of the families who lived at the end of this street around the time of the mining accident!" she shouted.

His brow creased. Clearly, he had either not heard or had not understood. Kate repeated herself several more times until he finally seemed to grasp her meaning.

"No, I don't," he said simply then stood there as if waiting for the next question.

"Well, thank you!" she shouted, deciding to give up.

"That all you wanted?" he asked, perplexed, as Kate made her way down the stone steps.

Kate merely waved and walked to the next cottage. This time, she knocked without hesitating. No one seemed to be home, however, so after several more knocks, she moved on to the next cottage.

At this one, a young boy answered. He was holding a baby, and a toddler wobbled beside him. The boy explained that his mother had gone into town but that she'd be home soon if Kate wanted to stop back. Kate contemplated explaining her errand for him to relate to his mother but then decided against it. It was too complicated. With a sigh, she thanked him and moved on.

There was only one cottage left at this end of Magnolia, and as Kate trudged toward it, she decided this had been a foolish idea. Still, she climbed the double stone steps and knocked. This time, a young woman about her age opened the door. Kate vaguely remembered her from school. Constance, she thought her name might be.

"Indian Kate! What are you doing here? Want to come in?"

Kate's face blanched. At being called "Indian Kate," her resolve wavered. She was tempted to pretend she had accidentally knocked on the wrong door, but she couldn't even come up with false name. "I . . . I know this sounds peculiar," she faltered, forcing herself to proceed, "but I'm just going up and down the street asking people if they remember anything about the families who used to live down at the bottom of Magnolia."

"The foreigners?" Constance raised her eyebrows. "Chief Meyers got rid of all them. Cleared 'em out. That was a long time ago, though. Why?"

"Who is it, Connie?" shouted a woman from inside. "Don't stand there with the door open."

Constance tilted her head toward the interior. "Better come in."

With a sigh, Kate followed her in, as there seemed to be no other option. It was very neat and tidy, and the front room featured an enormous radio, from which the sound of an orchestra emanated. The smell of something cooking lingered in the air. Pork chops, if Kate had to guess, and her stomach rumbled.

"Who is it?" asked the woman, coming into the room as she wiped her hands on her apron.

"It's Indian Kate . . . I mean, Kate . . . Kerwyn, from school, Ma. She's asking about the foreign families that used to live down at the end."

The woman's face crumpled in suspicion. "Why? We don't know anything about them. They're all gone now."

Kate wished she could remember Constance's surname. Ginter? Green? Gerber? She was pretty sure it was Gerber . . . "I'm a friend of Harriet and Rosemary Mueller, Mrs. Gerber," she explained, deciding to guess.

"Oh, yeah?" Mrs. Gerber's frown relaxed slightly.

"I . . . I was talking to Rosemary about the families that lived here around the time of the accident. The mining accident, I mean. Apparently, there was a man who died in it and whose wife died later of diphtheria. The kids were all taken in by a relative from Shullsburg." She looked at her hopefully. "Does any of this ring a bell? They were called Espo, I think. At least that's what Mrs. Mueller seems to remember."

Mrs. Gerber's lips twisted in thought. "Well, I do seem to remember something like that, come to think of it. There were so many sad stories, hard to remember them all." She looked to Constance for help, but Constance, who would have been little more than a toddler, was of no assistance. "I do think I remember that woman, though."

Kate held her breath.

"Long black hair she had; always wore it up in an old-fashioned bun. Probably what they did back wherever she came from. Always creeping up here begging for milk–as if we had milk to spare!"

"Do you remember the name? Was it Espo?"

Mrs. Gerber thought for a moment and then shrugged. "Mighta been. Couldn't tell ya. Rosemary knew more. She only had the one kid, while I was raising five. Didn't have time. And Rosemary . . . well . . . she always was a little different. But I suppose you already know that."

Kate silently acknowledged that Rosemary, with her big generous heart, was assuredly different.

"Not worth learnin' their names," Mrs. Gerber went on defensively. "There were packs of 'em comin' an' goin'. Filthy, they were. Lice-ridden. Hundreds of kids running around." She drew herself up. "Disgusting is what I say. Thank God Chief Meyers and Sheriff Norris got rid of them."

Kate could not get the image of what might have been her mother begging for milk from this kind of woman.

Mrs. Gerber's eyes narrowed. "Why are you so interested, anyway?"

Kate cleared her throat. "No reason, really. I . . . I thought I might know someone that was related."

"Well, I can't help you, I'm afraid. I need to get on with dinner. Good luck to you. What did you say your name was?"

"Kate. Kate Kerwyn." She turned to go.

"It was good seein' you, Kate!" Constance called as Kate made her way down the steps.

Once she was back in the street, Kate paused forlornly, wondering what to do next. The Gerbers' cottage was the last one on this end of Magnolia, with only weeds and spindly trees beyond. She stared at the scrub brush for a few minutes. Where had all of these "foreigners" lived? In tents? Or had their dwellings subsequently been knocked down?

With a heavy sigh, she started walking back up the hill and checked her wristwatch. If she wanted to get back home by suppertime, she would need to start now, but she desperately wanted to inquire at the cottages at the high end. She tried to calculate how much time it would take . . .

She paused, however, when she saw a man exit the furthest one, a bundle of lumber under his arm. Upon taking a few steps closer, she recognized the dark curls and realized that the man was none other than Henry Crawford! She had forgotten that the Crawfords were working on the Murphy cottage for Frank and Julius.

Quickly, she spun around. She had no desire to speak to the likes of Henry Crawford. He and Mary had stopped by the farm several times since the debaucherous party, though Kate couldn't understand why, unless it was an attempt on Henry's part to see more of Louisa. Or, she thought darkly, on Mary's to see more of Edmund. Curiously, though, neither got much of a chance, as Henry stayed mostly outdoors with Edmund and Mr. Kerwyn, who oddly did not seem to remember having met the brother and sister the night of Ray's party. According to Edmund, Henry was always offering to help, but when actually tasked with a project, he was of little real aid. Edmund found his ignorance extremely amusing, and took what Kate thought was valuable time to try to instruct him in the milking of cows, sharpening of plow blades, and the greasing of the tractor engine.

Likewise, Mary was stuck inside with the women. Like her brother, she tried, in her own small way, to be helpful, but she was also not very successful. For example, she had several times attempted to suggest to Mrs. Kerwyn how she might spruce up the front room by moving the furniture, or adding small tassels to the curtains, or perhaps painting the walls a different color other than white–and other ridiculous ideas.

Additionally, she seemed eager to make a best friend of all the Kerwyn girls, but most especially Kate. She was always trying to get Kate alone, and when she did, would ask all sorts of exasperating questions about Edmund. Kate was tempted to tell her to ask him herself, but she didn't want to give the precocious young woman any extra reason to lure Edmund into conversation. Already he turned red and sheepish whenever she spoke to him.

A few times Kate had been tempted to warn him of . . . of what? Making a fool of himself? But before she could ever get the words out, Edmund would thwart her by declaring how lovely and perfect Mary was. "Isn't she, Kate? I've never met someone so . . . so refined, I guess you would call it, but down to earth at the same time. I can't explain it. Can you?"

Kate couldn't. Neither could she explain Edmund's apparent growing attraction for her. It was obvious to her that Mary was toying with him, perhaps for lack of anything else to do. It simply wasn't possible that a woman so elegant and cultured and . . . well, *urban*, would be interested in a lowly farmer like Edmund Bertram. Was it possible that a woman could break a man's heart out of boredom?

"Kate!" Henry shouted.

Kate's shoulders drooped. She had started down the Muellers' stone path to escape his detection, but having been spotted, she turned.

"What a delightful surprise!" he called as he jogged up. "What are you doing here in town?" He dabbed his forehead with a silk handkerchief. She was surprised that he was perspiring, as back at the farm, he did more talking than heavy lifting. She had just witnessed him carrying a plank of lumber, though, so he must indeed be doing something.

He was in shirtsleeves, yet he still managed to look elegant, attired as he was in a brown velvet–*velvet?*–waistcoat and plaid serge trousers. He was, Kate admitted as she pulled her gaze away from his dark curls and deep green eyes, extremely handsome. It was a shame that his character was not, she thought, reminding herself of what he had done with Louisa in the kitchen.

"I was shopping for Mom." She held up her basket. "And I was just going to call in to say hello to Mrs. Mueller," she fibbed. "So, I'll say good afternoon." She tried to turn away, but he stopped her.

"Well, since you're here, why don't I show you our progress on the cottage?" he suggested eagerly, gesturing further up the hill.

Kate checked her wristwatch and feigned surprise. "Oh, my! I didn't realize the time. I need to get back. Mom will be worried."

Henry glanced up and down the street. "How'd you get here?"

"I walked."

"Walked? That's much too far. Allow me to drive you."

"No, really, Mr. Crawford. Please."

"Henry," he corrected her.

"I'm happy to walk. It . . . it clears my head."

"No trouble at all! Don't go anywhere!"

He jogged backward for a few moments as if to make sure she was staying put, then grinned, spun back around and continued up the hill.

Kate refused to be commanded by the likes of Henry Crawford. She began walking briskly toward Chestnut. She had gotten three-fourths down the block before she heard his motorcar chugging behind her.

"You're a stubborn one, aren't you?" he said with an amused expression, directing the car in front of her path.

Forced to pause, Kate flashed him an irritated glare. "I could say the same."

"Come on." He gave her a wink. "You'll be late otherwise. And I was headed out there anyway."

Kate could think of no way out of this, so she sighed and climbed reluctantly into the passenger side of his Pontiac Six. As soon as she was seated, Henry immediately threw it into gear, as if afraid she would change her mind.

She couldn't tell the make of one car from another, but this one was quite nice inside, not like Edmund's rusty old "beast."

"You don't like me very much, do you?" Henry said, looking over at her with yet another grin. Honestly, was that all he ever did? Grin?

She made a point to look out the window. "I don't think it matters much either way, Mr. Crawford." She was not only shocked by his bluntness, but by the fact that he found her dislike of him amusing.

Henry laughed. "But why?"

Why? Because you seduced my sister, who is engaged to another man! she wanted to say, but she refrained.

Kate had half expected Louisa to break her engagement with Vernon in the weeks that had followed the party, but she had not, though she still continued to stare adoringly at Henry whenever he did happen to come into the farmhouse. For his part, Henry seemed immune to these rather obvious overtures, or pretended to be, at least.

It was a shock, then, when just yesterday, Louisa had surprised them all by announcing that she and Vernon had decided to move up the date of their nuptials from October to May. She looked directly at Henry as she said it, but he did not react in the slightest. Later, after everyone had gone, her parents had given Louisa their blessing, though they hoped that the rush was not due to something . . . inconvenient.

"Look, whatever you might think, I'm actually a rather decent chap," Henry insisted. "I could help you, if you'd let me, you know."

"I wasn't aware I was in need of help," she said dryly, her eyes alighting on the tombstones as they passed the cemetery now.

"I mean, I could help you with your art."

She turned away from the window. "I wish people would stop calling me an artist," she said sharply. "I don't make art. I make baskets for money, pure and simple. There's nothing artistic about them!"

Henry let out a little laugh. "But there is. The color, the patterns. Anyone who can make something so beautiful out of twigs and weeds and string is an artist. Think what you could do if you had real materials!" He turned down High Street. "I have friends in Chicago. Artists, playwrights, actors. You should meet them. Discuss your work. I'd be happy to introduce you."

Kate felt her stomach clench. He was starting to sound like Frank and Julius. Did he really see her as an artist, or was he teasing her? She wavered a little in her decision to dislike him. "Introduce me? As what? A poor country bumpkin you met during your dreary sojourn in the wilds of Wisconsin?" she asked, deciding to test him.

Henry shifted the gears. "You're much too hard on yourself, you know. And in that way, you're just like every other artist. All you lack is confidence."

She drew in a breath. He was right. She *did* lack confidence.

"Confidence, my dear Kate, is half the battle. There's a certain . . . *je ne sais quoi* about it all. If you think of your work as just a bunch of twigs stuck together for money, then that's what it is. If, however, you see it as a beautiful creation emanating from your heart, a conduit for the divine, if you will, then it is."

Kate looked out the window again. A "conduit for the divine" felt a bit far-fetched, but she did feeling stirrings of . . . well, something when she was weaving together the patterns she saw in her mind. Then again, simply believing something was art didn't make it so.

"Well, suit yourself," Henry said jovially when she failed to answer. "But remember, I'm happy to help if you decide you can bear it. Maybe someday you'll grow to trust me."

Kate's wandering thoughts snapped back. That was the problem. She *didn't* trust him. But she wanted to, she conceded, which was what was so unsettling. She wanted to believe what he was telling her about herself–about her art, if nothing else. But there was something about him that unnerved her. At times she still felt as she had at the potluck, that he could somehow see right the way through her, and she continued to feel exposed and vulnerable around him, on edge. She didn't like it.

She gave him a final glance. Thankfully, his eyes were on the road, but he still wore that idiotic grin.

She shifted her body slightly away from him as they bounced along the country road toward home and remained silent for the rest of the way.

CHAPTER NINE

"There you are, Kate!" Mrs. Kerwyn exclaimed when Kate slipped through the back screen door. "What on earth took you that long? Did you stop and see Ray? I nearly sent Edmund out to find you. Oh, Henry! You're here, too."

Kate had hoped that Henry would merely drop her off, but, of course, that was hoping for too much.

"I stopped by the Muellers' for a moment, but no one was in," Kate fibbed. "Henry saw me and gave me a ride home."

"Well, that was kind of you, Henry. But you've taken him away from his work, Kate," Mrs. Kerwyn scolded.

"Not at all!" Henry interjected. "I was hoping to have a word with Edmund anyway. As it happens, I have a note for him." Henry pulled a small envelope from his inner breast pocket. "From my sister."

So, he had had an ulterior motive in giving her a ride. *She should have known.* Wearily, she tied on an apron and approached the pile of potatoes near the sink. Nettie, whose job it normally was to peel potatoes, was instead lifting hot cookies off of a pan and onto a platter.

"Here, Henry! Have a cookie!" she urged, carrying the platter to him. "I just made them." Ever since Louisa had moved up the date of her wedding, Nettie seemed to presume Henry hers for the taking, but her attempts to snare him were not only obvious, but thus far ineffective.

"Why, thank you, Nettie!" Henry said, as if she were a child, which she some days seemed to be. He selected a cookie and took a bite. His face twisted in genuine surprise. "Delicious! You're quite a baker."

Nettie again smiled widely. "I've learned quite a bit working at Ben's."

"How are you at cakes?"

"Cakes? Oh, I can make all sorts of cakes. Would you like me to make you one?" she asked eagerly.

"Not for me. I was thinking one for Kate, since it's her birthday Friday." Kate froze in the peeling of the potatoes.

"Her birthday?" Mrs. Kerwyn said. "Well, I suppose you're right. It *is* Kate's birthday on Friday."

Mortified, Kate kept her back to them, hoping that if she didn't face them, they would all just go away.

"We should have a party," Henry suggested.

"A party?" Her mother's voice was wary.

Kate turned, her face burning. "How do you know it's my birthday?"

"Mary told me." He grinned. "No secrets between us."

"I don't need a party, Mom." She turned toward her mother and begged her with her eyes to say no. "I don't want any fuss. Honestly."

"What's this about a party?" Louisa asked, hurrying down from upstairs. "Oh, hello, Henry! I didn't realize *you* were here!" An obvious fib. And why wasn't she down here helping get supper ready?

"I was just suggesting we have a party for Kate's birthday, since she's never had one."

"Well, we weren't ever sure when her birthday actually was," Mrs. Kerwyn said defensively.

"I meant no offense, Mrs. Kerwyn!" Henry said hurriedly. "I just thought it would be nice."

"Why does Kate get a birthday party?" Nettie whined. "I've never had one either!"

"Yes, you did," Louisa corrected, picking up one of the cookies and taking a bite. "When you were ten. Don't you remember?"

"That was at Grandma's house, so it doesn't count."

"What a spoiled child you are, Nettie!" Louisa scolded.

Nettie glanced nervously at Henry. "I'm not spoiled, and I'm hardly a child!"

"What do you say, Mom? Oh, please say yes!" Louisa begged, clearly deciding that any excuse for a party was a good one.

Mrs. Kerwyn glanced at Kate, who shook her head, trying one last time to thwart the idea. "Well," she said hesitantly, clearly not picking up the signal. "I suppose we should."

"Oh, thank you, Mom!" Louisa gushed. "How fun! We need something to cheer us all up."

Cheer us up? Not many brides-to-be need cheering, Kate thought ruefully.

"Now. Who should we invite?" Louisa asked, taking another bite of the cookie.

Mrs. Kerwyn's eyes widened. "Invite? Well, it's just going to be us, Louisa. Not some big party like Ray threw. Your dad would never go for that."

"No, of course not. But surely you mean to ask Henry and Mary." She glanced at Henry, who had taken to leaning against the wall, one hand in his pocket as he listened to the conversation.

"Well, yes, of course," Mrs. Kerwyn faltered, glancing at Henry. "We'd be happy for you to join us." She paused, seeming unsure. "Though it won't be anything fancy, like."

"After fending for ourselves these past weeks, I can assure you, Mrs. Kerwyn, that my sister and I would be delighted with whatever you prepare." He flashed Louisa a grateful smile.

"And don't forget Vernon," Nettie added with false sweetness.

"Obviously Vernon." Louisa threw her sister a little dart. "And I suppose if we're asking the Crawfords, we should probably ask Frank and Julius. And what about your friend Harriet, Kate? She was here every day when you were sick."

"Oh, Louisa, not all them," Mrs. Kerwyn complained. "This is getting out of hand, now. I agreed to a simple family supper, not a big reception."

"But, Mother! It will be awkward to invite the Crawfords and not their hosts!"

"Oh, alright." Mrs. Kerwyn wearily rubbed her brow. "But where are we all going to sit?"

* * *

As it turned out, extra seats were not needed, as Frank and Julius politely declined with the excuse of having already procured tickets for a performance of The Pirates of Penzance at the Merriweather Opera House. Everyone else, though, accepted, including Harriet and John, and of course Edmund, who also thought the idea of a party for Kate a splendid one.

Kate spent the afternoon of the big day up in her room. Mrs. Kerwyn had insisted that Kate be absolved from helping to prepare her own birthday dinner and banished her from the kitchen for the day. It was an extremely generous gesture, whether her mother was completely aware of it or not, as it meant more work for her, seeing as how little Louisa, Nettie, and Minnie actually contributed. Indeed, Kate easily accomplished more each day than the three of her sisters put together.

Being stuck in her room was proving worse to Kate, however, than sweating over the stove. She considered venturing outdoors to inspect her old badger hole, but the day was unfortunately rainy, and having washed her hair last night, she didn't want to spoil it for the party. So, instead, she spent the afternoon trying to work on a basket, which did not come out well, and a sketch, which did.

Finally, about an hour before the party was supposed to begin, she decided she should probably change into one of her Sunday dresses, neither of which she really liked. While living in the badger hole, she had taken to wearing trousers and shirts, as it suited living in the wild better, and had found it very freeing, almost exhilarating. But Mrs. Kerwyn did not approve, nor did her father. She might get away with wearing trousers on her birthday, but she didn't want to risk a scene. Instead, she slipped on a pale green dress, which accented her dark hair and dark eyes.

She was just buttoning the last button at the nape of her neck when there was a knock. Before she could even say, "Come in," Mary Crawford poked her head around the door.

"May I come in? Oh, don't you look divine!" Mary gushed, opening the door wide and revealing yet another splendid ensemble. Tonight she had arrayed herself in a wool tartan skirt in reds and greens paired with a crisp white silk blouse that featured a small lace collar and puffed sleeves that tapered at the cuffs. To complete the look, she wore a short black velvet vest upon which was pinned a silver Celtic brooch, and her curls were tied up with a plaid bow cut from the same material as her skirt. Again, she looked as though she had just stepped out of *Vogue*, albeit the country edition, if there was such a thing. Kate wondered where she procured such outfits. Certainly not in Merriweather!

"Happy birthday!" Mary gushed.

"Thank you."

"Here, I brought you this!" Mary held out a tiny box. "It's my birthday gift to you, but I thought maybe you'd want to open it now."

"You shouldn't have gotten me a gift," Kate murmured. This was exactly why she hadn't wanted a party! She hated receiving gifts and being the center of attention. And now, because of the Crawfords, she would have to endure a whole night of all eyes focused on her.

"Nonsense! Of course I should have. Here, take it."

Kate reluctantly took the box and pried it open. Inside was a delicate gold chain. In spite of herself, Kate let out a tiny gasp. "Oh, it's too much!"

"Do you like it?" Mary asked eagerly.

"Like it? Of course I do. It's beautiful!"

"Try it on!"

"Now?"

Mary let out a little laugh. "Yes, why not? That's why I came up early. I thought you might want to wear it to the party. Here," she took the box from Kate, "I'll help you."

Before Kate could protest, Mary had draped the chain around Kate's neck. Once she had fastened it, Mary moved to assess her handiwork. "Oh, it's beautiful. It really suits you, Kate." She glanced around for a mirror and spotted one on the dresser top, its brass edges gilded and worn. She held it up for Kate.

Kate was not accustomed to looking at herself, but she forced herself to do so now. She had pulled her long black hair up for the evening, and, she admitted, she did look pretty tonight, especially with the gold chain glistening at her throat. "Thank you, Mary," she said, turning to her. "It must have cost a fortune."

"Not really. It was a gift from Henry last Christmas. I hope you don't mind."

"Oh no!" Kate's fingers flew to her neck. "I can't possibly accept this, then."

"I insist! I already had a gold chain, which, if Henry was observant in any way, he would have known. And, to put your mind at ease, I asked him if he cared, and he said he didn't. Not at all. In fact, he said it gave him an idea of what to get you."

"This is plenty between the both of you."

"No, it isn't." She set the mirror back on the dresser. "Unless you mind taking something that was first mine. Is that it?" She stared intently at Kate. "Because I wouldn't mind taking something that was first yours," she said slowly, deliberately.

Kate returned the young woman's stare until Mary's deeper meaning became apparent. She could feel her cheeks redden. Edmund wasn't hers! "No, that's not it at all," Kate replied quickly. "It's just that . . ." She faltered, not knowing how to say that she didn't wish to wear anything that had been a gift from Henry, even a secondhand one.

"Look, let's talk about the party, shall we?" Mary took both of Kate's hands in hers. "I assume Edmund is coming?" she asked, her tone suddenly gay.

"Yes, I believe so."

"He's very handsome, isn't he?"

Kate furrowed her brow. "I guess so."

"He's just the sort I like, you know. The strong, silent ones."

While Edmund was certainly strong, Kate did not view him as being particularly silent, but she didn't argue.

"I wore this just for him," Mary said brightly, gripping the edges of her skirt. "He told me he liked it when I was out at his farm last week, so I thought I'd wear it again."

Kate blinked. "You were out at his farm?"

"Yes, last Sunday. I met his mother and everything. She's such a sweet woman. She seemed to like me. At least I hope she did."

Kate had met Mrs. Bertram countless times, but she had become more and more of a hermit these past years. She and Edmund rarely entertained. "Did he . . . did he *ask* you to visit?"

Mary sat on the edge of the bed and crossed her legs. "Well, not *exactly*." She smiled demurely. "You know how men are. I suggested it, and he agreed!"

Oh, why was Edmund so blind?

"It's quite a big farm, isn't it?" Mary continued. "And as the only child, he'll inherit the whole thing, won't he?"

"Yes, I . . . I suppose so." Kate considered mentioning that the fate of the Bertram farm was up in the air, as Edmund was planning to join the military, a fact which she herself had forgotten of late. He might have already left had her father not been in such need. The thought of him going away made her feel slightly sick.

"Listen, Kate. Would you do me a favor?" Mary urged. "Seeing as you and Edmund are so close–like brother and sister, it seems to me–do you think you might ascertain his feelings for me? I'm fairly certain he cares for me, but I'd like to be sure. I've given him so many hints, but you know how men are."

Kate drew in a sharp breath, stunned by Mary's boldness. "Well, I–" she began hesitantly, but was thankfully interrupted by a call from below.

"Kate!" It was Minnie. "Supper's ready!"

Kate gave Mary a weak smile. "I guess we'd better go down and get this over with."

"Get it over with? What a funny creature you are, Kate! You'd spoil your own birthday party if it were up to you. But remember what I said!"

Mary looped her arm through Kate's as they left the tiny garret. Kate disengaged, however, at the top of the stairs and let Mary descend first.

Gripping the rail, she took a deep breath. Her heart was fluttering, the usual desire to run upon her. She wished she could flee back to her room or to the badger hole or anywhere but downstairs where everyone was waiting. She took several more deep breaths and imagined Edmund beside her, reassuring her, putting his arm around her. After a few moments, she was able to make her feet move and began to descend slowly.

Mary was already at the bottom of the stairs. Kate gave her an uneven smile before they entered the dining room together.

"Happy birthday!" everyone shouted.

The Kerwyns and their guests were all squeezed around the table, and despite her anxiety, Kate did feel a wave of happiness. Her eyes went briefly to Edmund, who winked, and then to Harriet, beaming beside John.

"Here, Kate, you sit here at the head," Mr. Kerwyn directed. He had gotten up and was holding the back of his chair for her.

"Oh, no, Dad! That's your spot."

"Not for tonight." He tilted his head. "Go on, then."

Mary gave her a quick kiss on the cheek and then made her way to an open seat further down.

Kate dreaded sitting at the head of the table, but she knew that to continue to protest would cause more of a fuss. "Thanks, Dad," she murmured and sat down.

He kissed her on the top of the head. "You look real nice tonight, Kate. Like a princess, doesn't she?" he asked no one in particular.

There were a few nods and murmurs, and Kate looked to Edmund to catch his reaction. He was, however, already whispering something to Mary, who had somehow found a way to squeeze in beside him. *Hadn't Minnie been sitting there?*

Just then, Mrs. Kerwyn entered carrying a bowl of mashed potatoes. Louisa followed, carrying a large platter bearing a roast ham. Nettie carried a bowl of green beans. Louisa set the ham in front of Mr. Kerwyn.

"Well, would you look at this?" he said proudly. "Last of the hams hanging out in the smokehouse. Come fall, we'll have to butcher more." He picked up the carving knife and began to slice while the women carried in several more dishes, including hot rolls, gravy, corn, and a sweet onion relish, Mrs. Kerwyn's specialty, which had won several awards at the county fair. In addition, there were two bottles of cider Harriet brought from the Merc. Normally, the Kerwyns drank milk with supper, so the cider was a welcome change.

Kate's plate was filled first, and there was now a happy buzz of chatter as the food was passed around.

"Mrs. Kerwyn, this is delicious!" Henry exclaimed after taking several bites. He was dressed as elegantly as his sister, much more so than her father and Edmund, who had arrived in his usual wool jacket, a plaid shirt underneath. Henry, on the other hand, had on a tailored charcoal-gray suit with a plaid shirtwaist that matched his sister's skirt. Even his tie, held in place by a silver tie pin, was plaid. *Did they always dress alike?* Kate wondered, slightly amused.

"Oh." Mrs. Kerwyn patted her hair as she took the seat next to Kate. "It's nothing fancy."

"But it really is very, very good!"

Mrs. Kerwyn smiled to herself.

"It *is* delicious, Mom. Thank you," Kate added.

Mrs. Kerwyn turned the smile to her. "We should have done this a long time ago. Oh!" she exclaimed as her eyes caught sight of her new necklace. "Where'd you get *that*, Kate?"

Kate blushed and touched the chain with her fingertips. "It was a gift from Mary. She just gave it to me upstairs."

"Well!" Mrs. Kerwyn exclaimed again, looking at Mary. "That's mighty nice of you, Mary!"

"It's just a small thing. It looks nice on her, don't you think?"

"Indeed, it does." Mrs. Kerwyn took a bite of her mashed potatoes and sighed. "I just wish Ray could have come," she said wistfully, causing Kate's stomach to instantly churn.

"Now, Caroline, let's not get into all that. Don't spoil the party by mentioning that good-for-nothing–"

"Mr. K, did I tell you I saw Mel Dalsing in town the other day?" Edmund smoothly interrupted. "He told me he's selling off his dairy cows. Moving to beef only."

"What?" Mr. Kerwyn paused, his fork halfway to his mouth. He lowered it. "I don't believe that. Why?

"Says it's less work. More profitable."

"That don't make sense. You need a lot of pasture for that."

"That's what I was thinking. Might sell him a few acres of ours. Maybe the back forty?"

Mr. Kerwyn took a thoughtful sip of cider. "I don't know, Ed. Why do you want to break up the farm? It's not my place to say, but I don't think that's what yer dad woulda wanted. I know you've been workin' too much over here. I'm sorry about that. I mean to hire someone to help."

"Thanks, Mr. K. I appreciate that. But selling some of the farm off would reduce the amount of maintenance needed, and it would give my mom a little nest egg to live on while I'm gone."

"Gone?" Mary perked up. "Where are you going?"

"I'm joining up." He turned to her. "I thought you knew that."

"Joining up?" she exclaimed. "As in the *army*?"

Edmund laughed. "Yes, as in *the army*."

"But why? Mary's previously jolly face melted into dismay. "There isn't any need."

"There will be if things keep going the way they are. I mean to beat the Nazis to the punch. I'm going to enlist before I get called up."

"But . . . but why?" she repeated.

"Because it's my duty," Edmund said, suddenly more serious.

"Duty?" Mary scoffed. "That's ridiculous."

Edmund shifted uncomfortably, and any stray chatter around the dinner table was suddenly halted. "I don't think serving your country is ridiculous. Especially if there's to be a war."

"War?" Mary said prettily, obviously trying to lighten the disquiet. "There isn't going to be a war!" She looked around the table for encouragement but found little. Only Nettie smiled back.

"He's right, you know," Henry finally responded, leaning back. "I don't think it's a matter of *if,* but *when*, by the way things are going in Europe."

"But there are other ways to serve, you know," Mary urged. "We need you here to . . . to plant food. Isn't *that* your duty?"

"Perhaps for some." Edward glanced nervously at Mr. Kerwyn, who was listening intently, his thick, calloused fingers steepled under his nose. "But this is something I need to do."

"I think you'll make a fine soldier, Edmund," Kate said quietly, suddenly very proud of him. "Edmund's father was killed in the last war, you see. So–"

"But what if you were to be killed as well!" Mary exclaimed, cutting her off. "There would be no one to carry on the Bertram name! Henry, tell him."

"Well, a man must do what a man must do. Seems his mind is made up, dear sister."

Mary placed a hand on Edmund's arm. "Well, I'm not giving up! I have all spring to try to persuade you!"

"When are we going to have the cake?" Minnie broke in, leaning her head on one fist, clearly bored.

"Yes, let's have no more talk of war." Mrs. Kerwyn stood up and collected her plate and Kate's.

"I can get it, Mom," Kate offered, standing as well, glad of the change in subject.

"No, you don't!" Mrs. Kerwyn patted her shoulder. "You sit down. Louisa and Nettie can help. Go on, girls," she said with a nod. "Gather the plates. Minnie, you bring the food."

"Aw!" Minnie whined.

"You heard your mother," Mr. Kerwyn growled, and Minnie accordingly jumped up. Mr. Kerwyn rose, too, but instead of going into the kitchen, he went into the front room. Kate was almost certain she knew what he was after, especially when she heard the scrape of the cabinet door open. Sure enough, when he returned, he was carrying what was left of his special whiskey and several little glasses.

"Oh, no, Dad!" Kate cried out. "Not that!"

"It's *my* whiskey!" Mr. Kerwyn declared, setting it heavily on the table. "And I'll say when we drink it! If this is your first party, we need to make up for lost time." He began filling the little glasses as Louisa and Nettie, and now Harriet, carried the rest of the dishes to the kitchen.

Mrs. Kerwyn appeared with the cake. It was a large chocolate construction, only slightly lopsided, with chocolate jimmies sprinkled on top. It produced immediate oohs and ahs from around the table.

"I made it!" Nettie announced, hurrying into the room behind her mother. Kate caught Nettie's glance at Henry, but, as usual, he was staring at Kate.

Kate looked away, again feeling as though he could see right through her.

"Here you are!" Mrs. Kerwyn declared. "Better late than never, I suppose."

"Thanks, Mom. And Nettie," she added. "It looks delicious."

Despite the very likely probability that Nettie had made the cake more to impress Henry than as a gift for her, Kate was, in fact, touched. She hadn't had a slice of cake in ages. Mrs. Kerwyn hadn't made her traditional Christmas cake this year on account of Kate being so ill.

Mr. Kerwyn began passing the small glasses, each holding just a tiny dram of his whiskey, around the table. "This is the last of it."

Kate felt horribly guilty to be the reason for the whiskey's extinction, but she was moved by her father's gesture. Ever since Minnie had tattled about all the goings-on the night of Ray's party–including Kate's lack of participation–Mr. Kerwyn had begun to favor Kate even more than usual.

"Here's to Kate!" he said, raising his glass. "Happy birthday, girl!"

Everyone echoed the sentiment and drained their glasses. Kate took a sip, her throat constricting a little at the burn. Edmund raised his already-empty glass to her before laughing at something Mary whispered in his ear.

Mrs. Kerwyn sliced into the cake and began passing plates of it down the table.

"Open your presents!" Minnie shouted. "Mine first!"

Kate groaned internally. It had been hard enough to sit through dinner with everyone's attention on her, but opening gifts would be unendurable. Before she could protest, however, Minnie grabbed the little pile arranged on the sideboard and dumped them in front of her sister.

"I couldn't accept these," she faltered, looking around the table. "Thank you, though."

"Don't be stupid, Kate," Louisa called from the other end of the table. "Open them!"

Louisa seemed in a particularly foul mood tonight, perhaps because Vernon had not been able to make it, or because Nettie was desperately trying to get Henry's attention, or, more likely, because she had drunk almost a whole bottle of cider herself.

Kate pushed her half-eaten cake out of the way to make room for the gifts.

"This one first!" Minnie declared, putting a small pink bag in front of her and then hovered nearby.

Kate examined it. The pink was intriguing. "Where'd you get this?"

"From the Merc," Minnie answered excitedly.

Kate shot a questioning glance at Harriet.

"Melody ordered a whole box of pink bags. That was before she decided to go back to Chicago." She gave a little shrug. "So Fred's using them up on the candy."

"Don't tell!" cried Minnie.

On that note, Kate opened the bag and pulled out a small assortment of candy sticks. "Oh my!" Kate declared. "Thank you!" The candy was only a penny a stick, but she appreciated that the girl had spent her few precious coins for a gift, though Kate did suspect that Minnie was hoping Kate might share the spoils. "Would you like one?"

Kate could tell that Minnie was tempted, but her sister refrained. "Well, maybe a half of one. Some other day, though."

"The cider was our gift," Harriet said, tilting her head toward John. "But there's one there from Mom."

"Oh! We should have invited your mom!" Kate cried.

"She wouldn't have come," Harriet insisted. "And, anyway, it's just a little thing."

Based on the aroma emanating from the package, Kate suspected the contents to be of an organic variety. Though it was wrapped tightly in tissue paper, it smelled faintly of lavender. Kate carefully pulled away the paper to reveal a small burlap sachet.

"She made it from herbs in the garden. Mostly lavender. It's for your bureau drawers. To smell nice."

Kate gave the sachet a deep sniff, her eyes closing involuntarily at the pleasant scent. It made her long for summer. "Thank you, Harriet! It's lovely. You'll tell her thank you, won't you? And thank you for the cider."

Harriet smiled her usual big smile, and Kate suddenly missed their old comradery. She wished she could talk to her friend alone.

The next package, this one wrapped in old newspaper, contained a new pair of stockings. "That's from me and Louisa," Nettie called out between bites of cake.

"Thank you." Though she *did* need a new pair of stockings, Kate suspected that the gift, like Minnie's, was a somewhat selfish one, as both her older sisters would undoubtedly ask to borrow them. She set them to the side.

The last package was small, too, though not squishy as Mrs. Mueller's. This one was in a proper box and was wrapped in fancy store-bought paper. It was obviously from Henry.

She frowned to see him staring at her eagerly, grinning his usual grin. She suddenly felt as though she were some helpless woodland creature and him a wolf who had her in his sights. She wished she could run out of the room. She had no desire to receive a gift from Henry Crawford, but to reject it without even opening it would be horribly rude.

Kate took a deep breath and tried to pry open the paper without ripping it. When she had finally pulled enough of it away, she gasped at the box's gold embossed lettering–*Van Dyke*–which told her immediately that it was jewelry of some sort. She prayed it was perhaps a watch, but the box was too small for that. She could feel the perspiration trickle down her back as she lifted the lid. Inside was a beautiful gold cross.

"It's to go on the chain from Mary," Henry explained. "When she told me she was giving it to you, I knew immediately what I should get." He paused. "Do you like it?"

"Well . . . of course I do, but it's . . . it's really too much, Henry. I can't possibly accept this."

"Why not?" He seemed amused.

"What is it?" Louisa called. "Pass it down. Let us see!"

Kate obeyed and handed it to Nettie, who looked at it briefly and then passed it.

"Honestly, Henry. I can't accept that." Kate looked at her mother for support, but Mrs. Kerwyn was absently chewing a bite of cake. Kate then turned her eyes to her father, but he merely smiled and raised his glass to her.

"Can't refuse a gift, girl. Take it."

"There! You see?" Henry leaned back in his chair, beaming.

"Well, thank you, I suppose," she said, averting her eyes. "Thank you, everyone, for the party. And for your gifts."

"Just one left." Edmund reached into his jacket pocket and pulled out a small oblong object wrapped in cloth. Standing slightly, he stretched across the table to place it in front of her.

Kate smiled, suddenly delighted. She hadn't been expecting a gift from Edmund! She carefully began to unwrap the cloth.

"Sorry I didn't have any paper. The cloth bit is actually a handkerchief. Ma made it for you. She thought you might need new ones after being sick for so long."

"It's lovely!" she said, noting the embroidered blue trim along scalloped edges. "You'll thank her for me, won't you?" She flashed him a smile. She further unwrapped the handkerchief to find that it held a beautiful black fountain pen.

"Oh!"

"It's for your sketching. Is it the right kind?" Edmund asked eagerly.

"Yes, of course it is!" She had never had such a fancy pen!

"I got it at Hartigs," he explained, referring to the stationer in town. "I thought it would be good for your cider labels. And your other art stuff. Your pictures and all that."

"Thank you, Edmund," she replied, looking intensely at him, as if they were the only two in the room. "I shall cherish this."

Edmund beamed. "The clerk at Hartigs recommended several, but Mary helped me decide." He gave Mary a sideways smile.

Kate's delight immediately dissipated.

"Why does everyone suddenly think Kate's an artist?" Louisa chided with a slight hiccup. "Just because she makes baskets and writes out labels for cider? I mean, they're nice baskets, Kate, but let's be honest." She hiccupped again. "They're just scraps you put together to make money while you were pouting in a hole in the ground. I'd hardly call them art!" She gave a little laugh, and Nettie nervously joined in.

"I never said they were art," Kate said quietly. *So much for birthday goodwill.* Well, what did it matter? It probably wasn't really her birthday, anyway.

"But they *are* art," Henry insisted. "Kate could have a showing in a gallery somewhere."

"What's a gallery?" Minnie asked.

"Henry's right. You should, Kate," Mary added brightly. "Why don't you come stay with us when we get back to Chicago? We'd love to show you around the galleries, wouldn't we, Henry?"

"Yes." Henry fingered his glass. "I've already mentioned to Kate that her talent should be nurtured." For once, his irritating grin was absent.

"Can I come, too?" Minnie squeaked.

"Don't be silly, Minnie. None of us is going to Chicago!" Mrs. Kerwyn cut herself another thin slice of cake.

"People *do* like your baskets, though, Kate," Harriet added. "We're down to just one left!"

"There you are, Kate. The public have spoken." Louisa hiccupped again. "I suppose it's not a bad idea to have a way to make money, seeing as you're not all that domestic. You're more of a free spirit, aren't you? Must be your Indian blood coming out." She forced a little chuckle. "I don't imagine you'll ever get married and have children." Her eyes darted to Henry. "It's just as well, I suppose. That way you'll have an income to help Mom and Dad when we're all gone. I mean, someone has to stay behind."

"That's enough, Louisa!" Mr. Kerwyn grunted.

"Well, it's true," she muttered, flopping back in her chair.

"I don't know." Henry cleared his throat. "Who says that matrimony and artistry are mutually exclusive?"

Kate could feel him staring, but she refused to look at him. Instead, she pushed back her chair and stood. "I think I need a little air."

"What? Now? It's dark out, Kate!" Mrs. Kerwyn exclaimed.

"I'm just going out on the porch, Mom."

"You'll catch your death. Put a sweater on!"

Kate dutifully grabbed the saggy gray sweater that always hung by the back door and shrugged into it. Outside, dirty piles of snow still littered the muddy yard, but the air was warm, causing a fog to hang near the ground.

She breathed in the smell of wet earth and leaned against one of the porch posts, her arms folded. How dare Louisa claim she wasn't domestic, especially since she was the one who did most of the housework while Louisa lay around claiming to be working on her trousseau. And how dare Louisa dismiss her work as little more than peddling! Though, she supposed it was an accurate statement. She bit the inside of her cheek. She wasn't sure what to think. She was the first to admit that the baskets had been made from necessity, but then Frank and Julius had declared them to be something more. Something of beauty. Now the Crawfords were calling her an artist, too. She had always been quick to dismiss that title, but now that Louisa had publicly denounced her, she realized how desperately she had been clinging to that idea. Could a woman really be an artist?

She peered through the fog and saw a rabbit dart from under the pine tree. The idea secretly thrilled her. Perhaps her real family were all artists. Maybe the Espos had been great artists who had been forced down into the mines due to poverty. She stared at the wisps of fog curling around the ground and wondered where her poor family had all disappeared to.

She heard the screen door bang softly behind her and turned, hoping it was Edmund, but, no, it was Henry. Disappointed, she girded herself for an inevitable conversation.

He sidled up beside her, his hands in his pockets as he peered into the fog. "Nice night, isn't it?"

"Mmm." Kate didn't look at him.

"Do you like the cross?

"Yes, I said I did. But it's really too much."

"Not for someone I admire."

She was pretty sure he didn't *admire* her, but she decided not to encourage him with any extra speech.

"I understand you, you know," he said softly. "Better than you think."

"Oh?" She kept her eyes on the base of the pine tree, hoping the rabbit would return.

"I know, for example, that you're in love with Edmund."

She took in a sharp breath and wheeled on him. *In love with Edmund?* "No, I'm not!"

Henry grinned. "But you *are*, sweet Kate. It's written all over your face. Even now I see it in those beautiful dark eyes of yours."

"Edward's like a brother to me!"

"It might have seemed that way when you were children, but he is *not*, in fact, your brother."

Kate's chest heaved. Harriet had hinted at this very same thing in the past, but Kate had denied it then, too. She stared at Henry, her face burning despite the wet air. *Was* she in love with Edmund? *Dear God!* Of course she wasn't!

"Unfortunately, Mary's in love with him, too," Henry continued. "As I've said, there aren't any secrets between us." He gave a self-satisfied little shrug. "I think young Edmund returns the feeling, if I'm not mistaken. It's not every day that a young man takes a young lady to meet his mother."

"But that was–" Kate was about to say that it had been Mary's idea, but she made herself stop. She refused to argue about Edmund with Henry Crawford!

"As much as I esteem young Edmund, I think you are better off without him, if you want my opinion," Henry said. "I don't agree with your sister. You don't belong on a dirty farm, tending to elderly parents or even to a husband and dozens of dirty, probably disease-ridden children." He tried to laugh, but she didn't join in. He rubbed his eye with his finger and his silver signet ring gleamed in the porch light. "Listen, Kate. I was serious in there. You should be in the city, pursuing your art, attending gallery openings, meeting other artists. I really could introduce you to a lot of people. Do you not believe me?"

She stared into his deep green eyes, so confident, so commanding, and wondered if she *could* believe him? After all, he was only corroborating what Frank had already told her. Perhaps she should take her work more seriously; maybe she should–

Henry broke her train of thought by reaching out and tucking a stray lock of her hair behind her ear. He was standing so close now that she could smell his cologne, rich and spicy, and she began to tremble just a little. Several alarm bells went off, but before she could appropriately respond, he usurped them by swiftly bending down and kissing her. She felt a rush of panic, but as he caressed her lips, tender and soft, it dissipated.

He broke the kiss but his lips hovered near, and before she could pull away, he kissed her again, this one longer and more intense. And, God help her, she returned it.

In the next instant, however, she came to her senses. "Don't," she stammered as she pulled back, her heart racing. *What was she doing?* Hadn't he done the same to her sister just a few weeks ago?

"But why?" His face remained close. "Don't tell me it's Edmund." He reached up to brush her cheek with the back of his fingers, but she turned her head.

"I saw you!" she blurted, taking a deliberate step back.

Henry's brow quickly wrinkled.

"The night of Ray's party? I saw you and Louisa in the kitchen."

His face relaxed into his usual grin. "Oh, that? That didn't mean anything. I had a bit too much to drink." He tried to chuckle, but it withered under her steely gaze. "It was just a bit of fun, Kate," he said, letting out a deep, exasperated breath. "And, anyway, it's obvious that it didn't mean anything to Louisa either. After all, she *is* getting married."

"She would have you in a second!" Kate retorted, then instantly regretted it.

"She would?" He was clearly surprised. "Well, what does it matter?" he asked after a brief pause. "I'm not interested in Louisa. I'm interested in *you*, Kate Kerwyn!"

"But why?" she said. "I've barely said a civil word to you."

"Maybe that's why. You are a challenge, you see." He cocked an eyebrow.

For a brief moment hesitated. But, no. She didn't want to be someone's challenge–especially *his*. She wanted–

"Won't you even give me a chance?" His face was still somewhat bemused.

"No." She shook her head firmly.

"But why?"

"Because I don't trust you. I could never trust you. Even if I wanted to."

Suddenly, she wanted to retreat. To be alone with all of her thoughts. She felt confused and, truth be told, not a little ashamed of having fallen under his charming spell. *Dear God, she had kissed him!* Was she any better than Louisa?

"I *can* be constant, you know," he insisted. "I'll prove it to you. You'll see. I daresay I'm not a little in love with you already."

His bold announcement shocked her, but she didn't let on. "Well, I'm not in love with you," she said as stiffly as she could and moved around him toward the back door.

"I'm never going to give up, Kate Kerwyn," he said over his shoulder. "And I mean it."

"Just stay away from me, Henry," she retorted as she ducked into the house and let the screen door bang behind her. Once inside, she leaned against the wainscoted wall and tried to catch her breath.

Just then, Edmund pushed through the swinging door from the dining room, Mary close behind.

"Oh, there you are, Possum!" he called. "We were just coming to check on you."

"Possum!" squealed Mary. "Oh, how delicious! Is that what you call her when you're alone together? I think pet names are ever so sweet! I want one, too!" She darted to the back door and pushed it open. "Are you there, Henry? We're coming out!"

As she stepped out onto the porch, Edmund followed. But then he poked his head back in.

"You coming?" he asked.

She stared at him, at his bright brown eyes and his dimpled cheeks. *Was* she in love with him? Her heart beating hard in her chest, she shook her head and retreated to the dining room, afraid that if she stayed any longer, she might burst into tears.

CHAPTER TEN

"Stay away from the window," Melody hissed. "He'll see you!"

Giggling, Cynthia and several other girls retreated from the huge bay window in Philomena Hall as the big black Duesenberg phaeton came to a stop in the circle drive. Most of the girls at Mundelein were from wealthy families, but Eustace Sinclair's wealth was excessive, even to them. Melody thought so too, but she didn't let on. She was trying to contain her emotions, but she was more than a little intrigued.

Melody and Eustace had had only five dates thus far (six if she counted the Winter Ball), but in that short time, he had opened up an entirely new world to her–one that she had hardly known existed. Admittedly just a little bit dazzled, she had consequently had less time to worry about the Merc and Fred and certainly Cal.

Melody allowed herself a peek out the window. The uniformed chauffeur was now stiffly opening the back car door. Eustace stepped out elegantly. Tonight, he was in white tie and looked divine. Melody nervously patted her hair.

"How do I look, girls?" She was wearing a salmon Vionnet. It was last year's style and borrowed from Cynthia (as she was running out of her own gowns), but still, she looked lovely. They were to dine at the exclusive Chicago Athletic Club and after to attend the opera.

"Heavenly!" Cynthia crooned. "You look like an angel."

All of the girls chimed their agreement. Melody was pleased that most of her former court had returned, but she had to admit that something felt lacking.

The front door opened, then, and the young ladies, minus Melody, scattered into the parlor, though Melody guessed they remained in earshot.

Eustace smiled as he handed her a small bouquet. "Good evening, Miss Merriweather. Might I say you look lovely."

Although they had recently evolved into using their Christian names, his address was formal, she guessed, for the benefit of Sr. Joseph, who was currently on duty at the front desk and who was quietly reading a book (or at least pretending to).

"Oh, Mr. Sinclair!" Melody gasped, examining the bouquet. It consisted of pink calla lilies, white carnations, red tulips, and trailed some ivy. It was utterly gorgeous, and had most likely cost a fortune given that practically nothing was currently in bloom.

Thus far, Eustace had shown up with a bouquet for every one of their engagements, even the one where they had just strolled through Grant Park. Early on, he had revealed his secret obsession with the language of flowers. For the Victorians, he had explained, flowers had their own language between lovers, a sort of secret code, which he found most fascinating. He seemed to find great pleasure in schooling her in this esoteric language, and, as a dutiful pupil, Melody tried to decipher the message in today's.

"Beauty?" she asked, pointing to a calla lily. He nodded, pleased. "Innocence." She pointed to a white carnation, blushing slightly. She fingered the ivy. "Affection. Friendship." That one was easy; he frequently included it. Her brow furrowed as she pointed to a red tulip. "I don't know this one."

"It represents passion. A declaration of love."

Melody's blush deepened, and she shot a worried glance at Sr. Joseph. The sister's head, however, remained bent over her book.

"I thought it appropriate for tonight's performance of *La Bohème*. It symbolizes the almost instantaneous love between Rodolfo and Mimi. Do you not see? Is it not perfect?"

Melody did not want to admit that she had never seen *La Bohème* or that she basically knew nothing of it. "Oh yes." She flashed him a smile. "How ingenious."

As soon as she said this, she regretted it, as she doubted "ingenious" was the right word to use. The fact was that she was never quite at her ease around Eustace and often had no idea what he was talking about. He seemed to sense this, and yet he still pursued her. In truth, she wasn't sure why. She was definitely not of his social set, she was younger than him by almost ten years, and she had yet to discover any shared interests. And he seemed . . . well, more amused by her than attracted, as if she were a charming younger sister for whom he felt affectionate proprietorship. He had never once attempted to press himself upon heror, always acting with the utmost consideration and courteous attention.

"It's beautiful, Eus–Mr. Sinclair. Thank you." She moved toward the thick walnut counter. "Will you keep these for me, Sister?"

Sr. Joseph peered at the flowers through her gold-rimmed spectacles. She brightened. "Oh, they're lovely, aren't they? I'll put them in water, shall I?"

"Thank you, Sister. Yes."

In the morning, Melody resolved to lay the bouquet at the feet of the Virgin in the chapel, as there was absolutely no more space in Melody's room. The flowers disposed of, she retrieved her black silk wrap from the back of one of the foyer armchairs. Eustace expertly laid it about her shoulders.

"Shall we?" he asked and then led her out to the waiting car.

* * *

The Chicago Athletic Club was a bit of a misnomer, as there was nothing "athletic" about it at all. It was a private club dating back to 1890. The Sinclairs, Eustace explained as they were shown to their table in the dark-paneled dining room, had been members since the club's inception, as had several of Chicago's elite families, namely the Palmers, the Wrigleys, the Fields, and the Comiskeys.

As Melody took her seat, she glanced around at the staid elegance. Crystal chandeliers hung from an elaborately carved wood ceiling and various oil paintings of distinguished-looking gentlemen, presumably early club members, lined the walls. At the back of the dining room, a quartet played on a stage in front of a small dance floor. Several couples were dancing.

Melody took the napkin unraveled by the waiter and placed it on her lap, resisting the urge to finger her necklace, a plain gold crucifix. In her Vionnet gown, she was not underdressed, per se, but she lacked the diamonds most of the women were bedecked with, including several tiaras! She wished Cynthia could see this, or Harriet. She smiled at the thought of what Harriet would say if John were to take her here.

"Something amusing?" Eustace asked, intrigued.

"No, I was . . . I was just thinking of home, I suppose."

"We'll begin with a cocktail," Eustace said to the waiter who had appeared, his spotless apron severely folded and tucked around his waist.

"Very good, sir," the older man said with a bow.

"Martini for me—Plymouth gin, twist. A Dubonnet for the lady."

The first time they had dined together, the night at the Empire Room, she had apparently ordered all the wrong things, the worst being a Tom Collins as an after-dinner drink. From that point on, Eustace was given to ordering *for* her, and though it took the pressure off her to have to decipher menus mostly written in French, it did make her feel like a child at times.

The waiter bowed again and hurried away.

Eustace directed his attention back to her. "Are you missing home?"

"Well, a little, I suppose."

"And am I never to meet these Merriweathers and the place you so lovingly call 'the Merc?'" He said it teasingly.

"There's really not much there to see." She cringed a little at the thought of Eustace touring the Merc. It would take all of five minutes. And then what? She would take him to meet Mums, of course, though she had a sneaking suspicion that her mother would somehow not approve. Eustace was what Mums would call "full of himself." Melody supposed that that might be true—Eustace *could* be somewhat priggish, but he didn't mean to be. The more time she spent with him, the more she realized that he had no concept of his own pomposity, so didn't that mean it should be overlooked? Mrs. Haufbrau would also not be impressed, though she knew Harriet would later gush accordingly. And Melody would positively *adore* introducing him to Cal, whom, she was sure, would have something choice to say in that surly way of his. But for once, she would have the upper hand!

"Still thinking of them?"

Melody shook her head slightly. "No, why?"

"You're smiling again. You know, your smile is your best feature. That and your eyes. You have the eyes of a . . . of a Vermeer," he said, studying her as if she were a painting. "Mysterious, luminous. Even beautiful," he added. "Yes," he mused, "I do think one could classify them as beautiful."

Melody felt her face grow warm. He was always saying things like this, sizing her up and comparing her to works of art. She basked in his compliments, and yet she didn't know how to respond beyond a smile and a "thank you." She was spared answering this time by the appearance of the waiter, who carefully set the drinks in front of them. Melody made a mental note to try to look up Vermeer in the Mundelein library.

"Is that a no, then?" Eustace asked, raising his glass and taking a sip of the cold liquid.

"Regarding?" Melody picked up her own drink. It was delightfully sweet.

"Visiting your home. Meeting your family. I long to see you in your pastoral origins. The shepherdess, as it were, amongst the fields. I can just imagine it now as a Rubens. Utterly charming."

"Well, it really isn't all that romantic, Eustace. I'm fairly certain you would be disappointed."

A waiter appeared then with an amuse-bouche and carefully placed a silver spoon on a delicate china plate in front of each of them. Melody stared at the contents of the spoon, which appeared to be a tiny miniature pancake covered in black gelatinous balls.

"We will begin with a consommé and a white Burgundy, perhaps a '34 Chablis, followed by the pheasant and the '29 Domaine de la Romanée-Conti. And the baked Alaska, I think."

The waiter bowed. "Very good, sir."

Eustace picked up his spoon. Melody did the same, hesitating. It smelled faintly fishy. "What is it?" she asked.

Eustace, who had at this point already consumed his, fought back a laugh. "It is caviar, my dear. Beluga, I'd say. I'm getting hints of the Baltic. My guess is Romanoff. Have you never had it?"

Melody shook her head. She had heard of caviar, of course, but had never had any, much less would she be able to distinguish the brand.

"*Ma petite muse*, you are too, too wonderful. You are a perfect innocent. Unspoiled in any way. I simply adore you."

Melody wasn't sure she would call herself a perfect innocent, but she refrained from responding in favor of following Eustace's example and placed the spoon's contents into her mouth all at once. The flavors swirled on her tongue, and she found the concoction to be rather delicious.

"You see?" Eustace said, reading the pleasure on her face.

* * *

The meal was easily the best Melody had ever had in her life, better even than the one she had eaten at the Empire Room. It wasn't just that it was delicious, it was artistic. The way the food was arranged took the whole experience to another level of delight and made her feel as if she were eating at . . . well, at a palace or something. She wondered if any of the girls at school had ever eaten such a meal. No one in Merriweather would have dined at such a place, except perhaps Frank and Julius. But if they had, she wondered, why would they give this life up to go and live in plain old Merriweather, where the nicest restaurant was the High Hat?

"Cigarette?" Eustace pulled a silver case from inside his jacket and held it out.

She shook her head and watched as he selected one, long and thin. Even his cigarettes were elegant, almost feminine. They reminded her of something her mother smoked on special occasions, not the thick, smelly Old Golds or Chesterfields the men of Merriweather smoked.

He lit one and inhaled briefly, almost daintily. Then he leaned his elbow on the table and flicked his wrist back, holding the long cigarette erect.

"Well, even if I'm not to meet your family anytime soon, you really must meet mine," he said somewhat coyly. "Mother will adore you." He took a quick puff of the cigarette.

Melody's eyes widened at the prospect. She had thought he was joking about meeting her family, a subtle way of teasing her about her agrarian roots, but if he really did want her to meet his parents, he must feel more for her than she had perceived.

"I'd be happy to meet your family." Melody hid her excitement by taking a sip of what was left of her cognac. *Wait till she told the girls!*

"Mother and Father are in Europe at the moment, however," he explained.

Melody felt herself deflate a little.

"They are visiting my sister. She is in Switzerland at Le Rosey."

"What is Le Rosey? A resort?"

Eustace laughed. "No, *ma chérie*. It is . . . well, I suppose you'd call it a finishing school. The very best, you know." He inhaled again and blew a light cloud of smoke over his shoulder. "Just the right place to make all the right social connections. Royalty and all that."

"Oh."

"From there they travel on to our villa in Lake Geneva until June."

Melody deflated further. By June, the semester would be over, and she would most likely be back in Merriweather for the summer.

"But perhaps you would meet my uncle." His eyes squinted as he inhaled deeply, studying her. The waiter appeared and set an ashtray at Eustace's elbow.

"Your uncle?" Melody's hope revived.

"Yes, he lives with us." Eustace flicked his ash into the tray. "He'd be delighted to meet you, I'm sure." He snuffed out what was left of his cigarette. "Shall we say next Sunday?"

"Yes, alright, then." She tried to say it as casually as she could.

"Delightful. I'll send a car. One p.m.?" He downed his cognac. "Shall we dance?"

Melody agreed eagerly. She had been wanting to dance all evening. "But do we have time?"

"Dearest, no one arrives at the opera until the second act. Come," he commanded, rising and holding out his hand. Melody placed her gloved one in his and allowed him to lead her to the small dance floor where several other older, mature couples were already waltzing. Melody dearly loved to dance; besides attending nearly every school-sponsored function, she and Cynthia and the gang used to be in the habit of going to the Aragon almost every other week. Compared to its crowds, where the increasing number of servicemen were all vying for space on the sticky dancefloor, the Athletic Club was utterly divine! No clumsy Loyola boys tripping over themselves or the here-today-gone-tomorrow young privates and lieutenants.

Eustace drew her close and carefully placed his other hand midway (never lower!) down her back before beginning to twirl them. Melody followed his lead. He was an exquisite dancer, and in his arms—and in this elegant place—she felt she must have died and gone to heaven. Freddy had been right. This *was* where she belonged. She had served her time in the dusty old Merc, and now it was time to enjoy herself.

They danced three waltzes before the fairy tale finally came to an end, Eustace eventually signaling for their cloaks and for his car to be brought round. He was gentle and careful while helping her into the waiting phaeton, and as they zoomed through the brightly lit city streets to the Lyric to watch the love story of Rodolfo and Mimi unfold, she was tempted to lean her head on his shoulder. She did not, however, as, upon getting into the car beside her, he had maintained a respectable distance between them.

She sighed with pure pleasure. Finding Eustace, she decided, as she pinched herself to be certain, was simply too good to be true.

CHAPTER ELEVEN

"Thought it was too good to be true." Mr. Kerwyn let out a deep, tired breath. "You sure, Kate?"

"Yes, of course I'm sure!" Kate cried. "How could you think that I would want to court Henry Crawford?"

Mr. Kerwyn looked blankly at his wife, sitting beside him at the worn kitchen table. "He said the two of you had a little conversation the night of your party. I thought you liked him."

"Not like *that*! And, no, we didn't have a 'conversation.'" *More like a one-way street*, Kate fumed.

Mr. Kerwyn rubbed his forehead. "Well, why don't you like him? Never dreamt you'd say no. He asked for my blessing to court you, so I gave it. Said we'd be happy to have him in the family. I'll admit, I was a little surprised, but, well, there you go. Can't always predict, can you?"

"I'm *not* courting him, and I'm certainly not marrying him!"

Mr. Kerwyn was genuinely perplexed. "Why not? Got a good job down in Chicago. An architect I think he said. Not bad lookin'."

Kate groaned. "Because I don't love him." Angrily, she pushed away the memory of him kissing her on the porch. Did he think that that had entitled him to speak to her father? How dare he!

"That all?" Mr. Kerwyn let out a little chuckle, which further annoyed Kate. "That'll come. You don't have to *love* him completely in the beginning. Tell her, Caroline."

"Well, I suppose that's true," Mrs. Kerwyn replied with a sigh. "Your father and I liked each other well enough at the beginning, but as the years went on, we grew to love each other."

Kate wanted to blurt out that Henry Crawford was *not* the type of man you could grow to love over the years. He was the type, she was sure, who would break any heart foolish enough to trust him. She had not told either of her parents what she had seen in the kitchen the night of Ray's party, but she was sorely tempted to now. But to say as much would incriminate Louisa, and even though Kate had no great love for her sister, she had no wish to ruin her engagement to Vernon Tierney.

But there was another reason for her refusal, one she dared not say aloud. She was, as Henry had infuriatingly pointed out, hopelessly in love with Edmund Bertram.

Ever since her party, she had been turning it over in her mind, examining every angle of her and Edmund's . . . *friendship*–she dared not use the words *understanding*, *relationship*, *attachment*, *attraction*, *fondness*, *devotion*, *loyalty* or *affection*, though each of them had come to mind at one point or another in this assessment. In the end, however, there was nothing left to do but to admit that it was true. Now, whenever she thought about it–about *him*–she found it difficult to breathe. She hardly knew what to do with her feelings now that she realized they were not familial nor platonic.

How could this have happened? Again and again, she reflected on their childhood together–how kind he had always been, and how attentive and helpful and encouraging he had become as they grew into young adulthood. It made sense for these kindnesses to have eventually blossomed into love on her part, but did he feel the same?

As she tossed and turned at night, she tried to reassess the little looks he had given her at the badger hole last summer when he had come to help her and how he had visited her every day during her recent illness, usually bringing some little thing with him to cheer her–some candies from the Sweet Chalet, a bunch of wildflowers, once even a small kitten for her to pet. Or just recently on the night of Ray's party, when had come up to find her, concerned as always.

He *may* have been a little in love with her, she realized despairingly, but she had failed to recognize it in either herself or him, and now it was too late. Now he was in love with Mary Crawford, and she with him.

By nature, Kate was not a jealous person, but it did bother her that something she had held in her grasp for so long had now slipped out due to her own ignorant stubbornness. How could she have been so blind? So stupid? Her heart raced with anger and regret whenever she thought about it, which was nearly every hour of every day.

"Listen, Kate," Mr. Kerwyn went on in response to Kate's silence, "we took you in, you're like a daughter to us, but the fact is . . ." He shifted in his chair. "The fact is . . . you *are* an Indian."

Kate's head shot up.

"Now before you get all hot an' bothered, what I mean is . . . not many men around here are gonna want to marry an Indian. You should be glad that someone like Henry Crawford is making you a respectable offer. You're not gonna get many chances, I don't think. Tell her, Caroline."

Kate stared incredulously at the only father she had ever known. To spare their feelings, Kate had decided not to tell them what she had uncovered about her origins from Sheriff Norris and Rosemary, but now she regretted it. Her parents still believed her to be a Sauk Indian, and though her heritage had never seemed to matter before, she saw with a stab to her heart that it did. She was "less-than," at least in her father's eyes. She looked to her mother.

"Well, he might be right, Kate."

For once in her life, Kate could think of no angry retort. The shock and the pain were too deep. She turned and fled the kitchen and began climbing the stairs by twos to her room.

"Now, don't you run off mad!" Mr. Kerwyn called. "We're just trying to help you, Kate!"

Kate pulled out a battered carpetbag from under her bed and began stuffing things into it. It was obvious she didn't belong here. She had blown her chance with Edmund, and she wasn't about to be pushed into a marriage to Henry Crawford. But more than anything else, she needed to get away from this wretched family who saw her as a second-class citizen. Julius Fairfax had once compared her to some medieval Chinese Cinderella who lived in a cave, which at the time seemed ridiculous. But the more she thought about it, perhaps it was all too true. She *was* a sort of Cinderella.

Well, this Cinderella had had enough. She took one last look around the room and pounded down the stairs.

"Where do you think you're goin'?" Mr. Kerwyn shouted from the kitchen.

Mrs. Kerwyn hurried into the little foyer. "You're leaving?" she cried, noting her small carpetbag. "Oh, Kate, you're not going back to that dirty hole, are you? It's supposed to freeze again next week."

Kate dropped the bag on the floor and pulled on her coat. "No, I'm not going back to the badger hole. I'm going to find my *real* family."

Mrs. Kerwyn's face went white. "But *we're* your real family." Mrs. Kerwyn looked as if she was about to cry.

Kate wavered.

"Now you listen here, Kate." Mr. Kerwyn strode in from the kitchen. "You're upsetting your mother. You've tried leavin' here twice before, and it ain't worked. Runnin' away is a little kid thing to do. You're too old for this. Time to grow up."

Kate's angry resolve instantly returned. "Yes, it *is* time to grow up, *Mr. Kerwyn*. Don't worry–I won't be coming back this time." Picking up her bag, she marched to the front door.

"Oh, Kate, please don't go," Mrs. Kerwyn pleaded, following her. "We were just trying to help you."

Kate turned around, her throat aching with suppressed tears. "Help me?" she hissed angrily, too low for her father to hear. "Why didn't you help me when Ray was fondling me in a closet?"

Her mother stared at her, stunned. "What?"

Kate was as startled by the words as Mrs. Kerwyn. She stared at her mother, trying to read her face for deceit, but then realized with further crushing sadness that it was something else, something worse. "You don't remember, do you, *Mrs. Kerwyn*?" A tear rolled down her cheek. "Well, I should have expected that."

"Kate!" Mrs. Kerwyn called, following her onto the porch. "Don't go!"

Kate heard her father shout from the kitchen, where he had retreated in disgust. "If she wants to go, let her go, Caroline. We've tried our best. If she ain't grateful, well, so be it."

Kate stomped down the steps.

"Kate!" her mother called, but Kate did not turn and instead marched hurriedly down the lane, angrily wiping her tears as she went.

She would find her *real* family, no matter what it took.

CHAPTER TWELVE

"Oh, hello, Freddy!" Imogene Kaufmann cried with delight as she stepped into the Merc, a shopping basket dangling on her arm. "Though I suppose I really should call you Fred, shouldn't I, seeing as you're all grown up and in charge now! You look just like your father, standing there behind the counter. The spitting image, I'd say. You know, I still can't believe he's gone. If I've said it to Mother once, I've said it a hundred times!"

Fred gritted his teeth. If he had to hear "you look just like your father" one more time, he might actually murder someone.

"Thank you, Imogene. Can I get you something?" Fred normally hid in the office, but since he happened to be at the front counter at the moment, he figured he might as well wait on Imogene. Perhaps he could hurry her along faster than Harriet would, who was so docile and accommodating that Imogene was likely to stay all afternoon.

"I remember when you were just so high." Imogene lowered a hand to her knee. "You and Melody and Elizabeth running all around the Merc. It was an utter delight to watch you. I used to tell Mother all about your antics. And she did enjoy hearing them, stuck upstairs as she was. She did so look forward to my tales. You were her favorite, you know, Fred. And now, here you are, running the shop. Can you believe it? First Melody, and now you. I can't imagine Elizabeth taking a turn, though, can you? Goodness me, no. She's much too delicate. Though she is terribly beautiful. Didn't have much time for me and Mother, though, did she, when we were staying with you? But that's probably on account of her being shy. At least that was Mother's opinion. She said that–"

"Can I get something for you, Imogene? Or did you just stop in to say hello?" He leaned forward, bracing his hands on the counter.

"Oh, hello, Imogene," Harriet said, coming up from the back with a box.

"Hello, Harriet! Aren't you a pretty sight for sore eyes! I stopped by and saw your mother the other day, since we live so close now."

"Yes, she mentioned it. How are you settling in?"

"Oh, good enough. Good enough. Change is so hard on Mother, but she'll come round, I'm sure. Oh, but let me find that list! Fred looks about to murder me!" She gave a little laugh. "Wouldn't blame you one bit, Freddy. Taking up your time like I am. Now, I have a list somewhere . . ." She shifted her basket and fumbled through her scuffed black handbag. "Here it is!" She pulled out a crumpled piece of newspaper and squinted at the handwriting scrawled along the edge.

Fred sighed at Imogene's frugality–she would never use a fresh piece of paper for something as lowly as a grocery list. During the Kaufmanns' stay at the Willows after their apartment above the Merc caught fire, Imogene had made a habit of collecting bits of paper from the trash that she declared were "perfectly good." It had nearly driven his mother crazy.

"It's all mostly for Mr. Churchill," Imogene said. "Let me see. A dozen candles, a pound of flour, a tin of sardines–that's for me and Mother–a pound of sugar, a package of lard, some salt, two tins of tomato soup, and . . ." She turned the paper forty-five degrees, following the scrawl that went right round the edge, her eyes narrowing. "Two bottles of cider."

She looked up triumphantly, as if proud to have read it all.

"I'll get it, Fred." Harriet paused in her refilling of the candy sticks, setting the ones in her hand back into the box. She moved toward the shelf of canned goods and began selecting tins of soup, not bothering to ask which brand, knowing that Imogene wanted the cheapest ones. "How's the old Murphy cottage coming along?" she asked.

"Oh, Mother and I like it very much indeed. Frank–and Julius, too, mind you, but he's so quiet and shy!–are very kind. And we've plenty to eat! I've often suggested to Mr. Churchill that Mother and I could get by on half the food he buys, but he only laughs and says, 'Nonsense!' They're very generous, almost to a fault. I've said as much to Mother, and she quite agrees."

"How are the repairs coming?" Fred asked, as he began ringing up the items Harriet had thus far set on the counter. It always baffled him whenever Imogene reported her mother's responses, as he had never once in his life heard the ancient crone utter even one word. If he didn't know better, he would think her a mute. Maybe she was, and all of her supposed responses were just figments of Imogene's imagination?

"Oh, fine. Very fine, indeed. He's got a builder–a arkie . . . arkick . . . oh! I can't think of the word."

"Architect?"

"That's it! One of those. Name is Mr. Crawford. Up from Chicago. He spends all day drawin' the cottage, telling Frank and the rest of the crew, which is mainly Ralph Borman and Del Werner and, let me see . . . who else? Well, sometimes Jack Rhomberg's been out. Not old Mr. Rhomberg, his son. But speaking of the Werners, did you hear their youngest won the spelling bee? Gets to go on to the state finals all the way up in Madison! Can you believe it? One of our own Merriweather students representing that way? It's enough to make you want to . . . oh, I don't know, sing a little song, I suppose. Me and Mother looked for a mention of it in the *Herald*, but we haven't seen anything yet. Maybe they're waiting to report until the final debate, though that ain't rightly fair, is it? Little George Werner should be celebrated just for making it to the state finals. Doesn't matter who wins, does it? Now, as I was saying to Mother–"

"That'll be $8.16," Fred interrupted. "Here's everything." He pushed the brown paper bag toward her. "Except the cider."

Imogene raised her eyebrows. "No cider? You sold out?"

"In a way." He shifted. "We've decided to discontinue it."

"Discontinue it? But why? Does Melody know?"

Fred gritted his teeth and wondered, for the hundredth time, how this had become his life. He had initially disagreed with Mrs. Haufbrau when she *strongly* suggested they discontinue the cider. It was making a profit–barely, but a profit was a profit. It had been one of Melody's better ideas, he had had to admit. But Mrs. H. had very cleverly backed him into a proverbial corner (though it might as well have been a real one given how he was secretly a little bit afraid of Mrs. H.), saying that his father would never have allowed such a thing and that they were sure to get in trouble with the law. Personally, Fred wasn't so sure his father would have disapproved since he himself had made a fortune during Prohibition by selling moonshine. Likewise, he wasn't sure Chief Meyers would care all that much either, seeing as he himself was known to frequent the Miner most days of the week.

"But it's not him you have to worry about," Mrs. Haufbrau countered when Fred had made that point. "It's Sheriff Norris. He's cracking down! Just last week, my cousin over in New Glarus told me that the local newspaper shop was shut down for selling liquor illegally."

Fred was inclined to think Mrs. H.'s fears a bit reactionary, but he did share her opinion that the Merc, under Melody's direction, had become too fractured. Why were they selling ladies' wear and hats and fancy baskets? They were, after all, primarily a grocers with other basic household items for sale, like brooms or mousetraps. After some consideration, he agreed that the Merc had lost its way. If this was to be his fate, he meant to bring the Merc back to its former glory by focusing on the "tried and true," as Mrs. H. put it."

"Anything else?" he asked Imogene, who had carefully fit the bag of supplies into her basket but was still lingering in front of the counter.

"Oh, no! I suppose I should get on, shouldn't I? I almost thought for a moment that I would be heading upstairs, but then I remembered, didn't I, that we don't live upstairs anymore. I don't know if I'll ever get used to it. Not that I mind the cottage! Oh, no, it's just that–"

"You'll excuse me, won't you, Imogene?" Fred interrupted. "I've some paperwork to do." He inched out from behind the counter.

"Goodness, no! Aren't you your father all over! I was just saying that–"

Fred did not stay to hear the end, which he knew was rude, but he also knew there would never *be* an end if it was left to Imogene to determine. Once inside his office, he shut the door and leaned against it.

He hated being compared to his popular, jubilant, larger-than-life father. It was one of the reasons he had left. After Marquette, he could have stayed in Milwaukee for law school, but instead he had set his sights on *any* school that took him away from Wisconsin. It was one of his Marquette professors, Dr. Knightly, who had encouraged him to apply to Harvard, and, with several letters of recommendation, Fred Merriweather had gotten in!

Though it meant that his son would be away for most of the year, Louis Merriweather had been over the moon at his son's success, so much so that he spent the entire summer before Fred left telling every customer that entered the Merc that his son had gotten into Harvard!

At the time, Fred had tried to downplay it, knowing as he did that he had chosen to move to the East Coast as a way to distance himself from his father, and here he was, praising him to the high heavens. It wasn't that he hadn't loved his father–he had! But he didn't have his father's boisterous personality and ability to talk to anyone from any walk of life. Fred was more reserved, and though he tried at times to imitate his father, he could never quite pull it off without feeling like an embarrassed fool.

Therefore, when August finally rolled around, Fred was excited to board the train east, hoping to make his own way in life.

And he had been successful in his quest. Granted, he was not one of the popular men on campus, throwing wild parties or creating havoc after football games, but he had crafted his own small circle of friends, a quiet, studious bunch who enjoyed heated debates about the law, tracking baseball scores, and frequenting the local pubs.

It had cut him to the quick when his three best friends had traveled across country to attend his father's funeral, but it had been worse to endure their reactions when he told them that he wouldn't be returning with them, at least not right away.

They were stunned, of course, but didn't wish to argue with him so soon after his father had been laid in the ground. They encouraged him to take some time off to grieve and settle his father's affairs, but they had not been so accepting when he had later written to say that he was giving up Harvard altogether to run his father's business. It was at that point that they had decided to speak and had all of them–Rufus, Alan, and James–written him separately, outlining the foolishness of such a decision and imploring him to return. Couldn't his sister continue on? they suggested. It made the most sense.

Fred, old boy, wrote his very best friend, James, *I know you must be cut up completely and your brain addled by grief, but surely you must see this for what it is. You are quite obviously suffering from some sort of neurosis brought on by masochistic feelings of guilt. In short, you are suffering from what Freud calls a "guilt complex."*

Yes, Fred agreed, as he crumpled his friend's letter, he was aware of that, but it couldn't be helped. He did feel immense guilt. Guilt that he had cost his father so much money to attend Harvard, for one thing. Had he known the family was in such dire financial straits, he would never have even entertained attending an Ivy League school. But more so, he felt guilt that he had not come home to visit as his father lay ill. Guilt that he had wasted so much time. Guilt that he had even gone away in the first place. He could have easily gone to law school in Madison or Milwaukee. But no, he had insisted on getting as far away as possible. If only he could have those years back, even just one day, with his father.

But how was he to know his father would die so young? he always countered. It was his *father's* fault that they hadn't had more time together, not *his*! Or maybe it was God's fault. Round and round his anger flew, first at himself, then his father, then God, and then back to himself again. In short, he was miserable.

He slumped into the chair behind his father's desk and stared at the picture on the opposite wall. It was an old sepia photo of his grandfather and Pops in front of the Merc. They both looked so proud, and he felt guilty (*again*) that he wasn't proud, too. He rubbed his brow. Not only could he not see himself being happy running a general store for the rest of his life, he mourned the fact that he was giving up a career in the law. He was genuinely interested and thought he might even be relatively good at it. He leaned back in the old swivel chair, still staring at the photo.

Was there a way to do both? Could he set up a law practice here in Merriweather? The idea sparked his interest for a moment or two before it fizzled out. His dream had been to go into corporate law, and stuck here, he'd be forced to do general law. Property disputes, wills, the odd divorce. And would he be able to run the Merc at the same time? Maybe . . . if he could get someone to help manage it for him. Not Harriet, of course. Perhaps Cal? Cal seemed a decent enough fellow, but he was bent on leaving. Fred didn't blame him. Mrs. Haufbrau? He thought about it for a few extra minutes before shaking his head. Of course he couldn't turn the Merc over to Mrs. H.

Granted, she was a dedicated, dutiful employee whom his father had greatly admired for some reason, but he didn't think his father would approve of him abandoning ship to her. She was good with the customers—or, he should say, a certain circle of customers who met her approval—but she was otherwise rather severe in her opinions and freely shared them. In truth, she bullied customers some of the time, which was certainly not good for business. She was a mystery for sure.

There was a brief knock, then, and Cal's head poked in. "Taking off now, Fred. Anything else needs doing?"

Fred glanced at the black clock on the wall. Was it already closing time? How long had he been sitting here? "No, I don't think so. Thanks, Cal."

Cal hesitated. "How's . . . how's Melody doing?"

"Melody? Oh, fine, I suppose. She barely writes."

"She still with that Douglas guy?" Cal brushed his hair back.

"She says she's not, but you know girls . . . wouldn't surprise me if she's back with him. He proposed, you know."

Cal didn't immediately respond and instead examined his thumb. "What did she say?"

"Turned him down, if you can believe it. Well, there's no accounting for taste, as they say. She'll come round, I imagine. She's probably just playing hard to get."

Cal looked as if he were about to say something else but instead just gave a curt nod and a little one-finger salute. "Yeah, probably. Goodnight, then," he said and walked out.

Fred stood up wearily, knowing that Mrs. Haufbrau and Harriet were waiting up front. He was loath to go home to the Willows, as it offered no comfort. Mums hardly came down to dinner anymore, and Bunny was forever banging away at the piano. It might not be so bad if she played something light and lively, like cheerful showtunes, but she was instead constantly playing horrible dirges. It was enough to drive a man to drink had he not already arrived there anyway. Pops had left a sizable wine cellar, which Fred was currently working his way through at a pretty steady pace.

He reached for his coat where he had tossed it on the burnished stand in the corner. Perhaps he *had* been too hasty in packing Melody off . . .

But, no, he thought, glancing at the sepia picture again as he shrugged into his coat. The Merc was *his* responsibility now. He owed this much to his father and grandfather. Somehow, he decided wearily, he'd have to find a way to make a go of it.

CHAPTER THIRTEEN

Melody glanced at the pictures hanging in the long hallway of the Sinclair family home, hardly knowing where to look first, as there were so many works of art crammed into this . . . this *mansion.* It could easily rival the finest art museums in the country, if not the world. And this, Eustace had explained, was only *one* of their homes. There was the villa in Switzerland, a house in Newport, and a "cottage" at Lake Louise, though Melody suspected it was probably a far cry from the old mining cottages in Merriweather or the fishing cottage her family had rented one summer in Door County.

At first, she had been inclined to study each portrait and landscape, but eventually she had given this up in an effort to keep up with Eustace, his somewhat quick pace through the house at odds with his bored (but only slightly) tone. They had thus far explored almost every room on both floors of this gargantuan home, which seemed impossibly bigger than it appeared from the outside, a perfect example of a Beaux Arts construction sitting prettily on Astor Street.

Melody blindly followed Eustace up staircases and down hallways and through a series of gorgeous rooms with painted ceilings, gleaming old wood, and golden chandeliers. She had early on lost all sense of direction and nearly all sense of decorum, so in awe that she had to repeatedly remind herself not to exclaim every other minute or walk with her mouth open.

They were currently on the second floor, walking toward what Eustace called the best room of the house—the statuary. *The statuary?* Melody wasn't exactly sure what a "statuary" was, but she hesitated to ask, as she was sure it would only cause Eustace to amusedly roll his eyes at her ignorance. They were fastly falling into the role of professor and student, which Melody did not so much mind, as she was learning much. More than she was in any of her classes. The statuary, Eustace had explained, was the heart of the house.

They continued down the red damask-papered hallway, Melody's excitement growing, until they reached a set of paneled pocket doors. Eustace paused dramatically and then pushed them open with a flourish.

Tentatively, Melody stepped inside and was initially a little bit surprised that "the heart" was so starkly white and cold. The vaulted room was filled with sculptures of every size and type, the larger ones on daises, but most on pedestals. There was nothing else in the room, not even a single chair.

Melody looked to Eustace for direction, but he merely smiled, resting a long, elegant finger against his cheek. He wanted to capture her reaction, as if he were the parent watching a child who had just come down on Christmas morning to find her gifts. He tilted his head, indicating that she should enter further. Tentatively, Melody began to peruse the room, her steps echoing on the marble floor.

Melody went from sculpture to sculpture, attempting to observe each one intently, as she was sure she was supposed to do, but they failed to impress her in the way a nice landscape might. Indeed, she felt almost as though she were walking through a graveyard of marble- and bronze-encased bodies portraying the last of their human emotions. Fear, rapture, love, despair.

One, however, did particularly strike her. She paused in front of the life-size piece at the room's center. It was of a woman, either asleep or possibly dead, being partially lifted and kissed by an angel, his arm protectively covering her breast. It was incredibly beautiful, and Melody wasn't sure what to make of it.

"Ah," Eustace murmured, his voice rich with pleasure. "You've uncovered the prize of the whole room."

Since it was the largest statue and also at the very center, Melody did not think that "uncovered" was quite the right word, nor was her action worthy of praise, but she did not say anything.

"Do you like it?" Eustace asked with a rare eagerness. "It is a copy, of course, but a very good one."

Melody continued to stare at the sculpture, entranced by the emotion it conveyed, and felt a corresponding stirring in her heart. To be kissed in such a way. "What is it called?" she asked softly, turning to Eustace now, suddenly feeling the urge to transfer the emotion welling up within her from cold hard marble to flesh and blood.

Eustace, however, did not seem to notice the longing in her eyes. "It is Canova's *Psyche Revived by Cupid's Kiss*, *ma petite muse*." He stepped closer to the statue. "It really is exquisite the way he was able to capture that moment of awakening, both literally and metaphorically. It's the epitome of grace, do you not think?"

"It's very . . ." Melody faltered, the moment gone, "lifelike."

"Indeed. A perfect example of neoclassism, quite different from Thorvaldsen, however. Here," he said, walking briskly toward a bronze statue atop a pedestal, "you can see for yourself. This is his *Jason with the Golden Fleece*. Still of the neoclassical school, but so much more masculine."

Melody peered at the statue of a naked soldier, a spear balanced confidently on his shoulder, a ram's fleece draped over one arm. Feeling her cheeks grow warm, she averted her eyes from the sculpture's midsection. Eustace's attention remained on the sculpture. She looked back at it as well, and an image of Cal with his cocky self-assuredness suddenly came into her mind. Quickly, she banished it.

Eustace pointed to Jason's face. "See here–the strong set of the jaw, the angular pose–classical heroism. Jason has been imbued with a sense of potential energy and demands attention, while Psyche"–he pointed to the centerpiece–"is a study in gentle curves and delicate balance. It invites contemplation, reflection."

Melody's eyes traveled from one sculpture to the other and back again. He was right.

"Canova," Eustace explained, "emphasizes ideal beauty and emotion, while Thorvaldsen focuses on heroic virtue and action. It is not unlike comparing a sonnet to an epic poem. Both are perfect in their own way."

Not for the first time, Melody marveled at the breadth of Eustace's knowledge. He seemed able to discuss, at length, any artistic subject, connecting symbolism and themes in a way she never dreamt existed.

Eustace gestured limply at a cluster of other statuary. "The rest of these are mostly Etruscan," he said with a note of disdain. "Though they *are* original, which is saying something. Father has a weakness for the Etruscans." He pulled out a perfectly ironed monogrammed handkerchief and delicately dabbed his nose. "Thankfully, Uncle does not, and most of the other sculpture in the house are his." He neatly tucked the handkerchief back into his breast pocket.

"Where *is* your uncle?" Melody asked. Having walked through what Melody was sure must be the whole of the house, they had yet to meet a single person beyond the servants, who tended to scurry away whenever they happened to come upon one–save the footmen, of course, who stood at attention at various points along the route.

"My uncle?" Eustace asked, as if perplexed. "He's upstairs, of course, in his apartment."

"His apartment?"

"Well, it's not really an apartment, it's the third floor. He has it all to himself. Would you like to meet him?"

Melody blinked. *There was a third floor?* "Well, isn't that why I'm here? To meet him?"

Eustace chuckled. "You are quite right, my dear. I had almost forgotten. Yes, let us proceed." He pulled out a gold pocket watch. "Yes, he'll be expecting us right about now. Come, we can return to this room later, if you wish."

Melody followed Eustace out of the statuary and down a short side hallway until he stopped in front of a small door which was cut into the wall. "This is the servant's staircase, but it's much closer than the main. You don't mind, do you?"

"No, of course not." Melody followed him up the narrow circular stairs. "What's he like?" she asked as they climbed.

"Uncle Alistair?" Eustace glanced over his shoulder. "Oh, *très amusant*. He's–what would you call it?–a bit eccentric."

"What does he teach, again?" Melody asked, trying to remember if Eustace had ever mentioned it.

"Antiquities."

Definitely not.

"Nordic archeology is his specialty." When they reached the top of the spiral staircase, Eustace turned to her fully. "He's spent years traveling the world, researching and picking up treasures. At the moment, however, he's writing a book."

"Oh, but won't we be disturbing him?"

"Not at all. He's quite eager to meet you."

So, he's told him about me! As he rapped lightly, Melody patted her hair, hoping she was still presentable.

"Come in!" called a surprisingly high-pitched but genial voice.

Eustace pushed open the little door and ducked into the room. Melody bent as well and followed him. She looked around curiously, surprised by what she saw.

With its dark-paneled wood and floor-to-ceiling bookcases, this room was the exact opposite of the stark statuary below. A roaring fire in the hearth gave the room a warm, pleasant glow, and in the very center was a broad mahogany desk, upon which were piled stacks and stacks of papers, open books, and several maps. In front of the desk, on a large rug that looked to be of an American Indian pattern, sat a rattan sofa and two chairs arranged neatly around a tea table. A multitude of lit candles gave the illusion that they had somehow stepped back in time.

"Uncle Alistair, allow me to introduce Miss Melody Merriweather. Miss Merriweather, my uncle, Alistair Fitzwilliam Sinclair," Eustace announced, leading Melody toward the desk behind which sat a rather plump man dressed in a very wrinkled, very outdated brown suit.

The old man stood and peered at Melody over his wire-rimmed gold spectacles. His balding head was encircled by a wispy ring of gray hair, but his eyes were extremely bright, almost merry, and though he was obviously old, he exuded an air of youth.

"My dear!" he boomed, coming from behind the desk and taking her hand. "How enchanting to meet you." He raised her hand to his lips and kissed it. "Eustace has told me all about you." He continued to peer at her above his spectacles. "And now I can see why he is so very enamored."

Melody blushed and glanced at Eustace, who did not return the look; in fact, his expression was impassive.

"Do sit down, my dear." Uncle Alistair gestured toward the sofa. "You will join me for tea, I hope?"

"Well, if we're not intruding," Melody said tentatively as she took a seat. "I don't want to keep you from your work." Her eyes darted toward the stacks of papers.

"Oh, that? That can wait. It's not often I am treated to such lovely company. Now," he said, perching himself in one of the armchairs, "you must tell me all about yourself. You are a Merriweather, did you say?" He looked up at the ceiling and drummed his fingers against his cheek. "I knew a Merriweather, I seem to remember." He turned his gaze back to Melody. "Any relation to Mordecai Merriweather? He is a physician in Albany."

"I'm not sure." Melody shifted uneasily. "I don't think so, though."

"No matter, no matter."

A butler entered carrying a rather large silver tea tray.

"Ah, Manfred," said Uncle Alistair, pulling out his pocket watch, noting it, and then snapping it shut. "Perfectly punctual."

The butler carefully set the tray on the table. It was laden with a teapot, three cups and saucers, and a rather large three-tiered stand with a variety of tiny sandwiches and pastries. "Will there be anything else, sir?"

"No, that will be all." Uncle Alistair inspected the tray with delight, and, approving, dismissed the servant. "I'll ring if I need you."

"Very good, sir." Manfred gave a slight bow and promptly exited.

"You be mother, Eustace," Uncle Alistair instructed his nephew, who had delicately taken a seat next to Melody.

Eustace obediently began arranging the cups and lifted the cozy from the pot.

"Melody is a student at Mundelein College, Uncle," he said as he poured.

"Indeed?" Uncle Alistair pushed his gold spectacles back with one finger and then took the cup offered by Eustace. "And what do they teach you there, my dear?"

Melody shifted, embarrassed to report that she was taking swimming and horseback riding. "Geography. Mostly," she fumbled, suddenly aware of how absurd this sounded. She didn't dare mention the shorthand.

Uncle Alistair tilted his head slightly, as if trying to understand. "Just geography? A bit unusual, is it not?"

"Melody has an abbreviated schedule at the moment, Uncle," Eustace explained. "She has recently returned from a sabbatical, if you will, at home where she was engaged in helping her family for a time. Her father recently passed, so she has been in mourning and is only gradually easing back into her studies." Eustace added several cubes of sugar to his cup.

"Ah. I'm very sorry for your loss, my dear. Very sorry. Was he a scholar, by chance? Your father, that is?"

"Um, no. He ran the town mercantile."

Uncle Alistair pursed his lips. "A man of business, then."

"Well, yes . . . you could say that." Melody wasn't sure she would have classified her father as a *businessman*, but she supposed it was true enough.

"During her exile in the wilds of Wisconsin," Eustace elaborated playfully, "Melody became quite an accomplished brewer and purveyor of cider, Uncle."

"Cider, did you say? Then you join a long line of women in history who were brewers. Long before the monks, you know. Or the nuns, for that matter. We need only to look at the Beguines. It's all there in the book." He tilted his head toward the desk.

"Yes, Eustace told me you were writing a book," Melody added, glad for a chance to guide the conversation away from herself. "What is it about?"

Uncle Alistair's bright eyes became even brighter. He vigorously stirred his tea. "Have you ever heard of Thule, my dear?"

Melody shook her head and took a sip of her tea. "I don't believe so."

"Ah. Well, allow me to explain." He cleared his throat. "Thule is a mystical land," he began in a mysterious, storytelling sort of voice, "a legendary land that many say doesn't exist. It is similar in this to the myth of Atlantis, though Thule is indeed real. Many have spent a lifetime searching for it. It is the birthplace of the Thulians, the ancient Aryans, who are said to possess great power and supernatural abilities."

"Oh!" Melody was not sure what to make of this. She wanted to glance at Eustace for some sort of confirmation, but she dared not.

"The Germans are most interested of late. Rudolf von Sebottendorff has written rather extensively about it, as has Heinrich Himmler. In fact, it is rumored Himmler is sending an expedition to the North Pole this summer to look for traces. I may join them if I'm able."

"How . . . how interesting," Melody murmured and took another sip of her tea.

"Yes, yes, isn't it?" Uncle Alistair bit into a tiny prosciutto and butter sandwich. He stood and retreated to a large pedestaled globe. It looked very ancient. He spun it slowly and then tapped the North Pole. "It is said that they retreated here into the center of the Earth."

Melody *did* glance at Eustace now, who raised his eyebrows slightly.

"Come, come, Uncle, let's not get into all of that now."

"But why ever not, my boy? Miss Merriweather *did* ask." He seemed slightly offended.

"Yes, but you mustn't neglect to tell her about your first book."

"You have another book?" Melody asked politely, taking her cue.

"Indeed yes, my dear." He came back to his armchair. "*Unobserved Symmetry: Diagonal Compositions in Minor Flemish Masters 1440–1460.*"

"It is a most enlightening work," Eustace added.

"Thank you, my boy." Uncle Alistair picked up another tiny sandwich, this one cucumber, and spent the next twenty or so minutes reviewing the work's main points, though to Melody it felt like hours. She did not understand most of what the old professor was talking about and was, in truth, fighting to stay awake. Finally, when there was a break in the exposition due to Uncle Alistair needing to breathe, Eustace spoke.

"Well, Uncle, we must get on." Eustace stood.

"Leaving already?" Uncle Alistair seemed surprised. "But you've barely touched the sandwiches. And I haven't even gotten to the second half of the book!"

"Well, you don't want to give it away, do you? We must leave Miss Merriweather in some suspense."

"Ah," Uncle Alistair mused. "I suppose you have a point. Would you like a copy, Miss Merriweather?"

There was nothing she wanted less. "If you . . . if you have a copy to spare," she managed to murmur.

"But of course, but of course!" Uncle Alistair said enthusiastically. He hurried over to one of the bookcases and slid open the glass door. After removing a thick volume, he returned, placing it in her hands. "There you are."

"Thank you, Professor Sinclair, I–"

"Oh, but you must call me Uncle Alistair!"

"Uncle Alistair, then. Thank you. I'll return it soon."

"Return it? No, it is a gift, my dear."

"Oh, well, thank you." She smiled weakly.

"Why don't you stay for dinner?" he asked eagerly. "I'm sure Manfred can arrange something with Cook."

"No, Uncle," Eustace said quickly. "We're dining at the Berghoff tonight."

"The Berghoff, eh? I haven't been there in years. The last time, I believe, was, well, it must have been before the war."

"You're welcome to join us of course, Uncle," Eustace said, though even Melody could tell it was an insincere offer.

"No, no." Uncle Alistair sighed. "Not today. You go on and enjoy yourselves. Miss Merriweather, it was a delight to meet you." He raised her hand to his lips again.

"And you as well, Professor . . . Uncle Alistair."

The older man then shot Eustace a quick wink. "You've chosen well, my boy. When will you make Miss Merriweather one of us?"

If Melody wasn't mistaken, Eustace's cheeks were now flushed. She had never once seen him ruffled, much less . . . was he *embarrassed*? He did not return her look.

"And have you taken Miss Merriweather to see the new gallery?" Uncle Alistair asked, as if this was the most natural follow-up question in the world. "The one on Michigan. Quite good, you know. Quite good."

"I haven't, Uncle, but I shall," Eustace answered vaguely, causing Melody to wonder which of his uncle's questions he was answering–the former, the latter, or both? "Goodbye, then," Eustace said with unusual curtness and gestured Melody toward the door.

As she followed him down the main staircase, Melody was acutely aware of the awkward silence between them now. She wondered if he might be somehow angry and was surprised when he paused abruptly on the first landing.

"I do apologize. He's a bit batty, but he means well. You might not guess it, but he really is the most intelligent man I've ever met. He's actually quite brilliant. You musn't mind what he says." He absently drummed his fingers on a small section of the banister.

Melody wondered what part of the conversation he was referring to–Uncle Alistair's outlandish tales or his comment about making her a Sinclair? She decided to play it safe. "About the people living in the center of the Earth?"

"Yes, that's it." Eustace's worried face relaxed. "That and other things . . ." His voice trailed off. They stared at each other, and Melody's heart began to beat a little faster. They were standing so very close. She remained silent, waiting for him to . . . well, to perhaps kiss her, but he did not.

He backed down a few steps.

"Are we really dining at the Berghoff, or did you just say that to get away?" she asked with a bit of a pout. *Would he ever kiss her?*

"Yes, we really are dining at the Berghoff." He smiled tentatively. "If you wish it, that is."

"I do wish it. I'm famished!"

Eustace laughed. Really laughed. The first time that she had ever heard him do so. He seemed lighter now. "Do you always say what you feel and think?"

Melody considered. "Usually, yes. Don't you?"

"Oh, dear one," he said, suddenly taking her hand and kissing it, "what a breath of fresh air you are in this dusty old mausoleum. You are like the last of the pink summer roses. You are simply waiting to be plucked, and I tremble before you at the prospect. Come, let us go."

Melody was a ball of confusion as they descended the remainder of the stairs, her arm linked in his. It seemed obvious that a proposal was on the horizon, and yet he had not yet told her that he loved her. A pink rose, he had called her. *First love, innocence.* Everything *pointed* to him being in love with her, but she wasn't sure.

And, more importantly, she had yet to decide if *she* was in love with *him*.

CHAPTER FOURTEEN

Kate leaned against a dead elm on the side of County Highway O, trying to decide if she should continue on to Shullsburg. She estimated that she had walked about three miles, and she was already cold and wet and tired. She had not grabbed a hat or gloves when she stomped out of the farmhouse, nor was she wearing boots, and her fingers and toes were now numb.

At one point, she had debated turning around and seeking refuge in her badger hole, but decided against it, as Christmas Tree Hill would be muddy and horrible this time of year. Plus, it would be the first place they would look, and she didn't want to be found by anyone, not even Edmund. Especially Edmund. She had likewise briefly thought of fleeing to Rosemary and Harriet's, but this, too, was too obvious. Plus, Harriet would simply implore her to work it out with the Kerwyns. Harriet was a good friend, but altogether too forgiving. And that was the one thing that Kate didn't want to be right now—forgiving. She was determined to leave the Kerwyns behind and seek out these Espos.

She had never been to Shullsburg, but it wasn't all that big, probably the size of Merriweather. Surely, it wouldn't be that hard to track them down.

With a heavy sigh, she scrambled up the little bank to get back on the road. At this rate, she wouldn't get there until after dark. Only a few automobiles had thus far passed by, and when they had, she had stood off to the side, waiting for them to rumble by. But now she wondered if she should try to flag the next one down. She was loath to ask for help, not to mention having to make small talk with someone all the way to Shullsburg, but she was desperate.

Almost half an hour passed before she heard something approaching behind her. She turned and saw an old truck. This was her chance! With her heart pounding, she stuck her hand awkwardly in the air and waved.

Mercifully, the truck slowed and then rolled to the side of the road, gravel crunching. The man driving cranked the window down.

"That you, Kate?" It was Merle Koenig. "What you doin' all the way out here? Runnin' away?" he asked, glancing at her carpetbag before barking out a crusty laugh.

Ugh! Why couldn't it have been a stranger? "No, I'm . . . um . . . visiting"–she almost said "relatives," but caught herself in time, as she knew that Merle Koenig most probably knew all the Kerwyn relations–"friends in Shullsburg."

"Oh, yeah? Who?" Mr. Koenig seemed genuinely intrigued.

Kate wanted to retort that it was none of his business, but she didn't want to be rude, nor ruin her chances for a ride. "The Espos?" she chanced.

"Never heard of no Espos." Mr. Koenig shrugged. "Aye, well, get in. Can't let you out here in this weather. Surprised Gus didn't drive you himself."

"He's . . . he's under the weather," Kate fibbed and then walked around to the passenger side. She pulled the handle as best she could with her numb fingers, then stepped on the running board and hoisted herself up.

Mr. Koenig's truck smelled vaguely of hay, manure, and coffee, which oddly comforted Kate. It smelled like their barn. She looked out the window, or tried to anyway, but the glass was so dirty that everything appeared as through a thick fog. She was tempted to wipe it clean with her coat sleeve, but she didn't want to risk offending Mr. Koenig. She looked out the windshield instead, which was passably clear.

Mr. Koenig, his fat, sausage-like fingers resting lightly on the gear stick, shifted into a higher gear, and they bounced along. Mr. Koenig was probably the fattest man she had ever seen, and she marveled that there was enough space between his protruding belly and the steering wheel for him to adequately drive. He was also the most talkative man she knew, and he chatted away about this and that for the whole of the trip.

Kate only half listened as they passed dreary farm after dreary farm. It had always surprised her that so many people named spring their favorite season when anyone who lived on a farm knew it was not beauteous in any way–it was simply oceans and oceans of mud.

When they passed a signpost that read "SHULLSBURG 2 mi," she suddenly began to panic a little. She hadn't a clue where to start looking for her family. Should she just start knocking on doors like she had on Magnolia? What had she been thinking? And what if, by some longshot, she *did* find them? Would they know her? Welcome her? Or would they be angry, disappointed? Perhaps they didn't want to be found . . .

"Well, here we are," Mr. Koenig said as they turned onto Water Street. He rolled the truck to the curb and halted it, the engine rumbling loudly. "Where's these Espos live? I'll drive you there."

"Uh, no thanks, Mr. Koenig," Kate said, trying to quickly open the door. It stuck, however, so she put her shoulder to it and pushed until it creaked open enough for her to slide out. "I . . . I'm going to do some shopping first." She nodded toward the first shop she saw, which happened to be a corner grocer. "Kirschbaum's" was written across a red-and-white-striped awning.

"Shopping?" Mr. Koenig said, leaning one elbow out the window he had just cranked down. "Nothing here that you can't get in Merriweather."

"Thanks, Mr. Koenig!" she called, trying her best to sound happy and carefree, as if she were about to embark on a fun day out with friends.

"You need a ride home later?"

"No, I'm staying here for a while!" she called and bustled into the shop, the bell above the door ringing briskly.

She paused for a moment, trying to get her bearings. It was similar to the Merc, but smaller.

"Can I help you, Miss?" asked a gaunt older lady behind the counter.

"Uh . . ." Kate hesitated. "I hope so." She tried to smile. "I'm looking for some . . . some old friends. The Espos? I was told they might live here. In Shullsburg, I mean."

"Espo?" The woman's brow creased. "Don't think so." She looked Kate up and down, clearly noting her damp, bedraggled appearance and shabby carpetbag. "Roberta!" she called with only a slight turn of her head.

"What is it?" a voice from deeper in the shop answered.

"You know any Espos?"

"Espos?" Another older woman, obviously Roberta, appeared from the depths of the shop. "Don't ring a bell. Why?" She noticed Kate, then, and peered at her over the top of her spectacles.

Kate sighed, wondering how many fibs she was going to have to tell in one day. "They're friends of my family. I'm from Merriweather. I'm . . . I'm looking for them."

The first woman raised an eyebrow suspiciously. "Well, you best go on over to St. Pete's. Mrs. Seitgart would be able to tell you."

"Ah, yes," agreed Roberta. "Now that's an idea, Norma! Yes, you go on to the rectory over at St. Peter's–it's just down the street. You can't miss it. Mrs. Seitgart keeps all the town records, you see. Used to mostly be over at St. Matthew's, but it burned down, what was it . . . ten years ago?" She looked at Norma questioningly.

"Ten?" Norma exclaimed. "More than that, Roberta. More like fifteen."

"Can't be fifteen. I remember because Sylvia was baptized there, and she just turned ten this year, so that would make sense."

"Roberta, you're thinkin' of the chapel–"

"I think I'd remember where my own child was baptized, Norma!" Roberta said, irritated. "Now, I'd swear on my life that that fire was just ten years ago, and I–"

Kate backed toward the door, hoping to slide out unnoticed, but even her slow, calculated motion caused the shop bell to betray her with a single tinkle.

"Where you going?" Norma asked.

"I'm just going to head over to St. Peter's. Like you said." Kate gestured vaguely. "Thanks for your help."

"You want me to go with you?" asked Roberta. "I don't mind!"

"You're not leaving me here to mind the shop on my own!" Norma exclaimed. "You're a busybody if I ever knew one, Roberta Campbell!"

"How dare you! All I'm trying to do is help this poor girl–"

Kate slipped out, hoping they wouldn't follow. She could see a church down the street and guessed it to be St. Peter's. After hurrying for almost half a block with no ladies in pursuit, Kate slowed her pace.

As she neared the church, she grew uneasy. Though the Kerwyns were paid-up members of St. Mary's, Kate privately had little use for their pastor, Fr. Eggert, whose moralizing homilies somehow made her feel worse than when she had gone in. Did she really want to explain her current predicament to a priest? The ladies at the shop had mentioned a Mrs. Seitgart, however, whom she guessed must be the housekeeper, but what if the priest himself answered?

When she finally reached the low iron fence that ran around the property, she realized there was an even bigger problem. Chiseled into the cornerstone was: St. Peter Lutheran Church 1907. *Lutheran!* She had assumed it was a Catholic Church. She was pretty sure that entering a Lutheran church was a sin. Hadn't Fr. Eggert said as much, over and over?

She stood in the street, looking at the church and trying to decide. Well. She had come this far, hadn't she? She had already told several lies that would need confessing, so why not add another sin to the pile? Although, she mused as she pushed open the low gate, she wasn't actually going in the *church*, merely the rectory–or whatever the Lutherans called it–which was probably not a sin. After all, it was just a house.

She walked up the few steps of the little stone bungalow, took a deep breath, and lightly knocked.

After only a few seconds, an older woman, in her sixties or maybe seventies, opened the door.

"That you, Burt?" The woman was wearing a neat floral housedress covered by a full apron and held a broom in one hand. "Oh!" She gave a little laugh. "Thought you were the mailman." Laughing again, she rested the broom against the wall. "How can I help you? Are you here to see the reverend?" she inquired in a pleasant, warm voice, her blue eyes very bright. "Why don't you come in?" She opened the door wider.

"Are you Mrs. Seitgart?"

"Why, yes I am, deary." She seemed surprised. "How can I help?"

"I . . . I know this might sound very . . ." Kate searched for the right word. "Irregular, but I'm looking for some friends of mine, and the ladies at the shop"–she nodded toward Kirshbaum's–"they thought you might be able to help."

"Did they, now?" Mrs. Seitgart put her hands on her hips. "Those two," she said with a little sigh. "Well, I suppose they were right, but it'll be all over town in less than an hour."

"What will be?"

"Oh, never mind!" she said cheerily. "Here, come in, child. It's cold, and you'll catch your death."

Mrs. Seitgart's comment reminded Kate of something her mother would say. She felt a rush of guilt–Mrs. Kerwyn was probably worried sick. She pushed the feeling away, however, convincing herself that the Kerwyns didn't really care. Well, her sisters might care, but only because her absence meant more work for them.

Kate tentatively set her carpetbag down and dutifully wiped her feet on the mat, curious to see what the inside of a Lutheran pastor's house looked like. She half expected it to be filled with crosses and religious iconography, and so was a bit disappointed when it was not. The front room looked like a normal parlor. Likewise, she had expected the house to smell of candle wax, or perhaps mothballs, but instead the aroma of chicken soup wafted through the air. Kate's stomach grumbled. The last thing she had eaten was a bowl of oatmeal at the crack of dawn.

"Do sit down, deary." Mrs. Seitgart gestured at the sofa. "What can I get you? Some coffee maybe? Something to eat?" She glanced at the big grandfather clock in the corner. "Reverend Rushworth won't be home for another hour. Out on calls, you see. But I could make you a sandwich?"

"Oh, no!" Kate exclaimed. "Just . . . just coffee would be nice. If you have some made, that is."

"Won't be a moment!" the older woman called and disappeared into what Kate assumed was the kitchen.

Kate used the time to look around. The furniture was smooth and polished, not dinged and nicked like at home, and atop each gleaming piece sat a perfectly ironed doily. Even the sofa back and arms had beautifully crocheted doilies. The room did not exude luxury, but it did possess a quiet respectability and a tidiness that the Kerwyn home most certainly lacked. Under the far window sat a low bookcase double-stacked with books. Kate was tempted to inspect the titles, but before she could decide whether she should, Mrs. Seitgart returned with a china cup of coffee and two small cookies balanced on the edge of the saucer.

"Just in case you're a little hungry."

Kate took the cup and saucer and forced herself not to immediately scarf down the cookies.

"Now," Mrs. Seitgart said, sitting down opposite her. She had divested herself of her apron. "About these friends of yours."

Kate wasn't sure where to begin. From what Norma and Roberta had said, Kate had half expected this Mrs. Seitgart to dig out some dusty ledger filled with recordings of baptisms and weddings and funerals, but the woman just sat there, waiting.

Kate gulped down the coffee and set the cup on the little table. "Have you ever heard of the Espos?" she asked, trying to restrain her heart from hoping too hard.

"Espo?" Mrs. Seitgart murmured. "Espo. Can't say that I have."

Kate's heart sank. She should have known this was a wild goose chase.

"Wait a minute now," Mrs. Seitgart said then, almost to herself, "there was a Tim *Esposito,* I believe." She looked at Kate eagerly. "That ring a bell? Had a farm just outside Shullsburg. Closer to New Diggings, really. That was years ago, though."

Kate bit her lip. "He's not still there?"

"Took his own life, I seem to remember. Bless his soul."

Kate felt her gut wrench. To have been so close to possibly finding a relative, only to lose him within seconds. "Did he . . . did he leave behind any family?"

Mrs. Seitgart stood. "That's just what I was trying to remember. Here, let me have a look." She went to the bookcase and pulled out a very thick black leather book, the corners of which were tattered. Mrs. Seitgart set it on top of the bookcase and opened it gingerly, careful not to let any loose papers fall, and flipped through several pages. She read for several minutes, during which Kate secretly devoured the cookies.

"Don't see anything under Tim," Mrs. Seitgart muttered to herself and then flipped to a different page. "Ah! I thought so. There is an Ann Esposito listed here." She had her finger on a line. "Might have been a sister to Tim. She's married now, though, so that's why I didn't think of her right off. She's Ann Price now."

Ann. Ann. Ann. Kate said it over and over in her mind, hoping it would jog some memory, but it didn't. Neither had the name Tim, if she were honest. Perhaps this was all just a big mistake!

"That's all I can see here." Mrs. Seitgart closed the book. "You might pay a visit to Ann. They live above Gordon's Tap, just down Third Street, on the second floor. You can't miss it. If she's not the one you're looking for, she might know where to find the rest of them. If there are any, that is."

Kate stood up uneasily. Suddenly the prospect of meeting someone from her original family was terrifying.

"You sure you don't want a sandwich? Or maybe some soup?"

"No, thank you, Mrs. Seitgart. I'm very grateful for your help." She would, in fact, rather stay and have soup, but that was simply delaying the inevitable. She was so close now!

"Don't mention it!" Mrs. Seitgart said cheerfully, opening the door. "Now, if it doesn't work out, you come on back here and have dinner with the reverend. Or you can have dinner with me in the kitchen. What's your name, deary?"

"Kate. Kate Kerwyn. I'm from Merriweather."

"Oh! I have a cousin in Merriweather! Irene Ehlers. Know her?"

"I . . . Ehlers rings a bell. My mom probably knows her."

Mrs. Seitgart looked her over kindly. "Well, Kate Kerwyn from Merriweather, if you don't find what you're looking for, you come back, you understand?"

Kate nodded and stepped back out into the cold, wet air.

CHAPTER FIFTEEN

Gordon's Tap was located in a large, ramshackle building that looked as if a strong wind might blow it over at any moment. It was made of thin wood siding, which had lost its paint long ago and now was just a dirty gray. As Kate got closer, she spotted a covered stairwell hugging the building's side, though the door leading up to it, if there ever had been a door, was missing. Several men were loitering under the front awning, clutching beer bottles. Kate was hesitant to pass, but she saw no other way to get to the stairwell.

"Hey, sweetheart! Where you goin'? Want a drink?" one of them called.

Kate ignored him and ducked inside the stairwell.

"Be that way, then!" the man called after her.

Kate hurried up the steps, eager to get away from them and from the rain that had just now begun pelting down, the sound of it loud and exaggerated on the tin roof. Thank God she had gotten here before she got drenched. It would have been terrible to show up on her long-lost family's doorstep looking like a drowned rat.

She paused on the first landing, remembering that Mrs. Seitgart had told her they lived on the second floor. The single door was dented in one place, and the trim was rotting, but there was no other, so this must be the place.

She stood there for a few moments, breathing deeply. This was it. She was about to meet her family. Her real family. Would they welcome her with open arms or reject her, tell her to leave? That seemed the most likely outcome, she warned herself. As why else would they not have come looking? Though maybe . . . maybe they thought she was dead? Oh! She hadn't thought of that.

Kate's chest was heaving as she gave the door a swift knock before she lost the sliver of courage remaining.

After only a few moments, the door opened wide to reveal a stocky woman with dark eyes and dark hair tied at her nape. A baby was balanced on her rather full hip. "Yes?"

Kate hoped for some stir of recognition, however faint, but there was nothing. She cleared her throat. "Are you . . . are you Ann Espo? . . . or Esposito?"

The woman's round eyes narrowed. "I used to be. I'm Ann Price now. Why?"

Kate was at a loss for words. She should have planned this out better! "I . . . I think I might be your sister," she said in an unusually high voice.

Ann rolled her eyes. "You one of the O'Connells?" She nodded at the apartment above. "Top floor. They've always got people turnin' up, saying they're relatives. Like Ellis Island up there." She began to close the door.

Kate remained immobile as these words sank in, but then panicked when she realized she was blowing her chance and blurted, "No, I'm not one of the O'Connells." Though she *could* be, she thought irritably, since she had no idea who she really was. "I'm . . . My name is Kate Kerwyn," she faltered, realizing as soon as she said it that this would mean nothing to the woman. "I'm from Merriweather. My family used to live there. I think. Somehow, I got separated from them."

"Who is it, Ma?" A little girl of about ten appeared at the woman's side and peered up at Kate. Ann handed her the baby and then folded her arms across her ample chest.

"I ain't exactly sure. Says she's my sister."

Kate shifted uncomfortably while the two continued to stare at her.

"Well, ain't ya gonna ask her in?" The girl plopped the baby onto her own hip, which was nonexistent, causing her to have to angle her body sharply.

"Aye." Ann sighed. "Reckon so. Come on in."

Kate, her nerves racing, followed the woman inside. She dutifully wiped her feet on the dirty mat and tried to take in her surroundings without making it too obvious that she was doing so. She was surprised by how small it was, but she liked small spaces, like her badger hole.

"What did ya say yer name was again?" Ann asked, putting her hands on her hips.

"Kate. Kate Kerwyn."

"Don't ring a bell." She shook her head slightly and pulled at her chin. "Had a sister, Marie, that went missing." She raised an eyebrow, waiting for Kate's reaction.

Marie? Marie? It meant nothing!

"You're from Merriweather, you say? How old are you?"

"Well, I'm not exactly sure, but I think I'm eighteen. Thereabouts."

Ann twisted her lips. "That'd be the right age." She peered at her closely. "How come you think you're an Esposito?"

Kate wasn't sure where to begin. "I . . . I was found wandering as a toddler outside of Merriweather and taken in by a local family–the Kerwyns?" Kate paused to see if there was any recognition, but there was not. "No one knew who I was or where I came from," she continued, "and it's only recently that I started to wonder. I . . . I started inquiring, and a woman in town–Rosemary Mueller?" Kate paused again. Still nothing. "Well, she seemed to remember that one of the men who died in a big mining accident years back had a large family and that the mother died shortly after of diphtheria. Espo, she thought their name was. Relatives from Shullsburg came and took all the kids back with them. So, I thought maybe I'd look for you. To see . . . to see what happened. I guess."

Kate's gaze during this speech had gone from Ann to the floor to the girl by her side and then back to Ann again, who now, Kate was surprised to see, had tears in her eyes.

Ann stared at Kate for several long moments, her brow furrowed deeply. "Are you . . . could you . . . are you really little Marie?" she asked hoarsely. Ann looked at the girl beside her as if to help her understand. "Marie?" she asked incredulously, turning her eyes back to Kate, who was beginning to tremble.

Was she Marie*?*

"Oh my God, Marie!" Ann exclaimed, deciding that she was. She threw her arms around Kate and held her tight. "Is it really you?" she asked, pulling back and looking her up and down again, joy written across her face. "I can't hardly believe it! Jenny," she said, "this is your Aunt Marie! Well, I'll be! Come on, come on! Sit yerself down in the front room, there."

Ann gestured toward a sagging sofa that might have been respectable at one point, but that now was rather shabby, with several rips and one large stain. It was piled with newspapers and various pieces of crumpled clothing, including a few dirty socks. "Jenny, put the baby down and clear a space."

The girl set the baby down, who immediately began to crawl away, and cleared a stack of newspapers from the sofa, enough at least for Kate to sit down. She then followed the baby to where it had crawled down a narrow hallway, scooped it up, and returned, plopping herself on the arm of a chair and staring at Kate with big soft brown eyes.

"You want something to eat?" Ann called from a makeshift kitchen, which wasn't its own room proper, but consisted of merely a stove and a sink and a couple of cupboards along the opposite wall.

Kate was about to answer in the affirmative when she caught herself, noting their obvious poverty. "No, I'm fine at the moment," she answered, glad that she had taken advantage of Mrs. Seitgart's cookies.

"Nothing? How about a slice of bread?"

"Well, if you . . . if you have enough."

"That's one thing we always seem to have, don't we, Jenny?" Ann called cheerfully and reached for the breadbox. "You want coffee?"

"If you have some made," Kate called.

"Won't take a minute." She plopped a slice of bread on a plate, covered it with something, and held it up. "Here, Jenny, give this to her."

The girl propped the baby back on her hip, retrieved the plate, and delivered it to Kate. It held a thin slice of bread with an equally thin layer of strawberry jam.

"We're all outta oleo," Ann called. "But with the jam, you don't really notice, do you, Jenny?" Ann carried in two cups of coffee and handed one to Kate. She picked up a blanket lying on a torn armchair, its stuffing poking through, and sat down heavily. She tossed the blanket on the floor.

Kate was suddenly not hungry, but she forced herself to take a bite. This was not what she had been expecting at all. Was this woman really her sister?

"My goodness," Ann said, wiping one eye with the back of her hand. "I never thought I'd see the day. Wait 'til yer da hears." She gave Jenny an excited little nod and then looked back at Kate expectantly. "What happened to you, Marie? I mean . . . Kate."

Kate swallowed the tiny bite of dry bread in her mouth and washed it down with a sip of very weak coffee. "I was hoping you could tell *me*."

Ann shifted in her chair. "Well, it's like that woman told you. Da died, then Ma, and we was left orphans. Weren't long before Uncle Al, that's Da's brother–Alphonse was his real name–and Aunt Dorothy turned up from Shullsburg to take us all in. Well, some of us. The older ones. So as we could help on the farm. You little ones got taken to Queen of Angels in Green Bay."

"What's Queen of Angels?" Kate asked, though a part of her somehow already knew.

"That's the big orphanage up there."

"But I wasn't taken." Kate gripped her mug tightly. "I was found crying and dirty near the Wareham farm. Does that mean anything to you?"

Ann shook her head slowly. "No. Don't know any Warehams. Uncle Al and Aunt Dorothy took us, and a neighbor took the three–or two, I guess–of you up to Green Bay."

"Who was this neighbor?" Kate asked, thinking she might be able to ask Rosemary about them, if she had a name.

Ann shrugged. "I don't remember, Marie. Kate. I was only six. I don't remember much at all."

Kate sighed and tried to think. "Well, wouldn't this neighbor have realized that there were only two kids, when there should have been three?"

Ann shrugged again. "Maybe they thought Aunt Dorothy and Uncle Al took one of you little ones, too? I don't know. It was probably kind of chaotic with the mine accident and all. Twenty-three men died, or so I've been told. I imagine most families either lost someone or knew of someone. Maybe you wandered away and no one noticed."

Kate's eyes suddenly filled with tears, but she blinked them back. She was used to being of little notice to anyone, but this time it hit harder than usual. "How many of us were there?" she asked, clearing her throat.

"Seven."

Seven? Just like the Kerwyns!

"There was Joe, Tim, me, Tom, Jean, Emma and you," Ann recited, counting on her fingers. "You, Jean, and Emma were the little ones." Ann nodded. "It makes sense now though . . ."

"What does?"

"When I turned eighteen," Ann said, "I wrote to Queen of Angels to see if I could find out what happened to you three. See where you'd all ended up. Jean apparently got adopted out to a family in Chicago, and Emma's a nun now."

"A nun?"

"Yes, cloistered, apparently, so I wouldn't have been able to talk to her, even if I did find her. Queen of Angels had no record of a Marie Esposito coming in. I suggested maybe you were listed under a different name, that you would have come in with Jean and Emma, but they claimed to have no record. I assumed it was a mistake, that you must have gotten adopted out. That or you died, and they didn't want to admit it."

A rebellious tear ran down Kate's cheek before she could angrily wipe it. "That's why no one ever came to look for me. All this time, you thought I was there."

"That seems to be the size of it," Ann declared and let out a deep breath. "But what *did* happen, Marie? You said a family took you in? Were they nice?"

Yes, they were nice, barring Ray, of course. Her mind went to Edmund, then, but he was not her family.

Kate nodded. "Yes, they're nice. They're farmers."

"Oh, like Tim. He had a farm on the other side of Shullsburg. He lost it, though, in the Crash, and he killed himself."

"Yes," Kate murmured. "Mrs. Seitgart told me."

"Mrs. Seitgart? From St. Peter's? What did *she* want?" Ann's ire seemed raised.

"She the one who told me to come talk to you."

"Did she now? Damn Lutherans. Busybodies, every one of 'em. Pearl Seitgart doesn't know the first thing about me," Ann huffed. "Why'd you go talking to her?"

Kate blinked, a bit perplexed by this new side of Ann. "Well," she faltered, "the ladies at Kirschbaum's suggested it. I–"

"Norma? Or was it Roberta?"

"Both, I think?" She wanted to add that Mrs. Seitgart had been extremely kind, but she didn't dare.

Ann let out a disgusted breath. "Can you believe that, Jenny?"

Jenny gave a quick dutiful nod.

"So, Tim died," Kate went on tentatively, desperate to turn the conversation back to what had happened to the rest of the family.

Ann sighed. "That's right. He was never all that strong, poor thing. Fr. Fahey says we're not to speak of him because he's in hell now, but I don't know."

"How sad," Kate murmured, feeling cheated all over again to have found and lost a brother in the space of an instant.

"Yeah, terrible sad. Evelyn–that's his wife–she got remarried a few years ago. Had three kids with Tim, and now she's got two more. Might have another on the way, not sure. Don't talk to her all that much."

"Well, what about Joe? And Tom, is it?"

"Joe ran off to Texas soon as he could. Hated Uncle Al. They were pretty hard on us. We used to be jealous of you three–well, of just Jean and Emma, I guess–that got to go to the orphanage. We always imagined their life was so much easier, but it probably wasn't, poor things. Least you seemed to have a nice life."

Another one gone. "And Tom?"

"Oh, Tom's a drunk, ain't he, Jenny?"

The girl gave another quick nod.

"He lives down by the river, or wherever he can find. Doesn't come around here no more, not since Sam finally threw him out. Almost came to blows. Told him never to come back."

"Who's Sam?"

"Sam's my husband. Sam Price. Used to be down the mines 'fore they closed, but now he's on the rails. Got a temper on him, though, don't he, Jenny?"

Kate's eyes rested on the girl in front of her. Her niece. "So, you're Jenny?" she said with a sad smile.

The girl nodded.

"What's the baby's name?" It was impossible to tell if it was a girl or a boy, as it had very little hair and wore only a diaper and a dirty cotton shirt.

"Barbara," the girl said shyly.

"So, you have two children?" Kate asked Ann.

Ann laughed. "Two? No, there's eight. There's Billy and then Susie, Herman, Charlie, Petey, and Vera. And Jenny and Barbara here."

Kate looked around, perplexed. "Where are they all?"

"Well, most of 'em is at school. 'Cept Billy–he works down at the lumberyard. And Herman's a hired hand down at the Bonnet farm. Stays with them. And I keep Jenny home to help me round here."

"That's nice of you," Kate said to the girl, but Jenny didn't react.

"Funny, ain't it? Us livin' so close all these years and not even knowin' it!"

Kate stared at the now empty mug still in her hands and felt . . . well, she didn't know what she felt. She had found her family, apparently, but it was somehow anticlimactic. In fact, she felt mostly sad. She had envisioned them as . . . well, she wasn't sure how she had envisioned them. Perhaps a little more artistic?

"Growing up, I thought I might be from one of the tribes up by Prairie du Chien," Kate explained. "The Sauk, maybe? Do you know anything about that?"

Ann's face was aghast. "Whatever gave you that idea? Ain't no Indian blood in us, that's for sure." She suddenly barked out a laugh. "Hear that, Jenny? Poor Marie grew up thinkin' she was an Indian!"

"Well," Kate said, unable to keep the irritation out of her voice, "what are we then? Mrs. Mueller thought Romanian? Or Hungarian?"

Ann scoffed again. "We ain't no gypsies. Who is this Mrs. Mueller, anyway?"

"Well, what are we then?" Kate repeated.

Ann thought for a minute. "Da, I'm pretty sure, was from somewhere in Italy."

Italy? "And our mother?"

Ann thought again. "Don't remember where Ma was from. Don't think I ever asked. Tom might know if you could track him down. Uncle Al or Dorothy mighta known, but they're long dead, ain't they, Jenny?"

More family lost. "But is 'Esposito' Italian?"

Ann shrugged. "Don't know about that. Maybe they were originally immigrants to Italy from somewhere else? Who knows?"

Another tear began its slide down Kate's cheek, but she quickly wiped it before it got very far. She was no closer to really knowing her origins. Just that she was half Italian. She supposed that's where her dark hair had come from. Her mother could have been anything.

"What were their names?" she asked quietly.

"Who?"

"Our parents. What were their names? I don't even know."

"Oh!" Ann laughed. "Well, Da was Cosmo, and–"

"Cosmo? Our dad was named *Cosmo*?"

"Probably short for something. I don't know. And Ma was called Maria, I think. Like you," she said, flashing a smile.

Maria. That told her nothing. Every nationality had a Maria. Or maybe that wasn't even her real name! She looked at Jenny, with her light brown eyes and light brown hair, and tried to detect any shared resemblance. There was none that she could see.

"What's Sam's nationality?" Kate asked.

"Sam? Sam's about as German as they come. Blond hair, blue eyes.

Again, the same as the Kerwyns!

"We made a good mix." Ann nodded at Jenny and Barbara approvingly.

Kate gave a weak smile.

"So now what?" Ann asked, her eyes wandering to Kate's carpetbag, left crumpled at the front door.

Kate hesitated. She hadn't thought that far ahead. As much as she was eager to get to know more about what was left of her real family, she wasn't so sure she felt comfortable staying here. But neither could she face slinking back home, her tail between her legs. Perhaps she should take Mrs. Seitgart up on her offer, but she had a sneaking suspicion that it would infuriate Ann, and she had no desire to alienate her family already.

"I . . . I guess I was hoping I could stay with you. For a while. Until I find a place."

Ann shot raised eyebrows at Jenny before returning her gaze to Kate. "Well, I reckon you can stay here for bit," she said slowly, "if you don't mind sleeping on the floor. We're all double and tripled up as it is."

"Oh, I don't mind at all. And I could help. Whatever you need me to do."

"Well, I don't know what yer da's gonna say," Ann said to Jenny and then looked back at Kate. "But you *are* my sister, after all." She scratched her chin. "Come on, then, you can help me with supper. You know how to cook, don't you?"

Kate obediently rose. "Oh! There's just one other thing I wanted to ask. Do you . . . do you know when my birthday is?"

For the first time, Ann seemed to look at her with weary pity. "I don't, Marie. I'm sorry. I was only a little girl myself when we lost you."

CHAPTER SIXTEEN

Melody slumped in her seat on the No. 30 bus, feeling weary and not a little lost. As much as she was enjoying her new relationship with Eustace, she was failing in nearly every other area of her life. No matter how hard she tried to catch up in her classes, it seemed impossible. She had gotten a D on her last geography quiz, and she was always the last to finish during the timed shorthand exercises. Sr. Margaret had been very understanding in the beginning, but even she was starting to lose patience.

Likewise, Cynthia was beginning to get frustrated with her as well, as Melody had declined her last three invitations. It wasn't that she didn't want to be with Cynthia and the gang; she simply didn't have the time. But, if she were honest, going to the pictures or dancing at the Aragon or the Merry Gardens now paled a little after her extravagant dates with Eustace. Eustace's world was a grown-up one filled with elegance and wealth and culture, while the world of the Mundelein gang now seemed frivolous and adolescent.

She should be in her room studying now, Melody mused, as she stared out the window at the city rolling by, but when Elsie had rung up to invite her to tea, she simply had to go. She desperately longed now to pour out her woes to her old friend, including all the specifics of her relationship with Eustace; though, she supposed, she shouldn't really regard him as a "woe."

There *had* been a shift, however, ever since she had gone to his home and met his uncle. Eustace constantly referred to them in the future tense now, as if their lives had already been cemented together. He described in great detail trips they would take to Venice and Paris and Budapest and such places and suggested the clubs to which they might someday belong. Likewise, he had more than once outlined for her his rather long lineage, which he seemed able to trace back to the *Mayflower* and beyond, to courtiers in the court of Henry VI and William the Conqueror. All of this without her having pledged anything to him. However, she could hardly say "But Eustace, we aren't engaged!" without prompting said proposal, and she wasn't sure she *wanted* him to propose, even if he was by all accounts perfect.

He was handsome, wealthy, cultured, refined, intelligent, and infinitely respectful. He could have easily taken advantage of her in one of the many rooms of his parents' empty house, Uncle Alistair safely out of earshot, but he had acted the perfect gentleman. And while Melody, was impressed by his gallantry, she was starting to think that he was a little bit . . . well, cold. Shouldn't he have tried to kiss her *at least once* by now?

She had tried asking Cynthia for advice, but, as was typical, her friend's response was rather unhelpful. Cynthia had encouraged Melody to marry Eustace as soon as possible (but to please not choose blue for the bridesmaids' dresses as she looked terribly washed-out in blue). The wedding, Cynthia had further advised, should be at an extremely decadent venue with absolute *rivers* of champagne, followed by a deliciously extravagant honeymoon to somewhere *très exotique*. And then, of course, she could settle down in the lap of luxury! What was there to decide? She had escaped her dreadful little hometown. While it was sad, she admitted, that Melody's father had had to die in order to get her brother to come home and take over, he had, so why should she continue to fret about a little mercantile in some small town in Wisconsin?

Elsie, Melody felt sure, would offer a different perspective. It did feel odd, however, to be the one seeking counsel from her previously shy, timid friend rather than the one giving it. In the past, when they had shared a room in Philomena, Melody had been wont to shower poor Elsie with advice, and she was still not a little proud of her role in Elsie and Gunther's union, as it had been one of her more stupendous successes. Well, she hadn't exactly *matched* them (after all, who would have thought to pair Elsie with the school's custodian?), but she *had* had a very big hand in their elopement. And now, they were happily married (*blissfully happy* is what Elsie had written to her once in a letter) and living in Palmer Square.

Melody pulled the cord above her, and the bus lumbered to a stop at Armitage and Humboldt. She alighted and headed north toward Palmer Square, which was not a square at all, she discovered, but a rather long oval-shaped park. Elsie and Gunther's home, No. 21, was a large Victorian brownstone, and though it was one of the smaller homes on the block, it was easily twice, if not three times as big as the Willows.

Melody rang the bell and waited a full minute for someone to answer before ringing again. Still nothing. She checked her wristwatch, wondering if she had the wrong time. She was just about to ring again when the door finally opened, albeit slowly. An elderly servant blinked big owlish eyes at her.

"Miss Merriweather, I presume?" His voice was deep and nasally. There was, Melody noticed, a small drip hanging from his left nostril, which he accordingly dabbed with the white handkerchief clenched in his rheumatic hands.

"Yes, I'm here to see Elsie. I mean, Mrs. Stockel."

"Very good, Miss. Madame is expecting you. This way." The old butler shuffled her down a short hallway and pushed open a door on the left. "Miss Merriweather," he announced and stood aside for Melody to pass.

Elsie was at the far end of the drawing room, arranging a bouquet.

"Melody!" she called, quickly popping the last stems into the vase. "Thank you for coming!" She embraced her friend. "It's so good to see you!"

"Oh, Elsie!" Melody exclaimed, pulling back and taking Elsie's hands. "It's good to see you, too. Look at you! Lady of the manor!"

Melody gave the room an appreciative once-over. The walls were papered with a pattern of pink cabbage roses and in front of the fireplace was an oriental rug in green and maroon. The rosewood furniture was arranged invitingly, with sumptuous cushions and pillows. Small treasures were artfully displayed on little tables and shelves, and a tall bookcase in one corner overflowed with books. It was just the cozy sort of room Melody adored, though, upon second thought, she knew that Eustace would have declared it *très gauche*.

"What a beautiful home. Did you decorate it? It has the look of you."

Elsie smiled. "Well, in a way. Grandfather said I could furnish the house as I'd like, but I didn't wish to waste his money." She cast her eyes around the room. "But I did move things around a bit. And there were ever so many pieces tucked away in the attic! I do think I've put some of them to good use. Here," she said gesturing at the maroon sofa. "Let's sit down, and I'll ring for tea."

As Melody took a seat on the sofa, Elsie gave the servant cord hanging beside the fireplace a quick tug. Then she sat next to her friend and took her hand. "Now, you must tell me everything!" she declared with a confidence that Melody almost didn't recognize in her friend and which Melody desperately wished she currently possessed. Marriage obviously agreed with Elsie–a point, Melody conceded, for Eustace.

"Oh, I hardly know where to begin!" Melody exclaimed but nonetheless promptly dove into all of the details of her relationship with Eustace, her woes over her failing schoolwork or even her worries about Fred and the Merc and everyone at home taking a far back seat.

Elsie listened with rapt attention and gentle accompanying murmurs. Only twice were they interrupted. Once when the servant returned with the tea tray, slowly shuffling across the room and seeming in such distress that Elsie got up and helped him. The second time was when a little girl silently appeared and came to Elsie, holding out her arms to be held. Melody thought that the girl was perhaps too old to sit on laps, but Elsie scooped her up nonetheless.

"Anna," Elsie remonstrated gently as put her arms around the girl. "Why aren't you up in the nursery with Nanny?" The girl laid her head against Elsie's chest and plopped her fingers into her mouth and stared at Melody. Elsie kissed her on the head and gently tapped the girl's fingers from her mouth. "Can you say hello to my friend, Miss Merriweather?"

The girl stared at her for a long time before finally murmuring, "Hello."

"Hello." Melody smiled, guessing her to be the child Gunther had brought with him from Germany and whom he and Elsie had adopted once they finally uncovered the tragic death of the girl's mother.

"There you are!" called a plump servant waddling into the room. "I'm sorry, Miss." She gave Elsie a slight curtsey. "I turned my back for a moment, and she just bolted. I do beg your pardon for disturbin' you." She threw a nervous glance at Melody. "Come on, Miss Anna. You've got to go back upstairs with me."

The girl buried her face in Elsie's chest and gripped her dress.

"Anna," Elsie whispered, "go with Nanny; that's a good girl. Papa will read you a story tonight if you're a good girl and do your lessons. Go on, now. Doris and Donny will be worried." Elsie planted another kiss on her head. "Go on. You're a big girl now."

"Come on, Miss Anna," Nanny urged. "I was just about to bring a plate of cookies upstairs. Why don't you help me pick them out?"

The little girl raised her head warily.

"Come on," Nanny urged with a smile, holding out her hand.

After just a few more seconds of hesitation, Anna slid off Elsie's lap and took Nanny's hand. Elsie waited for them to exit and then apologized to Melody. "I'm sorry. She's still very traumatized. She's beginning to speak now, though, so we are quite encouraged that she might be getting better. But please go on."

Melody suddenly felt rather foolish that her own troubles consisted mainly of the pros and cons of a life with the likes of Eustace Sinclair, should he ever decide to propose, while Elsie had to manage a giant house with an invalid mother; a gruff, controlling grandfather; a pack of children consisting of her younger siblings plus Anna; and a handful of what looked to be elderly servants. All this as a fairly recent bride. By her own comparison, Melody's life sounded ridiculously silly. She wondered if Elsie viewed her the way she herself now tended to view Cynthia and the gang at times, as adolescent and shallow.

"Oh, don't worry about me," Melody tried to say with a little laugh. "Let's talk about you now. Tell me everything! How's your mother?"

Elsie gave her a forgiving smile. "I agree; Eustance certainly seems perfect. You must follow your heart, though, Melody. Do you love him?" She took a sip of her now somewhat cold tea.

But that was just it! She wasn't sure.

"Perhaps you just need more time," Elsie continued. "You can't rush affairs of the heart. And you've only just met him, really."

Yes. Maybe she *was* rushing things.

"Is it really over with Douglas?" Elsie's expression was concerned. "You seemed to have so much fun together."

Melody sighed. "Yes, that's all over. He's with Vivian Anderson now, though he doesn't seem all that happy."

"Hmm." Elsie peered at her over her teacup. "And is there no other?" she asked softly.

"No, of course not!" Melody forced out a little chuckle.

The grandfather clock chimed four, then, and with a sigh, Melody set her cup and saucer on the little table. Eustace would be arriving at Philomena soon to take her to a new gallery opening, and she still had to dress.

"I should go," she said, standing, and Elsie followed suit.

"Are you sure you can't stay for dinner? It's a little chaotic with the children, but you'd be most welcome. Gunther would love to speak with you, and we've recently gotten a new cook. She's quite good. Much plainer meals than the old one. I think she's preparing meatloaf tonight."

As tempted as Melody was to have a meatloaf dinner (her favorite, actually) and to spend a little more time in this house that exuded peace and hominess, it was impossible. Eustace had been looking forward to this opening forever, and he would be cruelly disappointed if she canceled.

"Another time," Melody promised.

"Perhaps you might bring Eustace." Elsie's eyes were bright. "Does he play rummy? We could have a game."

Melody cringed at the image of Eustace eating a meatloaf dinner and sitting down to anything besides bridge or whist. "Yes, maybe," she said noncommittally. The fact that she knew Eustace would probably not approve made her not a little sad. It was a decided point against him, if she were indeed tallying.

* * *

The bus ride home provided more time for Melody to consider her future, and she eventually concluded that she would follow Elsie's advice to give it time. She was being too hard on Eustace. After all, people didn't just immediately fall in love, and she did, in fact, very much enjoy his company. He was perfect for her, as Elsie herself had agreed, and it was just a matter of time before her heart caught up with her mind.

When she stepped off the bus at Sheridan and Kenmore, it was nearly five o'clock. She would have to hurry. Even so, she paused at the front desk to check the mail basket. She quickly rifled through, hoping for a letter from home just as she used to long for letters from Cynthia while stuck back in Merriweather. How the tables had turned! Rarely did she get a letter from her family, except an occasional note from Mums that told her little beyond Helenka's daily routine, as if Melody cared about which days Helenka scrubbed the kitchen floor. Didn't Mums have anything else to write about? Her committees? Her women's clubs? Before Melody left for Chicago, she had gotten her mother to promise, albeit reluctantly, to try to go back to all of her old activities, but Melody saw no evidence of that, at least in her mother's letters. Melody worried that her mother might never be able to shake the depression she had fallen into, and she internally scolded Freddy and Bunny for not doing more.

Ah! There *was* a letter for her! It was from Harriet, as usual. Harriet, who despite her horrible penmanship, had proven thus far to be Melody's most faithful correspondent.

Melody hurried up the main staircase and dumped her books on her desk before plopping onto her bed. She ripped open the envelope and pulled out a piece of lined notebook paper just like they had used in school. Harriet had obviously not graduated to stationery.

Dearest Melody,

How are you? Things here are the same as ever for the most part. It has been raining a lot, which is delaying the farmers from getting the fields ready, though it has been good for the daffodils, which are blooming in record numbers. But maybe it's just me taking extra notice of them this year because I am so happy. That's strange, isn't it? (Not my happiness, but that when someone is happy, they notice pretty things more, don't they?).

Anyway, I hope things are going well for you and that you are enjoying all your studies. We (well, I) certainly miss you at the Merc. Fred is not an unkind boss, but he certainly has different views on things. He and Mrs. Haufbrau have formed what you might call an alliance. They are "tightening up this bloated ship" is how they phrase it. Never thought someone as ancient as Mrs. H. (I'm just going to write Mrs. H. now to save time and ink. You don't mind, do you, Melody?) could get along so well with such a young man. Mom says it must be because Fred reminds Mrs. H. of your dad. In looks, yes (though Fred is thinner and has more hair, of course), but in personality, no. (I mean no offense.) He doesn't seem to have "the gift of the gab" for customers like your dad did.

But, regardless, he and Mrs. H. are two peas in a pod now and have changed the shop window displays to what they used to be before you came and rearranged them. They also got rid of our little supply of ladies' dresses, cardigans, and stockings, saying that it was ludicrous for a mercantile to stock ladies' wear. But isn't variety the point of a mercantile? Personally, I think it was Mrs. H.'s way of getting rid of all the fancy hats and gloves and scarves you purchased. Nothing was specifically said, of course, but that is just my guess. (But aren't I wicked to think so?)

The biggest change (and, Melody, you aren't going to like this, I'm warning you now) is the cider. Mrs. H. has convinced Fred to stop selling it. Fred was hesitant, but somehow Mrs. H. got her claws into him and convinced him otherwise. So, the cider, for now, is gone. Which is a shame, because we had people coming in this past week asking for it.

Melody stopped reading. How dare Mrs. Haufbrau!

Likewise, they have done away with all the homemade products—Kate's baskets and Imogene's soaps and candles. Frank has tried to offer his suggestions, but Fred seems not to value them. I have never seen Frank so dispirited as when he looks around the Merc now, but, thankfully, he has Julius, and his guests, Henry and Mary Crawford, to keep him otherwise occupied. The Crawfords, by the way (you remember them from the potluck, don't you?) seem to have acclimated to the town very quickly and are often out at the Kerwyn farm, though I'm not exactly sure why. I asked Kate the last time she was in, but she said she hadn't the slightest idea. You know how she is. Speaking of, I haven't seen Kate in a very long time, which in some ways is a good thing because I haven't the heart to tell her we've no more need of her baskets.

John and I are very busy getting ready for the wedding. He is a perfect gentleman and so kind. I know you didn't approve of him at first, Melody, but I hope you might grow to admire him as much as I do. He's not just a farmer; he reads, too. In fact, he has a collection of books. And he spends every Friday evening at the cottage with me and Mom for dinner and a game of cards, and I spend every Sunday with his family. Oh, Melody, he is a dream! I can't wait to be married. He has a little spot of land picked out for us, and he's going to start building as soon as the ground thaws a little more. He won't be done by the time of our wedding, of course, so I've agreed to live at his parents' until the new house is finished.

I suppose I don't have much other news. The Merc, besides what I've told you, is the same. Many customers have asked after you and asked me to send their best wishes. Mrs. Borman, Mrs. Portzen, Mrs. Dixon, and . . . Oh! I can't remember them all! But you are missed, Melody, which is such a nice feeling, isn't it? To be missed?

And speaking of missing people, the only one I've missed mentioning, I suppose, is Cal. As usual, he keeps to himself, and Fred doesn't bother much with him. I did hear Cal tell him, though, that his Uncle Lyle would be ready to come back soon. Apparently, he's well enough to work now and wants his old job back, so Cal told Fred he's going to be moving on. Which is sad, isn't it? I've always liked Cal, and I know you do, too, Melody, despite the fact that the two of you are always arguing.

Always arguing?

You know, I did once think that maybe you and Cal might end up together, but I guess it wasn't to be. You're in Chicago with all of your lovely friends, and Cal's leaving anyway. Well, I should go. Mom needs help getting the spring onions in the ground. And I have no more news. Write when you can, but I'm sure you're very busy.

Your friend,
Harriet

Melody let the letter slip from her fingers, thoroughly distressed. *How dare Fred stop the cider sales?* Did he not know how hard she had worked to produce it?

She stood up and began to pace. And what about all of the local products and the plan with Frank and Julius to make the Merc a part of a new artisanal version of Merriweather? And how dare Fred call the Merc a "bloated ship"! And why would Cal not stay on to make sure Lyle was up to the job? She was tempted to immediately dash off a letter to Fred, but what good would it do?

As for Harriet's insinuations about her and Cal, she decided to simply ignore them.

She went to her tiny window and looked out at Sheridan Road below, the cars rumbling by. It was raining again. Why was it always raining? She couldn't remember a soggier April. But *why had* Harriet said that about her and Cal? She tried to conjure up an image of Eustace instead, of the two of them in a romantic embrace, like the Cupid and Psyche sculpture in the Sinclair statuary, but it was not Eustace she saw over her, it was Cal, strong and taut and poised like the Jason, his dark eyes boring into her as he pushed his dark hair back with a calloused hand, his lips parted slightly . . .

There was a swift knock, and she jumped.

"Melody?" It was Sharon from down the hall.

"Yes?" Melody called, her heart pounding.

"Sr. Joseph sent me up to tell you your 'gentleman caller' has arrived."

Melody groaned. She hadn't even started to dress.

"And you should see the flowers he's brought! They're absolutely gorgeous!"

Melody sighed. "Tell him I'll be right down!"

As Sharon retreated, Melody went to her closet and pulled out a bias-cut red silk gown from Fields. Granted, it was not designer, but it was quite stylish. She wasn't sure it was the right choice for tonight, but it would have to do. As for her worries about home–they would have to wait.

CHAPTER SEVENTEEN

"When'd you say yer goin' home?" Sam asked Kate, stuffing his pipe with tobacco.

Kate paused in the clearing of the dinner table, but Ann spoke first.

"Oh, you be quiet, you! Marie ain't goin' nowhere anytime soon. Spent my whole life without a sister, and now that this one's come back from the dead, I ain't givin' her up just like that!"

Kate wearily carried the stack of plates to the sink. It was generous of Ann to defend her, especially when it was obvious that her sister, more than anyone, felt the strain of having another person in the house to feed. Kate had been with the Prices almost two weeks now, and though she had scrubbed the whole apartment from top to bottom, mended clothes, cooked meals, and minded the children, the fact remained that there was only so much help she could provide when there was only so much food to go around.

She couldn't stay here forever. What was harder to accept was that she actually didn't want to.

She supposed she loved Ann and her family, but she had not found much to actually *like* about them, which opened up a whole new fissure of guilt. She had spent so many years imagining them as either proud, noble Native Americans or, more lately, as exotic foreigners with artistic sensibilities, that now she was, well, more than a little disappointed.

Ann, though kind in many ways, seemed overly prone to gossip and complaint. According to her, the Prices had been dealt a raw deal, and she was openly jealous of nearly everyone else in town. And Sam, though hardworking, expected to be pampered at home and frequently shared his own wide-ranging complaints. Thankfully, his bark was worse than his bite, but Kate had already grown tired of his rants and hated when he flew off the handle at Ann over some real or imagined infraction, to which she would respond with her own brand of vitriol. The two of them could argue for hours.

But what to do? She had no money, and though she had asked around at the shops, even at the Tap below, no one was hiring, especially a woman. She would have to move on to Dubuque, or maybe Milwaukee or Madison, though she did not relish being in a big city alone with nowhere to stay.

The one thing she knew for sure was that she could not return to Merriweather, especially not after what her father had said about her running away yet again. She refused to be the prodigal a third time.

Worried about her mother, however, she had eventually broken down and written the Kerwyns a letter, telling them where she was and that she was safe. The fact she had not yet received a reply told her all she needed to know. She *had*, however, received a letter from Henry Crawford, of all people, but she had torn it in two, unopened, and tossed it into the garbage.

Kate felt a tug and looked down to find Vera clinging to her dress. "We want Aunt Marie to stay forever, don't we, Ma?"

Ann gave a little bark of a laugh as she scrubbed the dishes. "Well, don't know about forever. Aunt Marie might want to get married someday and have her own bad children!"

"Will you tell us a story again tonight, Aunt Marie?"

"If you're good," Kate said, trying to remove the clinging girl from her dress. Her new nieces and nephews had initially been cautious around her, but they now wanted to be entertained every night with either a story or a game. This was all fine and good, except that Kate was not particularly fond of children and also didn't know that many stories. Likewise, there was not a single book in the house. Still, the children seemed to enjoy anything she came up with, and she found she sort of liked it. It was at least better than having to sit and listen to Sam read aloud bits of the paper or Ann's latest gossip.

"You leave yer aunt alone!" Sam bellowed between puffs of his pipe. "She's busy right now!"

"Aw!" came a collective cry.

"Shut yer traps!" Sam yelled. "Who's goin' with me tomorrow?"

"I'm workin', Da," Billy said from where he sat on the floor by the radiator, trying to extract what little heat was emanating.

"Alright, then, Charlie and Petey can go with me."

"Why can't I ever go?" piped Susie, who was not all that much older than Jenny, which made Kate wonder why Ann allowed Susie to go to school but kept Jenny home to help. Maybe it was because Jenny was quieter and more obedient, which really wasn't fair.

"Girls can't go huntin'!" Charlie cried.

"Well, I could walk along. I'm real good at spottin' squirrels. Can't I go, Da?"

Sam took a deep puff. "Up to yer ma."

Susie immediately wheeled on Ann. "Can I, Ma? Please?"

"You know Sunday's laundry day, Suze. You don't fool me one minute. You ain't got no interest trampin' through the woods; you just want to get out of your chores," Ann scolded.

"Aw, but, Ma! Aunt Marie's here to help now. And Jenny, too."

Ann's brow wrinkled as she debated. "Oh, alright," she grunted. "But next week you ain't gettin' out of it."

"Yes, Ma!" Susie said, cheerful now that she had gotten her way.

Kate tried to catch Jenny's reaction to this turn of events, but Jenny's face was blank. Kate took the baby from Jenny's arms. "I'll take her for a bit," Kate said and balanced Barbara on her hip. "Come on, how about that story?"

"Yay!" was the collective cheer, but Kate ignored the others and looked only at Jenny, who finally gave her the slightest of smiles. Jenny, Kate guessed, was a deep soul. She reminded Kate of herself at that age.

Kate led the way to the broken-down sofa, which had since become her bed. Billy, whose bed it *had* been, was now forced to sleep on the floor, which was likely why he had not particularly warmed to her. Holding Barbara on her lap, she patted the seat next to her for Jenny, and Vera climbed up on the other side. Petey wedged himself in at the end, and Susie squeezed in at the other. Charlie sat on the floor. Though he was all of thirteen, he still seemed interested in hearing Kate's stories.

"Which one?" Kate asked.

"A new one!"

"A new one?" Kate racked her brain. The only story she hadn't yet told was the Chinese Cinderella story she had initially heard from Julius Fairfax.

"Do *you* want a new one, Jenny?" she asked, looking down at the girl squeezed beside her.

Jenny nodded.

"Alright, then." Kate let out a deep breath, trying to remember. "Once upon a time there was a young girl named Ye Xian. Yeh-hsien. She lived in a cave deep in China. Her father–"

"Why you have to tell that foreign baloney?" Sam interrupted. "Why can't the cave be here? Or leastwise in Kentucky? Plenty a caves down there!"

"Da! You're ruinin' the story," Susie whined.

Kate paused to see if Sam was going to continue his rant, but he instead picked up the newspaper and flattened it out on the table in front of him.

Kate continued. "Ye Xian's father was the chief of the people there, and her mother was very lovely. Unfortunately, Ye Xian's mother died when Ye was just a little girl. Her father remarried a cruel woman and had a child with her, another girl." Kate paused and took in their eager faces. "Ye's stepmother hated Ye very much and made her do all the chores while her sister was spoiled rotten. Ye was by far the prettier and more skilled of the sisters, which made the stepmother all the more envious and cruel."

"Hey! This ain't a new one!" Charlie interrupted. "This is the same as Cinderella."

He was sprawled across the floor on his stomach, his head propped on his fists. Kate was impressed that he had so easily recognized it.

"You're right, Charlie. It *is* like Cinderella, but it's a little different. You'll see."

"Keep goin'," Vera murmured, pulling Kate's sleeve.

"Ye was given ratty clothes and very little to eat. And every day, she had to go get firewood and fresh water from a pool further down the mountain. One day, when she was getting water at the pool, a beautiful fish appeared. It was a carp, ten feet long, with red fins and golden eyes." Kate held out her hands to indicate the fish's size.

"Golden eyes, my ass," Sam grunted, though he kept his eyes on the newspaper. "And anyway, carp ain't no good to eat."

"The fish became Ye's only friend," Kate continued, ignoring him, "and she soon realized that it was her mother reincarnated."

"What's that mean?" Petey interrupted.

"It means that after she died, she came back to life as a fish," Kate explained.

The children's eyes went wide.

"Now *that*," Sam exclaimed, slamming his hand down on the table, "ain't Christian. And I'll not have that heathen crap told in my house."

"Oh, you be quiet," Ann scolded. "You ain't been to church in months, so I wouldn't get all high and mighty. Go on, Marie. What happens next?" Ann pulled out a chair across from Sam and perched herself on it, leaning her chin on her propped arm.

"The fish was Ye's only friend," Kate went on, "and whenever Ye went to the pool, the fish would stick its head out of the water and greet her. Ye, though she had very little food, always saved some and would give a portion to the fish. Things went on this way until somehow Ye's stepmother learned of the talking fish. She grew very jealous and so devised a wicked plan. The very next day, she gave Ye a new dress and told her to go to a different pool to gather the day's water. Ye obeyed and set off, happy to have a new dress. The stepmother then put on Ye's old ratty clothes and went to the pool where the magical fish was. Pretending to be Ye, she lured the fish out with a bit of food. Once the fish appeared, Ye's stepmother grabbed the fish, took out a knife, and killed her!" Kate made a quick slashing movement with her hand for effect, and Vera actually screamed.

"Did she really kill her?" Petey asked.

Kate nodded. "She did. When Ye discovered what her stepmother had done, she was heartbroken and sat by the edge of the pool and cried for her lost friend, her lost mother. As she sat there sobbing, she heard her mother's voice in the wind, telling her to take her bones and hide them. Ye did as told and hid the bones, which had magical powers."

"What kind of magical powers?" Charlie asked.

"They could grant wishes," Kate explained.

"Wishes? Well, why didn't she wish for her mother to become alive again, then?"

Kate let out a sigh. "I don't know."

"Stop interrupting!" Susie complained.

"It was just a question!" Charlie argued.

"You have a question about everything!"

Kate waited for the two of them to settle.

"Go on, Aunt Marie! Finish the story!" Petey urged.

"Ye rarely ever used the bones," she went on, "but when the annual village festival came around, she asked her mother's bones to produce a fine dress and shoes for her to wear. Instantly, a dress and shoes appeared! The dress was made of feathers, which shimmered in the light like a kingfisher, and the shoes were tiny and golden. Ye was not supposed to go to the festival–"

"Why not?" Petey asked.

"Because she was supposed to stay home and work, right?" Susie asked.

Kate nodded. "Yes. She was supposed to stay behind, but after her stepmother and sister left for the festival, Ye put on the beautiful dress and shoes and slipped out. She was so beautiful that even her stepmother and stepsister did not recognize her. As the evening continued, however, Ye began to notice her stepmother looking at her with more and more curiosity. Fearing that she would be recognized, Ye fled the festival, but in the process, lost one of her golden shoes."

"This *is* like Cinderella!" Charlie exclaimed again.

"We know that, Charlie! Shut up!" Susie cried.

"The golden shoe was found, and passed from villager to villager, all of them wondering to whom it belonged. Finally, it reached the young king of the land, who was fascinated by its tiny size and beauty. He began an official search throughout the whole of the kingdom to find the shoe's owner. When he and his entourage finally reached Ye's tiny village, there was great excitement. All the young women and girls of the village tried on the slipper, including Ye's stepsister, but it fit no one. Finally, the only one left was Ye. To everyone's amazement, it fit! Ye's stepmother claimed that there must be some mistake, that the beautiful girl at the festival couldn't possibly have been Ye. But when Ye produced the other slipper, which she had hidden in the depths of a cave, the king proposed, impressed by both her beauty and her kindness. Ye accepted and went to live with him in his beautiful palace, where they were happy forever. The end." Kate looked around at each of them and smiled. "Did you like it?"

"But what happens to the stepmother and the sister?" Billy asked from beside the radiator.

"They get punished for being so mean."

"That *was* the same as Cinderella," Charlie complained.

"No, it wasn't!" argued Petey. "There's no magic fish in Cinderella."

"Well, I liked it!" Susie declared.

"Me, too!" Vera wiggled next to Kate. It was clear she had to go to the bathroom.

"Well, I didn't," Sam said, tossing the newspaper. "Lot of rubbish, that one."

"It's a story," Ann emphasized. "And it wasn't for you. It was for the children."

"Right, well, time for bed. Get on with you!" he shouted at the kids, and they scrambled toward the two bedrooms. "We leave at dawn!"

Kate waited for the room to clear and then unfolded the quilt stacked by the side of the couch. She was glad that Sam and some of the kids would be gone for at least several hours tomorrow. It would allow for a little peace and quiet. Maybe she would even try to go for a walk if she and Ann finished the laundry early enough. Though she hated to admit it, she longed for the solitude of her attic garret where no one ever disturbed her. Except Edmund. Wistfully, she thought about the last time he had sought her out there. It had been the night of Ray's party, and, if she wasn't mistaken, he had perhaps been about to say something before Mary had barged her way in. She wished she could talk to him now, to tell him all about the Prices, to ask what she should do next . . .

But, that was all over now. He had not followed her here, nor had he written. And she was not going back.

CHAPTER EIGHTEEN

Kate's hopes for a walk the next day lessened with each passing hour. Given that it was unseasonably warm, Ann had decided to strip all of the beds in addition to all of the regular laundry, and Kate predicted they would not finish before Sam and the kids returned.

The little group had departed early to make the two-mile walk to a stretch of woods far west of the town. Sam had lately been bringing back rabbits, as squirrels were harder to find this time of year. Officially, it was illegal to hunt them out of season, but Sam figured he was above the law in this regard, especially as he had eight children, and now his wife's sister, to feed. And besides, he knew the game warden.

Kate paused and wiped her brow. Even with the windows open, she was perspiring. She plucked another shirt out of the gray water in the tub and squeezed out the excess water before feeding it through the ringer. Her mother changed the water frequently, but when Kate had suggested doing so, Ann had balked at the waste of soap.

"Da's back!" Jenny called from the back window, where she was folding towels. "Looks like they got something!"

"Already?" Ann said, pursing her lips as she surveyed the laundry mess. "Right, then, let's get this cleaned up."

Obediently, Jenny and Vera began dismantling the laundry apparatus. Vera carried the clean laundry back to the bedrooms, while Jenny and Ann dumped the big tub of dirty water. Ann quickly gave a final press to one of Billy's shirts and then set the iron on the table to cool. She was just folding up the ironing board when Susie burst triumphantly through the door.

"Look what we got!"

She held up the carcass of an animal Kate didn't recognize, which, having grown up on a farm, was saying a lot. The creature resembled a small beaver . . .

"Muskrats!" Susie said. "Da got three of them!"

Kate swallowed hard. *Muskrat?* Growing up on a farm, Kate had of course partaken of many meals in which the main course was some type of game–rabbit, squirrel, grouse, deer–but never in her life had the Kerwyns resorted to eating what they considered to be large rats, even in the darkest days of the Depression.

Sam tramped in then and tossed two more carcasses on the table, knocking over the iron.

"Muskrat, eh?" Ann said, looking them over. "Haven't had that in a while. No rabbits?"

"Didn't see a one, did we, Charlie?"

"Nah," Charlie said as he set his gun behind the door. "Saw a few squirrels, but we missed."

"Got any coffee, woman?" Sam barked as he threw himself onto the sofa. "Jenny, get these boots off! Charlie, you start cleanin' the guns, and

Petey, you carry those down the back." He nodded at the stiff bodies on the table, which was now smeared with blood, and held out a foot to Jenny.

"Hold your pants on!" Ann shouted, pouring a cup of coffee. "Marie, you go down and get started skinnin'."

Still appalled, Kate wanted to protest, but she realized how pretentious, not to mention ungrateful, it would sound. She had never skinned a muskrat, though she assumed it was the same as any other wild animal . . .

"Mind you, don't throw away the tails," Sam called as she picked up a couple of knives and a large enamel bowl. "That's where the best meat is."

"The tails ain't no good!" corrected Ann. "All bone and grizzle."

"Well, I like 'em!" Sam grumbled.

"I'll be down in a minute," Ann said, though Kate suspected it would be far longer than "a minute" before Ann appeared to help.

Kate trudged down the stairs and walked around to the back of the tavern, which abutted a scraggly lot consisting of half gravel and half weeds. The back door of the Tap was dented where someone had tried to kick it in, and the windows were barred, though one was broken and had a rag stuffed in the hole to stop the cold air. Nearby, a plank of wood sat atop two barrels upon which Petey had hefted the creatures. Whether this makeshift structure had been constructed by the Prices or by the owner of the tavern was unknown, but both the Prices and the staff of Gordon's used it for a variety of purposes.

Kate stepped over a broken whiskey bottle and surveyed the muskrats.

"Want me to help?" Petey asked eagerly.

"If you want to," Kate said gratefully, holding out a knife. "If you know what you're doing, that is," she added, not wanting to incite Sam's wrath by incorrectly dissecting his trophies.

Together they worked for almost an hour, with Kate periodically checking Petey's progress. She was impressed with his skill, especially given that he was only eight. When they were finally finished, Kate tossed the grizzled chunks of meat into the bowl and carried it upstairs while Petey disposed of the hides and entrails.

Ann had a pot of water already boiling and was finishing up kneading dough for bread. Sam's snores reverberated from the couch, his boots lying haphazardly on the floor. Ann took the bowl and tossed the meat into the pot of boiling water. Jenny silently plopped several onions in after it.

"Helps with the musky taste," Ann confided.

"I thought you would bake it. Or maybe batter and fry it?" Kate peered into the pot.

"Nah, they'll go further as a stew. Be ready in a few hours. Charlie, aren't you done cleaning those guns yet? Get a move on. Susie, you can wipe that table. Get the blood off."

* * *

Several hours later, the pungent aroma of muskrat stew filled the tiny place. Ann had added a few potatoes and carrots and had likewise roasted the tails, which were for Sam alone. Though the thought of eating muskrat initially nauseated her, Kate's stomach was growling. She had had only a slice of bread early this morning. Ann was giving the grayish mass a final stir when a sharp knock sounded on the door.

"Who the hell would that be on a Sunday afternoon?" Sam barked from the sofa, his eyes suddenly popping open.

"Well, how would I know?" Ann wiped her hands on her apron. "It's probably Randy," she muttered, referring to Sam's bachelor friend from the railroad. "If it is, don't ask him to eat with us. There ain't enough."

"I'll invite who I like, woman!" Sam shouted, pulling himself up. He shuffled over in his stocking feet and threw open the door. Kate turned from where she was slicing bread and nearly dropped the knife she was holding when he saw that it was not the mysterious Randy in the doorway, but Henry Crawford holding a large bouquet.

All the color drained from Kate's face.

Henry shot her a tiny wink and then addressed Sam. "Mr. Price?" he asked smoothly.

"Whatever it is yer sellin', Sonny, we ain't buyin'!" he snapped and began to shut the door.

"No, wait! I'm . . . I'm not selling anything. I'm . . . my name is Henry Crawford." He nodded toward Kate. "I'm here to call on Kate. If I may. If I'm not interrupting."

"Kate?" Sam was momentarily puzzled. "Oh, you mean Marie? Marie!" he said, stepping back a pace. "Someone here for ya. How come you didn't tell us you had a fancy man?"

Kate gritted her teeth. *How dare Henry follow her here!* "He isn't my fancy man," she said bitterly, but moved slowly toward the door and stood beside Sam.

Henry's face was one of outrageous delight. "Kate!" he gushed. "It's wonderful to see you! You have no idea how worried we've been."

Kate wondered who he meant by "we." Angrily, she pushed away a stray image of Edmund.

He held out the bouquet. "Here, this is for you."

Kate's eyes traveled to the bouquet. It was, she had to admit, stunning. It contained tulips, daffodils, hyacinths and even some lilies of the valley. It must have cost a fortune. Still, she refused to take it. He continued to awkwardly hold it out, his arm beginning to waver slightly.

"Take it, girl," Sam barked. "Don't leave a man hangin' that way!"

Kate roughly took the flowers and without even so much as a passing whiff, handed them to Ann, who was hovering near.

"Ain't these pretty!" Ann declared.

"May I come in?" Henry asked.

Sam gave a small shrug and stepped aside, waving his hand in an exaggerated gesture of welcome. As Henry stepped tentatively inside, he flashed Kate a smile. He was dressed in an argyle sweater-vest with blue and yellow diamonds, a navy-blue herringbone jacket, and sported a light blue tie with thin yellow stripes. He looked so completely out of place that Kate was tempted to laugh. Wickedly, she wondered what Mary was wearing today. A matching herringbone cap?

With a nod to Ann, Henry removed his herringbone cap.

"Well, ain't ya gonna' tell us who this is?" Ann asked. "Must be your beau, I'm thinkin'. Susie, find a jar for these flowers."

"Aw! Why me? I want to hear! You always make me do everything!"

"Alright, then, little Miss Nosey. You get it, Jenny."

Jenny silently retreated.

Kate pressed her lips together tightly. "Henry Crawford, this is my sister, Ann, and her husband, Sam Price."

Henry, whose eyes had been surreptitiously observing the interior, held out his hand to Sam.

"And he's not my beau," Kate added quickly. "He's from Merriweather. He's a friend . . . of my *sister's.*" Kate said with exaggerated relish and enjoyed watching his smugness temporarily vanish.

"Friend, is it?" Ann asked, one eyebrow raised disbelievingly.

"Kate is correct, Mrs. Price, with one small exception. I'm actually from Chicago. I'm just in Merriweather temporarily for work."

"Oh, yeah?" Sam scratched his head. "What kinda work?"

"I'm an architect."

"Golly. You rich?" Petey asked excitedly.

"Peter Price!" Ann scolded. "Don't pay him any mind, Mr. Crawford."

Henry gave a false little chuckle. "Not at all. And please do call me Henry."

"Alright then, Henry," Ann said, plopping the flowers into the jar Jenny had fetched. "Why don't you come on in and join us for supper? Got a real nice muskrat stew."

Kate had to bite back a smile at Henry's discomfiture.

"Ah." He shifted. "How very kind of you, but I fear I must decline. I'm only here for a short time, and I particularly wanted to speak to Kate. In private, if I may." He looked around the tiny apartment again as if searching for a place in which they might be alone. Finding none, he frowned. "Perhaps you might favor me with a walk outdoors, Kate? There's something very particular I wish to speak to you about."

Kate let out a deep breath. *Would he never leave her alone?* As much as she had desired a walk, this is not what she had envisioned. "You may speak to me here," Kate said, folding her arms across her chest. "There are no secrets between us," she said with mock sweetness, delighted to be able to use his favorite phrase against him.

"Ooo!" Ann clucked.

"But it is a very *private* sort of matter," Henry insisted.

"I can't possibly hold up supper," Kate retorted. "You'll either have to join us or come back some other time."

"Don't be a fool, girl," Ann declared. "You go on, and we'll save you a bowl. The man's come all this way. Least you can do is hear him out!"

Kate rolled her eyes. "Very well," she said stiffly, "come along."

She picked up her old wool coat from the row of hooks behind the door and stomped past him down the stairs.

Henry hurriedly followed. "Nice to meet you!" he called to Ann and Sam, who were still standing in the open doorway.

Kate walked quickly down Third, wanting to get as far from the apartment as possible, knowing Ann would try her best to listen. Her mind was racing. She had to admit that it was nice to see someone from home, though she would have preferred it to be just about anyone other than Henry Crawford. *What was he doing here?* Her two worlds were colliding, and she didn't like it.

"Hey! Wait up!" Henry called.

She wheeled on him. "What do you want, Henry?"

"I . . . I . . . how are you?"

"Fine. As you can see." She pulled her coat tighter around herself.

"Did you not get my letter?"

"I didn't read it."

"I see." He thrust his own hands in his coat pockets. "Why do they call you Marie?" He grinned. "Is it an alias?" He tilted his head slightly as he peered at her, and the setting sun illuminated his curls and his long lashes.

Kate looked away. "It's my original name, apparently."

He looked back toward the apartment. "It doesn't suit you."

"The name or the place?"

"Both.

"Well, as it happens, your opinion doesn't matter." She continued walking.

"Wait! Kate!" He caught up with her again. "I'm very glad you are . . . being cared for, but do you not miss home?"

"Not at all," she said brusquely, ignoring the fact that this wasn't *entirely* true.

"Well, we all miss *you*. Very much. Your mother, in particular, has been most distraught."

Kate ran her tongue along the inside of her cheek. He obviously knew how to get to her.

"Mr. Kerwyn is the same, as you might expect. Louisa and Nettie are quite caught up in Louisa's wedding plans, and little Minnie positively pines for you." He glanced at her. "As do I," he added with another grin.

She steeled herself and kept her gaze on the street. "How is work progressing on the cottages? When do you think you'll finish?"

"Soon perhaps. By the way, Frank is thinking of converting one of the cottages into a little shop or a tearoom, seeing as the Merc has stopped selling local ware."

She turned. "It has? Why?"

"Yes, had you not heard? As I understand it, Melody has returned to Chicago, and her brother is now handling the Merc's affairs. Let's just say he has a different idea of how things should be run."

"Oh." Kate felt oddly deflated.

"Frank says that he would be happy to sell your baskets–or anything else you make–in his little shop, though. If you're interested." He looked back over his shoulder at Gordon's Tap. "Though it doesn't look as if you've had the time." He stared at her for several long moments, and his eyes were suddenly vulnerable, pleading. "Kate, this is madness," he said softly.

She swallowed hard and bit her lip. Why did he have this effect on her? *She didn't like him!* "They're good people."

"Yes, I'm sure they are. But we're good people, too. And we miss you. Mary sends her love and implores you to return. She is going back to Chicago soon. Edmund is to follow at some point."

Kate's stomach immediately clenched. "Follow? Why?"

His eyes searched hers. "Has he not written?"

Dread filling her, Kate gave her head the slightest shake. "Are they engaged?" she murmured.

"Yes, I believe so. At least there is . . . an understanding."

Kate suddenly wanted to run. Run anywhere to be alone, to think this through, to be anywhere besides here, having to talk to Henry Crawford. *Had Edmund really proposed to Mary?*

"Kate." Henry laid a hand on her arm, but she immediately pulled it away.

With a grunt, Henry transferred his hand to his hair and rubbed it through. "Look," he addressed the ground, "I behaved badly the night of your birthday party. I regret it very much." He gave her a sideways glance. "I'm ashamed of myself, to tell you the truth. I beg your pardon. Please."

"Fine, I forgive you. Now, let's leave it at that." *None of that mattered now!*

There was a moment of silence as he stared at her. "Could you not grow to care for me, Kate?"

Kate made herself look at him. Her world was fracturing again, and she felt that this time, a part of her might truly die. It wasn't just that Edmund clearly did not love her the way she loved him, it was that he was blindly choosing Mary, who was completely wrong for him! Kate would happily give him up if the woman he was choosing was worthy.

A tear ran down her cheek, and she angrily wiped it. *Oh, Edmund, how could you?*

Henry reached out and brushed away the next one. "Don't cry, Kate," he whispered as he stepped closer, as if he were lulling a child–or attempting to trap a wild animal. "I've got you now." Slowly, he wrapped his arms around her and held her close. "I've got you." He gently stroked her hair.

Several more tears fell as she remained in his arms, absorbing what little comfort they afforded. *Oh, Edmund!*

Henry kissed the top of her head. "Kate, I really am in love with you, you know." She stiffened slightly, but he persevered. "I meant what I said before. You would make me a better person," he said earnestly. "I know you would. Honestly, I need you. And I want to help you, too. Support you. Rescue you from this. Does it not make perfect sense?"

Kate groaned and pushed herself away. "Nothing makes sense anymore, Henry."

"Say you'll marry me, Kate," he urged. "Please. You'll grow to love me. I know you will."

Kate stared at him, her cheeks wet with tears. Edmund was gone, and what was she to do now? Perhaps a part of her had secretly believed he would come and rescue her, but she saw now how ludicrous that was. Except Henry really had come to rescue her. Did it matter at this point who it was? What other choices did she have? Her father had been right; she had none. She could move on to a bigger city and hope to find work, or she could accept Henry and return to Merriweather–or wherever he wanted to take her–and resume her art. She was tired of fighting. Tired of running.

"Kate?" Henry asked, looking at her hopefully.

"I'll think about it," she conceded. "That's all the answer I can give right now." Another tear rolled down her cheek.

Henry's signature grin immediately reappeared. "Oh, Kate! You've made me so happy!"

Kate's eyes narrowed. "I didn't say I'd marry you, I said I'd think about it."

"Yes, yes, I know," he said, putting his arms around her. "But I just know that you will. I know you think I'm inconstant. And I have been. But not anymore. With you at my side, I can be the most trustworthy, constant man. You'll be able to set a clock by me. I can see it now! 'Henry the Constant, Henry the Dependable, Henry the Faithful' is what people will call me."

Kate, already filled with regret, allowed herself to be led back to the apartment.

CHAPTER NINETEEN

"Are you alright, darling?" Eustace asked as he led Melody past an impressively large wall of art. "You seem . . . how shall I say it? Distracted? Do you not like the exhibition?"

Melody glanced around L'Avenir Gallery, which was very chic, all glass and silver. "It's wonderful," she said and took a sip of her champagne. It really was a magnificent setting, but she was having a hard time focusing. Her mind continued to drift toward the letter she had received this afternoon, and she was still fuming at Freddy's audacity.

"There is a radiance about you tonight, *ma chérie*, that sparkles, even in this crowd. Like a brilliant cornflower in a field of hay, or a tender lily of the valley amongst the bracken."

Melody smiled weakly. At first his compliments had been unexpected and welcome, but now he had showered her with *so many* that they were beginning to lose their meaning. She had begun to wonder if he merely liked the sound of poetic phrases. And, if she were being critical, she would bet a large amount of money that he had never seen a hayfield in his life!

"I have a surprise for you, you know," he said, leaning toward her conspiratorially. He seemed in an exceptionally good mood tonight, which, sadly, was the opposite of hers.

A flicker of curiosity, however, rippled through Melody before she tempered it, remembering that Eustace's last surprise had been a leatherbound book of Latin sonnets.

"Oh?" She took another sip.

"I wonder if you can guess?"

She twisted her lips. "Probably not."

"I've had a letter from Mater and Pater!" he announced with relish.

Definitely would not have been her guess. She opened her eyes wide, feigning interest.

"They are returning early! They will arrive next week, and I must introduce you as soon as possible. I've been writing to them, you see, with much more frequency than usual, with the intent of procuring their blessing regarding a . . . well, let's just say it is in regard to something–no, *someone*–who is very dear to my heart."

He said this last part close to her ear, and as he hovered, she felt sure he might kiss her cheek. Instead, he pulled back and tapped her on the nose with one long finger.

"And I just received this very morning their consent regarding a question I have been longing to ask you for quite some time. There. That's all I will say for now, my little blossom. Do not attempt to tempt me further!"

Melody drained her glass, not liking the sound of this. She was pretty sure she could guess what question he wanted to ask, and she prayed he would not do so tonight; she was not in the right state of mind.

"You . . . you haven't mentioned anything about the art," she faltered and gave a weak nod toward the exhibits, hoping to distract him.

Eustace turned on his heel. "Ah, yes! Yes, well, they have some interesting pieces, I'll say that, but it's certainly not Roullier's."

He looked at her knowingly, and she nodded, pretending she could tell the difference between the two galleries.

"Yes, a bit too heavy on the modernists." Eustace glanced around the gallery again as if to confirm his opinion and then looked down at her. "But what do you think, my pet? Is it to your taste?"

Melody wasn't sure what to say. Most of the paintings around her were dull and colorless, the people bent and distorted amongst cartoon-like machinery or buildings. There was emotion in them, she decided, but none of them held any joy or hope, which was what she needed.

"Well, it's certainly . . . different."

Eustace laughed. "You are a gem, my dear, a perfect diamond in the rough. All you need is polishing. Mother will adore you!"

Melody squirmed under this praise–if it could even be called praise. She did not, for example, appreciate being referred to as "in the rough."

"Eustace Sinclair!" came a jovial voice.

Two tall, thin young men, each with red carnations in the buttonholes of their white suits, were making their way through the crowd. Eustace turned, and a genuine smile erupted across his face. He clasped one of the men's hands. "Biggsby? What are you doing here? And you, too, Collins? I haven't seen you in an age!"

The two men laughed heartily.

"Darling, we sail on Tuesday on the *Aquitania*," the one called Biggsby declared. "We are touring Europe for the summer. You simply *must* join us."

"Alas, *mes amis*, if only I could, but I have duties here."

"Don't be beastly, Stacey. You know you have no duties," Collins pouted. "You're always pretending you do, but then you don't. Not really." He peered at Melody now. "But who is this divine creature?"

"Ah! Waldorf Biggsby, Mortimer Collins, allow me to introduce you to Miss Melody Merriweather. Miss Merriweather, Mr. Biggsby and Mr. Collins. Good friends of mine from Yale," he said proudly. "But what are you doing here at L'Avenir?"

His voice had changed somehow. It was more entreating, and pitched higher to match Biggsby's own somewhat effeminate tone.

"Thought we might as well come for the opening, seeing as we're in town. Rather a waste of time, as it turns out, except for the happy chance of meeting you, dear Stace."

"Yes, it is rather a disappointment," Eustace agreed, gesturing weakly at the paintings.

"Pitiful, is it not?" Biggsby added.

"Oh, I don't know," Collins drawled. "I rather like it." He looked around appreciatively.

"But they've got it all wrong, Morty," Eustace exclaimed. "The balance is off. A whole wall of Sheerer? One, maybe. But a whole wall? It's positively obnoxious."

"Steady on, old dog. I rather like Sheerer."

"I'm not saying I don't like him. I appreciate his intellectual precepts—his attempt to enshrine the mundane of the current era and yet still ensconce universal truth. Though, personally, I think Albright does a better job of that. But what I object to is not having *any* classical pieces, at least for context. One cannot truly appreciate modernism without understanding what it's responding to. It strikes me as, well, a little too unbalanced for my liking."

"Agreed," Biggsby added. "But then it's symptomatic of everything that's wrong with the current art scene in Chicago. Art has become a commodity, like everything else, and this, apparently"–he gave his head a languid tilt backward–"is what the market wants."

Melody set down her empty glass. She was trying to follow the conversation but found it horribly dull. What struck her more, however, was the realization that Eustace rarely ever spoke to her in this way. Seriously, or intellectually. It was all fluff and metaphors and poetic verses. It was suddenly becoming clear that despite his worshipful compliments, he did not regard her as his intellectual equal. She was more like a statue he wished to possess for his statuary, something he could worship or adore, not love or respect. But why was this surprising? Most men did not regard their wives equal to them, she knew, and yet her father had seemed to. Well, in most things . . .

"You're much too reactionary," Mortimer argued. "There has ever been a chase after the new at the expense of tradition throughout all of history. You're confusing–"

"Excuse me," Melody murmured to no one in particular, "while I powder my nose."

Eustace abruptly turned his attention to her. "But of course, *ma petite muse*. Shall I escort you?" he asked, as if she were a child who needed her hand held to find the ladies' lounge.

"Thank you, no. Excuse me, won't you?" she said to Biggsby and Mortimer.

The two men each gave a slight bow. As Melody retreated, she heard Biggsby's voice.

"She's quite pretty, Stace. A little young perhaps. Surely you haven't professed yourself in love, have you?"

"As a matter of fact–"

Melody increased her pace, not wanting to hear anymore, though she imagined Eustace's smug face as he answered his friends. She thought she heard laughter.

Once out of earshot, she slowed, stopping in front of a piece she hadn't yet seen. She peered at the tiny brass plaque: *Winslow Homer*. She had never heard of Homer, but several of the paintings in this corner were his. They were of a more pastoral nature than the other exhibits, filled with light and color and a certain raw innocence. The people in them seemed very real, and yet the scenes had a sort of gauze over them, as if they were memories, fuzzy, from the past.

The piece in front of her, *Hills of Pennsylvania*, was a landscape of rolling hills with poppies in the foreground. It could easily be a painting of the hills of southwest Wisconsin, she decided, despite the title.

It made her suddenly want to cry. She moved to the next one, transfixed. It was of three children lying, carefree, in a field, and she felt another tug. The next was of a girl on a tree swing. Out of nowhere, her grief rose up and pierced her. The painting reminded her of the swing in the backyard of the Willows and how her father had pushed her on it when she was a little girl.

Melody's eyes bounced between all of the paintings, and she felt somehow in the presence of what could only be described as . . . well . . . as the Divine, as corny as that sounded. For an artist to be able to capture what was in her heart was extraordinary. But it wasn't just the composition (she had learned that word from Eustace) that evoked such emotion, it was the sense of place. She flicked her eyes to the big windows at the front of the gallery and watched the motorcars rumbling by, the city illuminated beyond it.

Suddenly, she felt an ache that nearly stopped her breath.

It was no use denying it anymore. She missed home. She needed to go back. She didn't belong here anymore.

"Ah!" Eustace said into her ear, causing her to jump. "You've discovered the Homers. And from your flushed cheeks, I detect an impression. Yes, most definitely an impression. But is it favorable, or no? My guess is . . . no," he ventured. "Yes, most definitely no. I can see it in your eyes. I quite agree with you, you know. Homer is technically accomplished, but on the whole, much too provincial." He let out a little sigh. "It's no wonder they have him displayed all the way back here by the lounges. They really do seem out of place–"

Provincial? Melody quickly looked them over again. She supposed he was right, but how could he so easily dismiss something that spoke so tenderly and yet so fiercely?

"Darling?"

She turned to look at him. Really look at him. *Why did he never call her by her actual name?* It was beginning to annoy her.

"I say, are you quite alright, my pet? You look rather peaked."

"Actually, no," she said, pulling her gaze from him back to the paintings. "I'm not feeling well. Perhaps you might call a cab for me."

"Call a cab? Don't be ridiculous. Clarence is outside hovering. He can take us."

"No, you stay with your friends. Where are they, anyway?" She perused the room.

"Oh, they've already gone on to Maxim's. They're meeting us there, if that's agreeable."

"Oh, no, Eustace! You go. Please. I . . . I want to be alone."

Eustace's face suddenly grew concerned. "What is it, *ma chérie*?"

"It's just . . . just a headache."

"Then we must by all means get you home." He held out his arm. "Come, I will escort you."

"I really am capable of getting home on my own," Melody protested, though she took his arm nonetheless, knowing that it was useless to argue.

* * *

There was very little conversation on the ride back to Mundelein. Eustace continued to ramble about the gallery, the weather, his parents' trip. Melody, under the guise of her headache, got away with saying very little and instead stared at the city lights as they cruised up Sheridan Road in the back seat of the roomy Duesenberg phaeton.

She fingered a fold in her red silk gown. Why was she here, wading around in luxury–luxury she couldn't really afford? For what? To find a rich husband, as Freddy, the nuisance, had suggested? She chanced a sideways glance at Eustace. Well, if that had been the goal, she was fairly certain that one was hers for the taking. But did she want him? She let out a sigh and looked back out the window.

Eustace, though perfect in almost every way, was somehow empty. He was a shell of a man who had nothing inside. For all of his enthused speeches about art and literature, he lacked any of the passion of the pieces he professed to adore. Nothing ruffled him–in a good way or a bad way. He proclaimed to worship her, but where was the feeling, the emotion behind the words? What good was having a love affair if it was devoid of love?

She thought back to Elsie's advice to allow time for love to grow, but she didn't think she could ever grow to love Eustace. Not really. She was tired of him, tired of the city. Admittedly, she had been charmed and attracted in the beginning, but Eustace was not, she had come to realize, actually attracted to *her*, just the *idea* of her–the young innocent country girl in need of culture and refinement at the hand of the wise professor. How long would it be before this grew old? Before she tired of his corrections and he tired of her faux pas? Already, he had begun to make small disapproving little coughs–like when she had gushed over the latest Errol Flynn film (seen with Cynthia and the gang, of course, not him, as Eustace claimed celluloid was not an acceptable medium for art), or when she laughed too loudly, or when she spoke to the servants as if they were equals. Recently, she had dared ask one of the maids if she might have the cook's recipe for the rhubarb tart so that she might send it to Helenka, at which Eustace had gone beyond the disapproving cough and twittered, "I say, Melody, is this wise? What need have you for such a thing?"

She wanted–needed–to go home. But what if her soulmate was somewhere else in Chicago? But maybe, she countered, her soulmate was waiting to meet her in Merriweather. Or maybe she had *already* met him . . .

Heat rose to her cheeks as her mind drifted again to Cal, though he was certainly *not* her soulmate. Even if she did admit she might be in love with him–*which she wasn't!*–he most certainly did not love her, so it didn't matter. *And* he was leaving. She let out a long, deep breath and looked back out the window. *Oh! How soon could she get back?*

The car came to a smooth stop in front of Philomena, and Eustace quickly exited. "I'll do the honors, Clarence."

"Very good, sir," the chauffeur responded dully.

Eustace elegantly strode in front of the car, the headlights briefly illuminating him. He opened the door for her, and she slid out, not looking forward to saying goodbye. After tonight, she doubted she would ever see him again, and a part of her did feel a little sad.

Once they were outside the thick, arched double doors, she pulled her arm from his and held out her hand.

"Goodnight, Eustace. It was a lovely evening."

"But will you not ask me in?"

The girls of Philomena were allowed to entertain gentlemen in the downstairs parlor until ten thirty, and Eustace had been in the habit of joining her there at the end of each evening together.

"Not tonight, Eustace."

"Very well," he said with reluctance. "Might I call tomorrow?"

"I . . . I don't think so."

Eustace's brow furrowed. "But why?"

"I'm going home, Eustace."

Eustace stared at her. "Home? But you *are* home, *chérie*."

"No, I mean Merriweather."

"You are?" He looked confused. "When?"

"I . . . I don't know. As soon as possible." She bit her lip, dreading the conversation she would have to have with Sr. Bernard.

"How long will you be gone? I was hoping to introduce to Mater and Pater this weekend," he practically whined.

"I'm not coming back, Eustace. It's no use staying here."

"What?" Eustace was aghast. "You can't possibly be serious, Melody." (For once, he was using her actual name!) "You are tired. Overwrought by that infantile Homer."

Melody groaned. "But I *am* serious, Eustace, I–"

"Tut-tut! Do not speak of it!" He put a finger to her lips. "You will no doubt feel differently in the morning when your headache is gone."

"No, I don't think I will. Goodbye, Eustace," she said, holding out her hand again.

He instead rubbed his brow. "Good God! You can't mean it, darling. I . . . I quite love you. I . . ." He paced on the front porch. "Oh, good God! This is not how it was supposed to happen, but–"

He broke off then and thrust himself down onto one knee. "Melody Merriweather, will you marry me? Will you be my wife!" he declared, managing a little triumphant flourish despite the anxiety he clearly felt.

"Eustace! No!" Melody hissed. "Get up!" She prayed Cynthia and the gang were not watching from behind the curtains.

"Melody, please," he said, rising now and clutching her hands. "Forgive the crude nature of this proposal, It was supposed to be in the drawing room next Saturday, with Mater and Pater looking on . . ."

"It's not the propsal, Eustace."

"Why then?"

Melody's stomach twisted. "It's because I don't love you, Eustace."

His face fell. "But can't you grow to love me? I'm certain that you will. Only tell me what to do, and I'll do it."

But that was just the point. She didn't want to have to grow into loving someone, like wearing in a new shoe.

"Think, Melody," he urged desperately. "Think what you'd be giving up."

She *had* thought about it and had determined that she would be giving up too much by marrying him, but she struggled with how to say this. She didn't want to hurt him unnecessarily. "It's not you exactly,

Eustace. It's . . . it's my family." (Which was partially true.) "I made a mistake. I should never have come back. Everything's a mess at the Merc, and I have to figure it out."

"Something that your brother, a Harvard Law student, cannot manage?" he asked incredulously.

"No, it *isn't* something he can figure out. *He's* the problem."

"Melody, this is insanity. Is the fate of a dry-goods store worth your future?"

Melody did not answer.

"I don't wish to be indelicate," Eustace hurried on, taking her silence as a crack in her defense, "but in marrying me, there will be certain . . . funds at your disposal. And I would of course never turn my back on my wife's family. They would be well provided for, Father assures me. So, you see, you don't really need this 'Merc.' You can allow it to gently, nobly pass away into the annals of history."

Melody's heart beat a little faster. Eustace made perfect sense, and his offer of financial assistance was tempting. She could use part of it to pay Douglas back for his ring! But how absurd would it be to take the money from one suitor to pay off the other!

And no, she could not bear to let the Merc "pass away." She wasn't about to abandon what had been her grandfather's store, and then her father's, and then . . . well, *hers*. Not Fred's, or anyone else's. *She* had saved it from utter ruin–she and Harriet and Kate and Cal and Rosemary and Imogene and, yes, even Mrs. Haufbrau.

"I don't think you understand," she said sadly.

"Perhaps not, but I want to, my pet. Very badly." He was staring at her quite intently now. "I'll wait for you."

Melody searched his face. *Why didn't he do something? Take her in his arms, kiss her, shake her, something . . . !*

"Kiss me," she suddenly demanded.

"Kiss you?" He looked around uneasily. "Here?"

"Yes. Here. Right now."

He hesitated for a few moments and then took a deep breath. "Very well." He clutched her upper arms and gave her a quick peck on the lips. "There you are!" he said almost triumphantly. "You have been kissed."

Melody opened her eyes. She had felt nothing. Nothing like how she imagined a kiss should feel, thinking back to Psyche and Cupid. "I'm sorry, Eustace. It's no use." She put her hand on the doorknob.

"But was it not good?" he asked hurriedly. "Let me try again!"

"No," she said sadly, not bothering to differentiate between his questions. "I just need to go home."

CHAPTER TWENTY

Henry Crawford left Shullsburg, but true to his word, he attempted to prove his constancy and his love by sending a different gift to her, and thus the Prices, every day thereafter. Indeed, there were so many delivery people creaking up the stairs the following week that Sam likened the dingy apartment to Grand Central Station, not that he had ever actually been there.

"And not that I mind!" he had declared gleefully, after a ham, a beef loin, a two-pound box of chocolates, a basket of flaky pastries, two bottles of cider, and another huge bouquet of flowers had been delivered. The last had just arrived this morning and was addressed only to Kate, with a note:

Dearest Kate,

It has been my utter joy and delight to shower you with gifts this past week, and I hope these small efforts prove the constancy I am capable of and the devotion I feel toward you. Would that I might have this privilege for eternity.

It was my intent to attend you tomorrow, but, alas, I have just now been called back to Chicago on some rather pressing business. I will return as soon as I am able, but I live in hope that I might write to you and that you might this time deem my letters at least worth opening.

Yours eternally,
Henry Crawford

Kate tossed the note onto the table and examined the bouquet. This one consisted of the palest blue irises she had ever seen. They were beautiful. After staring at them for several moments, she allowed herself to sniff them, but, alas, they had no perfume. All show and no substance, Kate thought bitterly. How appropriate.

"He's sure sweet on you, ain't he?" Ann asked from where she was mashing potatoes over the oven. "You gonna go for him? Susie, find her a jar for those."

Susie began searching the cabinets while Kate momentarily studied the ceiling. "I don't know, Ann. He's . . . he's not . . . well, I'm not in love with him, if you know what I mean," she revealed.

Surprisingly, Ann did not have her usual quick retort. "There ain't no shame in marryin' for money, Marie," she said into the potatoes. "*I* married for love and look where it's got me." She glanced sideways at her. "You could do a mite worse than this Henry Crawford. Not like he's a stranger. A friend of your friends. They can vouch for him, can't they?"

"Found one, Ma!" Susie declared. "Had to dump out the buttons, but I–"

"There's someone comin'!" Jenny interrupted from where she sat by the front window, Barbara on her lap. In the rare times when she wasn't working, Jenny could usually be found by the front window, staring, like a caged bird peering out at the world. What Kate could never ascertain was whether she was happy as such, or if she, like Kate, perpetually longed to fly away.

For a moment, Kate feared the visitor might be Henry. It was something he would do–write her a note saying he was going away and then show up as a surprise.

"Good Lord!" Ann exclaimed delightedly. "Another delivery? Wonder what it'll it be next?"

"It's not a delivery, I don't think," Jenny said. "He doesn't have anything in his hands."

Footsteps sounded on the rickety stairs now.

"Is it Mr. Crawford?" Ann asked.

Jenny shook her head. "I don't think so."

Still holding the bouquet of irises, Kate flung open the door, ready to chastise Henry for his prank, only to come face-to-face with Edmund Bertram.

"Flowers?" he said sheepishly. "For me?"

Kate stared at him disbelievingly for a moment or two and then threw her arms around his neck, crushing the flowers in the process. "Edmund!" she cried. "Come in! What are you doing here?"

Edmund removed his hat and stepped tentatively into the apartment. He looked around cautiously, his eyes meeting Ann's.

"Edmund, this is my sister Ann," Kate said quickly. "And this is Susie and Jenny," she said, pointing to each of them. "This is my friend, Edmund."

"Yes, we can see," Ann commented with a wry smile. "Another one."

Kate handed the crushed flowers to Susie, who placed them in the jar of water without bothering to pick out the broken stems. She was much more interested in what was unfolding before her.

"Won't you sit down?" Kate asked, gesturing toward the front room. She could barely think what to ask first.

"I'm afraid I haven't time. I . . . I've come to take you home, in fact. If you'll come, that is."

Kate stopped and looked at him, confused.

"Your mom is very ill, Kate, and your dad sent me to get you," he said in a low voice. "Please come. It's rather serious."

Kate's stomach dropped. "What do you mean she's ill?" Fear filled her.

"They're not sure, but the doctor suspects diphtheria."

"Good Lord!" Ann declared. "You best go, Marie."

Kate looked desperately around the apartment, trying to think. "Yes . . . yes, of course I'll come. I'm sorry, Ann. Let me just get my things," she mumbled, moving toward the corner where she had stored the old carpetbag.

"Are you comin' back?"

It was Jenny. She had crept up, Barbara on her hip.

Kate was surprised to see tears in Jenny's eyes. Kate's throat suddenly ached. In truth, she had no qualms about leaving the Prices. But she did feel bad about having to leave Jenny, to whom she had grown oddly attached. "I hope so," she said softly, putting a hand on the side of the girl's head. "But I guess I can't live here forever, can I? Taking up your sofa?"

"I don't mind." Jenny's voice quivered. And then, despite the fact that she was still holding Barbara, the little girl threw an arm around Kate's waist. "Don't go!" she mumbled into Kate's dress.

Kate kissed the top of her head and then squatted down. "I'll come back," she said softly. "I promise." She brushed a finger along Barbara's downy cheek.

"I wasn't the evil stepsister, was I?" Jenny whispered, staring at Kate with big, desperate eyes.

"Oh, Jenny," Kate said, embracing the two of them again. "Of course you weren't. None of you were. I'll come back. I promise."

Jenny didn't say anything, but she maintained her grip.

"Kate," Edmund urged quietly.

Kate rose. "I have to go now. But here–" She rummaged in her carpetbag and pulled out a worn, leather-bound sketchbook. "Here, you take this."

Jenny set Barbara on the floor, who immediately plopped a finger in her mouth.

"What is it?" the girl asked, turning the book over, her sadness momentarily quelled.

"It's my sketchbook. You take it and fill it with your own drawings or maybe stories. Then when I come back, you can show me. Okay?"

Jenny smiled her tiny smile and then threw her arms around Kate again. Kate gave her a final kiss on the head. Jenny released her then and furiously rubbed her eyes with the back of one hand.

Kate picked up her bag and hurried to the front door where Edmund was still waiting. She paused to give Susie a quick hug and Ann a longer one.

"Thanks for everything, Ann. I'll come back. Tell Sam and the boys I said goodbye."

"I will. They'll be sad to see you gone."

"Well, we both know Sam won't." Kate smiled. "But maybe the boys will."

"Oh, don't you mind Sam. His bark is worse than his bite." Her eyes looked sad, too. "You will come back, won't you, Marie? At least to visit, like?"

"Yes, I will. I promise."

* * *

Edmund had left his old Studebaker running. He helped her up into the truck, tossing her carpetbag in the back, and then swung himself into the driver's seat. As he thrust the old truck into gear and pulled away, Kate gave one last look out the back window at the ramshackle Gordon's Tap. She had thought that maybe Jenny or Susie or even Ann might follow her down the stairwell, but there was no one.

Neither she nor Edmund spoke until he had turned onto the main street.

"I'm sorry we had to meet like this," Edmund said, shifting into a higher gear. "I would have rung you if they, the Prices, I mean . . . if they had a telephone."

"Is she bad?"

"Yes," Edmund said, chancing a glance at her. "I . . . I don't know if she's going to make it, Kate. I'm sorry."

Tears sprang to Kate's eyes. "How long has she been sick?"

Edmund cleared his throat. "A couple of weeks."

A couple of weeks? Why hadn't Henry mentioned it? "Oh, Edmund! This is all my fault!"

"*Your* fault?"

"I should never have gone away. I've been so stupid and selfish!"

"You? You're the least selfish person I know." He gave her a sad smile. "This isn't your fault at all. You know she's never been the same since Eula and Fern." He broke off. "She's not strong."

Blearily, Kate looked out the side window. "What about Louisa and Nettie? Aren't they there?"

"Louisa's been at your Aunt Bea's in Milwaukee to get some things for the wedding, and Doc Hodges advised that she not come back for fear of her getting it, too."

"And Nettie?"

Edmund let out a little sigh. "Nettie's there, but she stays in her room mostly, terrified of catching the fever herself."

"So, they sent for me," Kate mumbled bitterly. "The expendable one."

"That's not true," Edmund insisted. "Your mom's been asking for you. Calling for you. 'Specially during the nights, apparently."

Kate buried her face in her hands, unable to hold back her tears.

"Hey, there, Possum," Edmund said soothingly and rubbed her back with one hand, his eyes darting between her and the road.

At the touch of his hand, a wave of comfort radiated through her, which, oddly, made her sob harder.

"Kate, hey. It's going to be okay. Whatever happens, it'll be okay."

With a supreme effort, Kate stopped her tears and sat up, wiping her eyes with the back of her hand. "How's Dad?"

"Worried sick." Edmund reached into his pocket and handed her a handkerchief. She wiped her eyes and then blew her nose. "What about you?" he finally asked. "How are you? You must be happy to have found your family."

She wanted to declare that they weren't her family, that the Kerwyns were, that *he* was . . . "Well, I did write a letter home, but no one responded."

"Yeah, your mom was telling me she got a letter," he said, missing the point. "That was before she got sick."

Kate didn't say anything.

"Henry mentioned you, too." He glanced sideways. "Said he paid you a visit."

"What did he say?"

"Just that you seemed . . . content . . . I think is how he put it. That he hoped he might yet still have a chance." Edmund pulled his eyes from the road and looked at her full on now.

Kate remained silent, but her heart was beating hard.

"Does he, Kate?" Edmund shifted into lower gear and rolled the truck to a crawl at a stop sign.

No, Kate suddenly realized. No, she couldn't. Being with Edmund again and feeling the way she did for him, like her heart was going to implode at any moment, convinced her that she could never marry without love. Maybe if she had never known love . . . but she did, and it was torturous. "No," she finally answered, trying to keep her voice steady. "No, I can't marry him."

"I don't see why." Edmund glanced both ways and then pushed the accelerator with his boot. "He's a very good man."

"Why does everyone keep telling me that?"

"Well, I don't know about everyone else," he said, "but I'm saying it because . . . because I guess I'd like to see you settled. Happy. Before I–" He looked out the side window and then back. "Look, I was going to tell you later, but I suppose now's as good as any. I'm thinking of proposing to Mary Crawford."

Kate felt a faint flicker of hope. "You aren't already engaged?"

"Nearly," he said with a sideways crooked smile.

Kate pressed her lips together so hard it hurt. Had Henry exaggerated for his own gain?

"I'm hopeless at this sort of thing," Edmund went on. "So, I was hoping that you might . . . that you might help me. You know, put in a good word for me, or think of a romantic way to ask her."

Kate choked back a new wave of tears and stared out at the stark, leafless landscape.

"You *do* like Mary, don't you, Kate? I want you to love her as much as I love you–as a sister, that is. That's why it would be absolutely perfect if you were to marry Henry. It would be like two siblings marrying two siblings! Then we'd really be family, just as we always imagined."

Kate's throat was positively aching. Several moments of silence passed. She should say something *right now*, but what?

"Can you not say something?" Edmund asked, a little nervously.

What could she possibly say when the only boy–no, man–she had ever loved was about to marry someone else and was asking her to help bring it about? If Mary were someone that Kate loved and trusted, she might find a way to be happy for him, but she did not feel that way about Mary, or Henry either. She suspected the Crawfords of something . . . underhanded? Perhaps that was too strong a word. Certainly, something disingenuous. Did no one else see this?

She cleared her throat. "I think Mary is a very lucky girl," she finally managed.

"I knew you liked her!" Edmund exclaimed, his eagerness rewriting her meaning. "I trust your judgement completely. And you know, she reminds me of you in so many ways. The similarity is uncanny, really."

Kate wanted to scream. Did he really think the two of them were similar? It was maddening! And if he trusted her judgement "completely," why did he not trust her refusal of Henry?

"But . . . but what about your plan to enlist? Has she come around to your way of thinking?"

"Well, you know," Edmund said with a little shrug, "guess that can wait. Guess it wouldn't hurt to wait and see what happens over in Europe."

"But that's what you've always dreamed of doing, Edmund!"

He paused. "Well, I guess two people have to sometimes sacrifice if they want to be together."

Kate clenched his handkerchief, irritated by how much Mary Crawford had twisted him around her finger. What was *she* sacrificing for this relationship?

There were several minutes of silence again before Edmund spoke. "You know," he said, slowing down to turn onto County E, "there *was* a time when I thought that perhaps you and I . . ."

She quickly turned, her anger dissipating as a specter of hope rose. She allowed her gaze to linger on all of his features, which had become so familiar and so dear to her—the sharp angle of his jaw, his tiny scar, his dimpled chin.

"Yes?" she asked, almost in a whisper.

"I just thought that . . . that maybe you and me might end up together." He tried to laugh as he turned into the Kerwyns' lane, but it died away. "I guess that was just foolish fancy," he said with an attempt at a smile. "Especially since I've met Mary."

Kate's lips flattened into a thin line. This was her chance to say something, but what? "Yes . . . yes, I thought there might be something between us, too," she finally managed.

His brow raised in surprise. "Is that so?" He glanced at her and let his gaze linger. "Well." His eyes reverted back to the lane as they rounded the bend. "I didn't realize."

The Kerwyn farmhouse came into view, then, and as happy and relieved as Kate was to see it, she held her breath, hoping that maybe . . . perhaps . . .

"Well, I guess that's all in the past now, isn't it?" He shut off the engine and turned to her again. His tone was light enough, but his face looked . . . a little sad? Regretful?

"Does it . . . does it have to be?" she dared, but she was immediately cut off by shouts from her father, who had appeared on the porch.

"Kate? That you?" he called, making his way across the muddy yard.

Kate swung the door open and slid out, suddenly filled with horrible dread.

"Aren't you a sight for sore eyes!" Mr. Kerwyn embraced her tightly, as if nothing disagreeable had happened between them. "Come on, girl," he said, his face deeply etched with worry as he picked up her carpetbag. "Let's get you inside." He tromped through the mud toward the farmhouse. "Thanks, Ed!" Mr. Kerwyn shouted over his shoulder.

"Yes, thank you, Edmund. I–"

"Come on, Kate! Hurry!" Mr. Kerwyn's voice boomed again. "Yer ma's been asking for you. Doctor was just here. She ain't too good, Kate." He turned around on the porch steps, and Kate read the panic in his face. "She ain't too good," he said in a strangled sort of voice and looked as though he might . . . might cry.

With a bang, Kate slammed the truck door and began to wade through the mud after her father. She did not have boots on, of course, which made it more difficult. Was her mother actually dying? What if she didn't get to say goodbye? She began to try to run, but it was like trying to wade through molasses.

After only a few paces, one of her shoes got stuck in the ooze, her stockinged foot coming free and landing with a squish. For a split second, she debated trying to pull the shoe from the mud, but she didn't want to take the time. She would come back for it later! She continued her slog until she finally reached the porch and banged inside. She kicked off her other shoe.

"Mom!" she called, running up the stairs. Her father lumbered after her.

Edmund, meanwhile, having retrieved Kate's shoe from the mud, slipped into the kitchen and sat down to wait.

CHAPTER TWENTY-ONE

"I'm home!" Melody shouted as she banged through the front door of the Willows. She waited. "Anyone here?" she called again, setting her bags down.

She hadn't told them she was coming, wanting it to be a surprise, but she hadn't anticipated that *no one* would be home. *Where was Helenka?* Melody removed her hat and coat and, out of habit, rifled through the mail basket on the Chinese table. Nothing of interest. She hoped, now that she was home for good, that her friends–Cynthia in particular–would prove to be better correspondents.

Cynthia, as predicted, had been beside herself when Melody confessed her plan to return to Merriweather before the term ended.

"But why, dearest? Is it Vivian? She *has* been a pill lately." Cynthia tapped her foot impatiently, thinking. "Oh! It's Eustace, isn't it?" she guessed excitedly. "Have you had a lovers' quarrel? Oh, please say that's it. You'll be back together in no time! Are you rushing away to see if he'll give chase? How clever!"

Melody sighed. "No, that's not it at all," she said forlornly as she leaned against Cynthia's bedroom window frame. "I've broken it off with him. For good."

Cynthia was aghast. So much so that Melody almost laughed.

"You can't be serious, darling. Why?"

"He's not for me, Cyn. I just don't love him."

"You've barely given him a chance!"

Melody fingered the curtain and watched the cars whiz round Sheridan's curve. She wasn't sure how much to confide in Cynthia, to whom, she had to admit, she no longer felt as close an attachment. She now much preferred the quiet staidness of Elsie or even the simple companionship of Harriet. Cynthia would never understand her desire to go back to her little hometown in Wisconsin, and she certainly wouldn't understand her giving up Eustace Sinclair, nor her undeniable feelings for a certain someone else . . . She let the curtain drop again, suddenly feeling flushed. She had not ever told Cynthia about Cal–*why would she?*–and there was no point in mentioning him now.

"Well, sometimes you just know, Cyn."

"Melody, he's *rich*. Fabulously rich. You could grow to love him."

Melody let out a deep breath at the echo of Eustace's similar plea. But she abhorred the thought of having to *grow* into loving someone. Shouldn't there be at least some spark in the beginning?

"Why don't *you* go for him, then?" Melody suggested.

"It's a thought." Cynthia twisted her lips, contemplating. "But dearest, you know I can't. I'm practically engaged to Charlie. I can see him trying to work out how to propose. It's really too, too funny!"

Melody gave her a weak smile.

Cynthia let out a little groan. "You're not any fun anymore, Mel. You used to always be up for a laugh, and now you're, well . . . you're so serious all the time."

Stung, Melody was about to retort when she paused. She supposed Cynthia was right. But wasn't that all the more proof she didn't belong here? She had thought she could slip back into these shoes, but they no longer fit. She no longer cared about being at the top of Mundelein's social ladder, and her "fling" with Eustace had been anything but light and fun. Now that it was over, she realized how serious and heavy it had become. And there was home to worry about, too.

Melody absently picked up a torn ticket stub lying on Cynthia's bureau and fingered it. Maybe the loss of her bubbliness lately had nothing to do with Eustace or worry over the Merc, or—God forbid, Cal. Maybe it was something else, something deeper and infinitely sadder . . .

"Well, my dad did just die," Melody said quietly. "Maybe that's it."

Having spoken her grief aloud, she suddenly missed home more than ever. She desperately wanted to see her mother. She would even be glad to see Bunny.

"Oh, darling!" Cynthia cried, jumping up and embracing her. "What an absolute beast I've been! Of course you are sad, poor thing! Of course you need to go back. It's perfectly understandable. What a selfish, selfish girl I've been!"

Melody allowed herself to be hugged for several moments before finally muttering, "You're not selfish, Cyn. I didn't mean to make you feel guilty." She took a step back, but one hand remained on her friend's shoulder. "But, let's face it; you're going to get married soon anyway, and I . . . I guess I'm just worried about things back home."

"Of course you are. Not another word. I'll help you pack." She looked under Melody's bed for a suitcase. "When are you leaving? Now? But you *will* come back for my wedding, though, won't you?"

Melody let the various bills and advertisements slip through her fingers back into the mail basket.

"*Rany boskie!*" exclaimed Helenka now, coming from the kitchen with a tray in her hands. "What are you doing? Something happen?"

"Hello, Helenka!" Melody smiled. "I'm back!"

"*Ja*, I see. But why?"

"I . . . I decided I missed everyone too much. So, I've come home!"

"For good?"

"Yes, I think so. What's that?" She nodded at the tray.

"For your mother. I take to her."

"Oh, let me!" Melody begged, taking the tray from a somewhat reluctant Helenka. "It'll be a surprise! Where is she?"

"In bed," Helenka said, as if it were obvious.

"In bed? Is she ill?"

A strange ripple crossed Helenka's normally stoic face. "Not ill, just sad. She's not the same. You know?"

Melody hadn't thought about how Helenka might be faring since her father's death. After all, she and Mums had been more like friends these past twenty-odd years.

"Not to worry," Melody said as cheerfully as she could then proceeded up the stairs. Helenka watched her for a few moments, as if contemplating following, and then silently retreated back to the kitchen.

Melody knocked briefly on her parents'–now just her mother's–door, but there was no answer. "Mums?" she called softly pushing it open with her hip.

"Just set it there, Helenka," Mums mumbled. She was lying on her side, her back to Melody. Melody hurriedly set the tray on the vanity and rushed around to the other side of the bed.

"Mums!" she said, trying to keep her voice cheerful. "It's me!"

Mums lifted her head off the pillow, her eyes fluttering open. "Melody?" Her voice was rough.

"Yes! It's me, Mums!"

Mums awkwardly struggled to sit up, and Melody was surprised to see that she was still in her nightgown.

"What are you doing here?" Mums asked. "What's wrong?"

Melody put her arms around her mother. "Nothing's wrong." She kissed her temple. "I missed you. I couldn't stay away any longer."

"How long are you home for?" Mums's face was not one of disapproval. Instead, the hope that fluttered there was more crushing than any scolding could have been.

"Forever, I think!" Melody said, straining to keep the cheer in her voice. "I found I can't live without you and Bunny and Fred, and well, everyone."

"Oh, Melody, really? I'm so relieved. Nothing's been the same since you left. I've been so . . . so tired. You can't imagine."

Her mother did, in truth, seem tired . . . and much older. She looked like she'd aged twenty years, and it set off a panic in Melody, as if she had somehow missed twenty years of her mother's life. She switched on the bedside lamp, hoping it would help dispel some of the gloom, but it only served to illuminate how unkempt her mother looked. She wore no makeup, and her hair looked almost matted, as if she hadn't brushed it in days. *Oh, why had she left! How stupid and selfish she'd been!*

"Not to worry, Mums! I'm here now!" She deposited another kiss on her mother's head and strode to the window, throwing open the drapes. The sun immediately flooded in, nearly blinding Mums, who quickly put one arm over her eyes.

"Melody! Close that! It's too bright!"

Melody obliged, though not entirely. She left the drapes open a crack to let in at least a sliver of light. It was clear she had a lot to do to make up for lost time.

"Would you like some of the tea Helenka sent up?" Melody asked brightly.

Mums shook her head slightly. "No more tea. I'm tired of it."

"How about I run you a nice bath, and then we can sit and have a chat? You can tell me everything that's been happening."

"No, Melody, I'm not in the mood for a bath."

By the look of her, Melody guessed that she had not been "in the mood" for a bath in several days.

"I think you'll feel better if you do."

"Now you sound like Helenka!" Mums chastised, raising her voice slightly.

"Helenka's very worried about you."

"What did she say?"

"She didn't say anything, but I can tell just by her face that she's sad that you're sad."

"Well, I have a right to be sad."

"That's true, Mums. No one knows that better than you," she added softly. "But we're all sad. We *all* miss him."

The few stray tears that ran down Mums's face nearly caused Melody's heart to break. She sat down on the bed and put her arm around her mother. "Come on, Mums. You've got to rally. That's what Pops would have wanted, wouldn't he? What is it he used to say? 'Can't lie in bed and sulk all day! People die in bed, you know!' "

Mums let out a little grunt that could have been a cry or a laugh. "He did say that, didn't he?"

"What does it even mean? Doesn't everyone die in bed?"

"Well, not if you're in a war, or something." There was silence for several long moments, and then her mother spoke again. "I miss him. I miss him, Melody."

"Me, too, Mums." Melody leaned the side of her head against her mother's.

They remained in comfortable silence until Melody lifted her head.

"Come on. Have a nice bath, put on something pretty. I'll do your hair and tell you all the news from Chicago."

"Oh, alright," Mums said wearily.

Melody immediately shot up and began running a bath in the adjoining room before her mother could change her mind. She added a generous scoop of bubble powder and rummaged through the closet for the fluffiest towel she could find. Thankfully, her mother insisted on undressing herself, and once she heard her step into the water, Melody knocked briefly and then poked her head around to make sure all was well.

"You soak for a while," Melody instructed, "while I unpack."

Melody hurried down the staircase to the foyer. She was just reaching for her suitcase when the front door opened, and Bunny bustled in.

"What are you doing home?"

"I've decided to come back," she said matter-of-factly, holding the case in front of her with both hands.

"Why?" Bunny rifled through the mail basket. "Are you on break?"

"No, I've come back for good."

Bunny stared at her, disbelievingly. "But why?"

"Oh, I don't know." Melody heaved the case onto the first step. "A lot of reasons."

"Does Mums know?" Bunny asked as she removed her coat and hat and hung them on the rack.

"I was just up there telling her. She looks terrible, Bunny." Her tone was slightly accusatory.

"Well, don't blame me!"

Melody sighed. "I'm not exactly blaming you, but I . . . I guess I'm just surprised is all. And worried."

"Well, we've all tried. Even Fred."

"You might have written me."

"So that you could do what exactly? Anyway, I thought Fred might have mentioned it."

"I did not receive a single letter from him. Or from you."

"Likewise."

Melody let out an irritated breath. She hadn't been home an hour, and she was already quarreling with Bunny.

Bunny squared her shoulders and gave her blonde hair a toss. "Listen, Melody, I want to discuss something with you. I wasn't sure how I was going to undertake it, but now that you're here, it just might work."

Melody's brow furrowed. "What is it?"

"I want to go live with Miss Elliot."

"What?"

"Just for the summer. I . . . well, the truth is, I want to try to get into Julliard, and Miss Elliot has agreed to help me prepare. It will require hours and hours of practice a day, and I can't manage that here."

"But what about school? High school, I mean?"

"Well, I am graduating next month, if anyone around here cares to remember. I'm not ten any longer, as you all seem to think." She rolled her eyes.

In truth, Melody *had* forgotten that Bunny was graduating, but she wasn't about to admit that. "Well, why can't you practice here?"

Bunny rolled her eyes. "On *this* piano? It's ancient. It barely stays in tune from week to week. Miss Elliot has a Steinway, and that's what I need. It's really my only chance."

Melody wasn't sure which item to address first–the fact that Bunny wanted to be away all summer or that she had hopes to go to Juilliard.

"Bunny, I . . ." She hesitated, trying to choose her words carefully. "I'm quite proud of how much you've been able to achieve and how . . . how dedicated you are, but I don't think we can–"

"Yes, yes, I know. We can't afford it. But Miss Elliot thinks I have a good chance at a scholarship. I've mentioned this before, but either no one is listening to me, or no one thinks I can actually do it. It's time everyone in this family treats me with some respect. I'm not a child! And Pops told me to try my hardest and never give up," Bunny said, her voice wavering slightly, "and I don't mean to. Why should I?" she added with more resolve. "Fred's quit school, and now you have, apparently. But I'm not going to! There's more to life than this stupid little town! I have a chance, and I'm taking it!"

Melody rubbed her eyes with her fingers. Not Bunny, too. "Okay, Bunny. I'll . . . let me think about it."

"That's what you said the last time, and you didn't. No one ever thinks of me. I need a decision soon!"

Melody let out a deep breath, trying to think on the spot. "Well, I *suppose* you could stay with Miss Elliot for the summer," she said haltingly. "Provided she's agreeable to the idea. Is she?"

"She's the one who suggested it!" Bunny gestured angrily.

"I'm assuming we'd have to pay room and board?"

"I don't know the particulars." Bunny folded her arms now. "I hadn't gotten that far."

"Okay, I'll . . . I'll think about it. I promise."

"And don't tell Fred."

"Well, he'll have to know at some point."

"Yes, but come to a decision first. You know what he's like, and he's become even more insufferable than he was before. He's one of the reasons I want to leave! I've tried complaining to Mums, but you can imagine how that went."

"Speaking of, I need to go help her out of the bath."

"You got her to take a bath?" Bunny raised her eyebrows.

Melody didn't answer, but hurried up the stairs, wondering how, in the space of an hour, she had somehow become the parent of not only her sister, but her mother as well.

CHAPTER TWENTY-TWO

Kate sat beside her mother's bedside, attempting to read a book, but she was distracted by her mother's irregular breathing. Doc Hodges had announced yesterday morning that it was his opinion that Mrs. Kerwyn had finally turned the corner, but he had warned that her recovery would be long and slow.

Still, Kate insisted on taking most of the shifts beside the sickbed, which the rest of the family seemed grateful for, especially her father, who had so far made no comment about her stay in Shullsburg nor the argument preceding it. Nettie and Minnie begged for stories about her "other" family, but Kate was reluctant, feeling like it would be a betrayal to report their poverty and eccentric mannerisms, especially when they had been so kind as to take her in. Louisa, meanwhile, had not yet returned from her sojourn with Aunt Bea in Milwaukee, though they had telephoned to report that Doc Hodges had given the all-clear. Kate sighed. That girl would do anything to avoid work.

Kate, on the other hand, was glad to be the one to sit by her mother, as it gave her a chance to make up for lost time and to really think about her experience with the Prices. Though the Prices were her blood relatives, the Kerwyns, she realized now as she took her mother's worn hand in hers, were her real family. All her life, every time she had heard the story of the Kerwyns finding her as a dirty, wandering toddler, she had always felt a deep sadness for that little girl, separated from her family and raised by one that looked so very different from herself. Now, though her heart still ached for that lost little girl, she was finally accepting that she hadn't lost her family–she had found them.

She was loved, and she belonged. She *had* been the lucky one, just as Sheriff Norris had insinuated.

She stroked her mother's hand and felt ashamed that she had called the only mother she had ever known "Mrs. Kerwyn." Her stubbornness, she feared, would someday be her downfall.

"Oh, Kate!" her mother croaked, her eyes fluttering open. "You're back?" Her voice was thick and raspy.

Kate jumped from her reverie. "Yes, Mom! I'm here now." She gently brushed her mother's hair back with her free hand.

"Oh, Kate, I've missed you. I'm so sorry."

"I'm the one who's sorry." Kate felt a lump rising in her throat. "I shouldn't have gone away."

Her mother closed her eyes again for a moment and then opened them. "Help me up, Kate," she said, her voice still weak. "I want to tell you something."

"Mom, don't talk right now. Just rest."

"No, Kate." Mrs. Kerwyn tried to sit up on her own but failed and fell back into her pillows. "I need to say something."

"What is it, then?" Kate asked gently, reaching behind her to try to adjust her pillows.

"I'm sorry about Ray."

Kate stopped her fluffing and sat back down.

"I'm sorry that he . . . that he hurt you. That I was too wrapped up in my own grief to notice. And, I'm sorry I didn't believe you when you were a little girl. I do now, though. And I thank God he let me live long enough to tell you that."

She closed her eyes again, evidently exhausted from her little speech. After only a few moments, though, she opened them and gave Kate a little smile.

"You're as much my daughter as Louisa or Nettie or Minnie," she went on hoarsely. "Maybe more so. I've always loved you, maybe the most."

Kate's eyes filled with tears. "Oh, Mom." She wrapped her arms awkwardly around her mother's frail body. "Oh, Mom. I'm sorry. I'm sorry I've been such a spoiled wretch."

Her mother tried to embrace her back, but her arms were weak. "Did you find your family?"

Kate convulsed into sobs now. "*You're* my family! I'm sorry I went away." After a few moments, she sat up and tried wiping her tears.

"We all need to know where we came from. Otherwise, we won't know where we're goin', will we?" Mrs. Kerwyn patted Kate's wet cheek and then closed her eyes. "I'm so tired, Kate. I'm gonna sleep now, okay?"

"Yes, you sleep," Kate urged and took hold of her mother's hand again. She remained at her side until her mother's breathing became deep and regular. Only then did Kate release her hand and creep from the room.

Once in the hall, she leaned against the wall, exhausted. It was tempting to retreat to her attic room and cry, but she supposed she should probably go downstairs and make sure everything was ready for the morning. The house was oddly quiet.

As Kate turned toward the stairs, Nettie was coming up.

"I'll sit with her for a while," she offered.

"Thanks, Nettie. She's sleeping pretty deeply right now." Kate passed her, but then looked back. "Where's Minnie?"

"In the front room, I think. Reading."

"What about Dad?"

"Still out in the barn."

Kate wandered into the darkened kitchen, only to jump when she saw the silhouette of her father, still in his overalls and work boots, hunched over in a chair.

"Dad!" Kate switched on the overhead light. "You nearly gave me a fright! What are you doing sitting here in the dark? Do you want some coffee?"

"No, that's alright." For the first time, he looked old to Kate. "I can't lose her, Kate," he said, looking at his boots. "I can't live without her."

"We're not going to lose her," she tried to say confidently, placing a hand on his shoulder. "I was just with her, and she spoke a little."

"She did?" He looked up eagerly. "What'd she say?"

"Not a lot. She was just glad to see me, I think. Nettie's with her now. She's sleeping."

"I'll go up," he said, pushing himself out of the chair. "I'll change first."

A light knock sounded on the door.

"That'll be Ed. Said he'd stop by. He's leavin' for Chicago in the morning."

Leaving for Chicago? Kate's insides roiled. Since she had returned, she had seen Edmund only at a distance, crossing the farmyard or going in and out of the barn, but she hadn't yet had a chance to speak to him. Even if she had, what would she say?

"Why is he . . . why's he going to Chicago?"

"Darned if I know. He ain't the big city type. I think he's chasin' after that Mary Crawford. Asked me what I thought of him marryin' her."

"What did you say?" Kate asked, barely above a whisper.

Mr. Kerwyn shrugged. "Well, I says, why not, if that's what you're thinking, but don't know if she's the farmwife type. She seems to like the finer things in life."

There was another knock.

"Come in!" her father called. "You know you don't have to knock, Ed!"

The door opened a crack, but it was not Edmund; it was Henry Crawford.

"Hello, Mr. Kerwyn. Kate," he said pleasantly.

"What're you doin' here, Henry?" Mr. Kerwyn asked. "Thought you were in Chicago."

"I came back to consult with Frank on one or two points. But I'm returning tomorrow, so I've offered to drive Edmund. It will be nice to have a companion on the road. But I couldn't leave again without calling in to see how Mrs. Kerwyn is doing. And all of you," he said, his eyes darting briefly to Kate.

"Well, that's mighty kind." Mr. Kerwyn thrust his hands into his overall pockets. "She's doing well enough; wouldn't you say, Kate? Holdin' her own."

"Yes," Kate said hesitantly. "She's improving."

"You want some coffee or somethin'?" he asked Henry. "Kate was just gonna make some. I'm goin' up to get changed. Sit with Caroline awhile. Have a good trip," he said absently and shuffled across the room.

Kate was tempted to beg him to stay, but it would be useless; he was too eager to get up to her mother, and maybe he still held out hope that she would change her mind about Henry.

Kate crossed to the stove and began busying herself with the coffee pot.

"How are you?" Henry asked gently.

"I'm fine." She filled the pot with water. "*Do* you want coffee?"

"No." He took a step closer. "Did you . . . get my note?"

She set the coffee pot down but still did not turn to him. "I did. I suppose I should thank you for all of the gifts." She turned finally. "The Prices enjoyed them very much."

"And the flowers?"

"Yes, they were lovely. You shouldn't have spent so much." She leaned against the counter.

He cleared his throat. "Have you thought about my proposal? Do you yet have an answer?"

Kate's stomach clenched. She dreaded telling him the bad news.

"Kate," he hurried on, perhaps sensing her hesitation, "I can't stop thinking about you. You occupy my thoughts night and day. Please say you'll have me." He crossed the room and stood in front of her. His deep green eyes probed hers. "Have I not proven I can be constant?"

"It's only been a week, Henry," she said wearily.

"Kate, please," he begged. "Marry me. Make me a better man. With you, I can be different. I'm sure of it."

Kate studied him a final time, making sure her decision was the right one. He remained the most handsome man she had ever seen, but it was no use.

"No," she said as gently as she could. "It's no use, Henry. I can't marry you."

"But why?"

"Because I love another, as you know," she added quietly. "And I always will."

"You're sure?" His voice was sharper than it had ever been, and a muscle in his jaw tightened. Several alarm bells inside of Kate began to sound.

"Yes, I'm sure, Henry. I'm . . . I'm very fond of you, but I just can't. Please understand."

Henry's face further contorted. "After all I've done for you? The money I've spent?" he snarled.

Stunned, Kate took a step back.

"This is absurd!" he cried, beginning to pace. "You're a fool. Edmund will never marry you, and who else is there? You'll die a spinster; mark my words!"

Kate stared at him, incredulous. "Are these the words of a gentleman?" she finally sputtered.

"Oh, don't get all high and mighty with *me*! You know, I–" He took a step closer and, for just a trace of second, she was afraid he might strike her. "I've been mistaken. Grossly mistaken. I hope you'll be happy here in the life you have chosen, Kate Kerwyn. Or should I call you Marie? Neither suits," he spewed with distaste. "I'm through with you."

He stormed out the back door, letting the screen bang behind him.

Her chest heaving, Kate watched him go and then dropped into one of the kitchen chairs. *How dare he!* She braced her head in her hands, her thoughts whirling. *She had been right about him after all!*

When she heard her father's heavy boots on the stairs, however, she straightened and twisted in her chair.

"Henry leave already?" he asked.

"Yes, he had to go," Kate said matter-of-factly and stood up. She moved toward the counter, trying to shield her face from her father.

"What's wrong? You upset? " he asked, concerned. "Is it cause of Ma? Or was it something Henry said?"

"It doesn't matter, Dad." She gave him a weak smile. "I'm alright."

"Still after you, is he?"

Kate raised her shoulders slightly and prayed he would not chastise her for rejecting Henry Crawford again, or worse, encourage her to change her mind.

Her father scratched his head. "You know," he began, but then paused. "I didn't mean what I said before. It came out wrong. I don't think of you as less-than, Kate. I just wanted you to be loved and cared for. I thought Henry might do the job. But you have to do what you think's best."

Kate wiped a tear and fought desperately to keep the rest at bay. "Thanks, Dad," she said hoarsely.

Her father looked awkwardly around the room. "They nice to you, those people in Shullsburg?" He rubbed his upper arm nervously.

"They were, Dad," she said, releasing a deep breath. "But I'm glad to be home."

CHAPTER TWENTY-THREE

Kate woke early the next day, unable to sleep. After today, she thought, staring at the ceiling, Edmund would be engaged, and there was nothing she could do about it. Or was there? Should she say something? Beg him to reconsider? Not for herself, she emphasized, but because she was sure he would be unhappy. Mary and Henry were two peas in a pod, and if the brother had a darker side, might not the sister?

But that was ungenerous. Would she appreciate being judged by the actions of Ray? Though Ray wasn't *really* her brother. Well, then what about her *real* sister, Ann Price? Would she like to be judged by Ann's actions? This, she knew, was also ungenerous . . .

Finally, when the first birds began to twitter, she pushed aside her quilt and got dressed. She crept down the stairs as quietly as she could and started breakfast. Not long after, her father came down, already in overalls, and pulled on his boots.

"How's Mom?"

"Slept pretty good." He had insisted on staying with her the entire night. "She's a bit better, I think. That coffee ready yet?"

He pulled on his jacket. Gone was any trace of the yesterday's emotion, but Kate was not offended. This was his way. She handed him a mug of steaming coffee.

"Call me when it's ready," he said, referring to breakfast, and stepped out onto the porch.

Kate heard the crunch of gravel.

"Ed's here," her dad said through the screen before clomping down the steps. Kate perked her ears, trying to determine if Ed was following her father to the barn, or if he was headed into the house. She braced herself when she heard his footfall on the steps. As she wiped her hands on a dishtowel, she tried to prepare what she would say.

"Hello!" Edmund called, opening the back door. "Got any coffee?" He was dressed in his good black suit and church shoes, and he must have put on cologne, because he smelled nice, like pine and soap.

She poured out a mug of coffee and handed it to him. "Thought you would've left already."

"Nearly. I'm riding in with Henry. Gotta go pick him up in a minute." He smiled crookedly. "Any last words of advice?" His eyes were bright as he took a sip of coffee. "I'm surprising Mary, you see. She doesn't know I'm coming."

Kate desperately wanted to continue the conversation they had begun in his truck, but she didn't know how. Should she simply blurt out that she loved him? But he obviously didn't love her back, not in that way, or he wouldn't be dashing off to Chicago to propose to Mary.

She cleared her throat. "Just be yourself." She forced a smile. "Always the best policy, I think."

He looked at her admiringly, a half smile tugging at his lips. "That's my Kate. Practical as always."

Practical? That wasn't how she wanted him to see her! Didn't he see her as pretty or funny or intelligent or . . . or anything besides practical? *Brooms were practical.*

"Well, goodbye, then, Kate." He bent and kissed her quickly on the cheek. "No running off while I'm gone, mind you!" he teased.

It was now or never, or she would have to forever hold her peace. She opened her mouth to say something, anything–

Mr. Kerwyn shuffled in. "Thought you were leaving today," he said to Edmund.

So, never, then.

"I am, Mr. K. Just came to say goodbye."

"Dressed mighty fine." He looked him up and down. "You'd think you were off to meet the queen. You'll be back in a couple of days, won't ya? Don't take but two minutes to get engaged, and we gotta get the corn in."

Edmund gave an embarrassed little laugh. "Well, I don't know about that, Mr. Kerwyn. About getting engaged, that is. She still has to say yes, like. But I'll be back by Sunday, either way." He plopped his hat back on his head. "Bye, then!" he said cheerily. "Wish me luck!"

And before Kate could say another word, he was gone.

* * *

Kate spent the weekend in a very dark mood. Time seemed to tick by with horrible slowness. Almost every hour of every day, she envisioned Edmund holding Mary, whispering things in her ear, kissing her. Her only consolation was that she was sure the newly wedded couple would reside in Chicago, so she would at least be spared seeing them on a regular basis. No chance of running into Edmund at the post office, or the Merc, or church. It would be as if he had joined the army.

Yes, she decided, this was how she would try to think of him from now on. Not blissfully married to another, but marching around in some army base or fighting somewhere in Europe. Maybe someday she would write him a letter, telling him her true feelings. But what good would that do? It would be too late. It was already too late; she had missed her chance.

She tried distracting herself by tending her mother, cleaning the house (again), and even enlisted Minnie's help to put in the garden. It was the one chore Minnie didn't have to be threatened or scolded into doing. She seemed to have a natural affinity for growing things, and she willingly raked up the dead growth from last year and dug fresh rows.

It was oddly comforting, Kate found, to dig in the earth with one's hands. It made her think of the badger hole, and she decided that she would return there as soon as she could, if only to use it as a workshop, as she could never leave her mother again, at least not for a long, long time.

Leaning on her hoe, she thought of Jenny Price, who would likewise probably be the one to stay behind and care for Ann and Sam in their elder years. Kate wished she could somehow rescue the girl, as she herself had been rescued from the very same family by an odd twist of fate! But she could hardly bring her here to live, so what else was there? Writing to her? Encouraging her? Sending her things? Maybe books or sketchbooks? But would the other kids be jealous and torment her as a result? And who knew if Ann would even give them to her.

Well, Kate decided, she would at least write to the girl and see if she got an answer. If not, she would make it a point to go and visit sometimes.

Through the open kitchen window, Kate heard the telephone ring. She dropped her hoe and hurried inside, glancing at the clock as she did so. It was likely Doc Hodges, calling to check on her mother's progress.

For a split second, she wondered if it might be Edmund . . . but she squelched that thought as she hurriedly wiped her hands on a dish towel.

"Hello?" she said eagerly into the receiver.

"Merriweather 657?" asked the operator.

"Yes, this is 657."

"Go ahead," the operator instructed the caller.

"Caroline?' It was not Doc Hodges, nor Edmund, but a woman. "That you?"

Kate was pretty sure it was Aunt Bea. But why would *she* be calling?

"No, Aunt Bea," Kate answered quickly. "It's Kate. Is something wrong?" Her thoughts ran to Louisa.

"Oh! Is your mother or dad there?"

"Mom's lying down, and Dad's out in the barn."

Aunt Bea groaned. "I suppose I'll just have to tell you, then. I have the most dreadful news! It's Louisa! I'm so very sorry! And so very vexed, mind you."

"What is it? Is she okay?"

"She's run off and gotten herself married!"

Married? Despite the shock, Kate let out a breath of relief. She had thought that maybe Louisa was . . . well, dead. "She and Vernon ran off?" Considering the pomp and circumstance Louisa had been insisting on for her wedding, Kate found it odd that she would simply abandon it all in favor of elopement.

"No! Not Vernon!" Aunt Bea's voice crackled over the line. "With some scoundrel by the name of Henry Crawford."

Kate suddenly felt faint. Henry Crawford? "When?" she asked hoarsely.

"Couple of days ago, I think. Never even heard her mention him. Said Ray was coming to take her back home, which was clever on her part, as she knows I can't abide Ray and wouldn't want him to come in to say hello. I must admit, I shamefully left the cleaning of her room for a few days–Uncle Elmer's gout's been acting up something terrible, and I had my hands full. But still, this is all my fault! If I'd gone into her room sooner, maybe something could have been done? Oh, dear, oh dear!" the poor woman cried.

"Aunt Bea, I don't understand."

"What I'm saying is that when I *did* go into her room to gather up the bedding, I found a note. Thought maybe it was a little thank-you note, but good Lord! I never thought it would be this! Oh, what are we going to do? Your mother will never forgive me!"

Kate wasn't sure that was the preeminent problem, but she did not say so. How could Louisa have done such a thing? Poor Vernon!

"I . . . I'd better get off and go tell Mom and Dad," Kate finally stammered.

"Oh, I can't think how your poor mother will take it. This might be the death of her, an all. Is she any better?"

"A little, yes. I'll ring you back, okay, Aunt Bea?"

"Oh, please do! Do you think I should come down?"

Kate tried to concentrate. "Not just yet. I'll let you know. Thanks, Aunt Bea." Kate hung up the receiver and leaned against the wall.

How dare Henry Crawford! What a wretch!

As horrified as she was, a tiny part of her felt vindicated. It had only been a few days ago that he had professed to love *her*. And now he had run off with Louisa! And what about Louisa? How could she betray them all this way? Betray poor Vernon? It would be all over town in a few days . . .

Kate pressed her fingers to her eyes. How was she going to tell her parents?

* * *

The family, as predicted, was thrown into an uproar. Not wanting to upset her mother in her precarious state, Kate told her father first. Kate had half expected him to throw a fit, but he had instead simply slumped into a chair and put one hand over his eyes. He was a different man lately–all the fight seemed to have gone out of him. Thinking back, Kate judged the change in him to have first started when Ray left. But then there had been her own rejection of Henry Crawford and her subsequent flight to Shullsburg, Mom nearly dying, Edmund wanting to marry and possibly leave, and now this.

Kate put her hand on his shoulder.

"This is going to kill yer ma," he said, lowering his hand from his eyes.

"I know, Dad."

"Don't tell her just yet. I'll think of a way." Mr. Kerwyn let out a deep, broken sigh. "Go get my brandy." He had since replaced his special bottle with cheap stuff.

Kate did not think it was a good time to start drinking, but she left the room and obediently returned with the brandy.

"Did Bea say where they went?" her father asked gruffly.

"No."

"Wonder if I could get the sheriff after them." He pulled out the cork and drank straight from the bottle.

"I don't think that would do any good, Dad. I think they're probably married by now."

"She better be." He slammed a fist on the table, causing Kate to jump. "How could she do this to us? What are we gonna tell the Tierneys? The wedding was only a month away!"

The screen door creaked open, and Nettie stepped in from her shift at Ben's. "What's wrong?" she asked, shrugging out of her coat. "Why the long faces? Someone die?"

"Louisa's eloped with Henry Crawford," Kate said quietly. "We just found out from Aunt Bea."

"What!" Nettie cried. "When?"

"A couple of days ago, we think."

"But what about the wedding! I've already got my dress fitted!"

"Well, the wedding is obviously off. And I think your dress is the least of our worries, Nettie."

"How selfish can she possibly be?" Nettie cried.

"Quiet down!" Mr. Kerwyn barked. "Yer ma doesn't know yet, so quit yer bellyachin'. It ain't gonna help."

Nettie walked to the kitchen table as if in a trance. She pulled out a chair and slid into it, cradling her head. "Wasn't it enough for her to have Vernon, but to take Henry, too?" Her eyes had tears of fury in them. "Now I'll never get married!"

"I think you're exaggerating a little, Nettie," Kate said ruefully.

"No, I'm not! No one'll court me with a sister like that! They'll tar me with the same brush."

"Just give it time. People forget," Kate tried to say reassuringly, but in her heart she knew that some, like herself, were not prone to forgetting.

Mr. Kerwyn rose heavily. "I'm goin' up to talk to yer ma." He shuffled across the room. "Then I'll have to go over to the Tierneys' and let them know. Wouldn't do to say it on the telephone. You two best get supper started," he said wearily, and tramped up the stairs.

CHAPTER TWENTY-FOUR

Melody managed to get Mums dressed and downstairs for dinner, a fact that seemed to surprise not only Bunny and Fred, but Helenka as well, who was utterly delighted that her mistress was up and about again. Melody had done her mother's hair and encouraged her to dress in her favorite red polka-dot dress, which, Melody observed sadly, was now rather too big. Thankfully, her mother did not seem to notice, even when Melody suggested tightening the belt a little.

Leola Merriweather had never been what one would call thin, even as a young woman, but she was the type whose extra curves were attractive. In short, she suited being plump, and now that she was not, she looked drawn and old. *How could she have lost this much weight in such a short space of time?*

Well, she had decided as she handed her mother a bright red lipstick, she would find a way to fatten her up. She had also found, while rummaging around the room, several bottles of pills, one of which appeared to contain sleeping pills! No wonder her mother had seemed catatonic. Why had

Doc Hodges prescribed them? She longed to question Fred, but she knew she would have to wait.

Dinner was pleasant enough. The food at Mundelein was exceptionally good, and she had been out for countless dinners with Eustace, but Melody welcomed one of Helenka's home-cooked meals. Tonight, she had prepared a lovely roast chicken, the skin golden and crispy, with fluffy mashed potatoes, gravy, early spring peas, a dandelion salad, and a lemon cream cake for dessert.

As they ate, Melody attempted to regale them with stories about Chicago, but she quickly realized that unless she wanted to reveal her relationship with Eustace, there was not too terribly much to tell. Likewise, seeing as she had thrown all that over for good, it didn't make sense to start explaining everything from the beginning.

"Did you see much of Douglas?" her mother asked pertly.

As much as she wanted her mother to participate in a conversation, this was not a subject she wished to dwell on. "Not much," Melody answered with a small shrug.

"But why not? He seemed so keen when he came at Christmas," Mums mused. "You haven't argued, have you? I really thought you'd be engaged by now, Melody."

Melody let out a little sigh. "Well, things didn't really turn out with Douglas, Mums. He's . . . he's actually seeing a friend of mine now."

"What?" Mums cried. "Well, it can't be anything serious. I know a man in love when I see it!"

"Yeah, Mel. How'd you screw that one up?" Fred asked as he bit into a roll slathered with butter. He had been as surprised as the rest of them to find Melody flitting around the house when he walked in the door after work and, like the rest of them, had initially queried what had happened.

Melody had breezily informed him that she had decided to come home and would explain it all later. She had no desire to battle Fred after what was probably a stressful day at the Merc. She needed him to relax before she sprang her ideas on him.

"I didn't 'screw it up,' Freddy," she retorted. "He proposed to me, and I rejected him."

"Rejected him? Why?" Mums exclaimed.

Melody shifted in her chair. She squirmed to think what they would say if they knew she had rejected yet another young man in the meantime.

"I don't know, Mums. He wasn't right for me."

"Wasn't right for you, my foot! In my day, girls weren't so choosy."

"Yes, but there was a war on then."

"I don't see what that has to do with it. I think you're just being silly, Melody."

Melody resisted the urge to roll her eyes. She didn't need Mums confirming what she sometimes suspected about herself. However, she was glad that Mums was showing some of her old spunk. She was glad she had removed all the pills, tucking them safely away in one of her own desk drawers.

"How is school, Bunny?" Melody asked in an attempt not only to change the direction of the conversation but to include her younger sister more. Perhaps then she wouldn't want to leave. "Only four weeks left, isn't there?"

"Yes. And it can't go fast enough. I don't see why I have to learn geometry and typing and home economics! It's all so meaningless."

"Well, I'm not sure about geometry, but I should think typing and home economics would come in handy. Thank you, Helenka. That was delicious," Mums said as the older woman began clearing the plates.

"I am glad you think so." Helenka beamed. "I will bring dessert now and coffee."

"They won't help me in the slightest at Juilliard," Bunny rebounded.

"Juilliard?" Freddy scoffed.

Bunny's chin jutted. "Yes, Juilliard, Freddy. I'm planning to apply." Bunny glared at Melody. "I thought you said you would talk to him."

"Well, I haven't exactly had a chance!" Melody retorted. "We'll talk about it later, Fred. Why don't you tell us about the Merc? I'm dying for all the news." And she really was. It was all she could do upon alighting from the bus from Chicago to not immediately rush to the store instead of trudging toward the Willows. Seeing how badly Mums was in need of help, however, she was infinitely glad she had resisted.

"News?" he said sourly. "There isn't any. Everything's the same. Nothing ever changes there. You know that."

Fred, however, had. In the past, he had always been a bit of a teaser, but now he was decidedly more bitter. Almost mean.

Melody knew from Harriet's letters that the Merc had *in fact* changed, but she didn't press the point. "Well, how's Mrs. Haufbrau?"

"Yes, how is Marcella? Oh, this looks delicious, Helenka!" Mums said as Helenka placed a piece of lemon cream cake in front of her. It was an extra-large piece, Melody noticed, and she was grateful that she and Helenka seemed to be of one mind regarding the fattening up of Mums.

"She's fine. The same," Fred answered.

"Well, how about Harriet? Is she ready for the wedding? It's June, right?"

"How should I know? I didn't even know she was engaged. Look, I don't get involved with the employees like you did, Melody. Maybe that was your problem."

"Well, Pops did," Melody retorted, taking a bite of cake and glancing briefly at Mums, hoping the mention of Pops would not upset her.

"Listen, I didn't critique you when you were running it, so maybe you can lay off," Fred snapped.

"No, but you're sure doing a good job at it now. According to you, I didn't do anything right!"

Fred shoved a huge bite of cake into his mouth. "Well, if the shoe fits!" he garbled.

Irritated, Melody was tempted to flounce upstairs as she might have done in the past, but she had no wish to leave her mother, who might then be tempted to go back to bed.

"Must you two fight?" Mums said tiredly. "You haven't been back two minutes, Melody, and now you've upset poor Fred."

Poor Fred?

Melody bit her lip. "Why don't we have a game of rummy after dinner?" she suggested.

"Oh, yes!" Mums replied with surprising eagerness. "I haven't played in ages."

"You three can, but I'm tired. I'm going to relax a bit." Fred tossed his napkin onto the table and rose. "I'm glad you felt well enough to come down, Mother," he said to Mums and then retreated to the parlor.

"See what I mean?" Bunny snipped. "He's insufferable!"

* * *

Several games of rummy later, Mums, Melody could tell, was exhausted. Not only was she making mistakes, but she kept asking whose turn it was whenever it was hers. Likewise, Bunny claimed to have homework and again complained about not being able to practice in the evenings because it bothered Fred. Helenka kindly offered to help Mums undress and get her into bed, so Melody took it as the perfect opportunity to approach her brother.

He was sitting in Pops's study, in Pops's old chair, a cigar smoldering in the ashtray beside him and a glass of what looked like whiskey on the side table. He was rifling through the newspaper. It was such an obvious attempt to be Pops that she didn't know whether to laugh or cry. She took a seat on the sofa near his elbow.

"Hey, Fred."

"Mmhmm?" he said from behind the paper.

"I think we should talk."

"About what?" He lowered the paper. "About what you're doing home? I have a sneaking suspicion that you quit, but I'm hoping I'm wrong."

Melody rolled her eyes. "Well, I did quit, Fred. I'm home for good, and I'm taking the Merc back!" she declared and then instantly regretted it. Hadn't she planned to carefully ease into the topic? In her eagerness, however, she had stupidly blurted it out.

"No, you're not!"

"Yes, I am!"

"No, you're not!" Fred crumpled the paper and tossed it aside.

"Look, Fred, this is silly. I'm not happy at school, and you're not happy here. Let's just go back to the way things were."

"We can't, Mel. Pops is dead, for one thing. And the Merc is in trouble."

"Yes, I'm aware. I was trying to do something about it."

"By selling baskets and bottles of cider?"

"Well, it was a start. Frank says that–"

"I'm not interested in what Frank and Julius have to say. They're a couple of pansies, if you ask me. If they want to waste their time and money buying up old mining cottages and trying to make them into tourist attractions, good luck. We need cash! Now."

"Yes, but reverting the Merc to what it was fifty years ago isn't going to do it. Think about it. In Grandfather's day, it was a supply store that outfitted men for the mines. Then when Pops took over, he expanded it and made it more of a general store. Now it's our turn. If Frank and Julius are going to bring tourists in, we should at least be considering that. Homemade, local things are appealing to travelers."

"I don't know, Mel." He took a drink of his whiskey. "The whole thing seems a bit harebrained."

She crossed her arms. "Well, I've got other ideas, too."

"Like what, sell luxury scarves?"

"No," she retorted. "I was thinking that maybe we could make part of the shop into an . . . an art gallery." She unfolded her arms. "Or . . . have performances. Or poetry readings. Something like that." These new ideas had emerged on the bus trip home, but now that she said them aloud, she admitted they sounded somewhat idiotic.

Fred laughed out loud. "You've gone crazy now! Chicago has ruined you."

"No, it hasn't, Fred. At least let me try. What harm can it do?"

"Well, we could lose the whole damn thing, that's what. We're about a month or two away from it, anyway. The books are in terrible shape, Mel," he said forlornly.

"Yes, I know. So, what harm can there be in trying something new?"

Fred stared at her for a few moments, thinking, and then buried his face in his hands. "This is all my fault."

"*Your* fault?"

"I keep thinking that if I had been here, maybe he wouldn't have had so much worry. I could have helped him. Maybe he wouldn't have had a heart attack. And I wasn't even here when he died!"

His shoulders shook. Melody couldn't remember ever seeing her brother cry.

"Fred, it's not your fault," she said gently. "It's no one's fault. It was just his time. And he *did* drink whiskey and smoke cigars every night. That *might* have had something to do with it." She glanced at the smoldering cigar. "You don't really want this, do you?"

He looked up blearily and shook his head.

Melody reached for the cigar and snuffed it out.

"I'm sorry I've been an ass lately," he moaned.

"You haven't been an ass, exactly. Maybe a little self-righteous."

Fred wiped his eyes with the back of his hand.

"It's okay to go back, Fred. I'll take the Merc back over, and if it fails, well, then it fails. We'll both know that we gave it our best shot to stop the ship from sinking. I know you feel bad about Pops, but this is not what he would have wanted. He was so proud of you."

Fred reached into his pocket for his handkerchief and blew his nose loudly. "I didn't even thank him. Not really."

"Mums was right before. If you're so concerned about us staying afloat, finish your law degree. That's the best thing you could do for the family."

"I'm worried about her, you know." He stuffed his handkerchief back into his pocket. For the first time, she noticed the bags under his eyes. He looked exhausted, too.

"Yes, I found sleeping pills in her room. Did you know about them?"

Fred rubbed his brow. "Yes, she wasn't sleeping. Having terrible nightmares. Some nights even sleepwalking. Doc Hodges said it was to be expected and that we should give her two tablets at bedtime. I . . . I didn't know what else to do."

Melody pressed her lips together. She wanted to reprimand him, tell him that he should have simply spent more time with her, but she had no desire to make him feel worse than he already did. "Well, I don't think she needs them anymore. I've put them in my room for the time being."

Fred stared absently at the opposite wall.

"So, are we agreed?" she asked tentatively.

Fred slowly turned his gaze to her. "About what? The pills?"

"No. You're going back to *school*," she said slowly, as if speaking to a child. "And I'm staying here to look after Mums and the Merc. Agreed?"

He blinked a few times. "You sure, Mel?"

"Yes, I'm sure." She held out her hand. He took it and gave it a firm squeeze. "To be honest," she went on, "I'm looking forward to getting back. I miss it, and everyone."

"Why?"

"Oh, I don't know. I suppose it reminds me of Pops."

"It reminds me of him, too, which is one of the reasons I don't like being there. It makes me sad all the time," Fred said. "Especially with Mrs. Haufbrau around. She's still fully arrayed in black, you know. She gives me the creeps."

"She's okay, I suppose."

"I know, but why all this excessive mourning?" He was silent for a minute or two. "You don't think . . ." he began.

"What?"

He stared at her for a few moments, as if deciding whether to proceed. "You don't think that there . . ." He coughed slightly. "That there might have been something between her and Pops, do you?"

"Pops?" Melody sputtered. "*And Mrs. Haufbrau?* How can you say such a thing, Freddy?"

Fred shrugged. "I don't know. It's just an idea."

"I could never imagine Pops . . ." Her voice trailed off. Though it might explain some of Mrs. Haufbrau's odd devotion to her father . . .

Fred stood abruptly and went to their father's desk in the corner. "Look, I found these." He opened the top drawer, pulled something out, and came back to hand Melody a small pile of photographs.

Melody looked at the top one. She had never seen it before. It was a picture of a very young Leola and Lou posed near a lake. The next one was of Pops holding a fish he had just caught, obviously from the same trip as the first photograph. Melody looked up at Fred questioningly.

"Just keep going."

The next one was of her and Fred and Bunny as little children. They were in a field somewhere. Melody's heart tugged a little. "Oh!" she murmured. "Isn't this sweet?" She held it up.

"Yes, but that's not the one I wanted you to see. It's the next one."

The last one in the pile was of a group of people posing outside the Merc. Melody recognized her grandfather, Pops, Imogene, Lyle, old Billy, and . . . she squinted . . . Mrs. Haufbrau? If it *was* Mrs. Haufbrau, she was a much younger Mrs. Haufbrau. Melody squinted again. The young woman definitely looked like a version of Mrs. Haufbrau, but what was different was that she was smiling. A big, wide smile, almost as if she were . . . laughing. *And*, she noticed with an odd chill, her father's arm was around her.

She looked up at Freddy again.

He raised an eyebrow. "See what I mean?"

"But . . ." She studied the photograph again. "Mrs. Haufbrau is probably old enough to be his . . . his mother or something."

Fred shrugged. "That's what I thought, too."

And why does she look so happy? I don't think I've ever seen her smile."

"Me neither."

"Did you show this to Mums?"

"Of course I didn't! Now is not the time. Maybe someday, but–"

"Maybe someday, but what?" Bunny asked, poking her head around the partially closed pocket door. She pushed it all the way open with a loud rattle.

Melody quickly tucked the photos under her skirt. "Nothing." She wasn't sure why she was being secretive; there was nothing to hide!

"Are you discussing my education, or simply rehashing your old love affairs?" Bunny asked pertly. "Because I won't be put off for 'someday' for much longer. Can I go and stay with Miss Elliot, or not?"

CHAPTER TWENTY-FIVE

"Come on, Kate, can I go over to the Koenigs' or not?" Minnie begged, her lower lip sticking out. "I never get to do anything fun!"

The two of them were working in the garden, though Minnie had been itching to leave all morning. Kate raised herself from the row of new peas and wiped her brow. Before she could answer, however, a vehicle rattled down the lane.

"It's Edmund!" Minnie cried. "He's back!"

Kate lifted a hand to shield her eyes from the sun and saw that it was indeed Edmund's old Studebaker. She carefully stepped over the rows and stood at the edge of the garden, wiping her hands on her apron, and watched the truck roll to a stop. *Be happy for him. Be happy for him.* She repeated this over and over. He had not returned yesterday as predicted, which Kate had not known how to interpret. Perhaps he was having such a marvelous time in Chicago with Mary that he had stayed an extra day. Or had he gotten caught up in the mess with Henry? Or should she say, his soon-to-be brother-in-law?

Her father had already been to see Mr. and Mrs. Tierney and poor Vernon, who had, Dad reported bitterly, actually cried. No one had yet been able to trace the runaway couple.

The door of the truck swung open, and Edmund emerged. He was again dressed in overalls and boots rather than the fancy suit and shoes he had left in.

"Hi, Edmund!" Minnie called, running up to the truck. "Did you bring me something from Chicago?"

"Minnie!" Kate scolded.

"Well, did you?" she asked, ignoring Kate.

"Matter of fact, I did." He handed her a small brown bag.

Minnie peeked inside. "Candy!" she cried. "Oh, thanks, Edmund!" She gave his middle a brief hug and then jogged across the yard toward the house.

"I didn't say you were finished!" Kate called after her.

"I'll be right back!" Minnie shouted and pounded up the back steps.

"Hi, there," Edmund said, looking at Kate with his crooked smile, his dimples showing.

Kate's insides twisted, and she had to momentarily look away. "You're back," is all she could think to say, finally forcing herself to look up at him, tenting her eyes with her hand. She inhaled a deep breath and then let it out. "Am I to congratulate you?"

Edmund let out a weak little chuckle. "Sadly, no."

"No?" *Had Mary rejected him? Or had he changed his mind?* "What . . . what happened?" She tried not to say it too eagerly.

"Turns out she wasn't there." He smiled sheepishly. "My big surprise failed."

"What do you mean she wasn't there?"

Edmund stuck his hands in his pockets. "She was staying downtown with a friend, apparently. At least that's what the housekeeper told me."

"Edmund, none of this makes sense! Start from the beginning."

"Well, there's not all that much to tell. Henry dropped me off at their house in Oak Park. Said he had some business to attend to, but that Mary would be there to entertain me."

Kate wondered if his "business" had been to drive back to Wisconsin and abscond with Louisa!

"He wished me luck, and all that. You see, I had asked him on the way for Mary's hand, seeing as they have no parents, and he said she and I could do as we pleased. That he had no jurisdiction over his sister and that she was free to choose as she liked. So in I go, but turns out there's no one home except an old housekeeper. She tells me that 'Miss Mary' is not at home. It was hard to understand her to be honest. Had a strange way of speaking."

"They live there alone?"

Edmund shrugged again. "Guess so. Their parents died. Left the two of them that big old house. It's nice enough, but it's a little shabby. Has a lonely feel to it."

"So, it was just you there?" Kate found this whole story incredibly odd.

"Well, there was the housekeeper, as I said. And a cook, I think. Maybe another maid. I'm not sure. The housekeeper was able to get me to understand that Miss Mary was staying downtown with a friend. She was clearly suspicious of me, though I tried to explain that I was a friend of Mary and Henry."

"How strange that Henry did not come in and explain . . ."

"Well, he was obviously unaware that Mary wasn't home. Seemed in a mighty big hurry." He scratched his chin. "Anyway, I finally got the housekeeper to understand me, and she took me upstairs to one of the guest rooms. Kept bringing me coffee and tea and cookies. I asked if she could telephone Mary or Henry, but she kept saying, 'No number, no number.' I stayed the night and the better part of the next day waiting for Mary to turn up, until I came to my senses." He let out a deep breath. "It was my own fault. I should have told her I was coming. I left a note for her and hitched a ride back home. So much for me trying to be romantic. I feel like an idiot." He smiled sheepishly again.

Kate stared at him, bewildered. But this meant that he was . . . that he was not yet engaged . . . "So you never saw either of them?"

He shook his head. "No, Henry never came back, either. I was tempted to just stay and look around the old place–so many rooms and nooks and crannies, and real interesting things on the shelves, stuff from Egypt an' all over–but I couldn't afford to do that, not with all the work back here."

"But . . . but what about Henry and Louisa?"

"Henry and Louisa?" He seemed genuinely confused.

"You haven't heard the news?"

"What news?"

"Henry and Louisa have eloped. That must have been why he was in such a hurry."

Edmund's face slackened. "What?"

"Yes, they . . . Louisa left a note at Aunt Bea's. It's been a few days already. He must have dropped you off and immediately drove to Milwaukee to run off with Louisa."

"But why drive to Chicago at all? Why not drive directly from Merriweather to Milwaukee?"

"Perhaps to get his affairs in order? Withdraw money from his bank?"

"He did say he had business to attend to. . ." Edmund broke off, obviously deep in thought. "But I thought . . ." He looked at her questioningly. "I thought he loved *you*."

Kate tilted her head and frowned at him in an "I told you so" sort of way.

"Kate, I–"

He was interrupted by the sound of another car bumping down the lane. It was a sporty Ford V8, and for a moment, Kate thought it might be the errant couple. The car rolled to a stop beside Edmund's truck, but it was not Louisa and Henry who alighted. It was Mary Crawford!

"Oh, there you are!" Mary called. "I've just been over to your house, but I should have known to look here first. You practically live here, don't you?"

She was all brightness and smiles, as if nothing bad was currently unfolding. She must not yet know.

"Oh, Edmund!" Mary gushed, laying her hand on his arm. "I can't believe I missed you at home! You don't know how I've been chastising myself! And that stupid Bella. I've instructed her a hundred times on how to use the telephone, *and* I left my number in the top drawer of the bureau. But she's simply hopeless, you know. I would have rushed back in an *instant* had I known you were in town! I blame myself profusely, of course! And it wasn't even a friend I particularly like, that's the rub. Instead, I could have been spending the weekend with you and having a jolly good time. There are so many things I wanted to show you. But you *will* come back, won't you, Edmund? I mean, you must have very badly wanted to see me if you came all that way. You must have felt yourself to be in such a queer predicament. And now poor Henry has gone and gotten himself in yet another pickle, hasn't he?"

"So, you know?" Kate asked tentatively.

Mary blinked rapidly. "Yes, he telephoned last night to tell me that he and Louisa are in St. Louis."

"St. Louis?"

Mr. Kerwyn appeared at the back door. "You back, Ed? Well, that's some good news, anyway." He made his way across the muddy ground. "What are *you* doing here?" he said to Mary and flashed her annoyed look. "Where's your brother?"

"Mary was just saying that she heard from Henry last night, Dad!" Kate said eagerly. "They're in St. Louis."

"St. Louis? Why? Are they married?"

"Yes, it seems so," Mary answered, her gaiety leveling a bit. "Typical Henry!" she exclaimed. "He's always getting himself in these sorts of scrapes."

"A scrape is what a ten-year-old gets himself into, not a grown man. And I don't think, Miss Crawford, that this is a laughing matter. It's almost killed my wife, and the Tierneys are right broken up about it."

"I do beg your pardon, Mr. Kerwyn," Mary said, adjusting her tone to one of gentle condescension, "but it's not a *tragedy*, is it? I mean, I'm sorry for Louisa's poor fiancé, but isn't it better for them to find out now that they weren't suited? And, really, this happens all the time," she said enthusiastically. "Personally I think it quite romantic."

She glanced at Edmund, who shifted uncomfortably and scratched his chin again.

"Romantic?" Mr. Kerwyn sputtered. "This ain't romance. This is just plain irresponsible. Disgraceful. Never thought a daughter of mine would do such a thing. And, no, it doesn't happen all the time! Not around here, anyway." Mr. Kerwyn glared at her. "And you're right bold to have even turned up here without an ounce of apology or remorse."

"Remorse? But why should *I* have remorse? If anyone should have remorse," Mary replied starchily, "it should be Kate."

Mr. Kerwyn's eyes bulged. "Kate?"

"Yes, if Kate hadn't rejected him–multiple times–he would not have been driven to run off with Louisa! She's really the one to blame here." Mary flashed her an accusatory look.

"Kate?" Mr. Kerwyn repeated incredulously. "Kate's the only one that isn't at fault in this situation. She read Henry correctly from the get-go. She knew. And I'm sorry I didn't believe her."

His face was red, redder than Kate had ever seen.

"It's okay, Dad," Kate said, rubbing his arm. She was suddenly worried he might be on the verge of a heart attack.

Mary tilted her head slightly, seemingly unaffected by his fury. "I don't think you understand the full situation, Mr. Kerwyn," she said, again condescending. "You aren't privy to some of the things that have occurred between Kate and Henry."

Kate's face blanched. *Nothing* had occurred between them! Was she referring to all of the gifts he had sent? Or was she referring to his kiss the night of her birthday party? *Had he actually told his sister about it?* Even if he had, she tried to counter, the kiss had meant nothing! She opened her mouth to retort, but before she could, Edmund interjected.

"And what would that be?" he demanded icily. "I won't for a moment believe that Kate has done anything improper."

"Who said anything about impropriety?" Mary said devilishly. "I simply mean there was an understanding of sorts between them."

"No, there wasn't!" Kate spewed.

"Do you deny he visited you, cheered you, bought you gifts?"

"No, but I didn't ask for them. And I certainly didn't encourage him!"

"Did you, or did you not, tell him that you would seriously consider his proposal of marriage?"

"Yes, but . . ." she looked frantically from her father to Edmund, "but I turned him down."

"Listen," Mary said calmly and suddenly looped her arms through both Kate's and Edmund's. "Let's not worry about whose fault it is. Henry is a very sensitive soul, and, well, when his heart was broken"–she looked pointedly at Kate–"he simply had to act. Thankfully, Louisa was there for him. All we can do now is simply to be happy for them and to help as much as we can."

Edmund pulled his arm away. "How can you defend Henry in this, Mary?" he asked, genuinely perplexed. "He has acted dishonorably on several occasions and still you take his part. Granted, there is sisterly affection, but this goes beyond that. You ask us not to point fingers, but you implicate Kate, who is completely blameless. All along she has stood her ground when no one else believed what a . . . what a liar Henry is. There. I've said it." He took a few steps away but then turned back. "It's like I don't even know you." He stared at Mary. "How could I have been so blind as to think I loved you?"

"Edmund!" Mary cried, again laying her hand on his arm. "There is no need for *us* to quarrel! All will be well!" She tried foisting her sugary sweet smile on him, but it failed to elicit any response.

Edmund's face remained hard as a rock. "No, it won't."

"Edmund!" There was a note of real panic in Mary's voice now. "Surely you are not so unjust as to judge me by my brother's actions?"

"No," he said, looking at her scornfully. "I'm judging you by yours."

With that, Edmund marched to his truck and threw himself behind the wheel. Kate watched as his truck tore down the lane, still trying to make sense of what had just happened.

CHAPTER TWENTY-SIX

Kate surveyed the damage in front of her and worried that there was no hope of saving it. She was standing inside her old badger hole, trying to assess the destruction done by the ravages of the past winter.

Part of the roof had caved in, and as a result, a pile of mud had mounded on the little table where she used to work on her baskets. With a heavy sigh, she picked up a stray piece of wood that had been formerly wedged into place to brace the earthen ceiling and tossed it outside.

"Throwing things at me now?"

Edmund! She had not seen him since that day he had broken it off with Mary. He still did morning and evening chores at the Kerwyns, but he did not eat dinner with them, nor did he come into the house at all. Several times, Kate was tempted to go out to the barn to speak with him, but she wasn't exactly sure what to say. Congratulate him on breaking with Mary? Offer him comfort? Neither seemed right, and the fact that he did not seek her out told her much. Well, she could live with that. She could live with not having him so long as he was not tied to someone unworthy of him.

"Thought I'd find you up here." He held his hat and flashed her a crooked smile. His face was ruddy from walking up the hill, and the wind blew the locks of his brown hair, longer than she had ever seen it before. It suited him, Kate decided.

"What are you doing here?" she asked.

"Looking for you." He smiled again, but his eyes were sad, pensive.

She wanted to say that he could have talked to her anytime he liked this past week by simply walking into the farmhouse or catching her while she worked in the garden, but she refrained.

He peered beyond her into the earthen shelter. "I don't know, Kate. This one might be past repairing. You might think about finding a new one." He glanced back at her. "You aren't really thinking of moving back up here, though, are you?"

"No, not really." She let out a little sigh. "But I was hoping to use it as a workshop. A place of my own where I can leave out my materials without them getting in the way or Minnie messing them up." In truth, she was itching to get back to her creative endeavors. She had accepted the fact–*happily* accepted, she emphasized to herself–that she would be her parents' housekeeper and her mother's nurse forever, but she longed to have something that was still her own.

"Are you sad that your real family aren't the artists or the Indians you wanted them to be?" he asked softly, leaning against the doorframe.

She was surprised by the question. No one had asked her that. Nettie and Minnie wanted gossipy stories and her father had asked if they had been kind, but everyone had mostly been preoccupied with Mrs. Kerwyn being ill, and now they were preoccupied with Louisa running off. Her mother had eventually inquired about her experience but only in the most general of terms. Discerning that her mother was uncomfortable, threatened almost, by the subject, Kate had kept most of the details to herself.

"The Kerwyns are my real family." Kate stepped past him out into the open air. The day was windy, but gloriously warm. She began to aimlessly walk along the path that led down to the creek.

"Okay, then, your *original* family." Edmund slowly followed.

"Maybe a little." She picked up a thin stick.

Every now and again, she whispered the names of her siblings to herself–*Joe, Tom, Tim, Ann, Jean, Emma*–hoping that some–*any*–memory would surface, but none ever did. "But I really only got to know one of them. Who knows what my other siblings are like? Or what my parents were like. Maybe someone had a propensity for creativity but didn't have an opportunity to express it."

She thought of her poor mama, bearing seven children in a mining camp in a strange country and then dying. She wondered where her grave was. She mourned her death, of course, but she also mourned the fact that she had never really known her. Her heart went out to this young woman, whoever she had been. Maria. Mama.

"Kate, I'm sorry."

"You needn't be. I'm happy that I ended up with the Kerwyns. I was lucky. I have to remember that." They had reached the edge of the creek now, which was full and rushing swiftly due to the recently melted snow.

"No, I mean I'm sorry I hurt you."

She turned, and her heart picked up a beat when she saw those sad, pensive eyes again.

"I'm sorry about the whole incident with Mary Crawford. I . . ." He picked up a rock and tossed it into the rushing water. "I guess I just sort of lost my head." He picked up another and again tossed it. "You were right about them the whole time, and I was wrong. But worse, I put you in a very difficult position. I'm sorry."

He looked at her so pitifully that she was tempted to put her hand to his cheek and comfort him. But she instead studied the creek.

"Well, anyway, I just wanted to say that. Get it off my chest. And also to tell you that I'm leaving."

For a moment, she was afraid he meant that he was returning to Chicago. "Leaving? Where?"

"I've joined up," he said quietly.

"Joined up?" Her heart sank. "Oh, Edmund. Does . . . does Dad know?"

"Not yet. But I have to do it, Kate."

"Yes. Yes, I know," she said, though her mind was trying to make sense of it. She herself had always defended his decision to follow in his father's footsteps, but now that it was upon them, she felt panicky. What if there actually was a war? What if he was killed? "When do you leave?" she asked hoarsely.

"In three days."

Her stomach lurched. "So soon?"

"Yes, unfortunately. They don't give you much time." He smiled ruefully. "I guess it's in case you change your mind. But I'm not changing my mind this time."

"No, of course not." Kate quickly wiped a tear with the back of her hand, angry that it had even appeared at all.

"There's something else, though."

Kate was afraid to hear whatever news could be worse than this.

"I . . ." He picked up another rock, a small one. He didn't toss it but instead rubbed it between his hands. "I've been thinking a lot about that conversation we had in the truck on the way back from Shullsburg."

"Which one?" she murmured, though she was pretty sure she knew.

Edmund dropped the rock. "Kate, did you really once think there might have been something between us?" He searched her eyes. "Because I know *I* thought it. For years and years, I've felt it. But you seemed to think of me as a brother, so I . . . I tried to think of you that way, too. As a sister, but . . ." He rubbed his hand through his hair. "And then when Mary came along, I thought maybe it was a sign from God that I was supposed to be with her. It seemed so easy and obvious. I could see that it upset you, though, which is why I pushed so hard for you to love Henry—to ease my conscience, I guess."

Kate remained silent, her heart truly pounding now.

"But it obviously wasn't love on her part. And it's become clear to me that it wasn't love on my part, either. I'm ashamed of myself, Kate. I've been such a fool, and I can't believe you haven't shunned me for my stupidity."

Kate smiled a tiny smile. "Well, I thought about it."

"Kate," he said, taking her hand, "I'm sorry that I hurt you. Sorry that I hurt the only woman I've really ever loved. Can you forgive me?"

Kate was dangerously close to tears. She scrunched her face to stop them and could only nod. She had only recently come to understand that she was truly loved by the Kerwyns, but now Edmund was telling her the same thing. That he loved her. That he had always loved her.

He gently kissed the hand he held. "Will you marry me?" he asked softly.

Kate let out a little gasp. "Marry you?"

"I know I don't deserve you, Kate," he said hurriedly. "But with you I know I can learn to be a better man. Perhaps you can grow to love me. I mean, in the way that I love you."

Two tears rolled down Kate's cheeks. "I don't need to grow to love you," she said with a little laugh. "I already do."

Edmund's face broke into a crooked smile. "So, you'll marry me?"

"Yes." She smiled. "Yes, I'll marry you, Edmund."

Edmund released her hand and wrapped his arms tightly around her. He kissed the top of her head and then pulled away to kiss her forehead, her cheeks, and then finally, her lips, gently, tentatively at first, and then deeply. Again and again, he kissed her, and she eagerly returned his them, feeling a longing inside her swell up.

Breathlessly, he broke their embrace and leaned his forehead against hers. "I love you, Kate Kerwyn. Or whatever your name is."

She laughed. "I love you, too, Edmund Bertram."

He kissed her again, and Kate allowed herself to succumb to the love rushing through her before an errant thought broke the moment of bliss. She pulled away. "Oh, but Edmund, you can't leave now!"

"'Fraid I have to." He kissed her lips again and then her cheek, her neck . . .

"Then I'm going with you."

He straightened, a rueful smile on his lips. "You can't."

"I could if we were married," Kate urged, her mind whirling.

"True," Edmund said slowly. "Except we're not."

"We could do it quickly. Before you go. I . . . I could use Louisa's wedding dress! Save it from going to waste. We'd have to do it at the courthouse–Fr. Eggert would never do it this quickly. You don't mind, do you?"

Edmund looked at her lovingly and tucked a stray lock of hair behind her ear. "Kate, I'd marry you anywhere, anytime. On top of this hill, if you wanted. Right now. But I don't want you to follow me. No, listen!" he said, cutting off her response. "I nearly lost you once because of my own stupidity. I don't want to lose you again. More than likely, I'll be sent overseas. I couldn't bear to think of you alone in some small apartment on the barracks. Stay here with your family, where you can take care of each other until I get back."

"But what if you *don't* come back, Edmund?"

"I will. I promise. But you have to promise me, too. Will you?" He looked at her steadily.

A million protests raged through her mind, but as she stared into Edmund's warm brown eyes, she was calmed. What he was saying made sense, especially given her mother's current weakened state. It really might be the final blow if Kate left now. And this way, she would also be near to Jenny, who, as it turned out, had written her a letter back, telling her, in very crooked handwriting, that she missed her. And loved her.

"Yes," she said faintly, letting out a long breath. "I'll wait for you."

"That's my girl." He put his strong arm around her and held her tightly. "Come on, Possum," he said, his dimples showing, "let's go tell your mom and dad."

CHAPTER TWENTY-SEVEN

Melody hurried down High Street on her way to the Merc, anxious to get back to work and try to undo all of Freddy's damage.

Melody had finally gotten him to agree to return to law school, a decision Mums seemed to be happy about, too. Mums was coming round more now, spending most of the day out of bed and downstairs. She even seemed to be interested in attending the Women's League meeting regarding the Memorial Day parade. At any rate, Melody was finally feeling comfortable enough now to leave her at home with just Helenka.

When Melody finally reached the old place, she paused in front of the big display window, hating the fact that Freddy–and presumably Mrs. Haufbrau–had put up the old "Get Ready for Spring" sign and displayed all the usual items: shovels, rakes, seed planters, umbrellas. Gone were the cider, the bicycle, the scarves, hats, baskets, and all of the other items Melody had tried to feature. She let out a deep breath. She certainly had her work cut out for her.

She pushed open the door, setting off the tinkling of the shop bell. Melody enjoyed the look of surprise on Harriet's face.

"Melody!" Harriet cried. "What are you doing here?" She hurried from behind the counter and embraced her old boss.

Delighted, Melody hugged her back. This was definitely the right choice–if she *had* had any doubts about her decision. Which she didn't.

"Fred didn't mention you were coming home. How long you back for?"

"For good!" Melody beamed.

"For good? But why?" Harriet's face looked worried. "Did something happen in Chicago?"

"No, I just decided that–"

"Why on God's green earth are *you* here?" Mrs. Haufbrau interrupted, coming up from the back, still dressed all in black. "Is your mother ill? Fred didn't mention it." She glanced worriedly at the clock. "Where *is* Fred, in fact? Never known him to be late. Is *he* ill?"

Melody sighed. "No, no one's ill, Mrs. Haufbrau. I've decided to come home. For good. I was just explaining that to Harriet."

Mrs. Haufbrau's face twisted in dismay. "What about Fred?"

"He's going back to school."

"Well, who's going to run the Merc?"

"I am, obviously."

"Good Lord, again?"

Melody gritted her teeth. Clearly, she preferred Fred. "Yes, again."

Mrs. Haufbrau let out a reluctant grunt. "Well, I suppose it's the best thing for him. That's what your dad would've wanted, I reckon."

"Indeed," Melody muttered.

"Oh, but Melody! Won't you miss school and everything?" Harriet fretted.

"I don't know. I've missed this place too much. And all of you," she added, her eyes darting quickly from Harriet to Mrs. Haufbrau and back again. "Though it looks . . ." Melody gestured widely and made a point of intensely surveying the shelves . . . "*exactly* like it did on the day I arrived from Chicago the last time." She dared to cock an eyebrow at Mrs. Haufbrau.

"Yes, it does," the older woman snipped. "There wasn't a thing wrong with it when your father was running things, Melody. I don't know why you had to go and change everything."

Melody let out a huff. "I had to change everything, Mrs. Haufbrau, because the Merc was in danger of going under. It's still in danger."

"It was doing fine when Lou ran it," Mrs. Haufbrau said snidely, as if the Merc's demise was *her* fault–not Freddy's, or God forbid, her father's.

"But it wasn't, Mrs. Haufbrau. He was deeply in debt. That's why I started brewing and selling the cider, which you've gotten rid of, I see." She was careful not to implicate Harriet by revealing how much she already knew from her letters. "It was the sales from the cider and . . . and other things"–she dared not mention Douglas's ring–"and the Christmas gift from all the shop owners that allowed me to pay them off. But according to *Fred*," she emphasized, guessing that his opinion probably meant more to Mrs. Haufbrau than hers, "the Merc is still not really solvent. So, we have to change. I'm thinking of devoting one wall to local art or maybe having poetry readings or some other type of performances in the evenings."

Mrs. Haufbrau threw up her hands. "Good Lord! I've heard everything now."

"We'll still be the Merc," Melody assured her, "selling saltines and candy sticks and the *Saturday Evening Post*, but we need to sell the cider and other local products, too. Like the baskets and the soap. Where *are* Kate's baskets, anyway?" She looked around. "Surely you didn't pull those from the shelves, too, did you?"

"We sold out of them!" Harriet put in. "Kate came in the other day—finally!—and asked about bringing more in. But I told her we weren't going to be stocking them anymore." She glanced worriedly at Mrs. Haufbrau. "I'm sorry, Melody! That's what Fred told me to say!"

"I know. You're not to blame. I'll speak to her." Melody rubbed her brow. "She's not still in that badger hole, is she?"

"No, she's back home. But, Melody! You'll never guess! She got married to Edmund Bertram!"

Melody was a little taken aback. Edmund Bertram was an extremely attractive young man. She didn't know much about him, to be honest, but Kate Kerwyn was not whom Melody imagined would catch his fancy. "They're already married? Kate isn't... is she?" Melody asked delicately, as there was usually only one reason for a rushed wedding.

"Oh, no! Not that," Harriet said hurriedly. "It's because Edmund joined up. He ships out soon."

"Oh."

"I can't believe Kate ended up married before me, can you?" Harriet gushed. "But I'm over the moon for her! She's never looked so happy. Wait till you see her, Melody."

"Well, it seems wedding fever is in the air," Melody said, trying not to think about Eustace. He had, up until the day she left, still had flowers delivered daily.

"Yes! And you know who else is getting married?"

The shop bell rang, then, and Mrs. Schaffer bustled in.

"Oh, hello, Mrs. Schaffer!" called Mrs. Haufbrau, making her way behind the front counter. "I've got that cloth you special ordered."

"I was hoping!" exclaimed Mrs. Schaffer. "I was passing anyway. Thought I'd stop in and see."

Mrs. Haufbrau pulled a bolt of cloth from under the counter and laid it out. It was a pale blue with rows of tiny yellow rosebuds.

"Oh, Marcella! Now that's just what I wanted."

While the two women continued to chat, Harriet leaned closer to Melody. "*I'm* glad you're back, Melody. And I like your new ideas."

"Thanks, Harriet," she said, patting her friend's arm. "I knew I could count on you." She gave her a smile. "Well," she said, her eyes darting toward the back. "I suppose I should go say hello to Cal." She had tried to say it as casually as she could. "Is he back there? Strange he hasn't come up."

"He might be in the cooler. Want me to go get him?"

"No, that's okay, I want to check the shelves anyway."

Harriet's face contorted into a rare frown. "Oh, Melody, I'm not sure you're going to be happy about Cal. He's–"

"Yes, I know. Fred told me. He's leaving next week. That's just what I need to talk to him about."

Melody proceeded toward the back of the shop, pausing to tidy various items as she went, though it was really just an excuse to rehearse the speech she had been repeating for days now. She had come up with an idea of how to get Cal to stay. She would offer him the position of co-manager. She wouldn't be able to pay him all that much more, but maybe if he had a stake in the place, it would make a difference.

With a deep breath, she finally made herself round the final row of shelves and saw him standing over the back worktable, slicing some hunk of meat, his dark hair falling over one eye. She watched him unawares for a few moments, and felt her stomach clench a little. She had certainly missed him. She hadn't realized how much.

Seeing her, he broke into a smile, which she eagerly returned. So far, so good.

"Heard you were back." He set down his knife and moved toward the little sink.

"Yes, I'm . . . I'm here for good," she said to his broad shoulders.

"For good? Why?" He turned as he wiped his hands on a towel.

"Well, I . . ." She faltered. "I guess it just made sense. Fred should really finish his degree, and Mums needs me. She was in a terrible state."

He leaned on the glass display case. "That all?" He rested his chin on his arms. His dark eyes peered at her, and she felt suddenly flustered. She had completely forgotten her speech!

"Well, I . . . if you're referring to Chicago, I guess it just wasn't the same when I went back," she admitted.

"Yeah?"

She considered elaborating, but she didn't want to explain her silly classes, her disillusionment with Mundelein society, and certainly not her failed relationship with Eustace. "The point is," she said, twirlingd a lock of her hair, "I've decided to come back. Turns out I kind of like it here in Merriweather. And, though it's probably hard for you to believe, I guess I like this dusty old place." She tried smiling at him. "I missed it. And everyone."

She had wanted "everyone" to come out suggestively, intimately, but it was more of a bark. She bit the inside of her cheek. "I . . . I've got a lot of new ideas. I was hoping to talk them over with you."

He came out from behind the counter and stood in front of her, leaning against the case.

"Well, maybe you could talk them over with Uncle Lyle. He's coming back on Monday. Didn't Fred tell you?"

"He did. But I was hoping to discuss that with you." For the life of her, she couldn't remember her speech; she would have to utter whatever came into her mind! "I . . . I was wondering if you might think about staying. If I made you a co-manager?" She peered at him, but she couldn't read his expression. "I couldn't pay you all that much more than you're already getting, but you could . . . you could help me run the Merc. You'd be more in charge than you are now." She looked at him hopefully. "What do you think?"

He rubbed a hand through his dark hair. "I don't know, Melody. You see–"

"I know things haven't always been smooth between us," she rushed on, "but . . ." She paused, not sure if she should reveal her true feelings. But if she didn't, he would be gone, and she would never get her chance, not unless she wanted to write a letter, which she did not. "I . . . I know it's been a while since the Christmas party at our house, but I . . . I guess I felt like there might have been . . . well, something between us." She winced at how badly this was going. "I thought maybe we could see?"

A muscle in his jaw twitched slightly, but otherwise she couldn't read his expression.

She tried to chuckle. "If I'm being honest, one of the real reasons I came back . . ." She paused. *Now or never.* "Was you." She bit the inside of her cheek and held her breath. Eagerly she searched his face, and when she saw it light up for just a fraction of an instant, a happy little laugh escaped her.

In the next moment, however, he rubbed his eyes with his fingertips and then briefly steepled them under his nose. He exhaled heavily.

"I don't know how to say this, Melody," he said in a low voice, "but while you were away, I got engaged to Jessie Lange."

AUTHOR'S NOTE

Uncovered in Merriweather is meant to be a retelling of Jane Austen's *Mansfield Park*, with the character of Kate Kerwyn playing Fanny Price. But what makes the character of Kate even more interesting (in my opinion) is that she is also based on a real-life person!

Catherine Clare (a.k.a. "Indian Kate") Jordan was born Sop-Ho-Kab in 1825 and was a full-blooded Sauk Indian. She and her people were living near Victory, Wisconsin, when the Battle of Bad Axe occurred on August 2, 1832, as part of the Black Hawk War. Sop-Ho-Kab was just seven years old at the time, but she managed to escape the battle and floated down the Mississippi River in a canoe. After floating for over fifty miles, the canoe eventually washed ashore at Olde Jordan's Landing (which eventually became Dunleith, Illinois, and then East Dubuque, Illinois). Sop-Ho-Kab was found, scared, starving, and exhausted, by Thomas Jordan, who operated a small ferry between what would become Dunleith and Dubuque, Iowa.

Mr. Jordan took the girl, whom he nicknamed "Indian Kate," home to his wife, Mary, and they raised her alongside their fourteen other children. They officially named her Catherine Clare, but she continued to be called "Indian Kate" by all who knew her well. She eventually married a Prussian immigrant, Probus Eberle, and raised a family of eight children with him on a nearby farm. She and Probus are buried in plots Nos. 1 and 2 in the East Dubuque Cemetery.

I discovered this information by chance on a trip back to my hometown, East Dubuque, when I noticed a plaque dedicated to her outside the East Dubuque library. Never having noticed this plaque before, I took the time to read it and was fascinated by the story. Immediately, I could envision Sop-Ho-Kab as an excellent character in a novel.

So, when I began writing the Merriweather series, which is set in this general area of the country, it seemed the perfect opportunity to weave this Native American woman into the story, and she became our "Indian Kate." Though the real Indian Kate lived almost a century before Kate Kerwyn, I still used elements of her story. I also chose the name "Esposito" to be Kate Kerwyn's original family name, as it literally translates into "exposed." It is an Italian surname historically given to foundlings–children who were abandoned and left in a public place.

Between Sop-Ho-Kab and Fanny Price, our Kate Kerwyn has a big role to play, and I hope I've done her justice. As stated previously, however, this retelling of *Mansfield Park* is a work of fiction, and all deviations from Miss Austen's original should therefore be accepted as just that–imagined deviations!

Having stated this, my hope is that Austen enthusiasts will delight to recognize other characters from the original novel, as follows:

Kate Kerwyn: Fanny Price
Edmund Bertram: Edmund Bertram
Henry and Mary Crawford: Henry and Mary Crawford
Louisa & Nettie Kerwyn: Maria and Julia Bertram
Ray Kerwyn: Thomas Bertram
Mr. & Mrs. Kerwyn: Sir Thomas and Lady Bertram
Sam & Ann Price: Lieutenant and Mrs. Frances Price
Vernon Tierney: Mr. Rushworth

And of course, we have the overlap characters from ***Matched in Merriweather***, who are playing the various parts from Emma, and other Austen novels:

Melody Merriweather: Emma Woodhouse/Elinor Dashwood/ Elizabeth Bennet
Cal Fraiser: Mr. Knightley/Edward Ferrars/Mr. Darcy
Harriet Mueller: Harriet Smith
John Schneider: Robert Martin
Elizabeth (Bunny) Merriweather: Marianne Dashwood
Miss Elliot: Anne Elliot

And if it isn't already apparent, the next novel in the series will be based on *Sense and Sensibility* and will focus on Bunny Merriweather in the role of Marianne Dashwood.

My plan is to release five books in the Merriweather series, each based on a different Jane Austen novel, including: *Emma*, *Mansfield Park*, *Sense and Sensibility*, *Persuasion*, and *Pride and Prejudice*.

What is unique about the books in this series is that they are all based in Merriweather, Wisconsin, and have overlapping Jane Austen characters to create one big same-world experience. It's been deliciously fun plotting it all out, and I hope you enjoy reading them as much as I have enjoyed writing them.

And speaking of Merriweather, as pointed out and elaborated on in the author's note at the end of ***Matched in Merriweather***, this fictional town is, in truth, a thinly veiled version of the very real Mineral Point, Wisconsin. You can read all about the history of Mineral Point and its connection to the series by reading the author's note there.

Thank you all for reading ***Uncovered in Merriweather***. I do hope you've enjoyed it!

THE HENRIETTA AND INSPECTOR HOWARD SERIES

If you're curious about Melody's origin, you might try The Henrietta and Inspector Howard series, which is set in Chicago and abroad in the 1930s, and where you, gentle reader, `will be first introduced to Melody, though she does not appear (full disclosure) until the fourth book, *A Veil Removed.* But I can promise that it is a very enjoyable read getting to that point.

"Henrietta and Inspector Howard make a charming odd couple, mixing mystery and romance in a fizzy 1930s cocktail."

–Hallie Ephron, *New York Times* bestselling author

"Brimming with a dark plot on every page, this unpredictable literary thrill ride will transport you to the heart of 1930s Chicago and the love story of a lifetime."

–PopSugar

"Henrietta and Clive are a sexy, endearing, and downright fun pair of sleuths. Readers will not see the final twist coming."

–*Library Journal* (starred review)

Start the series for free!!

Download A GIRL LIKE YOU now!

ACKNOWLEDGMENTS

Once again, I'd like to thank everyone who helped bring this book into the world. As is the case with most second children, I wasn't quite ready for how fast this one wanted to come out. There are a lot of moving pieces in bringing a book into the world, however, so without my amazing team, it wouldn't have all come together as quickly as it did. Thanks to all of you for compensating for my lack of any kind of proper timeline.

Without further ado, then, I'd like to thank, first and foremost, my developmental editor, Andrea Robinson. Every time I work with Andrea, I come away a better writer–at least I hope I do. At any rate, she has again helped to shape this book into the very best version of itself. As ever, any errors that remain are mine alone.

I'd also like to again thank all the others who had a hand in this book's production: Kari Brownlie for another beautiful cover design and graphics, Kaitlin Schmidt for copyediting, and Ashley Santoro for formatting. I'd also like to thank Lisa Dailey of Sidekick Press for website management and Yolanda Facio for newsletter formatting. Likewise, I'd like to thank my street team for being early readers, reviewing, helping me to get the word out, and for all around general excellence. I love working with each and every one of you, and your support is truly invaluable!

Lastly, of course, but certainly not least, I'd like to thank my family for putting up with me these last few months while I've spent an unusual number of hours (even for me) locked in my office to get this book finished. Thank you for your patience and encouragement and for occasionally vacuuming. Thanks especially to my husband, Phil, who doesn't complain when he hears keyboard taps at 5:00 a.m. or when I continue to try to get in laptop time no matter where we are–in hotels, on planes, on trains, and even in the car. Recently, on a weekend trip to Kentucky, my laptop ran out of battery, and I insisted on getting off the highway in some small town, finding a hardware store, and buying an extension cord to plug into an outlet at the back of the van. It turned into a larger fiasco, which I won't go into here, but Phil did not complain . . . much.

Phil, thank you for everything. You will always be my sweetest song.

Michelle Cox has always been obsessed with stories of the past and has spent a lifetime collecting them. She is the award-winning author of historical fiction, including **the Henrietta and Inspector Howard** series, **The Fallen Woman's Daughter**, and **The Merriweather Series**. Cox also pens the wildly popular, "Novel Notes of Local Lore," a weekly blog chronicling the lives of Chicago's forgotten residents.

To date, she her novels have won over eighty international awards and have received positive reviews from *Library Journal* (starred), *Booklist* (starred), *Publishers Weekly*, *Kirkus*, BookLife (editor's pick), *Foreword*, *Historical Novel Society*, and various media outlets, such as *Popsugar*, *Buzzfeed*, *Redbook*, *Elle*, *Brit&Co.*, *Bustle*, *Culturalist*, *Working Mother*, and many others.

She lives in the northern suburbs of Chicago with her husband, an assortment of children who continually leave and then come back, and one naughty Goldendoodle. Unbeknownst to most, she hoards board games she doesn't have time to play and is, not surprisingly, in love with both Cary Grant and Jimmy Stewart. Likewise, she is happily addicted to period dramas and big band music. Also marmalade.

www.ingramcontent.com/pod-product-compliance
Lightning Source LLC
Chambersburg PA
CBHW021403110726
47901CB00008B/2034